Love Walked into The Lantern

by

NICOLE PYLAND

Love Walked into The Lantern

Chicago Series Book #3

Summer Taft is a twenty-seven-year-old billionaire, who founded a tech start-up with her brother while she was still in college. As that company's CEO, she feels stuck and underappreciated. She also has to take care of the company while her brother goes off exploring the world, leaving her holding the bag. The company recently opened an office in Chicago, where Summer has met some new friends. As Summer decides to uproot her life and make the move to Chicago, she meets Lena.

Lena Tanner has had no luck in her love life after divorcing her husband of several years before, after finally admitting to herself that she was gay. Lena had been exploring and having fun in the new life she'd made for herself. But now, she's ready to find the one and settle down. After a blind date gone wrong, she ends up at The Lantern where she spots her group of expanding friends and a newcomer.

Lena had never been brave in her personal life. And Summer has always had difficulty making decisions, small and large. The two women settle into a quick friendship that turns more flirtatious. But is either of them ready to dive right into something new that could be lasting?

To contact the author or for any additional information visit: **https://nicolepyland.com**

You can also subscribe to the reader's newsletter to be the first to receive updates about upcoming books and more: **https://nicolepyland.com/newsletter**

This is a work of fiction. Any names or characters, businesses or places, events or incidents, are fictitious. Any resemblance to actual persons, living or dead, or actual events is purely coincidental. No part of this book may be reproduced or transmitted in any form or by any means, electronic or mechanical, including photocopying, recording or by any information storage and retrieval system, without written permission from the author.

BY THE AUTHOR

Stand-alone books:

- The Fire
- The Moments
- The Disappeared

Chicago Series:

- Introduction – Fresh Start
- Book #1 – The Best Lines
- Book #2 – Just Tell Her
- Book #3 – Love Walked into The Lantern
- Series Finale – What Happened After

San Francisco Series:

- Book #1 – Checking the Right Box
- Book #2 – Macon's Heart
- Book #3 – This Above All
- Series Finale – What Happened After

Tahoe Series:

- Book #1 – Keep Tahoe Blue
- Book #2 – Time of Day

- Book #3 – The Perfect View
- Book #4 – Begin Again
- Series Finale – What Happened After

Celebrities Series:

- Book #1 – No After You
- Book #2 – All the Love Songs

CONTENTS

CHAPTER 1 1

CHAPTER 2 8

CHAPTER 3 23

CHAPTER 4 32

CHAPTER 5 43

CHAPTER 6 50

CHAPTER 7 60

CHAPTER 8 73

CHAPTER 9 83

CHAPTER 10 93

CHAPTER 11 102

CHAPTER 12 109

CHAPTER 13 118

CHAPTER 14 134

CHAPTER 15 150

CHAPTER 16 164

CHAPTER 17 177

CHAPTER 18 189

CHAPTER 19 200

CHAPTER 20 210

CHAPTER 21 218

CHAPTER 22 231

CHAPTER 23 241

CHAPTER 24 255

CHAPTER 25 268

CHAPTER 26 281

CHAPTER 27 292

CHAPTER 28 319

CHAPTER 29 330

CHAPTER 30 338

CHAPTER 31 346

EPILOGUE 356

"Yeah, I'm going to start looking for a more permanent place. We're going to tell the world about my relocation on Monday, because, apparently, where I live is something people care about." Summer looked over at Ember and Eva, who were staring at something on the phone and giggling. "Hey, you two."

"Hey, Summer." Eva then looked up and smiled at her, with Ember following. "Sorry. Al sent us a video of the kids playing in the water. They're so cute."

"Lizzy looks just like Alyssa," Ember said. "Do you guys think they'll have more?" she posed to the group.

"Why? To have a couple that look like Hannah?" Charlie asked her.

"I don't know. Maybe," Ember replied.

"When are you two planning to start?" Hailey asked, and Summer watched her smirk.

"What's so funny?" Summer questioned Hailey's expression.

"They hate when people ask them that," Hailey told her.

"It's like, the moment you meet someone and say you're serious, people start asking when you'll get married; and then, when you'll have kids. It's annoying," Ember said.

"Em is still working on her Ph. D. We'll wait to see how that shakes out before we even begin talking about it seriously," Eva revealed. "Right now, I'm just happy to be Aunt Eva to those two little ones."

She held out her phone and showed the paused video image to Summer, who smiled at it.

"They are adorable."

"So, now that you're staying here, what are your plans?" Charlie asked and sipped on her wine.

"Plans for what?" Summer turned.

"Your life outside of work," Hailey added for her girlfriend.

"Oh, that." Summer laughed lightly.

"Ladies." Emma Colton stood in front of the booth

and glanced down awkwardly at Summer, who caught her eye only for a moment before turning her head back to Charlie.

"Hey, Em," Hailey greeted her ex-girlfriend and now a close friend.

"Can I get you two something? Refills for anyone?" Their female server asked as she carried an empty but wet and dirty tray, noticing Emma's arrival.

"Scotch and soda," Summer requested.

"Martini. Dry, two olives," Emma ordered politely and took a seat next to Eva on the opposite side of the booth.

Summer and Emma locked awkward eyes again before Charlie finally broke the tension with a conversation.

"So, Sum... You still haven't answered the question."

"What question?" Emma wondered.

"I asked Summer what she was planning on doing with her personal life now that she's moving to Chicago permanently," Charlie said.

"You're moving here?" Emma asked Summer.

"Yeah."

Summer and Emma shared a secret. When Summer first met the other woman, Emma was dating Elizabeth. The relationship soured when Eli confessed to cheating on Emma numerous times. The two finally ended things, and a few weeks after that, Summer got a text from Emma, saying she was going to be in San Francisco for a work convention. Summer was in town, and they decided to meet for drinks. The drinks led to going back to Summer's house in Palo Alto. They talked and watched a movie while they snacked on popcorn and drank wine.

The following night, Summer and Emma went to dinner. Even though neither of them overtly stated that it was a date, it felt very much like one. They'd had a few drinks, but Summer knew neither of them was drunk or intoxicated enough to cloud their judgment as they wound up on Emma's bed, and later, naked, under the thin hotel blankets.

When Summer woke up the following morning, she had no regrets, but she was also cautious, because Emma had only just gotten out of a serious relationship, where she had been betrayed by the woman she loved. Summer left while Emma was still asleep. They hadn't spoken about their night together since, and Summer suspected that if Emma wanted to bring it up, she would have by now.

"What made you want to move here?" Emma asked.

"I spend more time here than at home, anyway. And other than the weather, this place is pretty great. Plus, it's close to our Detroit office, and closer to New York, where I have to go for meetings at least once a quarter."

"What about school?" Charlie asked her. "Don't you have a few classes left?"

"I have six classes left," Summer said. "And, I don't know. I'll have to reach out to the university and find out what they're willing to do."

"I'm sure they'll make allowances, given who you are. We've had a few high-profile students at the college since I started. The administration makes arrangements," Eva said.

"Northwestern did that for me, and I'm not high-profile," Ember added.

"Yeah, but you're special, Em." Eva turned to her wife. "You *are* high-profile in certain circles, and they're counting on you being even more high-profile when you graduate."

"No pressure," Ember joked.

"Well, we should be celebrating Summer's relocation with drinks," Hailey suggested just as the server arrived and placed the martini in front of Emma, and Summer's drink in front of her.

"Perfect timing." Summer placed both hands around her glass.

"To Summer's move!" Hailey raised her wine glass.

"To Summer in Chicago," Charlie echoed.

"To Summer," Emma said from across the table and raised her martini glass while offering Summer a shy grin.

CHAPTER 2

LENA SAT across from her blind date, Marsha, who was chewing her steak loudly and causing Lena to grit her teeth in response. Her friend from work thought Marsha, the forty-two-year-old woman, who worked down the street from their O'Shea's Grocery Mart corporate offices in a bakery that she owned, would be a good fit for Lena.

Lena had spent the better part of an hour listening to Marsha talk about her three children from her previous relationship. The woman and her partner had been together for twenty years, before separating two years prior to this date. Lena was already regretting agreeing to it, and it was only half over. She glanced down at her watch and noticed the time. She had told Charlie and Hailey she would be at drinks tonight, but that she also might not if this date went well.

After her own marriage had ended and Lena had officially come out, she wanted to explore a little. She had been doing that for a while now, though. Lena had hoped that the more dates she went on, the more likely it would be for her to find someone. Now, she wanted to settle down, and, at thirty-six, she was ready for it.

"I just got a text from my sister." Lena stared down at her blank phone. "She hasn't been feeling well and needs me to check on her. I'm sorry. She has two kids, and her husband is out of town this week."

"Oh." Marsha paused the fork that was about to place another piece of steak into her mouth. "Should I get the check and drive you–"

"No, that's okay. You finish." Lena grabbed her wallet and pulled out some cash to cover their meal. "I'll grab a car and head over there. Thank you, though."

"Should I call you?"

Lena had gotten this question a few times at the end of the first dates. She'd also asked it of her dates, thinking that the dates they'd just been on were good ones, but finding by their lack of immediate response or their facial expressions that they did not want her to call, nor would they call her. Since the first experience with this, Lena had promised herself that she would always be honest with her dates.

"Probably not," she said. "This has been nice, but I don't see it going anywhere. Sorry, I feel like I should be honest."

"Honest about that?" Marsha placed her fork on her plate. "But is your sister really sick?"

Lena sighed at the realization that her honesty shouldn't come in parts but as a whole.

"No. I don't have a sister," she confessed.

"You really *didn't* see this going anywhere," the woman stated. "To create a sister seems a little dangerous if we moved forward," she added and then smiled politely. "I understand. I can still drive you home."

"No, it's okay. I'll be fine. Thank you."

Lena felt bad about leaving Marsha mid-dinner, but she could not handle watching the woman chew for a moment longer. She ordered an Uber and headed toward The Lantern to meet her friends. They always seemed to enjoy Lena's bad date stories, especially since they were all happily coupled off now.

She pushed the door to The Lantern open and glanced around quickly for her friends. She knew Hailey and Charlie would be there and suspected that others would join them, but she hadn't heard for sure. So, she looked for Hailey's long blonde hair and Charlie's pixie cut darker locks. She found them along with the long dark hair of another woman she recognized; not because Lena had met her before, but because that woman's face was all over the world these days. Summer Taft was a young CEO and a total success story. She was also gorgeous, with striking features and dark eyes that seemed to match her hair to the shade. Lena had been aware that Hailey worked with Summer, and that Charlie and Summer were friends outside of that relationship, but she hadn't yet met her, and she hadn't expected to see her at the bar tonight.

"Lena!" Charlie yelled and waved her over. "We'll need a chair," Charlie added when Lena got close enough to hear.

The bar was only somewhat crowded. Lena had gotten accustomed to The Lantern. It became the place she would come to after a hard day at work or a trip, to unwind and to just sit at the bar to see if any interesting women caught her eye or vice versa. She had picked up a few or had been picked up by them at The Lantern since coming out, but she had rarely slept with the women she met.

For her, it wasn't about just having some meaningless sex with women because she finally could. At first, it was about discovering the type of woman she would even be attracted to or would want to have sex with. Then, it was about spending time with them talking and finding a connection. If one existed, they would go on a few dates. If she felt like there was a possibility of something real, she might have taken it that far, but that had been rare. Since coming out, Lena had slept with three women, and only one of them more than once. She had dated Reagan for two months over four months ago. They had never been an official couple, though, and she knew Reagan dated other women. It hadn't bothered her. On one of her trips for work, Lena found herself thinking about that very thing. Reagan had ended their phone call to get ready for a date with someone else, and that hadn't bothered Lena at all.

Shouldn't it have bothered her that a woman she was sleeping with was going out with someone else?

"Hey! Glad you could make it," Hailey greeted as Emma stood and headed over to a table where there was an empty chair.

"I needed to come. My date was a train wreck," Lena said. "Thanks, Emma."

Emma had pulled the chair over in front of the booth and then motioned for Lena to take her old seat so she could take the chair.

"Train wreck?" Ember asked.

Lena hadn't spent much time with Ember and Eva, but they had been out with Charlie and Hailey a few times, and she had gotten to know them enough to consider them both friends now.

"Lena, I forgot," Hailey began. "This is Summer. Summer, this is our friend, Lena." Hailey motioned to Summer Taft.

"Nice to meet you," Lena offered and lifted her hand from beneath the table to shake Summer's.

"You too," Summer replied softly.

"Summer has been hanging out in Chicago for a while, but she's making the official move now," Hailey said. "We're here to celebrate."

"Congratulations." Lena shrugged, not knowing if that was the right reply.

"Thanks." Summer chuckled lightly. "Let me get you a drink. I have to run to the bathroom, anyway."

"Oh, okay. I'll take a gin and tonic," Lena said.

"I'll be right back." Summer offered a smile and stood.

"I have to go, too. I'll join you. Anyone need a refill?" Emma stood and asked the group.

Heads shook from side to side, and Lena watched Summer and Emma walk off together.

"Something is up with those two." Hailey pointed at the two women who were walking toward the bathroom.

"What are you talking about?" Charlie asked her.

"I know Emma. She's weird around Summer."

"You think she likes her?" Ember questioned.

"I don't know. Maybe," Hailey said.

"Do you think Summer could like her back?" Eva questioned in Hailey's direction.

"She's never said anything, but I guess she could."

"I think you just like playing matchmaker, Hails," Charlie offered her girlfriend.

"Emma was really hurt after that cheater, Elizabeth. Summer is single. Why not?"

"Summer is gay?" Lena questioned.

"She's bi," Hailey explained. "She's been single for a while. I think it's time she finds someone new."

"What if she isn't looking for someone new?" Charlie asked.

"She doesn't have to date anyone if she doesn't want to date them. I just think she and Emma would be cute together," Hailey suggested and pointed at the two women who were standing in line next to one another by the one-stall bathroom.

Lena chanced a look in that direction. She noticed neither woman was speaking to the other. They seemed to be staring at the floor in front of their feet until the door opened and Summer went inside, leaving Emma standing and waiting. Lena turned back around to the rest of the group.

"Okay. So, spill. How bad was the date?" Hailey asked.

"I don't normally notice people chewing, but I have never heard someone chew so loudly in my life. It was driving me crazy."

"Misophonia," Hailey said. "I read about it. It's a real condition. People can't stand to hear other people chew, among other things."

"I don't think I have that," Lena said. "It was just really loud and annoying. Her mouth was even open sometimes. I could see her steak. It was gross."

"So, no second date, then?" Charlie asked her.

"She still isn't over her ex. I can tell," Lena continued. "They were together for twenty years. That was something my friend – who set us up – failed to mention. That, inherently, I don't have a problem with, but they also have three kids together, and they are still trying to figure out the custody situation. I'm not even sure I want kids. I don't think I want to deal with any that aren't mine in a complicated situation like this."

"What about kids?" Emma asked when she approached the table.

Summer was right behind her and placed Lena's drink in front of her before sliding into the booth across from Lena again.

"Lena was just telling us about her terrible date tonight. The woman has three kids with her ex." Ember took a drink.

"All under the age of ten," Lena added. "Too much for me."

"You've never really wanted kids, though, right?" Charlie asked her.

"Not really," Lena confirmed. "With my ex, I thought it was because I didn't want kids with him. I suspected that the marriage could end."

"Why?" Summer asked her.

"Because I'm gay, and he and I rarely actually had sex. After the first few years of marriage, he stopped pushing for it. He had also never expressed interest in having kids. I'm pretty sure he was glad I never brought them up. I'm also pretty sure that he didn't mind about the lack of intimacy in our relationship because he was getting it elsewhere, but I don't fault him for that. I shouldn't have married him in the first place."

"Why did you?" Summer asked a probing question.

"Well, these are deeper topics than I thought we'd get into at a bar," Ember said. "And I hate to break this up, but we're driving to Iowa tomorrow, to visit Eva's sister and her new baby, so we should get going. I still have to pack."

13

"Because you didn't do it earlier, like I told you," Eva teased.

"Yeah, yeah." Ember rolled her eyes. "Come on, let's go." She took Eva's hand, and Lena stood to allow them to climb out before climbing back in herself.

"Safe trip," Hailey said. "And we want pictures."

"When are you two going to start having them?" Ember wagged her finger back and forth between Charlie and Hailey in jest.

"Get out of here," Charlie laughed out.

Ember and Eva said their goodbyes and left the bar, while Emma stood and carried the chair back to the table she'd taken it from earlier. Afterward, the woman slid in next to Lena. Lena watched as she and Summer stared at each other for a moment. Hailey had been right. Something was definitely going on between the two of them.

"I guess I should find a real estate agent here," Summer broke the silence. "I want to buy something here, and maybe something in Detroit, to be near the other office. You could stay there when you need to travel there, Hailey."

"That would be nice," Hailey replied.

"I have a friend in real estate. His name's Hayden. I can get you his number. He helped me find my place after the divorce, and we became friends. He's good," Lena said.

"That would be great. Thanks," Summer replied with a smile.

She pulled her phone from under the table, and Lena took that to mean she was ready to get the number now.

"Sure." Lena pulled out her own phone and logged in with her password. "What's your number? I'll send you his contact info."

Summer gave Lena her number, and Lena then sent Hayden's work cell and email address to her while also saving Summer's contact information in her own phone.

"Where are you looking to buy?" Emma asked Summer and took a sip of her martini.

"Honestly, I have no idea. I think I just want to look

around for the right place and hope it's in a good neighborhood," Summer said. "I would prefer a condo in the city itself, if possible."

"There are some places for sale near me," Emma suggested. "They're new. Finished in the last year or so. They look pretty nice from the outside."

Summer nodded and gave Emma a shy smile.

***

An hour later, Charlie and Hailey had dismissed themselves, while Emma, Lena, and Summer remained working on their drinks. Emma and Summer didn't seem to want to engage in conversation with one another, but they had no problem engaging with Lena. The three of them talked for a little while longer, until Emma's eye caught someone at the door. Lena turned to see a woman enter, with another woman in tow.

"Do you know her?" Lena asked Emma.

"That's my ex with her current," Emma said through her gritted teeth.

"Sorry, Emma," Summer replied.

"I think I'm going to go. I don't feel like dealing with her tonight." Emma slid out of the booth and stood. "Sorry to cut this short, but it's still weird for me."

She glanced in the direction of the two women who hadn't noticed her and who headed toward the bar. Emma waved at both Lena and Summer. Then, she left the bar.

"There's a story there, right?" Lena questioned Summer when they were alone.

"Eli, her ex, was cheating on her for a long time, apparently."

"Oh, that's terrible," Lena replied.

"I think she's still trying to get over the whole thing."

"So, you two aren't…" Lena realized the question might be a little personal, given the fact that she had just met Summer.

"Emma and I? Oh, no. We're not together."

"It seemed like there was something going on there between the two of you."

Lena finished her drink. Summer reddened almost instantly. Lena found the blush cute.

"Something *was* going on. Well, it happened once, but nothing since."

"Oh."

"It was one time, while she was in California on business. We haven't exactly discussed it. That's probably what you're picking up on," Summer explained. "But, no one else knows, so if you could keep it to yourself, I'd appreciate it. I don't know how Emma feels about telling the rest of them."

"I won't say anything," Lena said.

"So, Hailey tells me you're a VP at O'Shea's."

"VP of Operations. It's a grueling job, sometimes, but I like it. I'm finally done with traveling for a bit, so that's good. I feel like I haven't had much time for my personal life these past few months. Hence the blind date tonight that went so well," she said sarcastically.

"I feel like I haven't had a personal life in years," Summer said. "I'm about ready to give up on the whole thing and just become a tired, old spinster."

"How old are you?" Lena laughed. "I don't think you can become a spinster at your age."

"I'm twenty-seven. I'll just stay single for a few years, then, before I try out the new title."

Lena laughed again and swirled the ice around in her sweating glass.

"Well, I'm almost thirty-seven. I think, if either of us is going to go by spinster, it should be me."

Summer seemed to consider that comment and stared at her thoughtfully.

"Did you always know you were gay but married anyway?" Summer finished the last gulp of her own drink.

"Oh, wow."

"Sorry. That's too much, right?" Summer questioned. "Was that rude?"

"No, not rude. It's just hard to answer that question, I guess."

"How so?"

"There are things I think I knew," Lena started. "There was a girl, in high school, that I thought was beautiful and spent a lot of time around, but I didn't know at the time, that it was anything more than a close friendship."

"I think a lot of people have been there," Summer said.

"I went to college and met my future husband. He was great. And I did fall in love with him, or at least that's what I thought it was."

"And you never thought of women?"

"I did, but I just pushed it out of my mind. My family was pretty religious growing up, and I spent every Sunday in the church until I was eighteen and went away to school. It was almost as if being gay wasn't even a possibility, because it didn't exist in my world. We didn't talk about it. I don't know if I even knew any gay people back then. He was my first real boyfriend, and it felt okay." Lena paused. "Okay, but not great."

"It wasn't like all the movies made it seem?"

"No, it wasn't. And then, we were married; and it was like the moment that happened, I started feeling trapped. He worked; I didn't have to, because he made more than enough, and we had family money. For a while, I associated the 'trapped' feeling to that, more than my sexuality." Lena watched what was left of the ice move around in her glass. "Suddenly, it was like, now that I was married, every woman was off limits to me, but attractive. I started thinking about things I shouldn't have been thinking about as a married woman. I then met a woman through an organization I volunteered for. It turned out, she was my neighbor. We became friends, but she was straight and married, so that wasn't going anywhere. It was also safe because of that. I allowed myself to have those feelings and thoughts."

"Let me guess. Then, you fell for a non-straight woman," Summer said.

"It was four years into my marriage, and I met Jackie through a friend of the family. She had been invited to a Christmas party. I didn't know she was gay, at first. If I did, I probably wouldn't have talked to her, because I wouldn't have had the guts. She was beautiful and kind. We went to lunch a few days later. She told me she was gay and that she had just broken up with her girlfriend. Then, it was terrifying. There I was, sitting across from a woman I was attracted to, and she was possible. I mean, I don't even know if she thought about me like that. She knew I was married to a man; so, probably not. But it didn't matter. It all came crashing down on me after that." Lena looked at Summer, who was staring intently at her. "It still took me a while to admit it to myself. I considered that I might be bisexual for a long time. I loved Damon at some point. Or else, I wouldn't have married him, right? But after I did some real soul-searching, I had to just admit it to myself, and later, to the man I married, that I liked women. I didn't want to be married to a man anymore. We divorced. I spent a couple of years after that just trying to figure out how to speak to a woman I found attractive. And that's how I met Charlie."

"You found Charlie attractive, too?" Summer smirked.

"Yes, I did," she admitted. "It took almost everything in me to work up the courage to ask her out. She was great with me, but I wasn't ready for anything serious then. It's why we're still friends."

"Are you now?" Summer asked her.

"Sometimes, I think I am. And, other times, I think I'm still searching. What about you?"

"My story?"

"Yeah, why not? I told you mine." Lena sipped on the water, formed by the melting ice.

"Well, I've kind of always known I was bi. I only dated guys in high school because even though I knew I liked girls, too, I wasn't ready to share that with the world. When I got to college, though, I started dating both, and I had my first serious girlfriend. I came out to my parents after that. My brother already knew because we've always been close. Right now, he's navigating the globe or something, but we still talk regularly and not just about the company. My parents didn't seem to mind. I've had more girlfriends and boyfriends since, but even the relationships that lasted the longest never really felt like they were going to be the last relationship of my life. I've never had that feeling that I've found the one. So, spinster it is."

"How do you even have time to date?" Lena asked. "I've read your bio. You've got to be constantly working. I know *I* feel like I am, and I'm not a CEO. On top of that, I read that you're still trying to finish your degree."

"It's one class a semester and not really a big deal, but yeah… I'm busy. It's easier when Seth is around, but I know he likes traveling. I'll handle things until he gets back," Summer replied.

"That's awfully nice of you. Have *you* ever left for that long before?" Lena asked.

"No, I don't think I've left ever." Summer shrugged. "I don't think I've had a vacation since we started this thing seven years ago."

"Summer, you deserve a break. If your brother gets a long one, I'd say you're due for one yourself."

"Maybe, but it's not a big deal."

"You say that a lot; that things aren't a big deal," Lena said.

"I do?" Summer's eyebrows lifted.

"You do," Lena confirmed.

"Um… hi. You're Summer Taft, right?" A woman stood at the end of their booth and looked down at Summer.

"Yeah."

"I saw you here, but didn't know if I should come over. Can I, maybe, get you a refill?"

"No, thanks. I'm fine." Summer looked across the table at Lena. "Right, babe?"

Lena was taken aback by that, but only for a moment, before she realized what Summer was doing.

"Right." Lena looked up.

"Sorry. You were here with a group earlier, so I didn't know you two were together." The woman started walking backward. "Sorry."

Lena and Summer smiled before Summer rolled her eyes at the whole thing.

"How often does that happen to you?" Lena asked her.

"Getting hit on?"

"Yeah."

"That wasn't exactly getting hit on," Summer began. "That – what she just did, happens to me a couple of times a week, or usually at least once a night if I go out." She pointed at the woman who had migrated to the bar. "That is what I call *'hitting on the name and not the person.'*"

"You think it's just because of who you are?" Lena questioned.

"If someone approaches me with my full name, I generally don't let them buy me a drink."

"Doesn't that prohibit you from meeting someone you might really like?"

"Maybe. But I don't want someone just walking up to me like that. I'd prefer they just ask my name, even if they know it. Maybe that's weird, though."

"I can understand, I guess." Lena lifted her empty glass a few inches off the table and then placed it back down. "Well, I should probably be going. It's getting late. And I've reached my drink limit for the night."

"Me too. I have some house-searching to do this weekend. I'll give your friend a call tomorrow, to see if he can help," Summer said.

"Good. Let me know how it goes."

Lena slid out of the booth and stood. As Summer did the same, they were suddenly standing face to face. They were the same height, Lena realized, or at least very near that. Summer's eyes sparkled a little in the lantern light. The Lantern used actual lanterns as a part of their décor, and many of them hung throughout the room. Lena had to guess that many people that hit on Summer, weren't just hitting on her because of her name. The woman was even more attractive up close and in person, than she was in pictures Lena had seen online.

"I will. Thanks for the help. Hopefully, I can find a place soon."

"Of course," Lena replied, and then, she considered something. "I have an idea… I'm still terrible with women and really want to avoid the loud chewers with three kids from now on. You seem to want to avoid a certain group of, well, groupies." Lena said and listened as Summer laughed. "Am I wrong?"

"No. I've just never thought about it like that before."

"What if we help each other out? We can go out together one night. Maybe here, or maybe somewhere else, and act as a wing woman for the other. I'll even go to straight bars for you, if you want. I don't really know how it works if you're bi and all your friends are lesbians."

"We go to Windy's and BBZ's sometimes, too," Summer said of the other two bars their group of friends frequented. "And I like the idea, but I don't think we should limit ourselves to just bars."

"That's probably a good idea." Lena nodded her head to the side, to indicate that they should start walking out. "Where else do you meet people outside of work and school?"

"God! Who knows?" Summer questioned as they made their way to the door. "Bookstores? Libraries? Is that even where smart people hang out anymore? I'd like a smart person, preferably. Do bookstores still exist?" Summer laughed as they made their way outside. She then typed something into her phone and looked back up at Lena.

"I think there are still a few around. There's the

farmer's market downtown. I bet people meet people there," Lena replied.

"People meet people at a farmer's market?" Summer seemed skeptical.

"I don't know. It sounded right." Lena laughed at herself.

"I just called for my car. We'll drop you off if you didn't drive." Summer nodded toward the street.

"You don't have to do that. I can grab an Uber or a cab."

"Why?" Summer looked back at her. "My car's here. Don't hold it against me. I'm not one of those crazy, rich people. I just hate driving in the city."

The car pulled up to the curb and Summer opened the door.

"Come on." She motioned with her free hand for Lena to join her.

"Okay. But if we're going in the opposite directions, it's on you," Lena told her and climbed into the car.

CHAPTER 3

SUMMER HAD the driver drop Lena off at her house just outside the city after he dropped her off at her apartment. She'd had a good time with everyone. It made the long day seem not that long at all. She had enjoyed listening to Ember and Eva banter with Hailey and Charlie, and even noticed that she, herself, was now more a part of it than before; meaning that the tight group of friends had opened up to her. They now shared their own inside jokes and histories. Summer smiled at that thought.

She'd had friends in high school and college but lost touch with practically all of them thanks to the company. She had always felt like she was missing something in her life. She was missing adult friends. She'd found that with these women, though. And now, there was the new addition of Lena to that group.

When Summer saw Lena walk into the bar that night, she had actually considered excusing herself from the table and walking over to wherever the woman ended up, to try to talk to her. Lena had this wavy blonde hair that was at about her shoulders. Her eyes were a color Summer hadn't ever seen before. They were blue, but not just blue. They were teal, maybe, or something similar. They didn't look real. They looked almost magical, as if Lena was really a character from a fantasy film, and she would soon reveal superpowers, or her wings would appear.

Then, Lena joined their table. Summer found it hard to look away from Lena the entire night. It was even more difficult for her because she couldn't exactly look at Emma, either. Summer hated this awkwardness between them. It was juvenile. She knew they needed to address it. She liked Emma. If Emma wasn't still hung up on that wretched ex-girlfriend of hers, Summer thought they might have had something after that night. But Emma had some things to work through before Summer would even consider that, and she had no clue if Emma was even considering it herself.

***

She called Hayden the next day. He was available to meet her for coffee. So, after readying herself in her casual hooded sweatshirt and jeans, Summer headed out to the coffee shop.

Hayden was a pretty good-looking guy; Summer had to admit to herself as she walked into the small café and took in the man who stood upon seeing her arrive. He was likely around 6'2" and definitely dressed for a meeting with a potential client, which made Summer feel like maybe she should have dressed a little better herself. The guy was wearing a gray pinstripe suit, with a tailored jacket, and a white undershirt with a light-blue tie. His hair was between blonde and brown and had been coifed back with gel. His eyes were kind and brown.

"Miss Taft, I'm Hayden Lewis. It's nice to meet you." He held out his hand for her to shake.

"You too." Summer felt vastly under-dressed and definitely wished she had done something more with her hair, other than just pull it back into a lazy ponytail. "Thanks for meeting with me so soon," she added.

"Of course." Hayden motioned for her to sit down first, which Summer did. He followed and opened the case on his iPad. "If you don't mind, I'd like to just hear a little about what you're looking for, take some notes, and if I know of any listings right now that fit, we can look at those on this first." Hayden motioned to his iPad. "If not, I'll get to work, send you what I find later, and we can arrange to see the ones you're interested in."

"That sounds good."

Summer listed off some of the amenities she had in her Palo Alto house that she would also like to have in Chicago. She added a few of them to the list and made sure to stress that she wanted something in the city and that a condo would be perfect.

Hayden nodded and took his notes in the process. As they reviewed three listings, he thought Summer might be interested in, she only wanted to see one in person. They had agreed to go out on Monday afternoon to see it, and he would keep looking to find what she wanted.

"What's making you relocate to Chicago?" Hayden asked as he sipped on his coffee.

"It makes sense for my business. We also have our new office in Detroit. I'm actually planning to buy something there as well. Do you handle anything outside of the city, or do I need to contact someone else for that?"

"I haven't worked in Detroit, but I can put some feelers out there for you and at least get you some listings you might be interested in. My office has a sister office in Ann Arbor. That's only about forty-five minutes away. I can work with them to find you something, I'm sure."

"That would be great. Thanks," Summer replied and finished the coffee. "I should head out. I have some work to do. Thank you for this, though."

"No problem. It's part of the job." Hayden stood when she stood. "I'll be in touch. And I'll see you on Monday."

***

"Hey, Seth," Summer greeted her brother.

"Hey, Sum."

"Where are you now?" she asked.

"Prague."

"Prague? Prague is nowhere near Thailand."

25

"I decided to come here on a whim. I've never been before. It's amazing. You should come."

"I can't. I have to run the company you started," she replied.

"We started." For some reason, he felt it important that Summer take credit for starting the business with him. "And no one is stopping you from taking a vacation. You know you're the boss, right?"

"Sometimes, it doesn't feel that way. When are you coming back?"

"I'm going to spend a couple of weeks here. I'll be back, then. And before you say anything... I've already booked my flight."

"That doesn't mean anything. How many flights have you missed because you decided to stay somewhere longer?"

"I know I need to get back, Sum. I've been traveling for a long time. I'm ready to come home, too."

"Well, there's something you should know, then, before it hits all the news on Monday. I'm moving to Chicago."

"You're already in Chicago."

"I know. I'm buying a place here and making it my primary residence."

"Oh. Is stuff really picking up there, or are you worried you need more of a presence at the new office?" Seth asked.

"I just like it here. I have a good group of friends. I enjoy the people in the office here. Plus, it's closer to the other office. I'll still keep my place in Palo Alto, and I'll go to that office when I need to, but I want to live in Chicago."

"Okay, Sum. Whatever you want works for me. Should *I* move to Chicago?" he asked.

"If you want to move to Chicago."

"I don't."

"Then, don't move to Chicago, Seth," Summer replied with a shake of her head.

"Then, I won't. I'll just crash at your place whenever

I'm in town."

"I'm getting a one-bedroom house, then, to avoid that," she joked.

"Sure, you are," he replied sarcastically. "I'll just crash on the couch, then."

"I'll buy the most uncomfortable couch I can find."

"And I'll replace it when you're out of the house."

"I give up."

Seth laughed and said, "Hey, I should go. My friends are ready to head out."

"Friends? You're traveling alone, Seth."

"Not anymore. I met these two British guys in Thailand. They're here with me. We've been having some fun."

"Picking up girls?"

Summer knew her extraverted brother well. While she was the one not to use her notoriety, Seth was somehow the opposite, and he used it whenever it suited him.

"Sometimes," Seth admitted. "But we're just doing a guys' thing right now. Anyway, I'll call you next week, okay?"

"Have fun. Be safe, Seth. I've seen the movie *Hostel*. People know you're a rich American. They'd pay millions to kill you."

A couple of hours into working, Summer received an email from Hayden, with more listings for her to check out. She put the web page on her smart TV and scrolled through the pictures of the four different condos he recommended. She messaged him back that there were two she was interested in seeing as soon as possible, since they'd just popped up on the market.

Summer went back to work for another few minutes before deciding to message Lena a thank you. She texted a quick message and then decided to go workout at the apartment's gym. She dressed and headed downstairs, placing her headphones in her ears and turning the phone's downloaded music on so that she could drown out the other sounds of the world around her. She was exhausted by the end of her workout and ready for a shower. After that, she changed into something she could go grocery shopping in and grabbed her keys to lock up.

She heard the familiar ping of her cell phone text notification and picked it up. She then smiled at Lena's reply and walked to the corner market, where she could pick up a few things she knew she needed. Her phone rang again later, as she was preparing a pasta dinner for herself. She gulped when she saw it was Emma Colton calling.

"Hey."

"Hi," Emma replied.

"What's up?" Summer tried to appear casual.

"I just thought we might want to talk," Emma said. "We haven't since that night, and things are weird now."

"You noticed, huh?"

"Yeah, I noticed," Emma replied with a small laugh. "I don't want it to be, but it is."

"I know. Neither do I," Summer said. "What are you doing now? I'm cooking pasta. You want to come over for dinner, and we can talk?"

"I can be there in twenty minutes."

"I'll see you then."

Summer boiled the water, moved to the small living room to place the throw blanket back over the couch, and plugged her laptop into the makeshift desk she had bought and put together herself next to the TV stand.

Living in this tiny apartment reminded her of a time when she didn't have much, and despite the claustrophobic feeling she sometimes had, it was also comforting to her. She hated what her mother's death had done to her father, because she loved her father, and that man was gone. He had been replaced with a pod person who was barely even there. Summer hated that he was still in so much pain, but he had lost the love of his life, and she couldn't fault him for missing her. Summer missed her mother, too. She had wished every single day that she could somehow have her back. She wanted to tell her about the company, school, and she wanted to get her mother's advice on the people she dated, like any daughter would; but she couldn't.

"Hi," Emma greeted her while holding a bottle of red wine. "I couldn't show up empty-handed. Sorry."

"You're apologizing for bringing wine?" Summer lifted an eyebrow. "Come on in." She smiled at Emma and motioned for her to come into the apartment.

Emma passed her the bottle of wine and glanced around the open space.

"I already opened that bottle." Summer pointed to a bottle of red that had been a gift from someone a few months ago, but she couldn't remember who had actually done the giving. "We'll save this one for later."

"Okay."

Emma and Summer carried bowls to the coffee table together. Summer returned to the kitchen to grab the bottle and two glasses. She then poured a generous amount into both glasses, feeling like they could both probably use the alcohol.

"Should I start, or should you?" Summer questioned after moving pasta around in her bowl for a few minutes while watching Emma do the same.

"I don't know. I've never done this before," Emma said. "I guess I just wanted to clear the air between us, because it feels awkward now. I don't want it to be."

"Neither do I," Summer said. "I don't regret what happened. I hope you don't think that's why I've been avoiding bringing it up. I wouldn't have left that morning if I didn't have to for my meeting."

"I know. I don't think that," Emma replied.

"What *do* you think?" Summer asked.

"That it probably shouldn't have happened, but it did," Emma revealed. "I was in a pretty bad place after what happened with Eli. I think I just needed someone to talk to, and you and I got along so well."

"And it just happened?"

"I don't regret it, either. But it probably wasn't a good idea then."

"No, I guess it wasn't," Summer said. "I am sorry we haven't talked about it since, though. That was stupid. We're adults."

"I know." Emma set her bowl down on the table. She had yet to take a bite. "But, here's the thing…" She turned to face Summer on the couch. "I *do* like you. I did then, too. I think you're smart, beautiful, and funny. That's why it happened. It wasn't just because I was trying to get my ex out of my system. I want you to know that."

"I do. But, thank you," Summer said.

"Do you think you'd want to go out for real?" Emma asked. "On an actual date?"

"Oh." Summer set her bowl down next to Emma's on the table. She had yet to drink her wine, and she was starting to regret that. "Emma, I don't know."

"Okay. Never mind," Emma said.

"No, Emma. Don't do that." Summer turned to face the woman and placed her hand on Emma's thigh. "I'm sorry. You just caught me off guard. I thought we were going to talk about what happened and put it behind us. I didn't know you wanted us to go out."

"If you don't like me like that, you don't like me like that." Emma's lips went into a straight line. "I must seriously have a problem."

"What do you mean?" Summer asked.

"I spent most of my adult life thinking about Hailey as the love of my life, and then – the one that got away. I finally moved on from that and met Eli. I fell in love with her and thought we would be together. It turned out, she still wanted her ex-girlfriend. But she couldn't just break up with me; she had to cheat on me for months. And I was too blind to notice it. Now, I'm into you, and you're not into me."

"I never said that," Summer replied.

"Never said what?"

"That I wasn't into you," Summer started. "I *was* into

you that night, Emma. I wouldn't have slept with you otherwise. We had a couple of great nights, I had fun, and that led us to what happened. It wasn't some drunken hookup for me."

"But you don't want to go out?"

"I don't think we should, Emma. Are you honestly sure you're even over Eli? It didn't seem like that last night," Summer said.

"I am entirely over her," Emma returned.

"I'm not judging. You loved her, and she hurt you. I just don't want to get involved with anyone if they're still thinking about someone else."

"I'm not thinking about her, Summer."

Emma's tone conveyed a different message. Summer wondered if Emma, herself, could tell.

"I think you're still working on it, and that's fine. But I don't think we should date. I like you. And I think we should be friends. If at some point in the future things change, we can see about more then."

"Because you still think I'm hung up on my ex-girlfriend?"

"I don't think you're hung up on her. I think you have to work through the pain; and that takes time."

"Yeah, I guess." Emma turned and rested back against the couch.

"I don't want things to be awkward between us anymore, Emma. I think people are starting to pick up on the fact that things are weird. I don't want that."

"Yeah, Hailey has been on my case for an explanation. She's convinced I have a thing for you."

"Well, you did ask me out," Summer said with a smile.

Emma turned her head and smiled back.

"I think we'll be okay. Just give me some time. I'll work through the whole Eli thing, and you and I will be fine," Emma replied.

"Okay." Summer picked up her bowl. "Now, eat. It's getting cold."

CHAPTER 4

LENA MET HAYDEN FOR dinner Sunday night. She hadn't seen him in a while, but there was something that made her want to reach out and meet up.

"Hey there." He stood and pulled out Lena's chair.

"Hey. Long time no see." She sat.

"I know. I've been busy. I seem to recall that you've been pretty busy, too."

"Things have finally settled down now. I thought we should get together."

"And this wouldn't have anything to do with the high-profile client you sent me this weekend?" He lifted an eyebrow.

"Summer? Why would you think that?"

"I wasn't sure, but *now* I am. You have a crush on Summer Taft." He pointed his finger at her.

"I do not have a crush on Summer Taft. I met her Friday night. She needed a real estate agent. I suggested you." Lena paused and glared at him playfully. "I'm starting to regret that referral."

"Hey, she's a beautiful woman, and she's smart. I could tell that during our meeting. You could definitely do worse."

"Sounds like *you* have a little crush on Summer Taft." Lena gulped.

"I could definitely do worse, too. But she's on your

team, isn't she?"

"I hate when people say that. Like we're all about to play a game of softball or something."

"Sorry, I didn't mean it like that. I just meant that she's gay, isn't she?" Hayden asked.

"I don't think I should be commenting on anyone's sexuality other than my own; seems wrong. But, are you interested?" Lena asked.

She nodded in thanks as the waiter returned with their drinks. They ordered the same meal they always ordered when they came to their favorite restaurant. When the waiter walked away, Lena folded her hands on top of the table and waited for an answer.

"I'm interested. She's gorgeous. She seems nice, too. But I'm dating someone. And I don't date clients, anyway. It's always messy."

"You're dating someone?"

"Yes. Her name is Lauren. She's a paralegal. It's nothing serious, but we've been out a few times, and I like it so far."

"That's great, Hayden. I'm glad."

"We'll see. But if Summer wasn't a client, I would maybe ask her out for a drink. Lauren and I aren't exclusive yet."

Lena gulped her wine. She wasn't sure why. She and Summer were friends and had decided to help one another find prospective partners. Summer was bi and, therefore, could date men as well. And Hayden was a great guy. He had been a great agent for her when she was going through her divorce. She had been happy to finally put that chapter of her life behind her. But she had also never lived alone and had gone through a lot of change in a short period of time. Hayden had been a good shoulder to cry on and a sounding board. That later led to their friendship continuing on past their working relationship. He had his own money because of his successful career in real estate, and he was intelligent and funny. Summer could do worse.

***

Lena got home after her dinner with Hayden. She enjoyed hearing about his successes in business and in his personal life. As she later sat on her sofa, she wondered about her own recent successes, or if she even had any. Certainly, she had professional successes. O'Shea's was thriving, and that was at least in part due to the decisions Lena was making regarding strategic locations for new stores and the management teams that ran them. Outside of her job, though, she had nothing else worth mentioning in a conversation with a friend; and that was a little scary to her.

It reminded Lena of how trapped she used to feel in her marriage. She hadn't worked back then, but she had volunteered with various charitable organizations, as she had watched her mother do the same growing up in Connecticut. Lena had attended Yale and had done well, but she had gotten married instead of graduating. So, she did what she knew – she volunteered. Outside of her volunteer work, she had a couple of clubs she had joined by recommendation, but she didn't really consider any of the women in the clubs her true friends. Lena had cooked, cleaned, and essentially, acted as a 1950's housewife. And she hated it. Her phone rang just as she was about to grab her computer and check some work emails. She picked it up to see that it was Summer Taft calling.

"Hi," she greeted the woman and realized that her tone likely came off as nervous.

"Hey. What are you up to tonight?" Summer asked.

"I just got back from dinner with Hayden. Why?"

"There's a book signing at Moreland's, not too far from my apartment. Any chance you're a fan of Joan Parkston?"

"I don't know who that is," Lena admitted while clenching her teeth.

"Most people probably don't know who she is, but

she's a brilliant computer programmer. She's got a new book out about her first years in programming. I just got an e-vite to attend. Technically, I got it a couple of weeks ago, but I just noticed it an hour ago. I've met her once, and she was nice. I feel like I should be supportive. I was hoping you'd come with me. I know it's last-minute; you probably have plans…"

"I don't."

"Are you interested? I'm sure it will mostly be a bunch of nerds like me in attendance, but there are some hot nerds out there. We might be able to find one for you." Summer laughed.

"Oh, right," Lena recalled their plan to help each other out in the dating department. "Sure. When should I meet you there?"

"In, like, thirty minutes, if that's not too soon."

"No, I'm still dressed from dinner."

"Do you want me to just swing by and get you? Or maybe not, just in case you meet someone," Summer teased.

"I'll meet you there. It would be out of your way to come here."

"See you then." Summer hung up.

***

Lena stood outside the bookstore and watched as several people headed inside. She wasn't sure if she should meet Summer inside or out, initially, so she had already gone inside and checked, but Summer had yet to arrive. Lena had gone back outside the crowded store to wait there instead. She had been correct in her assumption.

"Lena, hey."

The woman's car had pulled up behind where Lena was standing, and Summer climbed out.

"Hi there." Lena gave her a small wave and took the few steps in that direction.

Summer was dressed somewhat casually, but she had

on a black sleeveless turtleneck, with a gray sweater over it, and black boots that had the woman looking a little classier than just casual. Her hair was pulled back, and she had on hoop earrings.

"Thanks for coming," Summer told her when she stood in front of Lena.

"Thanks for the invite."

"Invitations weren't required. It's more about letting me know that it's happening than an actual invitation, but I'm glad you could come. Wanna go inside?"

"Sure."

Lena followed Summer inside the local bookstore. It had been in the city for over sixty years and had that kind of old, comfy feel to it. It had two stories and a staircase in the middle. The crowd of people, that were there for the signing, was headed to the back, behind the stairs. Summer was ahead of Lena as they walked. Lena watched as people noticed the other woman and did double takes. Some took out their phones and snapped pictures. Summer either didn't notice or just didn't care. Lena surmised that she was probably just used to it. As they approached the side of the stairs, though, Lena looked down to see that Summer had reached her hand back to her to help guide her to their destination.

Lena took it and allowed herself to be pulled, because Summer gave off this kind of confidence Lena rarely saw. She sometimes had to have it herself at work – and that was especially true since her company was dominated by males in other VP positions, but she turned it off as soon as she left the office, because it was exhausting. Summer just seemed to possess it naturally, though, and Lena found it attractive. Actually, Lena found it sexy. Even the back of Summer's long neck, as the woman walked, was sexy to Lena.

Finally, they arrived at the open space, where there were some chairs for the audience to sit in – that were already full, and a table at the front of the room.

Bookshelves lined the walls around the space, and people who hadn't secured seats, were standing in front of them, mainly staring down at their phones.

"It's interesting, isn't it?" Summer half-whispered to Lena, as Lena stood beside her after Summer dropped her hand.

"What?"

"That we are in this room filled with books, and everyone is just staring at their phones. Most of them are probably reading something."

"I would think someone in your line of work would have liked that." Lena turned her head toward Summer. "Technology business and everything."

"I actually have a surprising book collection," Summer revealed.

"You do?" Lena wrinkled her eyebrows.

"Eva's approved of it, actually," Summer shared of their friend Eva, the Doctor of Literature, who had a pretty large collection herself. "I have some first and second editions of the classics; some older stuff, too. I buy new stuff in places like this and, sometimes, in airports as I travel." Summer then paused and looked around. "I have e-books, too, and some audio, but I prefer the paper."

"Why's that?"

"Partly, because I like the smell. Books have an amazing smell. It reminds me of my mom. I guess, the other reason is that I had these built-in bookshelves in my house and needed to fill them with something," Summer said that last part rapidly, making Lena wonder why she had glossed over the mention of her mom. "Oh, here we go." Summer pointed at a woman who had entered the space through an employee-only entrance and was waving Summer over.

"Where are we going?"

"VIP spot." Summer took Lena's hand again and walked her around a few people in the direction of the woman.

It was then that Lena really noticed: the room was

filled with women. There were a few men, here and there, but the space was probably filled with 90% women. She would have expected the opposite, considering the author's field.

"Hey, Alana." Summer let go of Lena's hand when she met the woman and gave her a quick hug.

"I'm glad you could make it," the woman Lena now knew was named Alana returned. "You didn't reply until tonight."

"I missed the email. Sorry." Summer pulled back and then motioned to Lena. "This is my friend, Lena. She's my plus-one tonight."

"Nice to meet you." Alana reached out her hand for Lena to shake.

"You too," Lena replied.

"Alana is Joan's manager," Summer explained.

"She's back here." Alana held the door opened for the two of them to walk through.

"We're going in the back?" Lena questioned but followed the women all the same.

"VIP," Summer reminded with a wink.

They made their way down a brightly lit hallway. One of its walls was lined with a floor to ceiling bookshelf, that Lena could guess had rows and rows of books that would soon line the shelves on the sales floor. The other wall had rows of carts with books that also needed to be shelved, it appeared. There was also a room off to the right, where Lena could see the staffers unloading more books from boxes. Then, they arrived at a door on the left, that Alana entered a four-digit code into and then opened the door. Lena followed Summer through the door again. Alana closed it behind them and then got in front of them.

"Joan, Summer's here."

"Summer!" Joan stood and embraced Summer with a warm hug and a smile.

Lena had expected Joan Parkston to be older, maybe even slightly chubby, and with acne all over her face. She wasn't sure why she had expected that, but that had been the image her mind brought forth earlier, when Summer mentioned her name and her genius with computers.

This woman was none of those things, though. She was around Lena's age, maybe a few years younger. She had blonde curly hair that landed just below her shoulders and almond-shaped brown eyes. She was an inch or two taller than Summer, and thus, Lena as well. The woman was also rail-thin and, apparently, had a pretty good sense of fashion, because she had a black and white sundress on with a cardigan over it and ballet flats. She was, in short, beautiful.

"How are you?" Summer asked Joan when they pulled away.

"I'm good. Things are going well. The book is selling." Joan turned to see Lena standing there, and her expression changed from smiling and happy to a perplexed one. "And who's your *friend*?" she asked and highlighted the word *'friend'* with her tone, as if checking on their relationship.

"This is Lena. Lena, this is Joan Parkston," Summer introduced.

"Nice to meet you." Lena gave her a hand to shake, which Joan did.

"You too. Thanks for coming." Joan nodded and then returned her dark eyes back to Summer. "I was worried you wouldn't come. Alana said she hadn't heard from you. I thought about calling you myself, but things have been so busy with the tour... We're usually only in one place long enough to host the signing, do a meet and greet, and fly off to the next place."

"I get a lot of invites to things. This one got lost in the shuffle. Sorry, I would have responded sooner if I would have caught it." Summer stepped back beside Lena.

"No harm." Joan glanced at Lena again. "So, how do you two know each other?" she asked and motioned with her finger between the two of them.

"Joan, we should head out there," Alana said, and Lena turned to see that she was standing behind them, with someone, who, Lena guessed, was probably the manager of the store, based on the lanyard around the woman's neck with her bookstore ID on it. "They're getting restless."

"Oh, right." Joan nodded at Alana and then glanced at Summer again. "I'm staying in Chicago for the night. Can we catch up after?"

"Lena and I can't stay long, unfortunately. We have plans tonight," Summer lied, and Lena's face must have shown her initial confusion, but she quickly pushed that expression away and nodded as Joan then looked her way. "I just wanted to stop by and say hello and congratulations," Summer added.

"And get an autographed copy?" Joan asked.

"Of course," Summer answered with a smile.

Joan signed the books for both of them and then hugged Summer again. Lena watched as the woman's hand lingered on Summer's forearm a little too long before she headed out into the store for her reading and signing. Lena and Summer were ushered out of the back offices and into the store, where they left Alana to her work and headed toward the staircase instead.

"We have plans tonight?" Lena checked as they headed up the stairs.

Summer laughed and made her way past a foursome of women who were heading down the stairs.

"And why are there so many women here?" Lena asked as well.

Summer laughed again and waited for Lena at the top of the stairs.

"The café's up here. Do you want something?" Summer asked

She pointed to a small café at the right back wall. Lena had never been to this bookstore, but she was starting to consider it a place she should visit more frequently. The café had a couple of tables, some warm-looking oversized love seats, and also leather chairs, where patrons could read and relax. To the left, there was a loft that allowed people to gather at the edge and look down at the open space, where authors would read and sign. Currently, there was a solid row of customers standing right there, leaning over; likely, waiting for Joan to begin her reading.

"Sure."

"And, about the whole plans thing... Sorry about that," Summer began. "I guess I should have warned you before, but I thought she would be over it by now."

"Over it?" Lena stood next to Summer in the short line and turned toward her.

"Joan's gay. Hence the number of women here. She's kind of a well-known coder and a lesbian. She has a lot of female fans. Some of them actually understand coding, and some just think she's hot."

"She is attractive," Lena said. "You two were a thing?"

"No. We've only met once before, like I told you. I figured out pretty quickly back then, though, that she was flirting. I flirted back – which was a mistake, because she's nice and all, but I'm not interested. It was at a function I had to attend. I genuinely like her, but she was a little... forward."

"What did she do?" Lena asked, and they moved up a position in line.

"She kissed me; and we'd known each other for, like, two hours. We were outside the party with a few of her friends, who were smoking. We were all just talking. They went inside, and she asked me to stay out with her. We talked for a few more minutes, and then, she leaned in and kissed me." Summer moved up another place in line with Lena following. "It took me a second, but I pulled back; mostly, out of shock, but then, because I didn't really want to be kissing her. I'd flirted back, and that was my fault. Sometimes, I don't realize I'm doing it until it's too late. Anyway, I told her I wasn't interested, and she said she understood. She then got my number from somewhere and texted me after with an apology. We just kept up a correspondence, I guess. A text here or there for a few months, until it stopped. I figured she'd gotten busy or moved onto someone else. Then, I saw the invite tonight."

"Why did you come if you're not interested?" Lena asked.

"Professional reasons. She's brilliant. I had Ember look over some of her stuff, because Ember is also at that genius level. She agreed that Joan is crazy smart. Her work could help my company."

"You want to recruit her?"

"No, she's not someone you recruit. But she is someone we might contract with one day. I wouldn't add her to my full-time staff. She's more interested in the fame, that comes with writing a book, and the fans, than she is with the actual content."

Just as Summer nodded in the direction of the women leaning over the banister of the loft, the sound of applause invaded the quiet of the store, and Joan was introduced.

"She's good at what she does," Summer continued. "But I'm not looking for some glory hound at work or in my personal life. I just may need her one day, to advance our code or help with a product. Plus, she is one of the few women – unfortunately, in this field at her level, and she's also gay and is more than out. I think it's important we all support one another in that way, too." Summer placed her hands on the counter as they arrived at the barista to place their order. "Can I get a large cappuccino and whatever she wants?" She motioned with her thumb to Lena.

"Same," Lena said.

Summer paid for their order, and they walked to the side of the bar to wait for their drinks.

"I appreciate you backing me up in there," Summer continued again. "I didn't mean to put you on the spot. I had no idea she'd want to hang out after this. I was kind of hoping she would think you and I were together if I said we had plans."

"Happy to help." Lena smiled at her.

CHAPTER 5

SUMMER PASSED LENA her coffee. Then, she took her own cup as they made their way to the condiments station to add some sugar and stir their beverages.

"The upside of that little awkward moment with Joan, is that we're surrounded by women. I'm sure many of them are single and, likely, also into women." Summer smirked at Lena. "Any of them stand out to you? We could pretend to be looking for a good book and strike up a conversation."

Lena took a long glance around the café and then over to the women hanging onto Joan's every word on the banister of the loft space.

"Won't Joan notice we're still here?" Lena asked.

"Joan will be reading and signing; she won't be paying any attention."

Lena seemed to be considering something. Summer took a moment to sip on her cappuccino and stare into those amazing blue eyes. God, they were so intense and gorgeous.

"I'm okay with just hanging out tonight. I guess I'm not really in the mood to meet anyone new. Sorry, I know that's why you invited me," Lena replied.

"That's not why I invited you. I know what we said before, but I called you because I liked hanging out with you. We don't have to pick up people together just to hang out," Summer said.

"No, we don't." Lena laughed a little. "Should we listen to the reading?" She motioned with her thumb over to where Joan was reading her new book out loud.

"I just got a copy, so I don't need to hear her. You?"

"No, I guess not," Lena agreed.

Summer thought for a moment, met Lena's eyes, and took out her phone.

"Do you want to go somewhere else?" She searched for a phone number.

"Where? It's Sunday night," Lena reminded.

"You ever been to the Adler?" Summer asked and glanced up at her from her phone. "The planetarium."

"No. Why?"

"It's one of my favorite places in the city. It's nearby. You wanna go?"

"I repeat; it's Sunday," Lena said.

Summer lifted her phone to her ear with a smirk on her face.

"Rebecca, it's Summer Taft."

***

Summer had the car pick them up at the store and drive them the short distance to the planetarium. They parked around the back of the building.

"So, you know someone that works here, and you can just come whenever?" Lena asked as Summer opened the car door for them both to climb out.

"Not exactly. I've donated a lot to this place since I discovered it, but I come by whenever they have a new exhibit. One time, I got recognized and did the whole picture thing with a few people. I made a comment to the escort – that they insisted I have, to get me where I wanted to go without having to wait. I wished I could just enjoy the exhibits without all that. She gave me a private number and told me to call whenever I wanted to stop by. I've done it a few times now. It's actually pretty cool. They always have staff on site, even if it's just security, and I get the place to myself," Summer replied.

The back door opened, and a security guard stood, waiting for them.

"Miss Taft," he greeted her.

"Hi," she returned, and they headed inside. "Can we do the walk through space and time?" she asked him and turned toward Lena. "I haven't done that one yet. Is that okay with you?"

"Yeah, sure. I don't know what that is."

Summer followed the guard down the hall, that was mainly lit by exit lights, in the direction of the exhibition hall, where they would be able to watch the night sky as told through film.

"Here." Summer handed Lena a program she found on a rack.

"Transport yourself to the distant corners of the cosmos and witness how the universe has evolved over 13.7 billion years, from the Big Bang to this morning's sunrise," Lena read out loud.

"You already knew I was a big nerd, right? I assumed the whole tech start-up thing gave it away." Summer glanced over at her.

"It sounds pretty interesting," Lena replied.

Summer stopped just outside the door to the IMAX theatre and turned to her.

"Sorry, I kind of just dragged you to a book signing and then here. Are you sure this is okay?"

"It's more than okay," Lena said after a moment. "I realized tonight that I need to get out more."

"Get out more?"

Summer smiled at Lena and motioned for her to walk past her and pick a seat in the expansive yet completely empty theatre. Lena headed down the aisle and chose a seat toward the middle. Summer sat down next to her on her right.

"Hayden had all these stories tonight, and only a few of them were about his job. I realized that all my stories were about work. I somehow went from being a woman who had no stories about work, because I had no work, to a woman who only has work stories, because she has no life," Lena explained.

Summer turned her face to Lena and took the woman in. Lena was staring ahead at the enormous screen that was both in front of and somehow around them as well. She looked lost, almost, and Summer's smile disappeared from her face.

"Well, at least you'll have a story to tell him next time. How many people do you know get private showings at planetariums?"

"I guess so."

The screen illuminated, and a few seconds later, their show began. The story began with the Big Bang. Summer's eyes were mostly glued to the screen, enjoying the colors and the beauty of the stars and other celestial bodies as the story of the universe unfolded before them. Every so often, though, she would catch herself turning to check on Lena's expression. She wanted to know if Lena was enjoying the experience, too, or if she was bored out of her mind. What Summer hadn't expected each time she turned slightly to look at the woman, was the play of the colors in Lena's blue, near teal-colored eyes. Watching the greens, grays, silvers, yellows, and full-color spectrum play out in Lena's eyes, only enhanced Summer's enjoyment. Compared to that, the giant screen in front of the two of them was nothing. Summer had only chanced brief glances, though, because she didn't want Lena to think she was staring. But, every time she turned back, she was again surprised with the vibrancy, despite having noticed it only a few moments before.

***

"Did you like it?" Summer asked as the show came to an end, and she turned to face Lena.

"I feel really small." Lena smiled and turned to face Summer.

"Small?" Summer asked with a look of confusion.

"When you think about how big the world is, it's usually abstract. But I just watched the Universe become the Universe. It's less abstract now. I feel really, really small." Lena laughed a little.

"It's interesting, isn't it? We feel like we're the center of our own world. We walk around all day, and all we know is what we experience, so we feel big in a way. I know I feel that way. And, sometimes, it's exhausting." Summer paused and sighed. "I don't think I was prepared for what came along with this app thing when Seth and I first started it. People take pictures and want autographs from me almost every day. It's strange. I'm not a real celebrity. I'm not an actress or a singer. I'm just a CEO of a tech start-up."

"So is Mark Zuckerberg."

"I never expected us to be as big as Facebook. When you start in a garage, with your wacky older brother, it's hard to picture the whole thing working out. Seth was the face back then. I was just along for the ride. But now, it's mostly me people are interested in. It can sometimes feel like I'm the center of the Universe because of that. I know that makes me sound egotistical."

"I get it," Lena told her.

"I like coming here because I can get lost in the experience. I find that I actually like feeling small."

Lena nodded in understanding and said, "I should probably go. It's getting late, and I have work tomorrow."

"You know, I'm meeting Hayden tomorrow, to check out a house." Summer stood and headed out of the row and into the aisle, as Lena joined her. "I could use a second opinion, if you can get free."

"I'm in meetings until four," Lena said as they headed out of the exhibition and back down the hallway, with their guard in tow. "I wouldn't be able to get away until after."

"Well, I'll take a look myself. The pictures look nice, but it could be terrible in person. No point in you wasting your time," Summer replied.

"I usually go to The Lantern on Tuesday nights, during happy hour," Lena began. "Cheaper drinks, obviously, and there's the hot bartender that only works Tuesdays and Sundays. I usually just sit at the bar and watch her work like a creep for about an hour."

Summer laughed, "Creep, huh?"

"I've never actually talked to her outside of ordering drinks," Lena confessed as they headed out the back door toward the car that was waiting for them.

"But you think she's hot?" Summer asked with a lifted eyebrow and a smirk.

"Have you seen her?"

"Can't say I spend a lot of time there on Tuesdays or Sundays," Summer shared. "Are you asking me to come this Tuesday, though?"

"I might work up the courage to talk to her if you're there." Lena climbed into the car.

"I have a meeting until 5:30. Is after that okay?" Summer climbed in next to her.

"Sounds good. Thanks. Next time, we can hit up a different bar," Lena said.

"Why?"

"In case you want to meet a guy," Lena suggested. "There aren't any straight guys at The Lantern that I've ever seen."

"Let's play it by ear." Summer looked ahead as they drove on. "Can I please take you all the way home? It's late."

"It's totally out of your way."

"I'll get dropped off first. The car can take you the rest of the way," Summer said. "I don't know why I'm asking." She then laughed at herself. "We're taking you home."

Lena laughed as they drove toward Summer's apartment. When Summer got home, after assuring Lena would arrive home safely by way of her driver, she grabbed a quick snack, checked her personal email, and climbed into bed. She had also received a text from Joan, that she gave a quick, standard reply to, about enjoying the reading. And then, she put her phone on do not disturb. She fell asleep with the vision of bright blue eyes and flashing stars.

CHAPTER 6

WHEN SHE FOUND her place in California, it had felt good. It wasn't her dream house, but it didn't have to be, either. It was her first house. The first house for someone was rarely ever their dream home. If Summer was going to stay in Chicago, she was hopeful that, maybe, the dream home was here. She hesitated to start looking now, because, ideally, her dream home would be someone else's dream home, too, and they'd share it together. She had a lot of work ahead of her, then. First, she had to find the person. Then, they had to find the house.

"We just sent the press release." Hailey leaned against the doorframe of Summer's office.

"So weird that a press release goes out because I decide to relocate." Summer leaned back in her chair.

"You're the one that had to go and create a successful business," Hailey reminded. "It's really your fault."

"Clearly." Summer smiled at her.

"Charlie's meeting me for lunch. You want to join us?" Hailey asked after a moment.

"No, you guys go ahead. I don't want to be the third wheel on your lunch date with your girlfriend."

"You know you're not a third wheel. It's not like Charlie and I are just starting out or something. We live together. And before that, we were best friends for more than a decade. I love her more than life itself, but sometimes, I could use a little relief." Hailey winked at Summer to indicate that she was joking. "You're heading out later to see that house, right? I'll just see you tomorrow?"

"Sounds good. Have a good night."

Hailey waved and headed toward her own office; likely, to grab her things. Summer sat behind her desk and reviewed the project her product team had put together and needed her to approve. The words in front of her began blurring together. She was bored. She knew it. She had known it for a while. The work wasn't exciting to her anymore. It was the same thing every day. Even if she was in a different office, the job was the same, and it no longer excited her. Of course, part of that was because Seth had been MIA for so long. And while Summer's heart just wasn't in it anymore, it wasn't like she could just step away from it all.

***

"Two beds and two baths, and you've seen the balcony." Hayden had been giving her the realtor speech since before they walked into the two-story condo.

"It's great," she returned, lacking enthusiasm.

"Is it? You don't seem to really think so." Hayden stood next to her in the empty master bedroom.

"No, it is," Summer replied and laughed lightly at herself. "I like it, I do. I just don't think it's the place for me."

"No problem." He took out his tablet and began tapping away. "Tell me what you don't like about it. I can make sure to find a better place to check out next time."

Summer turned to face him and said, "I don't know." She gave him a shoulder shrug. "I know that's not helpful. I'm sorry. I just don't get that feeling."

"That feeling?" Hayden looked up from his tablet for a second, and his phone rang in his jacket pocket. "Sorry."

He pulled the device out, glanced at the screen, and hit ignore.

"You can take that."

"It's okay. I'll call her back later. So, that feeling you were talking about."

"I don't know how to explain it, but it doesn't feel like my place."

"It doesn't feel like home," he said. "I hear that a lot in my line of work. Not a problem, though. We'll find that place for you." He tapped back on his tablet. "It took me four months and about thirty showings to find Lena her place."

"Really?" Summer asked as they headed out of the master bedroom back toward the stairs that led to the street level entrance.

"Don't tell Lena I told you, but she was very picky," he said with a wink. "I understood, though. She had never lived on her own. The place she had lived in with her ex-husband was actually her parents' old place. They gave it to them as a wedding present."

"They gave them a house?" Summer questioned as they made their way back outside.

"I guess you can get away with things like that when you're crazy rich. It was only one of their houses, I think. Anyway, she didn't get to pick it out herself. After the divorce, she stayed with a friend, got the job out here, and needed to find a place. I helped her find the perfect house. She's been there ever since." He put the key to the place back into the lockbox. "She hadn't told you that story yet? Am I going to be in trouble?"

"I doubt it. We just met the other day. We have the same group of friends, but I guess she had been traveling a lot. I came here for work every so often, but it was only recently that I really started sticking around on the weekends. We've done a little getting to know one another, but I'm sure we'll do more of that in the future. She did fill me in a little on her past, so I'm not totally surprised."

Hayden stopped in front of his car. Summer's was right behind it.

"Can I ask you a totally inappropriate question?" He tossed his keys from one hand to the other after placing his tablet back in his leather messenger bag.

"I guess." Summer lifted a perplexed eyebrow.

"I'm not asking as your agent. I'd be asking as a friend of a friend."

"Go ahead."

"Are you–" His phone rang again.

"You really can get that, you know?"

"It's the woman I'm seeing. She knows I'm working. I'll call her when I get in the car."

"You want to know if I'm gay, don't you?"

"I promise, I'm not one of those guys." Hayden put up his hands defensively. "I just love Lena like a sister."

"What does Lena have to do with anything?"

"Nothing, I guess."

"I'm bisexual, okay? Sometimes, the press has a hard time understanding that, so they say I'm gay. I don't really care about that, though, because it doesn't change who I am. I've had boyfriends, *and* I've had girlfriends."

"I'm sorry. I shouldn't have even asked. I don't know why I did, honestly."

"It happens. I'm used to it now. People have been curious about me and who I'm dating since I was outed. It's not a big deal."

"I remember hearing about that. Sorry." He seemed genuinely sympathetic.

"It happened. The worst part wasn't being outed, actually. It was what came after. Suddenly, every time I was with a guy, he was a beard. Every time I was with a woman, I was just leading her on before I went back to men. I was told to pick a side, which I can't do, because that's not how it works for me. I was branded a slut because I dated more than one person in a lifetime. It wasn't much fun then. It's died down, but it's still not much fun now." Summer glanced over at her car. "I'm just a regular person, looking for love, like everyone else."

"I'm sorry, this conversation got a lot more personal than I planned."

"It's okay." She took a step backward toward her car. "I have a dinner meeting, though. It's on the other side of town."

"I'll have new listings in your inbox tonight. Let me know which ones you want to check out. And we still have those other two to look at on Wednesday," he reminded.

"I'll be there."

***

Summer walked into The Lantern feeling guilty for being a little later than she had planned, but couldn't help the city traffic during rush hour. She saw Lena absently stirring a martini at the bar. The crowd was thin, which was expected for a Tuesday. But, as Summer approached, she took in the bartender, who was mixing up a drink for another customer, and she was a little surprised at Lena's taste in women. The woman seemed barely five-feet tall. Summer felt like when she got to the bar, she should look down behind it, because that woman must have needed an elevated floor or a step stool to do her job. She also had a stocky build and was wearing a black bandana and a studded choker.

"So, that's your type?" she asked in a hushed tone as she sat down next to Lena.

Lena looked over at her with those teal-colored eyes and a soft smile.

"No." The woman rolled her eyes. "I guess my type called in sick."

"That's good, because I think I'm a little too intimidated by her replacement to try to be your wing-woman with her. She seems intense," Summer replied.

"Well, you definitely do not have to worry about it. She

is not my type." Lena smiled and then went back to twirling an olive around in her glass. "Do you want to go somewhere else?"

"Why do you always assume I want to go somewhere else?" Summer asked just as the bartender approached. "Can I get a Rum and Coke?"

The bartender nodded solemnly, as if she wasn't paid on tips, and then headed off to make the drink.

"I don't know. I guess I don't want you to feel like we're always at places where you'd meet women."

Summer laughed as her drink was placed in front of her.

"I told you not to worry about that, remember?"

"I know." Lena took a drink and turned a little on her stool to face Summer. "Do you want to get a booth?"

"Let's go." Summer slid a bill onto the bar to cover her drink and the tip, and they headed to the booth nearest to the bar to then sit across from one another. "So, how was work?" Summer asked after they settled in.

"Oh." Lena seemed a little surprised that Summer would even ask her about that topic. "It was good, actually. We locked down a deal with a wine distributor to be exclusive to our stores in the Midwest. We were able to get it for less than we originally anticipated, so it was a good day." Lena smiled and lifted her glass to her lips. "You?" She took a drink.

Summer looked around the room and took in the other customers. They were all women, and there were about twenty of them in total, that she could see at least. Some of them were coupled off already, or at least, they appeared to be. There was a table of four, that seemed to be on a double date, based on the way the arms were wrapped over the top of the booth on both sides.

Outside of that, there were still a few somewhat lonely-looking souls sipping on drinks. Summer dismissed two of them right away, because they looked about eighteen or nineteen. She doubted they had been carded upon entry.

That left the three women in the bar. The first, Summer observed, looked to be about forty. She had an incredibly pointy nose and very thin lips that made her look like a Disney movie villain come to life. The woman, two stools down from the first one, was eyeing the scary-looking bartender, so Summer checked her off the list as well. That left the woman in the corner, who Summer immediately recognized once her vision was no longer obscured by the two women playing darts.

"Emma's here." She nodded her head in Emma's direction for Lena to follow her eyeline.

"Oh, I didn't see her." Lena turned to check.

Summer hadn't spoken to Emma since Sunday. She had no idea that the woman would be at The Lantern. Maybe Tuesday nights at the bar was Emma's thing.

"I didn't, either," Summer said and watched Emma take a drink of her beer as she stared off into space.

"We should invite her over," Lena suggested.

"I'll go get her." Summer went to stand but stopped herself as she saw someone else she recognized approach Emma's table and sit down across from her. "Or not." She stayed sitting. "Why is she talking to her ex-girlfriend?" she asked about Eli.

"The one that cheated?" Lena turned more fully to spy.

"I didn't know they were still talking." Summer realized she was staring, and she shouldn't be. "I probably shouldn't just gawk at them, huh?" She returned her eyes back to Lena's.

"Probably not. My guess is that they could use their privacy."

"Not too much, though," Summer suggested without looking back at them.

"What do you mean?"

"I just hope they're not talking about getting back together or that Emma's not going to become the other woman, since Eli has a girlfriend."

Lena nodded solemnly and gripped her hands around

her thin-stemmed glass.

"Are you sure there's nothing going on between you two?"

"Emma and I?" Summer rolled her eyes at Lena's question. "I told you about the hookup. But, that's it."

"So, your concern is only that of a friend?"

"Yes," Summer stated definitively. "She came over to my place on Sunday, and we talked. I guess that's why I'm really concerned."

"Is she okay?"

"She asked me out."

Summer took a sip of her Rum and Coke. It was a little stronger than she would have liked, but she took another sip anyway, before setting it back down.

"I thought you said nothing was going on."

"Nothing *is* going on. I said no. Mainly, because I'm pretty sure she's still hung up on Eli, or at least needs more time to get over it," Summer replied.

"Mainly, huh?" Lena lifted an eyebrow.

"Emma's great. I told her that if we were both 100% available, we could have maybe gone out. But that's not the case."

"So, you do like her, then?"

"It's hard to explain." Summer laughed. "I haven't spent that much time with her. The time we have spent together, she mostly spent talking about Eli and their relationship. It's like, it's hard to separate that from the rest of our conversations and find out if there's anything there. Does that make sense?"

"I guess," Lena replied. "So, how was work?" She repeated her question.

Summer took another look around to see if there were any other possibilities.

"Hey, what about her?" she asked Lena and nodded toward a woman who had just walked into the bar.

"What about her?" Lena asked.

"Is she more your type than a scary bartender?"

"Oh." Lena seemed surprised again. Her eyes flitted over to the woman and back to Summer. "I think anyone is more my type than a scary bartender."

Summer laughed and asked, "Even a guy?"

"Maybe not *anyone*." Lena smiled. "Can I ask you a question?"

"I'm not into the scary bartender either," Summer replied playfully.

"I've asked you about work twice now. You keep avoiding the question."

Summer thought about the question. She had dodged giving Lena a reply, and she knew why.

"It's the same as it always is," she answered her vaguely. "I sit in on meetings, review reports, check emails, have conference calls with India and Japan, with translators and time differences."

"Sounds like a lot," Lena said.

"It is, sometimes. But I can't exactly complain."

"Why not?" Lena finished her martini.

"Because I'm the CEO of a massively profitable company."

"Why can't you complain about that?"

"I have more money than I could ever actually spend. I already have a huge house, and I'm looking at two more houses. I even have an assistant who does things for me." She paused. "Crap. I didn't even think about her."

"What?"

"She lives in California. I don't always have her travel with me. I told her, obviously, but I didn't actually think to see if she wanted to move here or if she wanted to stay, and if she wants to stay there, how that would work. Would I hire someone here to replace her? Do I hire someone here and keep her on because she's great? Am I the person that has two assistants? I can't be that person," Summer said more to herself than Lena.

"Hey, calm down." Lena reached across the table and took Summer's hand. "You don't have to decide it tonight."

"I'm bad with decisions. I've been told that on numerous occasions. Like, the move here? I should have decided that months ago. I've been here a lot more than home. I knew that I liked it here and that it made sense, but it still took me forever to make the decision. This whole house thing is already more work than it should be."

"How so?" Lena pulled back her own hand, and Summer stared down at her now empty hand next to her still mostly full glass.

"Hayden and I went to that place on Monday. It was amazing. It looked like what I wanted, but I just felt like it wasn't. And then, he sent me five more listings last night. I've looked at all of them, and they're exactly what I'm asking him for, but I don't know about any of them. We're going to two of them tomorrow. I doubt they'll be what I want, though."

"Summer, do you maybe think you just don't know what you want?"

CHAPTER 7

SUMMER STARED AT HER from across the table, as if Lena had just dropped some massive bomb on her.

"Summer?" Lena tried again after a moment of silence.

"Sorry, what?"

"Nothing. I'm in meetings tomorrow, but only in the morning. Do you think you could still use that second set of eyes?"

"Really? That would be awesome."

"Maybe you, Hayden, and I can grab lunch and then go see the places," Lena said.

"I have a lunch date with Hailey and a few members of our legal team, but I can meet you two after. Maybe you and I can grab dinner when it's all done? We can use that as an opportunity to plan our wing-woman nights."

"Sure," Lena replied with a smile.

Lena had a problem, and she knew it. The moment she had arrived at the bar and discovered that the bartender who normally worked on Tuesdays wasn't coming in, she thought about leaving and texting Summer that she had to cancel, or at least change their meeting place. She didn't, though, because she wanted to see Summer. She worried that at least part of their friendship was based on this whole helping one another find someone idea. Lena had wanted an excuse to see Summer again and often, but she was starting to regret the whole concept of helping her find someone else.

Lena definitely had a problem. She liked Summer Taft. It was probably just a crush. Summer was attractive, funny, and clearly a kind person, who was loyal to her friends, like Emma. Those were all qualities that Lena wanted in a partner.

She and Summer parted later. Summer insisted that her driver take Lena home after dropping Summer off at her apartment again. Lena made a joke that she could get used to this kind of treatment. She was surprised to see Summer's shy smile as they pulled up to her apartment.

Lena liked not having a car. It was an excuse to join others, walking about the city or on the train. She felt like she was a part of this city now, and that was important to Lena because she needed to feel like she was a part of something. Since coming to Chicago and leaving her old life behind, she had gradually started to feel more herself than ever before. Yet, she still felt as if there was something missing. She wasn't sure exactly what to do about it.

***

Lena arrived at her first meeting of the day with coffee in hand. She was prepared to deliver the presentation she had worked on for the past several weeks and showed no signs of nervousness as she stood in front of the other VPs of O'Shea's, walking them through their quarterly numbers and explaining their projections for the next quarter and the remainder of the fiscal year.

In her company, Lena always possessed only assured confidence. She dressed the part and always wore sleek business suits. She straightened her naturally wavy blonde hair. Today, she had pulled it back at the base of her neck and wore her glasses. Lena rarely wore them. In fact, she mainly reserved them for meetings like this. Lena was a woman, and she was also blonde and blue-eyed. She found that by wearing glasses in a room filled with stuffy, older men, her IQ jumped ten points in their minds. She only needed them for reading, and even so – to the chagrin of her eye doctor, who told Lena to wear them anytime she was at her computer, she didn't follow that instruction.

She always found it interesting that, in her work world, she could exude such confidence, but once she was talking to a beautiful woman, it evaporated entirely. It took all the courage she had to ask Charlie out the day they met, and it still took a lot for her to work up to speaking to a woman in a bar.

She hated the office coffee, and after suffering through one cup of it, Lena decided to take a break and walk down to the nearest coffee shop, Strange Joe's, to pick up a mid-morning cappuccino. She stood in line, checking email on her phone, until it was her turn to order. She paid and headed to the other end of the coffee bar to await the cup as she typed a response to an email into her phone.

"Cappuccino for Lena," the barista announced and set the cup on the counter for her to take.

"Thank you," Lena replied and picked up the cup.

As she noticed her name written on the cup, as it usually was, she also noticed something else.

"Anytime," the barista, who'd placed the cup down, replied.

Lena stared at the cup and then glanced up at the voice's owner. The woman was probably about thirty years old, and Lena could only tell she was blonde because of the wisps of hair emerging from under her hat. Her eyes were brown, and her smile was wide.

"Is this–"

"My number? Yeah. And my name, too." She pointed at the cup. "It's Vanessa, by the way. I wrote *'Van'* there because that's what I go by."

"You're giving me your number?" Lena looked back down at the cup and then at the woman again in disbelief.

"Sorry, was I wrong?" Van asked her.

The woman then walked out from behind the bar through a little half-door and stood in front of Lena. She was likely only an inch or two shorter than Lena, but Lena was also in three-inch heels, so that meant Van was probably an inch taller than her.

"I saw you in here with a woman a few months ago. The two of you seemed like more than friends. You were in here with her again, a few more times, but then, you've been in here alone since, so... I was thinking maybe you were single now."

"I am," Lena confirmed for some reason.

Van smirked and took a step away for a moment so that another customer could retrieve his drink.

"I could join you for that coffee, maybe," Van suggested.

"Oh, I'm taking it to go. I have a meeting in ten minutes," Lena said. "Sorry."

"That's okay. You have my number now," Van replied. "You could call me."

"I'm sorry. I'm confused. You just give random customers your phone number?"

Van smiled and let out a small laugh, "No, I do not give random customers my phone number. I've done it exactly one time, and you're holding the evidence." She pointed at the cup. "Like I said, I've seen you in here a lot. I don't know... I just thought it would be nice to actually talk to you for once. I'm not a crazed stalker or anything, I swear." Van smiled again, and Lena smiled back this time.

"Well, I should be going."

"Right," Van replied, and her tone led Lena to believe that she felt a little embarrassed.

"But I come in here a lot," Lena added to help. "I'm sure I'll see you next time."

Van's smile returned, and she nodded without words.

"Large vanilla latte for Michael!" Another barista's voice had interrupted their moment.

"Have a good meeting," Van said.

"Thanks," Lena replied.

***

As Lena sat in the conference room minutes later, trying to listen to her Director of Midwest operations walk through his hiring plan for the next quarter, she had a very hard time doing that. She kept glancing down at the cup in front of her, with a name and the phone number written on it. Lena had never been hit on like that before. She wasn't sure how she felt about it. In a way, it was a good thing, since she had such a hard time striking up conversations with women. Van was attractive, and she had a nice smile. Her initial arrogance, or at least what Lena had taken her forwardness for, had disappeared completely the moment the woman thought she had been off-base by hitting on Lena. Van had been embarrassed and a little shy after that.

***

Lena wasn't able to make lunch with Hayden after all, because he had gotten a call from a client and had to take care of something. She met him at the first place Summer wanted to see instead. They had beaten Summer there and stood outside by Hayden's car.

"She just wrote her number on the cup?" he asked.

"Yeah, just like that. Here's my name and number. Call me," Lena replied.

"Was she hot?" Hayden lifted an eyebrow at her.

Lena rolled her eyes and crossed her arms over her chest.

"She's hot. I've seen her in there before. I might have even stared a couple of times."

"Really? This is good news. She's into you."

"She doesn't even know me," Lena replied.

"You could call her, and she could get to know you.

Come on. You keep talking about how you want to find someone, but you have a hard time picking up women. This one picked you up. At least, give her a chance," Hayden suggested as Summer's car pulled up. "Unless you're hoping for someone else…"

Summer climbed out of the back seat and said, "Am I late?"

"No, we were early," Hayden replied as she arrived on the sidewalk.

"Wow," Summer said as she looked at Lena.

"What?" Lena asked her.

"You just look different," Summer replied.

"I came straight from the office."

Summer seemed to be taking her all in, while Hayden unlocked the door to the condo they would be seeing.

"How was lunch?" Summer changed the subject and walked toward where Hayden was staying.

"We didn't go." Lena followed.

"I had a client emergency," Hayden said and ushered the women into the house. "So, I'm going to wait here and let the two of you walk around for a while. Just let me know if you have any questions."

"Thanks," Summer replied and took the lead.

She turned around and motioned for Lena to follow, which Lena did.

"You don't want to take a look around by yourself first?" Lena asked as they headed through a hallway further into the house.

"I'd rather have my second set of eyes now," Summer answered with a smile.

Lena smiled back and followed her through the house. They made their way through three bedrooms, two bathrooms, and a massive kitchen with brand new appliances and countertops. Then, they were outside on the balcony, which overlooked part of downtown.

"Well?" Lena asked as they leaned over the rail next to one another.

Summer had been relatively silent while she was exploring. Lena had matched that silence so as not to interfere with the woman's process.

"It's great," Summer replied after a moment. "But it's not the right one. See? This is my problem. I can't make a decision to save my life, sometimes."

"It's the second place you've seen, Summer. It took me forever to find my place. Ask Hayden."

"He told me about that the other day. I just get frustrated with myself."

"Let's go see the other place, okay? Maybe it's the one. If it's not, that's okay, too," Lena said.

"I should just keep renting my tiny apartment. It would be easier." Summer pushed off and moved away from the railing to go back inside.

"Well, aren't you the eternal optimist?" Lena joked.

***

The second place obtained much of the same reaction from Summer. Lena wondered if that was because she had some kind of a mansion back in California, that there was no way a condo in Chicago could live up to. But, based on Summer's lack of enthusiasm in regards to both places, Lena guessed there was something else going on.

"It's a little early for dinner, but you could come to my house. I could cook us something," Lena offered.

"That sounds good, actually. I'm not sure how much help I can be. I'm not much of a cook. Should we stop? I can buy wine or dessert?" Summer offered.

They stopped at an O'Shea's near Lena's house. When Lena showed Summer the wine selection from that new distributor she had just locked down, Summer insisted on buying six bottles of red wine so that they could try it all. Lena laughed as she grabbed one of those cardboard wine bottle carriers, piled them all inside, and then carried them toward the checkout stand. She also suggested ice cream for dessert, which gave her a chance to pick up some heavy cream and cheese for a sauce she liked.

***

"This is your place?" Summer asked when she stood fully, after picking up a few bags off the ground, and took in the two-story all-brick home in front of her.

"This is it," Lena answered and turned to see the look on Summer's face. "Not what you were expecting?"

"It's not that." Summer shook her head. "It's beautiful. Will you give me the tour before dinner?"

"Of course. Come on." Lena walked with her own bags toward the front door. "I took that porch swing from my old house. It was on the porch of my first house growing up. I took it with me when I got married. Then, I brought it here. I've had it refinished a couple of times." She pointed with a nod in the direction of a wooden swing hanging from the porch ceiling by the chains.

The floor of the porch was brick that matched the house, and Lena had changed the original front door to a solid oak one when she had first bought the place. She wanted a homier feeling to the house. And while she had loved the bones of the place when she had just bought it, it also had been entirely way too modern for her taste.

Lena unlocked the front door, after shifting the bags to one arm, pushed the door open, and walked inside. She allowed Summer to enter as well before closing the door behind the woman.

Summer's eyes were darting around the open space. The foyer was one of the reasons Lena had purchased the house. It was bigger than any of the others she had seen in the city. It had dark hardwood floors that she kept because she fell in love with them immediately. While the stairs were straight ahead, due to the size of the entryway, they didn't feel like she ran right into them when she entered the house. The large dining room was off to the right, and the kitchen was behind it.

"It's amazing," Summer said and met Lena's eye.

Lena smiled at her and started moving past the stairs.

"Let's put this stuff in the kitchen. The tour starts there."

Summer followed her into the room. Lena placed the bags she was carrying onto the marble island, and then, she took the bags from Summer and did the same.

"How did you even find this place?" Summer asked.

"I told you Hayden was good. I did a lot of work on it when I first moved in. It had a very modern feel to it. I like some things about modernity, but I wanted something a little comfier, I guess."

"So, like the opposite of what we saw today?" Summer asked.

"That would be your house, so my opinion on it doesn't really matter. *This* is what *I* wanted. I did some of the work here myself, but not the tough stuff, of course. I had the plumbing and electrical work done by professionals. Last year, actually, Charlie helped me redesign the bathroom. I had a contractor take care of most of that, but I refinished all the floors myself and hung the swing. I even did the tile in here on my own."

Lena pointed to the backsplash behind the sink that was patterned with soft hues of pale pinks and barely grays. Summer approached the tiles and touched them, as if that action would supply her with an answer to her own house confusion.

"You did this on your own?"

"I read a book. It took a lot of extra tiles, but yeah, I did it on my own. It was important to me to work on this place."

"Show me." Summer turned back to her.

"Let's start upstairs."

They headed back to the staircase. Lena climbed up the stairs, which led to the open loft that overlooked the foyer, and Summer followed right behind her.

"There are two guest rooms, but I've turned one into a home office. There's a pull-out sofa in there, in case I actually ever have two people stay over at the same time. I can't say that I've ever even had one person stay over. I doubt I'll need it. It's down here."

Lena headed to the end of the hallway and waved Summer to the open door of her office.

"It's nice," Summer offered as she stood in the doorway.

Lena was also standing in the doorway. Since there was little room for the two of them to share the doorway, they had both turned their bodies to face one another as Summer's eyes were still searching the room.

"It works when I need it. I usually just put my computer on my lap in the living room, though," Lena replied.

She didn't look at the office, though. She kept her eyes on Summer's face. She noticed a few freckles under the woman's jaw, near her left ear.

"I do the same thing. But I don't have a choice, since my apartment here doesn't exactly have an office," Summer replied.

"Well, you can borrow this one anytime," Lena said.

"When I was in school, I mean, on campus and, like, nineteen," Summer paused, as if trying to sort out how to complete that thought, before she continued, "I was at Stanford, just going through my pre-requisites. I was majoring in business, but I had no clue what I wanted to do with it. I guess I thought I would have time to figure it out, since I'd have to go for my MBA, anyway. I took a bunch of classes outside my major. Do you know what my favorite one was?"

"What?" Lena asked, surprised by the change in subject.

"Creative writing. The business major liked creative writing the best. Well, that and this philosophy course I took; but, mostly, creative writing."

"You thought about being a writer?" Lena asked.

"Not professionally or anything. I just enjoyed the class. Business courses are pretty cut and dry. There's not a lot of creativity involved."

"I remember," Lena said.

"I've never asked. I'm sorry. What was your major in school? Where'd you go?"

"I went to Yale," Lena replied.

"You went to Yale?" Summer's hand came forward to touch Lena's briefly before returning to her side. "Smarty."

"Says the woman who went to Stanford."

"Still going, technically."

"I majored in business, too."

"Why didn't I know that?" Summer asked herself more than Lena. "I mean, of course, you did. You're a VP of Operations. That makes sense."

"I guess. It came in handy when I wanted a job after the divorce." Lena moved out of the doorway and headed to the next room, needing to get some space from Summer. "This is the other guest room."

"Nice," Summer said.

"So, creative writing?" Lena pointed as they hit the guest bathroom immediately after the guest room. "Bathroom, obviously."

"It was fun. We wrote short stories and read each other's work. I don't know... I just liked it." Summer paused and glanced into the bathroom. "I've been approached by three different publishers to write about the founding of the company and my business advice or techniques; things like that. Seth has been approached by, like, six publishers because he's the genius, or maybe just because he's the guy."

"Probably the guy thing." Lena smirked at her. "Lastly, up here is my room."

Lena walked them to the end of the hall, closest to the staircase. She allowed Summer to walk into the room first before following the other woman inside. Summer took in the space. The room was rather large for a home this size. The bed was a king and a four-poster at that. The floors of the upstairs had all been carpeted when Lena had first moved in; with the exception of the bathrooms, of course. But Lena had pulled the carpet out, replaced it with hardwood, and updated the bathroom tile to match her taste. She had a TV mounted above the dresser, and two bedside tables. There was also an old rocking chair in the corner. The paint on the walls was satin light-blue, and the molding was white. Lena watched Summer walk through it and head toward the master bathroom. She followed her slowly.

"This is perfect," Summer said as Lena walked up behind her. "You have an old claw bathtub," Summer added.

"I do. Although, I don't use it all that often, unfortunately. I'm usually just taking quick showers and heading out the door."

Summer turned to see the two above-counter sinks in the same marble Lena had chosen for the kitchen and the walk-in closet off the bathroom.

"You have an amazing house, Lena," Summer said after turning back around to face her.

"Thanks. Do you want to see the downstairs?"

"Yeah." Summer followed her out of the room and back down the stairs.

"Why haven't you taken any of those publishers up on their offers?" Lena asked when they arrived in the living room.

The living room had the same dark hardwood floor and white molding, but Lena had chosen an off-white for three of the walls, and a rich amber color for the accent wall behind the fireplace.

"Is that wood burning?" Summer asked, surprised, and pointed at it.

"I thought about getting gas, but it seemed wrong, considering all the other changes I had made."

"It would have been."

Summer turned to see the opposite wall with the TV mounted to it just above a small shelf with the speakers and a cable box, among other items. The sofa and two chairs faced the center of the room, instead of either the fireplace or the TV.

"I like this," Summer said and pointed back and forth between the sofa and the chairs facing it. "It's like you want people to actually talk to each other, instead of just staring at the television."

"That was the thought. But I don't have people over often enough for it to work. It does help *me*, though. I can lie down and watch TV, or flip around and watch the fire behind me as I work on my laptop or something. Or, I can just face the window." Lena pointed at the large bay window that faced the small backyard.

"You have a freaking garden?" Summer headed toward the window while Lena laughed.

"It's not really a garden. I have flowers. I don't grow vegetables or anything. I've never had a green thumb. I'm surprised those are surviving," Lena said of the flowers outside the window.

Summer stood staring outside. The sun had nearly finished setting and illuminated the world outside with oranges and pinks. Lena watched the scene in front of her and felt, for a moment, that it was perfection; Summer, taking in the bright colors of the sunset and flowers through Lena's bay window, looking beautiful and bright herself. Then, Lena shook herself out of it again and headed back toward the kitchen. Summer's phone rang just as she joined Lena at the island to start unpacking their groceries.

"Hey, Seth," Summer greeted her brother, and Lena went about placing items in the fridge so as not to seem nosy.

CHAPTER 8

"HEY, SUM. I'm thinking about—"

"No way," Summer replied into her phone as she watched Lena open one of the bottles of wine she had bought earlier.

"I met some guys who are going to Australia to surf. I haven't been to Australia yet."

"Neither have I, Seth. I've hardly been anywhere, because you're always everywhere. Get back here, like you promised." Summer turned around and walked toward the bay window to stare out of it. "Seth, I need you here," she said it in a more hushed tone, not wanting to make a scene in front of Lena. "This is your company more than it is mine."

"I know. I'm sorry, Sum. Look, I'll stay here until the end of the week, and then, I'll head home, okay?"

"I've heard those words before, brother," she replied.

"Sum, what's going on? Is someone giving you a hard time?"

"No, it's not like that." Summer matched his sigh with one of her own. "I'm just doing it all by myself. I don't even know if this is what I want to be doing, Seth. I've fallen behind in my courses, because I'm the face and the CEO. And the board is driving me nuts, still asking for me to try to find another, more qualified CEO. We just opened this office and the one in Detroit. I'm trying to buy a house, and–"

"Okay. Okay," Seth interrupted. "I'm sorry. I'll come home. I will this time. You should take some time off, Sum. You've been dealing with all this. I know that some of it is my fault, but you should take a vacation or something."

"I'll let you know when that happens. I've got to go. I'm at someone's house. We're about to have dinner."

"You're on a date?" Seth teased.

"It's not a date, Seth. I'm with a friend."

"Male or female?"

"Her name is Lena."

"But it's not a date?"

"Seth, just come home. Get back to work at the HQ, please. Stop by the other offices to let everyone see your face and that you're back to work and that you're done taking vacations for a while," Summer said.

"Yes, boss. I'll see you soon, I guess."

"You better."

Summer hung up the phone and stood in front of the window for another moment, just staring outside. God, she loved Lena's house. She'd thought so the moment she got out of the car and laid eyes on the exterior with shuttered windows and beautiful brickwork. She loved the swing, the wood on the floor, and the dining room table that she had seen in passing. The kitchen was a perfect combination of new and old. Summer loved it all. Even her house in Palo Alto couldn't compare. This place was so near a major city but maintained an old-world sensibility and quietness that Summer found calming. She smiled at the thought and recalled her idiot brother's comment about a date. That caused Summer to withdraw her smile, because this wasn't a date. She and Lena were friends. And, for some reason, Lena seemed to want to hook Summer up with a guy, despite her protestations.

"Everything okay?" Lena asked her when Summer returned to the kitchen.

"Everything's fine. My brother's an idiot, but

everything's fine." Summer sat in front of the island on a stool and watched Lena pour her a glass of wine and then one for herself. "He thought he could extend his trip even longer, but I told him to get his ass back here."

"That's good."

Lena took a sip of her wine and stood on the other side of the island, facing her. Summer took her in. Lena's hair had lost some of its straightness and had gotten wavy, which Summer preferred. Her suit jacket was hanging on the back of the stool Summer was sitting on, revealing the still tucked in light-green buttoned-up shirt more fully. Summer, on the opposite end of the spectrum, was wearing another hooded sweatshirt with skinny jeans and tennis shoes; the uniform of millennial start-up workers.

"What can I do to help with dinner?" Summer asked and rolled up her sleeves.

"Honestly, nothing." Lena shrugged. "It's pretty easy. I just bake the chicken and make the sauce. I guess you can make a salad or something. I have everything in the fridge."

"I can do a salad."

Summer stood and moved toward the refrigerator. She opened it, stared inside, and then felt a warm body just behind her own.

"Lettuce is down there," Lena said over her shoulder.

"Okay. Thanks." Summer gulped.

Lena moved back to the counter and began working, while Summer removed all the items she would need. The two worked in relative silence until Lena pressed a button on a sound system, and some light background music filled the entire downstairs space. Summer smiled at the perfect combination of new and old. She then smiled again as she watched Lena stir a pot on the stove. The woman had rolled up her sleeves, too, and the back of her shirt was coming slightly untucked.

"So, he'll be back when, exactly?" Lena asked her without turning around.

"I don't know. Probably Monday. He said he's staying

until the end of the week. He'll head to California first."

"That'll be good, right? Having him back?" Lena turned around and took a drink of her wine while Summer held up two small bowls of salad.

"Where do I put these?" she asked.

"Do you want to eat in here or in the dining room?" Lena asked.

"Either is fine."

"Let's use the dining room. I never use that table I paid so much for."

Summer headed into the dining room and began setting the table, making trips to the kitchen as she needed to, for silverware, plates, and glasses.

"It will be good to have him back from his endless vacation. I need his help with some stuff, and I miss my brother."

"You should take a vacation of your own, Summer." Lena plated the food.

"He's the one that's always had the wanderlust. I'd be more or less content with just lying around for a few weeks and not doing anything," Summer said.

"Then, take a staycation. Just lie around and relax."

"I'd have to go back to California to do that. And I can't go back right now. I just told people I'm moving here. My apartment is about the size of this kitchen; not exactly relaxing."

Lena seemed to consider something as she took the plates in hand.

"Stay here," she said and walked toward the dining room, as if she hadn't said anything of importance at all.

Summer waited until Lena joined her to respond, "Here?"

"Why not? You can stay in the guest room. I'm at work pretty much all day. You would have the place to yourself. You could still look for a house, if you want, without the distractions from your office, and maybe write that book about your business tips and tricks."

Lena placed the plates in their respective positions on the table. Summer sat down across from her.

"Lena, I can't just stay at your house."

"Why not?" Lena sat and picked up her fork.

"I couldn't impose on you like that."

"It wouldn't be imposing. I just invited you. It's up to you, Summer. If you don't want to, it's not a big deal. If you could use some time to recharge, or get away from the office, my house is definitely big enough. And, I don't know..." Lena paused for a second as she cut a piece of chicken. "Maybe it's me being a little selfish, too."

"What do you mean?"

"It might be nice having someone else around here." Lena smiled and took a bite.

Summer smiled back and did the same. They ate and talked about other things, while Summer kept Lena's offer in the back of her mind. The meal was fantastic. Summer wished she had learned to cook from her mom, but there had never been any time, with her mom being so sick, and then Summer growing up and moving out. Summer could make pasta, grilled cheese, and a few other things, but she rarely cooked a full meal like this one. She missed having a home-cooked meal. She finished every bit of it and sipped on her wine as she watched Lena do the same.

"Dessert in the living room?" Summer suggested.

"Dishes later." Lena smiled and stood.

They carried their plates and glasses into the kitchen and deposited them in the sink. Summer removed the ice cream, along with the toppings, and placed everything on the counter. Lena pulled out the bowls. Summer scooped the ice cream. She insisted on giving Lena three scoops, despite her protestations and an attempt to block Summer from her bowl to no avail. Lena finally let her go through with it. Summer laughed as Lena squirted whipped cream accidentally in the air before connecting it to her sundae. They cleaned up that small mess and took their dessert into the living room, where they sat side by side, facing one another on the sofa.

Summer's phone chimed, and she carefully pulled it out of her pocket while holding onto her bowl in the other hand.

"Oh, it's Hayden. He's got more listings for me," she said.

"Do you want to borrow my computer to check them out?" Lena asked.

"I have mine. It's in my bag."

Summer passed Lena the bowl to hold for her while she retrieved her messenger bag that she had left by the door. She grabbed it and sat back down on the sofa, while Lena placed Summer's bowl on the coffee table.

"Put them up on the TV. We can look at them together."

Summer smiled at her as she booted up her Mac. Lena turned the TV onto the Apple TV input so that Summer could project her screen up onto the massive one. Summer faced the TV, connected to it, grabbed her melting dessert from the table, and set it in her lap. Lena remained facing the chairs but turned her head to watch the listings appear on the screen.

"I like the countertops," Summer said about the fourth place.

"They're nice," Lena offered and finished her dessert, placing the bowl on the table.

"I'm not a fan of the master bedroom not having a master bath," Summer said.

"Yeah, that's a little weird. The first place had an amazing master bath. I could live in there," Lena said.

"I guess." Summer closed her laptop, disconnecting the TV from her screen.

"What's wrong?" Lena questioned as Summer placed the computer on the table.

"Nothing. I just can't seem to like any of them."

"You should tell Hayden what you really want," Lena said.

"I did." Summer shrugged.

Lena turned toward her, and they both sat Indian style on the sofa.

"Be honest with yourself, Summer. Whatever you're telling him isn't working, right? How many listings has he sent you that were exactly what you told him you wanted?"

"A lot; I know. I'm just indecisive."

"You're not indecisive."

Lena placed a gentle hand on Summer's knee. Summer felt the touch radiate from her knee and down to the tips of her toes as she met Lena's bright eyes.

"I can't decide on a place to buy."

"You don't want any of those places. You seem to think you do, but you want something else. What is it?" Lena asked calmly.

"This." Summer pointed up to the ceiling.

"Heaven?" Lena laughed.

"No, this place." Summer opened her hands to the sky. "I love your house. It's perfect."

"My house?" Lena lifted a curious eyebrow. "Are you thinking about stealing it from me?"

"No. I just mean that this is what I want, and I didn't know that before. I thought I wanted a condo in the city, but I think I've seen every available condo in Chicago, and I don't want any of them. Your house is like my dream home, Lena," she said.

Lena pulled her hand back off Summer's knee and smiled wide.

"It's official. You're staying here."

"What?"

"Summer, you like it here. And I have the space. Just stay here. Take the time that you need to find someplace like this one, instead of pretending you want a condo in the city. Tell Hayden what you really want. You and I are friends, and you seem really stressed. You should take some time to figure things out. And, I don't know, maybe it's a bad idea, but I just feel like it's not," Lena said.

"You feel like it's not?" Summer wasn't sure what she meant by that.

"It would be nice having you around. I don't know… We can hang out. We can still do the whole help each other thing if you want, but we can also not. I'd be okay with just not. I mean, not for me. I'm not great at talking to women for myself, but I'm sure I could do it for you if you want, and—"

"Lena, we don't have to try to hook the other person up just to be friends. We *are* friends. We can postpone that or cancel it altogether and just be friends," Summer said.

"Yeah?"

"Of course." Summer looked out the front window for a moment and caught the darkness that she hadn't noticed before. "Do you really mean it? Me, staying here? It wouldn't be for long, but I could use a little time away, without being too far away. I could catch up on school stuff, figure out what I'm going to do to transfer, and find a place I actually want to live in."

"Yes, I mean it." Lena stood. "You can even start tonight, if you want." She picked up their bowls. "I have stuff you can sleep in. You can go to your place tomorrow and pick up what you need. If not, I'll just give you a key. You can come by whenever you want, okay?"

"Lena, this is really nice of you."

"You can repay me by helping with the dishes." Lena winked and headed toward the kitchen.

Summer smiled back at her as Lena walked away, and then sighed; in part, out of a sense of relief. She could really use some time to relax here. The other part of her sigh, though, had her concerned.

Lena Tanner was gorgeous and had her life seemingly well put-together. The woman was kind, funny, and really knew how to work a business suit just as well as she could work a pair of jeans. Summer wasn't sure if she would just make things worse for herself by staying just a bedroom away.

***

Summer didn't stay at Lena's that night, but she did stay there for another couple of hours. She enjoyed just sitting on the couch, talking to the other woman. Lena, in just a matter of a few days, had become someone Summer felt closer to than practically anyone else in her life, save her wandering brother. Even Seth couldn't understand her that much when he was never around to try these days.

When Summer woke up the next morning, she felt instant relief that she didn't have to go into an office and play CEO. She had told everyone that mattered, via email, that she would be taking some time off. Now, all she had to do was pack. Although, she wasn't even sure for how long she should pack. Summer threw enough stuff for a week into a large suitcase and had the driver take her over to Lena's place to drop it off. Then, she went to the same O'Shea's store and picked up food for them to have for dinner. It was the least she could do. Summer wasn't sure exactly what Lena would like, and she had a very limited repertoire in the kitchen, but she was determined to at least try to make the woman a decent dinner.

"Hey," Lena greeted her through the phone just as Summer was about to get in the car.

"Hi. Please don't tell me you've changed your mind, because I've already dropped my stuff at your place," Summer replied as she climbed into the back of the car.

"I haven't changed my mind." Lena laughed. "I wanted to let you know that I was on my way home. I thought I'd pick up dinner."

Summer smiled at the thought of Lena coming home and Summer being there when the other woman arrived. She had never really had that before. Sure, she'd had long-term relationships before, but she had always kept whoever she was dating at a distance. She rarely stayed for more than one night at a time, or had them stay over at her place for more than one night at a time. Summer had always been so busy with work, and she tended to date people that were the same way. It sometimes made having a significant amount of time together difficult.

"I just got some stuff from the store, actually. I'm on my way back to your place now."

"Oh, okay."

"I know I said that I wasn't a good cook, but I can do some stuff. You can pick something up just in case I screw it up, though. I mean, if you're worried."

Lena laughed, "I'm not worried. I trust you."

"Are you hungry now? I can start cooking when I get there. I think I remember where you keep everything."

"I'm starving, actually. I skipped lunch."

"I'll be there in ten and start cooking."

"I should be home in about a half-hour," Lena said.

"I'll see you there."

"Yeah, you will," Lena replied playfully.

CHAPTER 9

LENA TOOK THE TRAIN and walked the rest
of the way to the house. It was about a mile, but she enjoyed
the walk after a long day at work. She also worked up even
more of an appetite by the time she opened her front door.
As she walked in, Lena had to resist the urge to shout,
"Honey, I'm home." She thought that might be a bit
awkward, given her intense and new attraction to Summer.

At dinner, the previous night, Lena had found the
woman both sexy and adorable in her usual sweatshirt and
jeans combo. Summer had looked comfortable, and Lena
found women that were comfortable with who they were
incredibly attractive.

"Hey. I thought I heard the door." Summer popped
out from the kitchen. "Dinner's ready. Do you want to eat
in here?" she asked and motioned behind herself with her
thumb.

"Sure. Just let me change first, okay?" Lena asked.

Lena dropped her bag at the door and headed to her
room, where she changed into her favorite pair of old jeans
and a V-neck t-shirt. When she headed back downstairs and
into the kitchen, she was barefoot, and her hair was a little
wavy but pulled back at the base of her neck.

"You look comfy." Summer placed two bowls down
in front of the stools at the island. "All I can do is pasta, and
I'm not 100% sure it's really that good, but it was either that
or grilled cheese."

Lena laughed and looked down at the fettuccine
Alfredo in front of her.

"I'm sure this is fine. And, for future reference, I love
a good grilled cheese sandwich."

"I guess we have tomorrow's dinner plan, then." Summer sat next to her. "I opened another one of the six bottles for tonight." She nodded toward their filled wine glasses.

"Thank you. This is great. I already like having you here." Lena dipped her fork in and began twirling the sauce and pasta around. "But I'll have to take a rain check on tomorrow night. I have a work dinner thing I have to go to, in Naperville."

"Oh." Summer took a drink of her wine and set the glass down. "The next night, then."

"Sounds good. I'll try not to order a grilled cheese at the French restaurant we're going to tomorrow night," Lena joked.

"How was work?" Summer smiled.

"Never-ending, I think. I like it, I do. I just have to remind myself of that some days," Lena replied as she took a bite.

"What happened?"

"I had to fire someone today. I hate firing people."

"That sucks." Summer turned a little more to face her. "I hate that part, too. It sucks, being in charge sometimes. I had to fire someone once for having sex with another employee on top of the copy machine," Summer said.

Lena had just taken a sip of her red wine and nearly spat it across the island at that unexpected comment.

"You what?"

"His name was Richard. I fired his partner in sex, too. His name was also Richard. He went by Rich, though, and the other one went by Ricky. I had my suspicions that they were either an item or were at least hooking up, but I saw it with my own two eyes, unfortunately."

"Oh, my God!" Lena exclaimed.

"Yeah, that's what Ricky said with his front pressed against the machine, while Rich was behind him."

Lena cackled at that, "Okay. Gross. I don't want the details."

"Neither did I. They thought that everyone had gone home for the day, but I had fallen asleep on the couch in my office. I woke up and went to leave when I caught them. The worst part is that we don't have a copy room or anything. The machine is just on the floor, with all the desks. There are no walls. I could see everything."

"Okay, you win." Lena laughed, and it felt so good to laugh with someone outside of the office. More importantly, it felt good to laugh with someone in her own home for the first time in a long time. "I had HR take care of most of the conversation. I was just sitting there, listening."

"Start-ups are different," Summer said and took another bite.

"I guess so," Lena replied.

"Hey, what are you doing on Saturday?" Summer asked after a moment.

"Saturday?"

"I made a couple of day spa appointments for us today."

"You did?" Lena turned with a lifted eyebrow.

"You're doing this amazing thing by letting me get away from my life for a while. I want to try to repay you. This dinner doesn't really count."

"But I was promised grilled cheese," Lena teased.

"And I will deliver on that promise, but I thought it might be nice for you to relax a little, too. Manicures, pedicures, massages, mud baths, and whatever else they have there."

"That sounds amazing. You don't have to do that, though." Lena paused and considered being in a spa with Summer for an entire day.

Summer would be wearing one of those puffy robes. They might even have to disrobe in a locker room at some point. Lena wasn't sure she could see all of Summer and not touch her, and she knew she couldn't hold back her blush when she was around attractive women.

"Maybe Charlie and Hailey can join us, or Ember and

Eva," Lena finally suggested.

Summer looked from Lena down to her pasta and toyed with it.

"I hadn't thought about that."

"I can text Charlie to see if they'd be interested."

"I'll send her the info for the place," Summer replied. "It sounds like fun. Thank you."

"This is a thank you to you. You don't need to thank me."

Lena took another bite, "This is really good, by the way. You may not cook much, but what you do cook is good, Summer."

Summer smiled and took another drink, "Thanks."

***

"I have a little more work to do," Lena said as they wrapped up the dishes.

"Okay," Summer replied. "I was going to watch some TV in the living room. Is that okay?"

"Yes, Summer. You're allowed to watch TV." Lena walked around Summer to head to get her bag. "I can work while you watch."

"You sure? I can watch it in the guest room."

"Treat this place as your home. If you don't, what's the point of you staying here?" Lena said.

Summer joined her on the couch, and while Lena sat facing the chairs again, with her computer in her lap, Summer propped her legs up on the sofa and faced the TV. Her legs were up, but her feet were pressed against the sides of Lena's thigh. It took a lot of focus for Lena to get through the reports she needed to review. She continued working when Summer got up without a word and headed up the stairs.

For a few moments, Lena thought the other woman had gone to bed and hadn't said goodnight. Her question was answered, though, when Summer emerged. She was now wearing a pair of gray shorts, fashioned out of old sweats that looked like she had cut them down, with the number seventeen written in blue on one thigh, and a green t-shirt, with the name of some random tech company scrawled across the front of it. Summer just wanted to get into her sleepwear.

"Seventeen?" Lena asked as Summer returned to her previously occupied position on the sofa.

"Huh?"

"Your shorts." Lena pointed at the number.

"Oh, I don't know. I bought them like this. Clothing companies put random numbers on clothes. Doesn't make any sense to me, but they're comfortable."

Lena smiled at her and returned to her work. She kept her eyes glued to the screen in front of herself, because if she looked to the left, she would see Summer's long and smooth legs. Her eyes would slide over Summer's body and meet her eyes. Lena would blush and give herself away. So, she just kept working. When Summer's toes slid under Lena's thigh, Lena kept working. Summer laughed, and it was a little higher in pitch than her normal laugh, but Lena kept working.

Then, Lena realized that she hadn't heard anything from Summer in a while. She turned to see that the woman beside her had fallen asleep in what must have been an uncomfortable position. Her torso was resting up against the arm of the sofa, leaving her head unsupported, as it kind of wobbled around while she rested. One arm was over the back of the sofa while the other was hanging off the edge. Her legs were still in the upside-down V, with Summer's feet a little more under Lena's thigh than they once were. Lena had been pretending to work for so long, she had missed Summer falling asleep. She then closed her computer and moved ever so slowly to set it on the table without waking Summer abruptly. Lena considered letting her sleep on the sofa, because the woman looked so cute and was clearly already asleep, but she knew Summer would wake up sore if she stayed in that position.

"Hey, Summer," Lena whispered. When Summer didn't respond, she reached out to her knee and rubbed it up and down, "Summer?"

"Hmmm?" Summer's reply was soft and sleepy.

Lena smiled when she heard it. She smiled again when Summer stretched, and she could see the smallest sliver of hip bone and the soft skin between her shirt and shorts.

"You fell asleep. Come on. Let's get you to bed," Lena said.

Summer's eyes opened, squinted, and then closed again.

"I'm good here." The woman attempted to snuggle herself into the sofa more.

"You're not sleeping on the couch. Come on. You have a bed."

Lena reached down, took both of Summer's hands in her own, and began to pull her up.

"Lena…" Summer whined and then realized she had to give in as she was pulled into a sitting position. "Fine. Fine." She stood, still holding onto Lena's hands.

Lena walked backward at first. Then, she let one of Summer's hands go so that she could walk the incredibly tired woman up to the guest room. Lena pulled her along up the stairs and smiled as Summer climbed into the guest bed without pulling back the blankets first.

"Summer, come on. Cooperate." Lena laughed.

"I'm sleeping like this," Summer muttered into the blanket, as she lay on her stomach with her face buried between two pillows.

"I'm not leaving you to sleep like this." Lena first moved Summer over to the other side of the bed, with a few persuasive pushes. She pulled back the blanket, organized the pillows into a less decorative pile, put them more into a useful shape, and rolled Summer over while laughing at her until the woman was on the sheet. Lena pulled the blanket back over her and stood up fully again. "Okay. I think you should be good now. I'm going to bed, okay?"

"Mmm," Summer said with her eyes still closed and a sweet smile on her face. "Good night."

"Good night, Summer." Lena laughed again and left the room, closing the door behind her.

When she got into her own bed, she was restless. When she received an email from Charlie, about one of the other renovations Lena wanted to do with her house, she knew the other woman was still awake. Lena texted her first, to make sure it was okay to call, and when Charlie replied that it was, she dialed her number.

"Hey. I didn't expect you to review the plans immediately," Charlie greeted.

"I didn't," Lena said of the proposed plan to open up her walk-in closet to accommodate additional shelves and space for more storage. "I have a problem… Well, it's not a problem exactly yet, but I think it might become one."

"What's wrong?" Charlie asked.

"Am I keeping you up? I can talk to you about it later."

"You weren't keeping me up. Hails is already asleep, but I'm in my office, so we're good," Charlie said.

"I think I have a crush on someone, and it's kind of weird."

"You have a weird crush?" Charlie asked with a slight chuckle.

"I think I have a normal crush, but it's weird because of who it is."

"A guy?" Charlie full-on laughed.

"No, it's not a guy. Why am I even talking to you?" Lena laughed at herself.

"No idea. Hails is way better at this stuff than I am. Ember is, too. I'm kind of the last person you should be talking to about this."

"Well, you're also my best friend, so you'll have to deal."

"Who is it, Lena?"

"Summer."

"You have a crush on Summer? You met her, like, once."

"That's not exactly true. I haven't talked to you this week," Lena replied.

"Have you two done something?" Charlie questioned.

"What? No! I said it was a crush. We hung out on Friday night, after you guys left, and then, we spent some time together on Sunday night. I saw her again on Tuesday. Now, she's kind of staying at my house for a while."

"Wait! What? She's staying at your house? Why? She has an apartment and, like, a billion dollars," Charlie asked.

"She needed a place to relax. Her apartment is so small. She's been looking into buying a house, but she doesn't know what she wants. She came over here last night and said that she loved my house. I suggested that she take some time off work, because she seemed so stressed out. I thought, maybe, if she stayed here and just relaxed, it would help."

"Where is she sleeping, Lena?"

"She's in the damn guest room. Come on. She's sleeping and not with me," Lena replied.

"But you want her to sleep with you?" Charlie asked without a teasing tone behind the question.

"I don't know." Lena sighed. "She's Summer Taft, Charlie."

"What does her name have to do with anything?"

"She's the CEO of a giant tech company."

"And?"

"And I'm just me," Lena said.

"What do you mean, you're just you?"

"She could have anyone she wants. I watched a woman flirt with her on Sunday night. I've seen how others, male and female, look at her. All she would have to do is give them the time of day and–"

"But does she?" Charlie interjected.

"No, not really."

"Summer's not like that, Lena. She doesn't care about

the notoriety that comes with the position she holds. She's not a constant flirt or someone that just hooks up with people."

"She almost hooked up with you," Lena returned.

"She had known me for weeks at that point. It wasn't like we had just met; we had hung out a lot. She was also slightly intoxicated, and even though I was the one that put a stop to it, I doubt she would have gone through with it."

"She hooked up with Emma," Lena revealed. "Shit!" Lena pressed her hand to her mouth. "Pretend I didn't say that. I wasn't supposed to say that."

"Summer slept with Emma?" Charlie asked.

"I didn't say that."

"Yes, you did. When?"

"Charlie, please. I'm sorry. I shouldn't have told you that. I promised her I wouldn't."

"Well, it's a little too late for that now. But if it makes you feel any better, I won't tell anyone else."

"You won't tell your girlfriend? The woman you once told me you tell everything to?"

"No, I won't tell Hails. She would understand this. It's not my secret to tell," Charlie replied.

"She and Emma had a night together when Emma visited California."

"So, that's what Hailey's been picking up on all this time," Charlie said. "She kept telling me that those two were up to something, or were about to be up to something. Is that what you're worried about? That you like Summer and she and Emma were—"

"No, not exactly. I mean, yes, but they're not together. I don't fault her for having sex with someone. I don't want it to sound like that's what I'm worried about. I've had my own one-night stand if you recall." Lena pointed out one of the reasons she and Charlie never went further than casually dating.

"I remember. But, what's the problem, then? Really?"

"I know she and Emma aren't together, but she did

say that she liked her. Emma just needs time to get over her ex."

"You're worried that if you tell her you like her, she'll what? Want Emma instead?"

"I don't know." Lena closed her eyes tightly in frustration and then opened them again. "You know how bad I am at this stuff. I have no confidence. What if I ask her out, and she turns me down? She's staying here now."

"Maybe wait until she's not staying there to ask her out."

"I don't know when that will be."

"You really like her, huh?" Charlie laughed. "You want to ask her out *yesterday* and don't want to wait."

"She's so cute, Charlie." Lena knew she sounded desperate. "Tonight, she fell asleep on the couch. I had to pull her up the stairs and then tuck her into bed. It was adorable."

"You've got it bad, girl." Charlie continued her laughter.

"What do I do?"

"Ask her out, Lena. If she says no, and it's awkward, she can just go back to her apartment."

"I hate that you're probably right."

"Babe, who are you talking to?" Lena heard Hailey's voice through the phone.

"Lena," Charlie told her. "I should go. Hails is up."

"Tell her I said hi. I'll talk to you later."

"You better. I want details," Charlie replied.

"Details about what?" Lena heard Hailey ask.

"I'll fill you in. I can fill her in, right?" Charlie asked Lena.

"Sure. Might as well let someone in on my misery and see if she has any better advice. If she does, text me," Lena replied.

"I will." Charlie laughed. "Good night."

"Night, Lena!" Hailey yelled.

"Good night, both of you."

CHAPTER 10

SUMMER WOKE UP and looked around an unfamiliar room. It took her a minute to figure out where she was, and when she did, Summer smiled, because she remembered Lena dragging her up the stairs into the room and tucking her into the bed.

She turned to grab her phone and checked the time. She wasn't sure what time Lena normally left in the morning. They hadn't exactly talked about how they would handle being temporary roommates. She sat up, rubbed her face to get her mind to wake up, grabbed her phone off the table, and headed to the bathroom.

Summer then heard sounds coming from the kitchen as she took each step slowly. She wasn't hearing sounds, exactly; she was hearing humming. Lena was in the kitchen, humming cheerfully. Summer's smile grew as she slowed her arrival to take in more of the sweet sounds. She landed on the first floor and headed into the kitchen where she watched a fully dressed and ready for work Lena pour coffee into a travel mug while continuing her humming. Summer stood in the entryway to the kitchen, listening and watching for another minute before Lena turned around and jumped.

"Oh, my God! You scared me."

"Sorry." Summer laughed lightly.

"How long have you been standing there?"

"I don't know. I think, about a minute."

Lena put the lid on her travel mug and asked, "You just let me embarrass myself?"

"What's embarrassing about it?" Summer lifted an eyebrow. "You have a nice hum." She smirked at her.

Lena laughed a little and said, "I didn't wake you up,

93

did I? You're on vacation. You should be able to sleep in."

"I don't usually sleep this late, so this *was* sleeping in. But no, you didn't wake me up." Summer sat on the stool. "Can I make you breakfast? I bought cereal yesterday. I'm good at cereal."

"Sorry, I have to get going. I'm running a little late. I have to catch the train."

"Hold on." Summer lifted her phone out of her pocket and took care of something.

"What did you just do?"

"Ordered you a car."

"Summer, I don't need a car."

"Yes, you do. I have a standing order. It will be here in ten minutes, to pick you up and take you wherever you want to go today. If you give me your phone, I can install the app and link you to my account. Order one whenever you need it. Like, especially tonight, after dinner. Don't take the train that late, okay? It's dangerous out there."

"I don't need a town car. I can order an Uber."

"Can you just let someone take care of you?" Summer lifted her eyebrows. "Lena, I pay them monthly whether I use the service or not. Just use it for me, please."

"Fine," Lena agreed.

"Good. And now, since you don't have to leave right away, I'm making cereal. I bought something sugary and something healthy, because I didn't know what you would like." Summer stood and headed to the pantry where she'd stored the boxes.

"Whatever you're having is fine."

"I'm having the sugary stuff. Hailey is obsessed with it. I ate it over there for dinner one night, with the two of them. Now, I always have it in my apartment." Summer pulled the box down and turned back around to see Lena clutching her coffee.

"I'll make you coffee. You, do the cereal," Lena said.

"Perfect." Summer smiled and got to work.

They shared a simple breakfast. Summer hooked up

Lena's phone to the driver app and her account. Lena still protested, but Summer insisted. She walked Lena to the door when the car arrived and waved her off. When she closed the door, Summer found herself smiling once again. She liked this. She liked waking up and having breakfast with someone. No, not someone… She liked waking up and having breakfast with Lena. She liked seeing the woman off to work, and the only thing she would change about the whole scenario, would be the fact that they woke up in two separate rooms.

Summer sighed, turned around, and faced the stairs. She then looked around, trying to figure out what she should do now. She had never taken a real vacation before, and she had no idea how to be on one. She settled for grabbing her computer and heading into Lena's unused office. She sat at the desk and checked the newest listings Hayden had sent her after she explained her new plan. He had found several home options that fit the bill. Summer liked some of them, and she sent him an email back with her thoughts on which ones she would like to see.

She felt bad about not understanding her own wants and needs and involving him in it. The guy had wasted days of work because of it. She would remedy that by being more self-aware and more upfront with poor Hayden.

He had also sent her the name of another agent she could work with in Detroit. There, Summer was certain, she only wanted a small condo, since it wouldn't be her primary residence. She then made a decision to go back to California soon and put her place there on the market. She would get a smaller place there for when she needed to be at HQ, but there was no need to keep that place when she wouldn't be living there full-time.

Summer wanted Chicago to be her home now. She wanted whatever house she bought here to be the one she could feel completely at home in, without feeling like she could sell it tomorrow, and it wouldn't really matter. She would have all her stuff moved out here, and sell or donate what she no longer wanted. That would officially represent her new start; her new life.

***

Lena made her way to the café for her mid-morning coffee. She hadn't been able to get it the day before, thanks to her crazy schedule, but she had set aside ten minutes today to get a caffeine jolt. She had always been able to do what she had to do at work, even if it meant being a little more outgoing and attending dinners like the one tonight. It came with the role of being a VP. But when she got home after, she was always extra exhausted. She knew that after tonight, all she'd want would be a nice glass of wine and a hot bubble bath, while she listened to soft jazz music playing in the background.

"This one's on the house," Van said, and Lena looked up from her phone.

She was still second in line, and she hadn't even ordered yet. Also, Van wasn't behind the counter. She was in front of it and standing next to Lena, holding a cup of coffee.

"I'm sorry?" Lena replied, a little taken aback. "You don't have—"

"You usually look so busy in here. I was in the office and saw you come in. I assume you have a meeting to get to somewhere." The woman handed Lena the cup. "Take it. I don't expect anything in return."

"Like a phone call, you mean?" Lena questioned with a sympathetic look in her direction.

"Exactly," Van replied. "You weren't here yesterday. I assumed you were avoiding the place because of me. Consider this a peace offering. I didn't mean to make you feel uncomfortable. I'm sorry. I'm glad you came back today, though."

"I was just busy yesterday," Lena explained. "I wasn't avoiding you. I'm just not very good at this."

"At what?" Van smiled and removed her hat.

Lena could see the blonde hair for the first time, outside of the wisps she had a glimpse of before. It was a short cut, and the woman had either curled it into the light, perfect waves, that landed just at her earlobes, or her hair was naturally like that. Lena was jealous. It was the perfect haircut for Van's face, and it took Lena a second to answer.

"With women. I'm not good at it."

"Do you have to go now?" Van asked.

"I do. I have a meeting in ten minutes," Lena said as she glanced down at her phone. "It takes me three minutes just to get back up to the office. I barely had enough time to get coffee."

"But you made the trip anyway?" Van lifted one side of her mouth.

"I needed the coffee." Lena lifted the cup and smiled back. "I should pay for this. I don't want you to get into trouble."

"It's my coffee to give away, and I want you to have it," Van said.

"You own this place?" Lena asked.

"I do. I bought it four years ago."

"But you don't look like–"

"I'm old enough to own a coffee shop? I get that a lot. I'm thirty-one. I bought it when I was twenty-seven, after grad school. I'm still paying off both the student and the business loans, but it's mine, and I love it. So, it's worth it."

"That's pretty amazing. Listen, I do have to go, but I don't have any meetings tomorrow, around this time," Lena said.

"You don't, huh?" Van smirked.

"Maybe I can stop by. We can talk."

"I'd like that," Van replied and tousled her hair before placing her hat back on her head.

"I have to go." Lena took a few steps backward, bumped into a stand that held several bags of chips, and knocked a few of them over. "Oh, crap." She managed to hold onto her coffee without spilling it, at least.

Van laughed and said, "It's okay. I've got it. Go to your meeting." She bent down to begin picking up the bags. "I'll see you tomorrow."

"Okay. I'm sorry. I'm a klutz."

"It's not a problem."

"Okay. Bye." Lena offered a pathetic wave and left the café.

***

Summer met Hayden a few miles away from Lena's place, at a house that just popped up on the market the day before. It wasn't as nice as Lena's from the outside, but that was because Lena had put a lot of work into making her house look the way it did. Summer would have to do the same thing with whatever house she bought. She couldn't judge the place based on its initial appearance. She had to try to visualize what it could look like. If it felt right, she'd know it was the place for her.

"So, it's a two-story, has three bedrooms and two and a half baths. The exterior hasn't had a lot of work done on it, and the homeowners were upfront about the fact that the roof will likely need work. They said they'd consider that coming out of the cost based on the inspection. The inside, though, has had a total facelift. Every appliance has been updated within the past year, the electrical work was also redone a few years ago, to accommodate the more modern technological needs, and the carpets in the bedrooms are all new."

"I hate carpet."

"It can be removed."

"I know. I know." Summer convinced herself. "Let's do the tour."

Twenty minutes later, she knew she wasn't buying this house.

"So, this is a no?" Hayden said the moment they hit

the front stairs. "I'm getting used to that look on your face."

"Sorry, but yeah… I hate that I'm being a problem client for you."

"You're not being a problem client, Summer. We've been working together for less than a week. It would have been a miracle if you found something this early. I'm just glad you figured out what you really wanted. I'll find something for you, I'm sure."

"The first problem I had was that I didn't really know what I wanted. But now, I do, and that's a problem."

"Why is that a problem?" Hayden asked as he clicked his remote to unlock his car.

"Because I want Lena's house," she said with a laugh.

Hayden laughed, too, and replied, "I think she'll fight you for it."

"It's not like that. It's her house. I can't explain it. I just pulled up in the driveway and felt at home. Then, I went inside, and it felt like home. Did she tell you I'm staying there?"

"I haven't talked to her since we were all together. Is something wrong with your apartment?" he asked and opened his door, leaning over the window to face her.

"Nothing's wrong. She just recognized that I needed some R&R. I told her I liked her place. She's letting me crash in her guest room and take a vacation."

"She's great, that Lena," he replied.

"She is," Summer agreed with a smile.

"Can I ask another totally personal question?"

"More personal than my sexual orientation?" Summer mocked.

"Do you like Lena?"

"Of course, I like Lena."

"No, I mean, do you *like* her?"

"Oh, like *that* ?" she asked.

"You've been spending a lot of time with her. Now, you're staying at her house, that, apparently, feels like home to you. I'm just curious, I guess."

Summer thought about how to answer his question best and decided to be honest.

"I want to tell her myself, okay?"

"Yeah, sure. No problem," he answered immediately.

"I like her." Summer then smiled and moved her head from side to side. "She's really sweet, Hayden, and she's smart. I like how she looks in those glasses she wears sometimes. I watched her work a little last night. She put them on for a while, and they were so cute on her. I don't think she likes me like that, though, so I'm trying to figure out if that's the case before I tell her."

"Why don't you think she likes you?"

"I don't know," Summer sighed. "Last night, I tried to initiate some totally innocent yet somewhat flirtatious touching. She didn't move or act like she wanted me to do it. She didn't push me away or anything, but I'm not sure she's into me like that. And our friendship is new. I think it's best if I keep it to myself for now."

"Summer, Lena's different than most people."

"How do you mean?" she asked and crossed her arms over her chest.

"She's not good at initiating with women. Even after her divorce, it took her a long time before she put herself out there. She's shy, sometimes. So, even if she feels something, she has a hard time expressing it unless she's pretty sure the other woman feels the same way."

"So, you're saying she does like me, she just doesn't know how to start the conversation?" Summer asked.

"I don't know how she feels about you. And even if I did, I wouldn't tell you. Just like I won't tell her how you and I had this conversation. I'm just saying you can't take whatever happened or didn't happen last night at face value," he replied.

"I guess that's fair. I'll play it by ear, for now," she said.

"Where's your car?" Hayden turned around, as if suddenly realizing there was no other car next to or behind his in the driveway.

"I didn't call one. I'm at Lena's, remember? It wasn't that far of a walk, so I just put my headphones in and came over."

"Do you want a ride back?"

"I'm good. Hours of music on here." Summer held up her phone and then put in her headphones. "I'll see you tomorrow for those other places."

"Sounds good. Have a good rest of the day. Oh, Summer?"

"Yeah?"

"Good luck." He winked at her and climbed into the car.

She watched him drive off before turning on the music and heading back to Lena's house.

CHAPTER 11

LENA HAD TO ADMIT how glad she was that Summer offered the car, because she definitely needed it after that dinner. It was with a prospective vendor that wanted to put their business inside O'Shea's grocery stores. It was happening more and more these days, that coffee places like Starbucks, banks, and other services wanted positions inside existing locations to increase their revenue and also to give their customers a place to visit while running their errands without having to go out of their way. It made sense, because the structure was already there; the overhead was much lower. But meetings like this were a pain in the ass for Lena, and she had no choice but to sit through an entire long dinner.

When the car pulled up in her driveway, and Lena got out and headed toward her front door, she was more than ready to pass out in her bed. It was late. She had been going non-stop since she got to the office. Her only break had come when she had gone to Strange Joe's to get her cup of coffee. She had thought about it a lot over the course of the day. Had she really just gone there to get coffee? She had thought about Van a few times, since she'd first been given that cup with her name and number.

Lena also knew that she had a pretty big crush on Summer, but, at least for now, she wasn't planning on saying anything to her about that. Summer seemed to be going through something right now and needed some time to herself. It was probably best that she not date anyone, but that wasn't up to Lena. If the woman did date someone,

Lena still wondered if that would be Emma or someone else entirely.

She unlocked the door, dropped her bag on the floor with an exhausted sigh, and made her way to the living room. Seeing no sign of Summer there, Lena walked around the downstairs and determined that the woman had likely gone to bed. Lena was disappointed. She wanted to see Summer and maybe talk about their days, even though she knew she needed to get some sleep. She would have stayed up if it meant she got a chance to talk to Summer and learn more about her while discussing the events of their hours apart. She tiredly dragged herself up the stairs and into her room, noticing Summer's door was closed. Then, she made her way to the bathroom, where she stripped and climbed into a hot shower. It wasn't the bath she had been hoping for earlier, but it would have to do for tonight. Lena wrapped herself in a towel and walked back out to her room to search drawers for clothes to sleep in.

"Oh, sorry," Summer said from the open doorway. "I didn't see anything."

She put her hand over her eyes and looked toward the floor. Lena clutched the towel to her still wet body and gulped.

"I forgot, for a minute, that you were here. I should have closed the door," Lena said.

"I heard you come in. I was on the phone with Emma. I thought I'd come see how the dinner went, but I'll leave you to get dressed. See you in the morning." Summer went to turn around, still looking at the floor.

"Just give me a second." Lena chuckled.

She was a little disappointed at the thought of Summer and Emma having a late-night call, but she still wanted to talk to the woman standing in front of her, wearing another adorable shirt and shorts combo. Lena watched Summer stop turning, but she continued to look away, giving Lena enough time to grab a shirt, throw it on, and pull underwear on under the towel. She also slid a pair of flannel pajama pants on and lost the towel. Summer lifted her eyes then and smirked at Lena for a moment.

"Sorry, I should have just left you alone," she said.

"I thought you were asleep already, or I would've let you know I was home." Lena picked the towel up off the floor to deposit back in the bathroom. When she returned, Summer was still standing in the doorway. "You can come in."

Summer sauntered into the room. Lena sat on her unmade bed, pulling the blanket back a little more to slide under it. She felt cold after emerging from the hot shower. Summer sat on the side of the bed and turned to face her.

"How was the dinner?" she asked after allowing Lena a moment to settle in.

"I hated it, but I survived," Lena replied.

Summer reached over and slid a piece of Lena's still wet hair, that had clung to her cheek, behind her ear.

"Why'd you hate it?" she asked, and Lena tried not to make it noticeable that her breath had just caught with Summer's touch.

"The guy was kind of a pig. He ordered two scotches before we even got the appetizers he ordered, but I didn't actually eat. Then, another two drinks followed during dinner. He also insisted on me getting a dessert I didn't want. While I played with it with my fork, he took his own fork and dug right in," she sighed. "He also asked if I was single and told me I have beautiful eyes in the same breath before finishing the fourth scotch."

"Oh, my God!" Summer leaned back on her hands. "That guy's an ass. I thought this was a business dinner."

"It was. He just had more than business on his mind, I guess," Lena replied and leaned her head back against her pillow.

"Who was he? I can have Seth hack his social media accounts and fill them with tiny dick pics or something," Summer offered.

Lena laughed so hard, she snorted through her nose

and then blushed with embarrassment.

"Oh, my God!" She covered her nose and mouth with her hand.

"That was cute." Summer laughed with her. "I'm serious, by the way."

"I don't know if that is the appropriate response." Lena removed her hand. "But, thanks for the support."

Summer continued to smile at her and sat up fully, placing her hands on her own thighs.

"I should let you get some sleep."

"How's Emma?" Lena asked and regretted doing so immediately.

She didn't really want to know how Emma was, because she was afraid of the answer. She just needed something to keep Summer in the room, because she wasn't ready to be alone yet.

"She's good, I think. She called to talk about Eli." Summer leaned back on her hands again.

"Are they back together?"

"Not exactly," Summer answered ambiguously. "Apparently, the ex broke up with the ex. Eli ended things with the ex, who she cheated on Emma with. She wants to start talking to Emma again. Talking? Like we're in eighth grade. Anyway, that's what they were talking about at the bar when we saw them."

"She cheated on her for months... Why did Emma even give her the time of day?"

"I don't know. I wouldn't. As soon as I find out someone's cheating on me, it's over."

"Does it count if you kind of want the person you're with to cheat on you because you don't want to have sex with him?" Lena shrugged.

"Your ex-husband, I forgot."

"It's okay. Like I said, I kind of wanted him to. It took the pressure off me. But if it was someone I was with now, I'm with you on that. What's Emma going to do?"

"I was on the phone with her for over an hour. I don't

think she knows. She talked to Hailey before me. Hailey scolded her for even considering it. I think she just needed someone to not judge her if she did decide to entertain it."

Lena smiled at Summer, who smiled back and then moved over Lena ungracefully to sit on the other side of the bed next to Lena. She kept herself over the blanket and stared straight ahead toward the blank TV.

"That was nice of you, to not judge her or tell her what to do. It's hard, sometimes," Lena said.

"Part of me just wants to shake her and tell her that Eli was a bitch, and she deserves better."

Lena turned her face to Summer and asked, "And the other part?"

"Realizes Emma's an adult, who has to make her own decisions. Even though I'm worried she'll get hurt again, it's still up to her what to do."

"That's very rational of you."

"I think so." Summer turned her face to meet Lena's stare. "That guy from dinner was right: your eyes are crazy beautiful," Summer complimented.

Lena's mouth opened on its own at those words.

"Anyway," Summer deflected. "I don't know what she's going to do. I just hope it ends up okay."

"Me too." Lena looked back toward the television. "You want to watch something?" She nodded toward it.

"I should let you get some sleep. I'm on vacation. You're not," Summer said.

"I usually just fall asleep with it on."

Lena picked the remote up off the table next to her. She flicked it on and settled on the news. Summer took the remote from her hand and started changing the channels.

"You fall asleep to the news? That's depressing. Goonies is on!"

Summer stopped changing channels. Lena laughed at her and settled into her own pillow a little more. Then, she reached for the blanket, which had gathered at her waist, but Summer pulled it up for her.

"Thanks," Lena said.

"You tucked me in last night. It's only fair." Summer turned her attention back to the TV. "Should I get the lights?"

"There's a button," Lena replied with an exhausted tone and pointed to the remote in Summer's hand.

"You have your bedroom lights on a remote? Amazing!" Summer said when she noticed the button that Lena had pointed to. She pressed it, and the room submitted to the darkness. "I love this house."

Lena laughed at her as she lay flat on the bed. She wasn't sure what Summer was going to do. Would she stay and watch the movie for a bit, or would she leave, now that Lena had been tucked into bed? Lena didn't find out the answer, though, because sleep took her almost immediately after the thought entered her tired mind.

***

Summer stared at the TV for several minutes before risking a look down at the sleeping form of Lena Tanner. She didn't know what she should do. Lena didn't seem to have a problem with Summer being there, in her bed. She was the one that suggested they watch something. Maybe it was okay that she stayed for a little while and watched the movie. When she looked down at the woman, though, she no longer had any interest in watching one of her favorite films. She smiled a smile of adoration at the peaceful face, the soft breath sounds, and the rise and fall of Lena's chest as she took air in and let it out.

Lena's hands were under the blanket, but Summer could tell by the form that they were clasped together on her stomach. Her body seemed tense. Summer suspected that had to do with the dinner and her long day. Summer would have punched the guy who treated Lena like that, if she were a violent person. She really did want to know the guy's name, though, so that she could have Seth hack his accounts. Maybe it wouldn't be tiny dick pics. Maybe she'd have Seth get him on a no-fly list or something, or screw up his credit. She squinted her eyes at the thought of someone hitting on Lena like that with no class.

Earlier, Summer had gulped audibly at the sight of Lena standing there, just in her towel. Even when she then had looked down and away to give Lena the time she had requested to change, Summer couldn't get that image out of her mind. Lena's legs had been long and entirely visible under the towel. They'd looked lean, likely, because of all the walking Lena did, and they had looked smooth. Lena's normally light-blonde hair had been darker with water, but it was still wavy, dripping a little on the hardwood of the bedroom. Lena's arms had been covered in water droplets that Summer wanted to remove with her tongue.

Now, Summer was sliding down a little onto Lena's bed, listening to Data say, *'booty traps'* instead of, *'booby traps,'* and watching Lena sleep. A few moments later, Summer found herself lifting the blanket ever so slowly and sliding her own legs underneath it. She then rolled on her side, facing Lena, and observed the woman's untroubled demeanor as she slept. Another few minutes went by before Summer could no longer keep her eyes open and gave in, closing them and submitting to sleep.

CHAPTER 12

W HEN SUMMER WOKE UP, Lena was still asleep. She watched her for another moment, grateful that she hadn't apparently attempted to spoon the other woman while she slept. Summer quietly slid out of bed and turned her head back only once she was at the door, to see that Lena moved ever so slightly toward the middle of the bed. Her arm went to the spot Summer had just occupied. Summer smiled at the thought of Lena touching that space and feeling her warmth there even after she had gotten up. She headed back to her own room, to pretend like she had woken up there instead, and waited until she heard Lena head down the stairs. She dressed in jeans and a t-shirt, grabbed her laptop, which she planned to use in the living room today, and walked down the stairs herself.

"Morning," Lena greeted her when Summer entered the kitchen, laptop and phone in hand.

"Sleep well?" Summer questioned, definitely curious as to what the response would be.

"I did, actually. I think I fell asleep on you, though. Sorry," Lena apologized and set a cup of steaming coffee in front of Summer at the kitchen island.

"It's okay. You had a rough day," Summer replied and looked down at the coffee to see that she'd already added the cream for her.

"Did you sleep okay?" Lena asked as she poured her own coffee into her travel mug.

"I did, yeah," Summer answered the question without revealing anything more.

"Good."

"I'm planning on doing a lot of homework today. But I'm thinking about going into the city, too. Do you, maybe, want to grab lunch?" Summer asked in a hopeful tone.

"Sure." Lena twisted the lid on her cup.

"Should I just meet you at your office?"

"Where are you going in the city? Should *I* meet you somewhere? I don't want you to have to go out of your way or anything."

"To have lunch with you?" Summer laughed lightly. "I think I can go a little out of my way."

There it was. She had flirted. It was out there. Surely, Lena would see that. Summer had commented about her eyes last night, done the whole hair tuck behind the ear thing, and was now offering to go wherever, just to see her for lunch.

"Summer…"

"I'm going into my office," Summer said as she attempted to internalize her disappointment. "I have to sign some stuff."

"You're on vacation."

"I'm a CEO. That's not really a thing we get to do. I just need to sign some paperwork for some plans. Hailey wants to meet after, to go over some stuff, but then, I'm done."

"What about your brother?"

"He's landing Sunday, at SFO. I talked to him yesterday. He's going to stay there for a week, fly out here for the following week, and then spend a few days in Detroit before going home."

"Will I get to meet him while he's here?" Lena asked with a lifted eyebrow.

"And why do you want to meet my lame-ass brother?" Summer took a drink of her coffee.

"Because I want to hear all the embarrassing stories about you as a kid, obviously."

"Am I going to get to meet any of your siblings?"

Summer realized something as she asked that question. "Wait. I don't think I even know if you have any siblings."

"I have a brother, too. He's three years younger than me." Lena looked down at her coffee and seemed to need a moment.

Summer let her have it.

Then, Lena looked back up more thoughtfully than before and said, "I used to have another brother, but he passed away when I was twenty."

Summer had not been prepared for that. She reached across the island and took Lena's hand off the cup it was clutching and clutched it in her own hand instead.

"Lena, I'm so sorry," she offered but knew it really meant nothing.

"It was a long time ago."

"What happened? You don't have to tell me if you don't want to."

"No, it's okay." Lena pulled her hand back and placed it back around the cup, as if it was a security blanket. "His name was Helios, and he was my twin. We were seven minutes apart. He was older."

"You had a *twin* brother?"

"I did. Helena and Helios. My maternal grandparents were very Greek and insisted that their Americanized daughter and son-in-law give their children traditional Greek names."

"Lena is short for Helena?"

"I started going by Lena as a kid. I've never been called Helena, really. Helios hated his name, too, but his was harder to abbreviate, so he usually just went by H." Lena paused. "My younger brother, Cale, came along a few years after us. He's the one that came up with calling him Leo. It wasn't so much an idea, as that was all he could pronounce back then, and it kind of stuck."

"Lena and Leo," Summer muttered under her breath.

"Yeah, both of our names meant light. Mine was Greek for bright, shining light, and his meant sun. Cale got a different one. His name means 'to be faithful'… No pressure there." Lena laughed at the thought and, likely, at the brother she still had. She then turned to glance at the time on the stove. "I should get going. I'm going to be late."

"Let me call you the car." Summer grabbed her phone.

"No, thanks. I think I need the walk and the train this morning."

"Lena, I'm sorry."

"You did nothing wrong," the woman interjected. "I just wasn't expecting to talk about this today. But I will see you at lunch. We can keep talking about it then, if you want."

"We don't have to talk about it."

"It's okay. Really, Summer. It was a long time ago. I can talk about it. Just, sometimes, it catches me off guard, but I'm fine."

"Okay," Summer replied, but she wasn't so sure she believed Lena.

***

The air was cool but not cold, and the wind wasn't strong enough to mess up Lena's freshly straightened hair. Thoughts turned from the breeze to Summer's question about her siblings, and she realized how little they really knew about one another. They'd known each other for about two weeks. Lena felt an intense attraction to the woman, and she knew it wasn't just physical. She liked Summer's spirit. The woman was funny and lighthearted. She was somehow able to maintain a carefree attitude about most things yet still be serious and in charge when she needed to. Summer also wasn't perfect.

When Lena had read about her in the past, before actually meeting her in person, Summer had appeared to be perfection in human form. Every article talked about how smart she was, and how she was ridiculously busy but still intent on completing her degree, which Lena more than admired. The pictures, which were always also perfect, had captured her intense dark eyes and beautifully shiny long hair. Her laugh was infectious. When she got excited about something, Lena got excited about it. That was new for Lena. She had not been an excitable person for a very long time. But when Summer tried to throw five cherries on Lena's sundae the other night and nearly toppled Lena over in the process, they'd both been laughing so hard, tears formed in Lena's eyes. Lena couldn't recall the last time she had laughed so hard and so frequently. She smiled at that before her thoughts turned to Leo.

She and Summer had spent time talking about their lives before meeting, about work and dating, but they hadn't gotten to the really deep stuff yet. *That was the important word*, Lena thought, as she boarded the train that would take her into the city. They hadn't gotten to it *yet*. She sat down in an empty seat and pulled out her phone. She would listen to music and drown out the sounds today. She wasn't in the mood to listen to the city sounds this morning.

When she got to the café, she saw that it was in the middle of a welcomed lull. There were two employees behind the counter. One was steaming some milk for a drink, while the other one was stocking bottles of flavored syrup above the back counter. Van was nowhere to be found. Lena waited for a moment, wondering if something had come up, before she considered how stupid she was being.

"Excuse me, I'm here to see Van," she said to the employee that was stocking the syrup.

"She's in the back. One sec." The guy climbed off the step stool to head to the back office.

A few moments later, he returned through the swinging door, and a moment after that, Van did the same, sans her normal hat. She had definitely dressed for the occasion. The woman looked great in a pair of dark skinny jeans and a white button-down. Her hair looked as if it hadn't been under a hat all day. She wore diamond stud earrings with a matching necklace that anchored high between her breasts, drawing Lena's eyes down for a moment before she returned to Van's wide brown eyes.

"Hi," the woman greeted.

"Hey. Sorry, I'm late," Lena apologized. "I got caught up."

"It's okay." Van motioned to one of the empty tables. "You wanna sit? I'll get you your usual."

"Sure," Lena said and moved to sit at a table by the window.

She took a moment to watch Van work behind the counter. Van's movements were so precise, so smooth. She clearly knew her café like the back of her hand. Lena found herself staring and then caught Van's eye for a moment, as she looked in Lena's direction. Lena blushed and turned her stare toward the window instead. The café was on the end of the block, so Lena had a view of the cross streets and the people moving briskly about the city.

"Here you go," Van said as she sat in front of Lena with her own cup.

"Thank you." Lena clasped the cup placed in front of her.

It was warm and offered a distraction for her as she glanced down at it and then back up and out the window again.

"Let's start again," Van voiced after a moment. "I'm Vanessa Chambers. I go by Van. I own this café." She motioned to Lena with an open hand.

"I'm Lena Tanner. I am the VP of Operations at O'Shea's Grocery Mart. My office is in the building next to your café."

Van smiled, and Lena smiled along with her at the ridiculousness of this moment.

"I'm sorry. I get nervous sometimes," Lena added.

"It's okay. You don't have to be nervous. And, for what it's worth, I think it's cute. Should we start at the beginning?" Van asked.

"Beginning?"

"Yeah, like where you grew up, what school you went to, or what led you to your current job; maybe your favorites, too, like color, movie, book, and other stuff like that. I already know your favorite coffee, at least." The woman smiled and pointed at the cup Lena still clutched.

"Oh, yeah. I guess we could start at the beginning, then," Lena replied.

"So, where did you grow up?" Van asked and took a sip of her coffee.

"Connecticut. You?"

"Here. Windy City, born and raised. Where'd you go to school? What did you major in?"

"Yale and Business. You?" Lena asked.

"Michigan and Business. MBA at Loyola."

"I didn't get that far," Lena replied.

"You became a VP at a company like that without an MBA? That's pretty impressive."

"I don't know about that. They said I was the right person for the role. They didn't seem too concerned about graduate school. I got into Yale's MBA program; I just didn't go."

"Why not?"

Lena lifted her cup to her lips and thought about how best to answer the question. She felt Van's brown eyes on her own, and they were piercing.

"I got married instead."

"Married?" Van asked.

"I was twenty-one, and I got married. I opted not to continue school after that," Lena replied ambiguously.

"So, you were married before, but... not now?"

"Yes. I have an ex-husband."

"Married to a man?"

Lena laughed and said, "I was married to a man, yes. We've been divorced for over five years, though. I haven't been with a man since. To answer your next question, I am gay, yes."

Van let out a sigh and said, "Not that I would have minded if you weren't specifically gay."

"Good to know, but I am."

"When did you know?" Van asked and took another drink.

Lena relayed her coming out story to Van, as she listened intently and asked questions when appropriate.

"So, for me, I knew I was gay when I got to college." Van took her turn. "I was a total cliché." She laughed a little. "I had a boyfriend in high school. We tried to stay together when we both went to separate colleges. He stayed here. I was in Michigan. It didn't last long. The weekend after we broke up, my roommate took me to a party, and I met Casey. Casey was amazing. She was hot and funny. I spent the whole night attached to her hip, and I started to think I wanted to be more than friends with Casey."

"What happened?" Lena asked.

"We kissed, but she was doing the drunk straight girl thing, and I was doing the, *'Holy crap, I might like girls'* thing. It took a few months before I actually got up enough courage to ask a girl out, and a few more months before I came out officially to my family. I haven't looked back."

"A few months? It took me a few years," Lena said.

"Everyone's different," Van replied.

"Yeah," Lena agreed with that but found herself unwilling to share any more on this particular topic. "So, why a café?"

"I wanted to have my own business. When I was in school, I wasn't sure what that was. But I spent most of my nights and weekends studying in coffee shops during grad school. I also started working in one, to pick up some extra money. I liked the atmosphere. Like I said, it's not in the black yet, but I'm on track to get there within the next three years. And I like what I do. I like being the boss. My employees are like my family. My customers are mostly great." Van paused. "You're included in that."

"Thank you." Lena smiled, and her phone buzzed. She

looked down and noticed the message from Summer, confirming their time for lunch. "I should go. I have some work I have to do."

"Oh, okay." Van seemed a little disappointed. "I should get back to inventory, anyway."

"Thank you for the coffee and the company," Lena said.

"Anytime."

"I still have your number." Lena stood and reminded her. "Could I still call you sometime?"

"Definitely." Van smiled as she stood.

CHAPTER 13

SUMMER WAS EXCITED. She'd worked on her school stuff for the better part of the morning. She'd met with Hailey, and she was now heading up the elevator to take Lena to lunch. She couldn't stop the smile on her face if she tried. She hadn't talked to Hailey about her attraction to Lena, though, because she wanted as few people to know as possible, and Hailey was the consummate matchmaker.

She knew that morning that she had brought up a sore subject for Lena. Summer hated seeing the look of pain on Lena's face when the woman remembered the brother she had lost. Had she known, she never would have brought it up. She only hoped it wouldn't close Lena off to her. She liked what they were doing. She liked getting to know Lena, and she wanted to know more. She wanted to know the deep stuff, the painful stuff, and everything Lena was willing to share with her.

"I'm looking for Lena Tanner. Any idea where I might find her?" Summer asked when she arrived at Lena's open office door and noticed the woman was heavily engaged in a fight with her keyboard.

"Hey." Lena looked up and offered a smile. "Is it time already?" she asked and then glanced at her screen.

The woman was wearing those glasses again. Summer smirked as Lena still squinted at her computer.

"It is. Sorry, I lost track of time. I've done that twice today already," Lena added.

"It's okay," Summer replied and took a few steps into

Lena's office. "Do you need a few minutes to finish up?"

"No, I'm good. Just let me send this." She clicked some keys. "And, I'm ready."

"Perfect. I'm starving. I was thinking about burritos. I've been craving them for a few days now," Summer said.

"I can do burritos." Lena smiled as she grabbed her purse and approached Summer. "Do you know a good place?"

"No, but there's an app for that." Summer pulled out her phone, and they proceeded toward the elevators.

***

They decided upon a small Mexican eatery about ten blocks away. Summer had ordered a car, but she found it challenging to start up a conversation while they were driving. Lena seemed distracted. She stared out the side window at the streets as they drove along. Summer wondered if it had anything to do with their earlier conversation. When they arrived at the restaurant that had gotten great reviews specifically for their burritos, they found it nearly packed, with only one tiny table available. It was clearly not a place people went to for ambiance.

Summer and Lena stood side by side in the line, waiting their turn for the employee in a burrito hat to take their order. Again, Summer felt the awkwardness that hadn't really occurred in her relationship with Lena so far. Summer grabbed the plastic stand that indicated their number, and they headed to the table. She placed the number thirty-four on the end of the table and stared at Lena, who had just finished typing something into her phone.

"I was kind of hoping we could talk about this morning," Lena said.

"Really? I've been trying to avoid bringing that up, because I didn't want to make you feel like you had to talk about it," Summer replied.

"Thank you, but it's okay. I want to tell you about it. I

just haven't talked about it in a while. I don't usually talk about it at all. I just told Charlie about what happened only a couple of months ago, and she's my best friend. No one else here knows."

"And you want to tell me?" Summer asked.

"I do." Lena gave a shy smile. "Is that okay?"

"Of course, it's okay," Summer replied.

"Leo was my twin, but personality-wise, he was my polar opposite," Lena began. "Where I was shy and a little withdrawn, he was loud and always a joiner. Where I focused on school and my future, Leo lived in the now, and he rarely studied. When I got into Yale, he barely made it into UConn, and that was with my parents greasing the wheels a little bit. My family is very well-off. My dad came from old money. He met my mom at a fundraising event for his older brother, my uncle, who was running for the US Senate. They fell in love."

"That's nice," Summer said when Lena took a breath.

"It was kind of like the movie *My Big Fat Greek Wedding*, actually." Lena laughed. "My dad is not Greek. My mom was born here, but her parents were born there. My mom has three brothers and a sister. I have a million cousins. Apparently, my grandparents did not approve of my father, but they married anyway. Leo and I came along two years later. Cale was born three years after that. He was kind of a surprise."

"Happy accident?" Summer laughed.

"Yeah, my parents thought they were done having kids. My grandma said that Greek women shouldn't stop having babies just because they had two at once." Lena laughed. "She wanted my parents to have more, but my mom stopped at three. I think Leo and Cale were both big handfuls."

The server approached and dropped off their drinks and two giant burritos, removing the number sign as she walked off.

"You weren't a handful?" Summer used her plastic

fork to open the burrito and check its contents.

"I kept to myself. By the time Leo and I were old enough to cause any real trouble, he had Cale to help him out. I was usually along for the ride, but a non-participant," Lena replied.

"What was something they did that pissed your parents off?" Summer asked with a smile, hoping it wouldn't bring up any bad memories for Lena.

"Oh, God. Just one?" Lena poked at her own burrito. "Well, my favorite story involved the prank they played when Leo and I were seniors, and Cale was a freshman. It was St. Patrick's Day. They broke into school the night before. They'd bought a bunch of food coloring online and then used it to die the pool green. They used sidewalk chalk and washable paint to make a giant rainbow that led to the principal's office. They filled *that* with those gold coin chocolates so that when he opened the door the next day, they poured out onto the floor."

"Wow!" Summer laughed.

"It's amazing what you can accomplish when you're a teenager, and your parents just give you a credit card. I took no part in it, of course," Lena said.

"Of course," Summer replied.

"They both got suspended, and my parents had to pay for the cleanup. The pool had to be completely drained and then refilled. The boys had to remove the paint and chalk themselves. At least, everyone in the school got chocolate, though, since the principal didn't know what to do with it. He just had students in and out of his office all day, picking up piles of it to take home with them."

"That *is* funny." Summer took the first bite of her burrito.

"It was," Lena said.

Then, her smile disappeared. Summer sensed the change in mood.

"When Leo was at UConn, he thrived. He started caring about school enough to get decent grades. He joined a fraternity and had a long-term girlfriend. He even ran for student office and won his sophomore year," Lena paused. "We were home for spring break. Our grandmother wasn't doing well at the time, so my mom asked us to stick around in case she took a turn. Leo gave up his trip to Florida to do as she asked. I wasn't going anywhere, anyway. Damon and I had been together for a while by then. He was local and wasn't a party kind of guy, anyway, so he wasn't interested in spring break festivities. Leo took Cale to the grocery store, to pick up stuff for my mom, who wanted to make a traditional Greek meal for us. On their way home, they got side-swiped by someone who ran a red light." Lena then dropped the fork on her plate. She had yet to take a bite of her burrito. "It was on the driver's side. Leo was killed instantly. Cale ended up with two broken legs, a broken collarbone, and a broken arm. He had a concussion, too. They had to do surgery to repair some of the major damage. He then had to go to physical therapy for a while, but he made a full recovery."

"Lena, I'm so sorry. I don't know what else to say but that."

"There's nothing anyone can say. Damon had taken me out that afternoon. My parents have a pretty nice estate there. There was this gazebo, and he had already asked my dad's permission. When he proposed, I was completely caught off guard. I thought that, if we took that step, it would be after we graduated. But I said yes, because I didn't know what else to say. I loved him. I'd thought about us getting married before that. But as he knelt down in that gazebo and held out a ring, I knew in that moment that it would be a mistake. I said yes anyway."

"Why?" Summer asked.

"I couldn't explain it back then. I had this gut feeling that I should say no, but he was on one knee. When I turned my head, I could see my parents in the kitchen window, watching the whole thing with smiles on their faces, and my mom had glassy eyes. I knew she was crying happy tears. It seemed like the right thing to do: say yes to Damon and worry about the rest later." Lena needed a drink and took a sip of water. "About that time was when the accident happened. After we got the call, we all rushed to the hospital to check on Cale. They'd told us about Leo when we got there. I remember watching my parents take a few minutes to grieve their lost son before they turned their attention to the one that was still hanging on." She paused again. "I had to do the same thing. We didn't have any other choice. Cale needed us then. But once he was out of the woods, it all sunk in; Leo was gone." Lena's eyes turned glassy. "I can't explain it to people who aren't twins. It's too hard for them to grasp, I think. It feels like you've literally lost your other half, and I mean *literally*. It set in for the first time when we brought Cale home and got him set up in his room. I walked past Leo's old room and realized he'd never set foot in it again. His dirty laundry was still on the floor, because he was a slob." She laughed a little laugh at the memory. "His schoolbooks were on his bed, because he'd actually brought them home to do work while we were on break." She paused again and inhaled deeply. "I cried for days after that, and Damon was there for me. It felt like I had already lost my brother; I didn't think I could lose Damon, too. I had already said yes. I just waited for a few months until things got at least somewhat back to normal and started planning the wedding. We waited until Cale was healed, and then, we just did it. We did the perfect Connecticut blue blood wedding thing, and I spent years pretending it was okay. It's interesting, sometimes, how one moment can change or alter your entire life path. Damon and I were good at that moment, but I had already been thinking about other things. I thought, at most, I was probably bi, for thinking about women, too. But it was enough to give me a pause on my relationship with Damon. Then, Leo died. My parents were devastated about him and about Cale's injuries. The one good thing they had in their lives was my upcoming wedding. I couldn't break their hearts. And I didn't want to break Damon's. But, sometimes, I wonder what would have happened. If the accident never happened, I still would have said yes to Damon. But I don't know if I would have gone through with it. I'd still have Leo in my life, and he was always so supportive of me. I know I would have come out to him first, and he would have been more than okay with it. He probably would have wanted to help me find girls." Lena laughed. "I think things in my life would have turned out to be very different."

"I understand," Summer said after a moment.

She wished that Lena could have her brother back, but the thought that the woman's life would have turned out differently and that with that turn she may never have met Lena, stung Summer in a way she hadn't expected. Lena's eyes were still a little glassy, but not as much as before. Summer admired them as Lena glanced out the window, and the sun hit them, making them even brighter.

"I'm sorry. You wanted to have lunch, and I'm ruining the whole thing."

"You're not ruining it. I'm glad you told me." Summer watched as Lena's eyes returned to her, and she seemed to be smiling a little at least. "So, tomorrow, you and I are hitting the spa."

"Oh, yeah, I almost forgot. Could anyone else make it?" Lena asked.

Summer's eyes got big, and she quickly looked down at her burrito.

"I kind of forgot to text everyone," she admitted.

"I guess it's just us, then. Unless you want to see if they can still go," Lena replied.

"I'm okay with it just being us," Summer said and wondered if Lena knew what she meant. "I can text Charlie and Hailey about it if you want, though."

"No, just us is good." Lena finally took a bite of her food.

"And tonight, there's grilled cheese in store for you," Summer reminded.

Lena nearly choked on her food with laughter and said, "I forgot about that."

"How could you? I'm hitting the store on the way home and picking up five different kinds of cheese."

"Oh, God!"

"I know. Just you wait, Lena Tanner." Summer squinted her eyes in playful mocking.

***

Lena wrapped up her workday, and just as she was about to head to the train, she got a text from Summer saying the car would meet her outside. She rolled her eyes and smiled at the gesture. She now had another problem with her feelings for Summer. She could really get used to having a town car drive her everywhere. She didn't want to take advantage of their friendship, but Summer seemed to want to offer, so she'd at least take advantage of it at the end of a long workday. She arrived home and walked in to the sounds of that soft jazz she liked running throughout the whole house. The lights were dim, and when Lena glanced in the living room, she could see the fireplace roaring.

"Um... Summer?" she yelled out into the foyer after dropping her bag by the door.

"Oh, hey!" Summer emerged from the kitchen. "Just in time for the first batch." She disappeared again and then reappeared one moment later. "And go change first," she ordered. "You should be comfortable," she added as she waved a spatula at Lena.

Lena laughed but did as she was told. She went up to her room, changed into her comfy jeans and a t-shirt, and decided to take an old UConn sweatshirt out of her drawer for the first time in a long time and put that on, too. She completed her look with fluffy socks and met Summer in the kitchen.

"So, you said *the first* batch before," Lena said as she entered the room.

She smiled at Summer standing at her stove, wearing an apron she hadn't seen before. It was black and white and checkered. She had a t-shirt and shorts on that had become her standard comfy look to Lena.

"I did." Summer turned around, still holding onto the spatula. "I've made the first ones with regular old cheddar. I'm currently making some with pepper jack, and then, I have three more cheeses to include. I also made tomato soup. And by *'made,'* I mean that I bought it, and I'm heating it up."

"You are taking this grilled cheese thing really seriously." Lena laughed and joined the other woman at the stove, where she watched Summer drop butter into a pan.

"You said you loved grilled cheese." She shrugged. "I thought it would be fun." Summer then turned to take Lena in. "You look comfortable. Well done."

"I follow orders well." Lena turned to see the already finished sandwiches on the island. "What should I do now, CEO?" she asked of Summer.

"Drinks," Summer said. "I opened the wine a while ago. It just needs to be poured. We're on bottle number three. So far, for me, two was better than one, but we'll see what number three tastes like. Then, we have three more after that before making a decision."

Lena couldn't help but smile. The implication of them trying all six of their recently purchased bottles of wine was that Summer would be around for a while. Lena liked the sound of that.

"I will pour the wine."

"And I was thinking, we could eat in here and then hang out in the living room. Maybe a movie tonight. I started a fire. I hope that was okay." Summer turned to her as Lena began pouring the wine into glasses. "I'm just kind of making myself at home here. Is that okay?"

"Of course, it is. I told you, I like having you here." Lena finished pouring the second glass. "Now, what should I do?"

"Just sit there and tell me about your day. I know we saw each other at lunch, but we didn't really talk about that."

"Let me help, Summer," Lena said.

"Hey, I'm on vacation here. You're the one that had to work today. Just relax, Lena."

Lena rolled her eyes and observed Summer flip sandwiches in the pan before sliding them onto a plate next to the others. Summer smiled and winked before going back to the pan for another round. Lena didn't say anything for the next several minutes. She just watched as Summer finished another round and then turned to go back to work again.

"Okay, the rest of these are getting cold. We should start eating. We can try the other cheese varieties you bought later." Lena pulled out the chair next to herself. "Sit," she ordered, and Summer squinted playfully before pouring out two bowls of tomato soup and setting them in front of both chairs.

"So, how was work?" Summer asked after she sat down.

Lena talked about her morning emergency and how she was now behind on a project, but there was nothing she could do but press on with it anyway. She also went on about one of her fellow VPs, who continued to try to get their way, and told Summer about how one of the directors was definitely out for her job. He had been upset that she'd gotten it over him, when he had been with the company longer and had a master's degree.

They'd finished their grilled cheese sandwiches with Lena telling Summer that the pepper jack was her favorite and that she still preferred wine number two over wine number three, but that the third one was better than the first. Then, they took their glasses into the living room. Lena watched Summer handle the fireplace as if the woman had been living in this house for years and knew just what to do. After Summer had added two more logs and made sure they took flame, she sat on the floor in front of it. Lena hadn't yet sat down, so she joined Summer, instead of taking the sofa.

"What movie do you want to watch?" Lena asked.

"Whatever is fine."

"The Goonies?" Lena sipped her wine. "Or did you finish that one the other night?"

Summer stared at Lena while sliding her legs underneath her body and sitting on her calves.

"It's just Goonies." She smiled. "I did not finish it the other night, but we don't have to watch that."

"I thought it was one of your favorites."

"Because it's awesome. You don't like it?"

"I've never watched it all the way through," Lena said.

"What?"

"I've seen bits and pieces when I've changed channels, but I've never seen the whole thing."

"Oh, my God! We are totally watching it, then." Summer's excitement grew, but then Lena noticed it fade as Summer glanced at the UConn lettering on her sweater. "Was that Leo's?"

"I haven't worn it in a long time. He gave it to me our freshman year. I gave him a Yale one, and he gave me this one."

"How are you?"

"I'm good, actually." Lena realized that was true the moment she said it. "I'm glad we talked about it. I've been holding a lot of that in for a very long time."

"I thought you said you told Charlie."

"I told her some of it. She knows Leo existed and that he died in an accident, but not the other stuff."

"But you told me?" Summer asked.

"I did. Now, can we watch this amazing movie?"

Lena stood with her wine and headed to the sofa. Summer joined her. It took no time for them to relax as the movie began. Lena sat facing the TV, with her legs on the sofa, much like Summer had been sitting the other night. Summer was sitting closest to the TV, with her legs propped on the table in front of her. Lena watched Summer watching the movie more than she actually watched the movie. She thought about Van that morning and how she had texted the woman later in the afternoon that they should maybe go out sometime. She had been brave in sending it. After her lunch with Summer, Lena had felt both excited about the fact that she had let someone in, when she hadn't done that in so long, and also worried more, because she had known why she had let Summer in on some of her secrets in the first place. Lena was in way further than she cared to admit. She thought maybe Van would be a distraction that could lead to something more. If she could be brave and text Van, why couldn't she just be brave with Summer? At that thought, Summer reached for Lena's feet and placed them and Lena's legs on her own lap so that Lena could extend her legs along the whole sofa.

"What do you think so far?" Summer asked a moment later as her hands found themselves on top of Lena's legs. "It's good, right?" Summer turned and smiled at her.

"It is," Lena said, and she wasn't referring to the movie.

"Don't say it if you don't mean it," Summer replied with a laugh.

Lena didn't say anything in return. She rolled her eyes at Summer and then turned her attention to the screen. By the time the movie ended, Lena's eyes were heavy. Summer lifted her legs up and took their empty wine glasses to the kitchen. When she returned, she pulled up on Lena's arms, and they headed up the stairs together.

"I had fun tonight," Lena said groggily as she stood in front of her bedroom door. "Thank you."

"Me too," Summer replied and reached forward to tug on the front of Lena's sweatshirt. "Do you need me to tuck you in again?"

Lena gulped. Summer was a foot away from her. She wasn't even touching Lena's skin, but even in this proximity, Lena could still feel it. There was an undeniable chemistry between the two of them. She should be brave. She should tell her.

"I think I can handle it," Lena said instead and watched Summer take a step back and drop her hand.

"Okay. Good night, then." Summer walked toward her room.

Lena turned around and stood still until she heard the door of Summer's room close. She looked down at her sweater, saw the UConn logo, and called upon Leo for some courage.

"Summer?" Lena asked as she headed down the hall toward her room.

The door opened. Summer stuck her head and then her whole body out.

"Yeah? Everything okay?"

"Go out with me," Lena stated and then gulped as she recognized she was now only a foot away from Summer again, and she had just ordered instead of asked a very important question.

"Okay," Summer replied almost immediately.

She smiled, and Lena put the word with the expression and registered that Summer had said yes.

"Yeah?"

"Yes." Summer emerged entirely from her room. "I've been wanting to ask you, but I didn't know if you'd want to. And then, I was staying here, so I didn't know if that–"

"I know. Me too," Lena interrupted and continued smiling.

"You really want to go out with me?" Summer smiled, and Lena watched as the smile met the woman's expressive dark eyes.

"You really want to go out with *me*?" Lena laughed, feeling like that was the more appropriate question.

"I do," Summer said after a moment. "I really do."

"How does this work? I mean, you're going to bed in this room, and I'm going to bed in that one." Lena pointed at her bedroom. "And then, tomorrow, we're going to a spa together. That's not exactly a date."

"I can cancel it." Summer took a step toward Lena.

"What would we do instead?" Lena asked. "Wake up and eat breakfast? We're basically living together, and we haven't gone on a first date yet."

"Do you want me to go?" Summer asked and stopped moving.

"What? No," Lena objected. "I love having you here."

"I love being here. I feel like I'm supposed to be here. Maybe that's a little much before a first date, but it's how I feel," Summer said.

Lena knew how Summer felt because she felt it, too. She felt like Summer was right where she belonged, but Lena had wondered if she felt that way because she wanted Summer there or if Summer actually felt that way herself.

"I know what you mean," Lena agreed.

Summer took another step forward. Her body was now inches away from Lena's. Lena could feel Summer's breath against her own skin. They weren't touching, but Lena's skin felt like fire.

"If you think about it, tonight was kind of like a first date," Summer said.

"It was?" Lena whispered out.

"We had dinner." The woman reached for Lena's hips and placed her hands firmly against them, causing Lena to stop breathing for a moment. "And then, we watched a movie. I even walked you to your door."

"In that case, that would make this the..." Lena trailed off and watched as Summer's eyes flitted to her lips and back to her eyes.

"This would be the goodnight kiss part," Summer finished for Lena as her hand slid from Lena's hips to around her waist.

Lena's hands remained at her own sides.

"Are you nervous?" Summer checked?

"Yes," Lena replied honestly.

"Why? It's just me." Summer replied with eyes so kind.

"Summer, you're–"

Before Lena could get her words out, Summer's lips pressed gently against her own. It was only an instant, and then, she pulled away.

"Good night, Lena," Summer said after a moment.

Lena's heart was racing. The kiss had been all too brief. It had also been sweet and chaste, and Lena wanted more, but Summer took a step back and released Lena's waist.

"Good night?" Lena asked tentatively and knew the disappointment rang in her tone.

Summer smiled at her and said, "Tomorrow morning, I'm going to go back to my apartment."

"What? Why?" Lena asked, concerned. "I thought–"

Summer reached out and took her hand.

"Not permanently. I need to get more stuff, anyway. But I'm going to hang out there instead of here. I think we should postpone the spa. I can come back here tomorrow night, and we can go on an actual date."

"Oh." It was all Lena could say.

"If you still want me to stay here after that, I'll bring my stuff and stay for as long as you can put up with me, until I find my own place." Summer paused and dropped Lena's hand. "But if you change your mind, that's okay, too."

"I won't."

"Lena, I want us to go out, and I think it's going to go well." Summer shrugged her shoulders. "I don't want you to feel pressure to let me stay here if it doesn't. Since I'm optimistic and think that that's not going to be a problem, I also want to protect it." Summer paused. "I don't know if that makes any sense, but if me staying here could get in the way of whatever might happen, I don't want to stay here."

"I understand."

"So, I'll say goodnight, and we can go on a real date tomorrow night?"

"Yes," Lena agreed and took a step back.

"Can I ask what made you ask me out?" Summer asked

before Lena could walk back to her room.

"I don't know," Lena replied and then thought about it for a moment longer. "Actually, that's not true. I realized something today, and then something else tonight."

"What?"

"Today, I told you about Leo and Damon, and a difficult part of my life that no one outside of my family knows." Lena took a deep breath in and then let it out. "I wanted to tell you about it. I wanted you to know that part of me."

"And tonight?"

"I have fun when I'm with you, Summer," Lena confessed. "I watched you in my kitchen. You just felt like you belonged there. We ate grilled cheese sandwiches and drank wine while we watched an 80s movie, and it just felt-"

"Right?" Summer asked.

Lena nodded and said, "So, I decided to be brave."

"I'm glad you were," Summer replied.

They stared a moment longer before Lena took another few steps back toward her room.

"Good night, Summer Taft."

The corner of Summer's mouth lifted.

"Good night, Lena Tanner."

CHAPTER 14

SUMMER WOKE UP EARLY on Saturday morning. She had set her alarm specifically knowing Lena would still be asleep. She dressed and packed up her stuff, leaving some behind, because she was, as she said last night, an optimist. She moved quietly down the stairs and into the kitchen, where she ate cereal in silence and then left the box out with a clean, empty bowl, spoon, the milk, and freshly made coffee. She also left a note for Lena on the counter and called for her car. Five minutes later, she was on the road. By the time she was home, had unpacked the dirty clothes, and threw them into the washing machine, Lena had texted a thank you for breakfast.

Summer smiled at the message and typed back that she would see her later. Then, she got to work on finding what she would wear to this date she hadn't yet planned. She repacked her suitcase with new, clean clothes, made sure to include some better underwear, in case the first date went well and turned into another and another.

She had heard from Hayden that there was another place to check out, and they agreed to meet there. Summer knew she needed to find a place, but she was even less excited about it than before. When she wanted to get out of the apartment, it was hard enough to get excited about a new house. That was mainly because Summer wasn't sure what she wanted. Now, she didn't really want a new house, because she liked the one she was currently living in.

She knew it was crazy. She and Lena hadn't even technically gone on a real date yet. She couldn't just move into Lena's house. But, the more time Summer spent there, the more she felt right at home. She had sat at Lena's desk for much of the morning yesterday, getting her work done for school. It felt comfortable and welcoming to her. She could see a shelf with her books in the corner and, honestly, other than that, she wasn't sure she would change anything about the room. She had cooked in her kitchen and done dishes with Lena next to her. They'd passed each other wet plates to dry without words. It felt so natural to Summer. She had never had anything like that with the people she had dated, including the ones with whom she had been in serious relationships.

***

"Hey, Hayden," Summer greeted him as she climbed out of her car.

"Happy Saturday." Hayden put the phone he had been typing on back into his pocket. "I have something important to talk to you about."

"Did this place sell already?" Summer asked him as she pointed to the two-story brick house in front of her.

"I've been promoted."

"Oh." She stopped in front of him. "Congratulations."

"Thank you. I'm going to be a partner in the agency. I've been working for this for a few years now. It's a really great opportunity for me."

"That's great, Hayden."

"Thanks. But it means that I'm not going to be in the trenches anymore, so to speak."

"You won't be doing what you're doing now; that makes sense." Summer paused. "What does that mean for me and my house hunt?"

"Well, you're a big client for us, so I'm going to stay on until we find you the perfect place, but I'm finding all my other clients other agents to work with."

"You don't have to stay on for my account. I'm happy

to work with someone else. Not that I haven't enjoyed working with you. You're doing a great job. I'm a pain in the ass. Anyway, you can pass me off to someone else."

"I'm happy to stay on."

"No, it's okay. Honestly, my heart really hasn't been in this whole house hunt. I'll still check out listings, and if I see something I want to check out, I'll see it. But, I think I need some time to adjust my expectations. I feel like I've been dragging you around from place to place. None of them are working for me, and that's not your fault. I think you should probably put some newbie on my account and focus on being a partner." Summer smiled at him.

"Oh, okay. Do you want to cancel this viewing?" He pointed at the house. "You didn't seem that excited about the place on the phone. We could grab lunch instead."

"Lunch?"

"Yeah," Hayden replied and then seemed to consider something. "I can show you some of the listings I've got in Detroit. We can try to plan when you can go there to take a look in person."

"Oh, sure," she said.

***

Lunch with Hayden was a little different than what Summer thought it would be. They had been at the neighborhood's bistro for twenty minutes now, had just received their meals, and he hadn't spoken once about Detroit listings or who would take over finding her a place in Chicago. Instead, he asked her questions about her childhood, her school years, and the business. If Summer hadn't known any better, she would have thought this was a date.

"Are you interested in dessert? They have this great cheesecake here."

"No, thanks. I actually have to get going," she said.

"Oh, of course," Hayden replied, and his phone rang

in his pocket.

"You can get that. I really do have to go." Summer went to pull her wallet out of her pocket.

"Oh, no. I've got this." He insisted and removed his own wallet while his phone continued to ring.

"Hayden, your phone."

"It's just Lauren," he replied.

"Well, Lauren seems to want to talk to you. I'll let you take care of that." She stood, feeling awkward with Hayden for the first time since they had met.

She didn't like it. Hayden knew that she liked Lena, and Lena was Hayden's friend.

"I'll see you later, or you can just have the new agent call me." Summer pushed her chair in.

"Let me drive you home." He stood, and the ringing phone stopped its intrusion.

"No, I've already got a car on the way. I'll see you around."

"Tell Lena I said hi." Hayden waved at her with a look of confusion on his face.

"I will. Bye."

***

"I'm stupid if I take her back, right?" Emma's voice came through the phone just as Summer unlocked her front door while clutching the phone between her ear and her shoulder.

"Hello to you, too, Emma." Summer laughed. "And what are you talking about? Eli?"

"Yes, I'm talking about Eli," Emma replied.

"Emma, I can't tell you what to do about this." Summer made her way inside and locked the door behind her.

"Charlie, Hailey, and I are going to The Lantern tonight. I'm calling in reinforcements to help me. Can you make it?"

"I can't, actually," she replied and set a bag on her sofa before sliding off her shoes and sitting down on it. "I have plans."

"Plans?" Emma asked.

"Yeah, plans. I sometimes have plans."

"A date?" Emma asked.

Summer wasn't sure what Lena would want their group of friends to know.

"No, my brother's back. He and I are going to FaceTime. I have to get him caught up on what he's missed."

"And that has to be tonight?" Emma asked.

"He's still on European time." Summer rolled her eyes at herself for the lies she was making up. "He needs to be brought up to speed on some stuff before he hits the office on Monday."

"All right, I get it. Want to grab lunch tomorrow, or will you still be debriefing the world traveler?" Emma asked.

"I'll let you know. I'm not sure what I have planned tomorrow," Summer replied ambiguously.

"I'll choose not to be offended." Emma retorted, though sarcastically.

Summer didn't want to make plans with Emma if something else with Lena might come up. If they had a good first date tonight, they might have a lazy Sunday together. She liked Emma, but the thought of spending a lazy day around the house with Lena was too tempting to pass up.

"I'll text you once I know," Summer said.

Her text notification sounded. She pulled the phone away from her ear to see that it was Lena texting. She worried for a moment, at seeing her name, that Lena was canceling their date. But as she read the message, she realized that wasn't the case.

"You okay?" Emma asked.

"Yeah, that was Seth. I should probably let you go," Summer lied again.

"Let me know about tomorrow."

"I will. Have a good night."

"You too."

The text was from Lena. Charlie had texted the woman that they're going to The Lantern tonight. Lena had been asked to invite Summer along. Summer thought for a moment about how best to reply. She opted to ask Lena if she wanted to cancel their date to go out with their friends. As Summer hit send, she immediately regretted it. She shouldn't be giving Lena an out. She wanted this date to happen. She didn't want Lena to cancel or even postpone because Emma needed some advice about her ex-girlfriend. The reply came immediately. Lena didn't want to cancel, either.

***

Lena sat on her sofa, waiting nervously for Summer's arrival. She stared at the clock she had on the mantle of the fireplace as it ticked the seconds and minutes away. It was 5:59 p.m. Summer would be there in one minute. It was so strange to her: Summer had been staying with her, they had already shared so much, but Lena was still nervous now about the fact that they were going on a date. When the clock ticked to the next minute, and Summer hadn't yet arrived, Lena began to worry. Maybe Summer had changed her mind. Maybe she didn't want to go out with Lena after all. Or, maybe the woman had chosen to go out with the others at The Lantern and hadn't texted or called Lena to let her know.

"A watched pot never boils," Summer said from behind Lena, who had stood to greet her. She then turned to take in the clock. "For the record, that clock is fast. My phone shows 5:58." Summer held up her phone and then pressed the button to illuminate the screen. "See?"

Lena smiled and nodded at her. She'd often wondered how was it fair that her twin got all the confidence of the two of them. Somehow, in the womb, Leo had gotten 100%

of it, and Lena was left with none. She'd made strides with her friends, and she had no problem at work, but that was out of necessity. If she weren't confident, she'd have no chance in that world. But, with Summer, Lena was nervous all the time.

"I'll have to fix it later," she replied as Summer slid the phone into the back pocket of her jeans.

"You look nice." Summer looked her up and down.

Lena had chosen to wear a pair of jeans and a light-brown button-down, three-quarter-length sleeve shirt. She had worn matching brown boots and left her hair down and wavy.

"You do, too." Lena reached out an open hand to reference Summer's look and then dropped it at her side.

Summer had chosen jeans, too, but she wasn't wearing her usual hooded sweatshirt. They were skinny jeans, with knee-high black boots over them. Her hair was down and over her shoulders. She had a simple black V-neck on, but it appeared to be silk. And while it wasn't exactly see-through, it did leave little to the imagination. Lena gulped at the sight and then lifted her eyes back to Summer's.

"So, I made a plan for tonight, but it involves a trip. Are you up for that?" Summer asked.

"A trip?"

"Can you pack an overnight bag?"

"That kind of a trip? Where are we going?" Lena took several steps toward her.

"It's a surprise. We can come right back if you want, but I booked a place to stay, and I think we should stay the night and come back tomorrow. Is that okay?" Summer asked.

"And you're not telling me where we're going?" Lena smiled and found that her nervousness was still present, but it was now due to the fact that Summer had sprung an overnight trip on her, and not because of Summer herself. "How do I even know what to pack?"

"Just pack stuff to sleep in and something to wear

tomorrow. It's not a big deal, honestly." Summer took steps toward Lena to take her hand, and then pulled the woman gently in the direction of the stairs. "Comfortable stuff only, though."

Lena allowed Summer to usher her up the stairs into her bedroom before she turned around to face her and dropped her hand.

"This is crazy," she said.

"I'll wait downstairs." Summer smirked at her and backed out of the bedroom.

"This is crazy," Lena whispered only to herself now.

She pulled out a roller bag from her closet and rolled it into her bedroom. She placed it open atop her bed, and then moved hastily into her drawers to find something to wear. Summer had said she should dress comfortably, but she hadn't specifically told her where they were going or whether the place they would be staying at had one bed or two, or even if they would be in the same room.

Lena wasn't sure if the comfortable clothing extended to the sleepwear, so she grabbed baggy flannel pants and a t-shirt, but she also grabbed something a little less comfortable just in case. She threw in her toiletry bag and made sure not to forget her phone charger. She tossed another pair of jeans, two shirt options for tomorrow, and zipped up the bag. As she placed it back on the floor, she couldn't believe she was about to go somewhere without knowing the destination and with no time to prepare herself. She smiled and took a deep breath in before letting it out. She left her room and found Summer standing right outside the door and just out of view. Lena nearly toppled over with surprise.

"Sorry, I thought I should help with your bag. I didn't mean to scare you." Summer grabbed Lena's roller for her.

Outside, the car waited for them. The driver took Lena's roller and placed it in the trunk, while Summer held the back door open for her to climb into the backseat. Lena did, and Summer joined her moments later.

"Are you really not going to tell me where we're going?" Lena turned a little to her side to ask.

"Can you not handle surprises? Is that something I should know about you?" Summer teased as the car moved in reverse.

"I'm not great with them, no," Lena said.

Summer stared at her eyes and brushed the hair away from Lena's face.

"I like your hair when it's like this; when it's natural and wavy. It's nice," Summer replied.

"Thank you."

Summer's hand remained in her hair just behind her ear for a moment, before she finally pulled it away. Lena missed the contact. Summer's hand there felt steadying. It felt like she was holding Lena together just with that one touch.

"So, do you want to tell me about your day?" Summer asked with a smile.

"My day? So, you're really not telling me where we're going that required me to pack a bag?" Lena asked.

"No, I'm not," Summer replied with a smile. "How was your day?"

Lena accepted that she would have to submit to Summer's surprise. She reminded herself that Summer's spirit is one of the things she liked about the woman most. About thirty minutes after they left Lena's house, they arrived at the airport, but not at O'Hare or Midway. It was a small, private airport. When Summer pulled her out of the car, Lena glanced around to find a small private plane less than fifty yards away from them.

"Why are we taking a plane wherever we're going?" she asked as Summer's hand took her own, and Lena was again pulled in the direction of the jet.

"Because it was the only option."

"What are you talking about?" Lena asked, the sound of the engine forcing her to get louder as they grew closer. "Where are we going?"

"Just come on, or we'll be late. It's going to take us three hours to get there," Summer said as they climbed the stairs to the private plane. "They've got our bags. Don't worry," Summer added when Lena turned to check on her roller.

Lena sat first in a seat on the ten-seat plane, before Summer stood over her and nodded for Lena to join her instead, on the small bench-like sofa, that lined one side of the aircraft. Lena stood and followed the woman, sitting beside her instead.

"Summer, I don't–"

"I swear, I don't normally use my money to take women on wild, whisk-away dates. This is the first time. I am perfectly content just sitting in your living room, watching a movie. But, when I was trying to figure out what to do tonight, there was an opportunity I couldn't pass up. And it wasn't local."

Lena smiled, as Summer turned to her, and said, "How not local was it?"

"Nashville," Summer replied.

"We're going to Tennessee?" Lena asked.

"Just trust me, okay?"

Lena nodded. Within fifteen minutes, they were in the air. A flight attendant offered them drinks and snacks. Lena was hungry. She hadn't eaten lunch out of nervousness, and then, decided not to eat after that because they'd likely be going to dinner as a part of their date. But that had certainly been a mistake, because they were now flying to Tennessee. Lena definitely hadn't been prepared for that. As she ate pretzels, nuts, and a variety of fruits and cheeses along with Summer, she contemplated where Summer could possibly be taking her in Nashville. Lena had never been there before, but she had never felt a particular pull toward the city, either. As far as Lena knew, there was nothing there she had wanted to see, and she couldn't recall mentioning anything to Summer about the city. She was at a loss for their destination.

While they snacked, they talked. Lena loved Summer's voice. It was so expressive. She could tell exactly how the other woman felt about whatever she was talking about without even looking at her, because Summer's voice gave her away. She also loved looking at Summer. She crinkled her nose, sometimes, when she smiled, and she had a small patch of freckles under both eyes that one could only see this close.

It felt like only minutes had passed when the pilot announced that they were about to land. Lena had never experienced that before. Even when she first started dating Damon, the time had never moved like this. She had always been aware of how long they'd been talking. With Summer, time stood still.

They deplaned and headed into another car Summer had waiting. Their bags were placed in the trunk. Lena began getting nervous again. She still had no idea where they were going or, more importantly, where they'd be spending the night. Lena wondered if Summer had more in mind for their night together. They were in the car for another fifteen minutes before it pulled up outside what looked like some sort of a club.

"We're here to see Esperanza Spalding," Summer said.

Lena's head snapped around to Summer, and she found the girl looking nervous for the first time all night.

"What?" Lena asked.

"You love jazz. When I was playing with your system the other day, I noticed you had a ton of it. Nearly every playlist had at least something in the jazz family. When I looked at the songs you played the most, Esperanza Spalding was eight of ten."

"I love her stuff," Lena said.

"I guessed that." Summer smiled. "I looked her up today. She's on tour. And she's here tonight. It's the last night of the tour. I didn't want you to miss it, or else, I would have just taken you somewhere else on another date and given you a little more notice."

"Summer…"

"Is this okay?" Summer asked.

"Of course, it is," Lena replied, and the driver opened her door.

"Good. She's on in, like, ten minutes," Summer said.

Lena climbed out of the car. Summer joined her on the sidewalk.

"This is amazing, Summer. I've never seen her live. I've wanted to, but I never found the time or had anyone willing to go with me. Not everyone likes jazz."

They proceeded to walk into the smoky lounge setting, with Summer showing tickets on her phone. Summer motioned to a booth off to the right that had a velvet rope in front of it.

"We're over here. VIP space."

"Summer, you–"

"It was available," Summer interrupted the soft background music and Lena, with a whisper into Lena's ear as she took her hand. "The rest of the place was sold out. I swear, I don't flaunt money around like this. I really am just a normal girl who likes normal dates."

"I think I know that by now, considering how many hooded sweatshirts I've seen you in and the fact that you spent an entire night making me grilled cheese sandwiches," Lena replied.

She sat in the booth behind the table. Summer slid in next to her. The booths around the outside of the room were all a deep red. The tables in the middle had red candles flickering light that bathed the whole room in red. It was an appropriate place for a jazz show. The tables were filling up with patrons as the show was about to begin. Lena was just trying to take it all in. She glanced at Summer, who was staring intently at her.

"I have to confess something," Summer said after a moment. "I know nothing about jazz. I'm more of a Top 40 girl, myself."

"Then, it's even more impressive that you brought me

here," Lena replied and then noticed someone approaching their table.

"What can I get you?" the man said.

"Sorry?" Lena wasn't sure what he was referring to.

"He's taking our drink order," Summer said.

"I've never been to a show where they take our drink order," Lena replied.

Summer smirked at her and then turned her attention to the man, dressed in what looked to be a 1920s-inspired ensemble.

"Martini?" Summer asked her.

"Sure."

Summer ordered two martinis, and the man disappeared. Just as he did, the main lights dimmed even lower. The walls of the room illuminated with red accent lighting, and a few moments later, Lena recognized the opening notes of one of Esperanza Spalding's songs.

Lena couldn't hold back her glee, as her eyes made their way to the stage. She was immediately captivated and engaged. She hadn't noticed when her martini was placed in front of her, and she almost forgot she was in a crowded room, watching one of her favorite musicians amongst at least a hundred other people. But then, Lena felt a hand on her thigh, and as the first song ended, she felt a pull in a different direction. She turned to Summer, to find the woman's expression reflecting nervousness. Lena found it endearing. Summer's eyes were flashing the reds and yellows from the flickering candles around the room. Her lips now had a sheen of recently placed gloss. Lena wondered if she had done that while Lena's eyes had been glued to the stage.

She placed her hand on top of Summer's and felt Summer's fingers link with her own before Summer pulled their now joined hands into her lap. Lena's eyes remained locked on Summer's until the second song was already in the slow, perfectly paced chorus. She flashed them to the stage and felt Summer turn forward to allow both of them to continue watching the show. Their hands remained linked, but Lena felt Summer's thumb slide back and forth over her hand by the time the fourth song had started. They both sipped on their drinks but hadn't finished their first round.

With the sixth song starting to play, Lena felt Summer let go of her hand. She immediately turned to express her disappointment, but before she could do that, she watched Summer place her arm around her shoulders instead, and Lena smiled. She hadn't been held like that in a long time. Summer's hand met her shoulder, and Lena slid her fingers into Summer's fingers. When Damon had used to place an arm around her shoulders, even early in the marriage, it was out of his own comfort more than anything. They had never linked hands like this. Lena's head went to Summer's shoulder while her free hand moved to Summer's thigh. It took only a moment for Summer to place her other hand over that one. They were as linked as they could be.

"Are you having a good time?" Summer whispered into her ear.

Lena lifted her head slightly and pressed her lips to Summer's ear.

"This is the best first date I've ever been on," she replied.

"Me too," Summer said and turned her head.

Esperanza began singing *Unconditional Love*, a song Lena knew by heart but had never seemed to relate to the lyrics.

This time, Lena tried to focus on really hearing the lyrics for maybe the first time. She had been in love before. She had felt a pull toward another person, but she had never felt it *this* intensely. She had been waiting for that magic the song spoke of. People always talked to her about the *'it'*. Charlie and Hailey had found it. Ember and Eva had as well. And from what Lena knew of Alyssa and Hannah, they had found it in one another years ago. Lena had never found it for herself and wondered if, at thirty-six, she ever would.

Then, she met Summer Taft. And as Lena stared into

those welcoming brown eyes and felt their fingers aligned perfectly together, she wondered if maybe she finally had.

Their faces were inches apart. Their lips needed only to reach out for each other, and they'd be linked as well. Lena knew it was what she wanted. Based on how Summer was looking between her eyes and her lips, it was likely what Summer wanted as well, but Lena couldn't close the distance for some reason.

"Don't be scared," Summer said.

She let go of Lena's hand and placed her own on Lena's cheek. Lena's heart thudded loudly in her chest. She hoped the sound of the music would drown it out. Summer leaned in just an inch more, and Lena waited. Her eyes flitted up and down, and up and down, as she watched Summer do the same. Then, their lips met. And, again, it was gentle. It was light, barely there, and Lena was burning inside. Fireworks burrowed out of her body, up through her lips, and through her fingers as she lifted her hand to the back of Summer's neck to pull the woman closer.

Within moments, those glossed lips were gliding against Lena's. The lips wove their way between her lips and sucked, for only a moment, on Lena's bottom one before letting it go. Summer found her top lip, and then, her mouth opened for Lena. Lena's opened in return, to welcome Summer's tongue as it tentatively made its way inside. Lena allowed it to explore while letting out a soft moan that seemed to entice Summer further.

Summer's hand slid down and around Lena's neck. Her lips moved faster against Lena's. Lena's breath came faster as Summer's arm around her pulled her even closer. Lena's body reacted in ways it never had. She wanted more. She wanted it now. But just as she was about to be brave for the second time in as many nights and place her hand high on Summer's thigh, the song ended, and applause erupted around them. The moment was broken.

Summer pulled her lips away but left her hands and the rest of her body in place. No words passed between them as they stared at swollen lips and glazed over eyes.

"Best date ever," Lena muttered under her breath as the next song started.

"We can do more of that later, but I don't want you to miss your show."

Summer kissed Lena's cheek and pulled away, keeping her arm around Lena's shoulder and pulling Lena back into her side. It was a position Lena was more than happy to occupy.

CHAPTER 15

SUMMER HEARD THE FINAL song in the set, but she wasn't really listening at this point. She couldn't stop replaying their first real kiss in her mind. Lena's lips had matched her own in pace and desire, and Summer wanted nothing more than to experience it again. She hadn't tried again because she'd brought Lena all this way to see the artist. They would have time after the show.

When goodnights were shared with the room, the crowd began to disperse. Lena downed the remainder of her martini. Summer left the last sip of her own for the server to pick up. She stood and waited for Lena to join her, reaching out her hand for the other woman to take. They waited until most of the crowd was out of the club. Then, Summer felt Lena tug on her this time. Summer smiled as she enjoyed being led out into the night.

"That was amazing," Lena said as they stood on the sidewalk.

People were moving around them. Some had stopped to have a smoke. Others stopped just to talk about the show or plan their next moves for the night.

"The kiss or the show?" Summer teased and reached for Lena's hips.

"Both." Lena giggled as Summer backed her up a few feet into the dark brick wall of the club. "What are you doing?"

"Kissing you again," Summer replied. "I'm going for magical this time."

Summer had to wait for Lena to stop smiling before

she leaned in to capture those lips she'd been dying to kiss again. It was soft, at first. Summer wouldn't take things any further, since they were in public, but she wanted to. She wanted to wrap herself up in Lena and have Lena be wrapped up by her. She had wanted to be with this woman like this since they had first met. It had been building inside her ever since. Lena's lips parted. Summer's tongue found what it was searching for, and the soft velvet made her whimper softly, as she considered what it might do to other parts of her body.

Summer's hands stayed at Lena's hips, not wanting to wander too much, because she knew she wouldn't be able to stop herself if they did. Lena's arms wrapped around her neck, as if that was where they should have been all along. Then, Summer's phone rang in her pocket. She kept kissing Lena, though, with gentle pecks, to bring them out of their reverie slowly and paced.

"Answer your phone." Lena laughed between those pecks.

"I don't want to." Summer pecked again. "That's Seth's ringtone."

Lena laughed, and Summer finally relented, but only because the laughter made it difficult to keep kissing her.

"Answer it," Lena insisted.

"Fine. I am going to kill him," Summer replied and took out her phone. "What?" she said immediately.

She kept one hand on Lena's stomach as if to make sure she'd stay there and not disappear. Lena's arms lowered from her neck but went to Summer's hips, where they stayed.

"Nice to talk to you, too, Sum," Seth replied.

"I'm a little busy."

Summer continued to stare into Lena's eyes. She found happiness mixed with a little desire in near teal eyes staring back at her.

"You're not having sex, are you?"

"You think I'd pick up the phone if that's what I was

doing?" She watched Lena laugh as she'd guessed what brought on that comment.

"I just wanted to let you know that I am back in the States, as commanded."

"I'm glad. Can I talk to you tomorrow, though?"

"You're not having sex, but you're about to, aren't you?" he asked.

"Seth, you're impossible. I'm on a date."

Lena started playing with the ends of her hair, and as she did that, Lena's hands grazed the tops of Summer's breasts. Whether it was as a by-product or on accident, Summer didn't know. But she didn't care. Those brief touches were causing her legs to go a little weak.

"You are *about* to have sex, then." Seth paused as he laughed. "Wait. Who with?"

"Seth, good night."

"I'll be in the office Monday morning. When are you coming here?"

"I'm not. At least not now. I'll come back in a few weeks, maybe." Summer took in Lena's eyes and saw their disappointment. "To put the house on the market and check in at the office, but then, I'm coming home." She leaned in, pecked Lena's lips again, and delivered the woman a shy smile. That was enough to bring the happiness back in Lena's eyes. "But I'm still on vacation. You're in charge while I'm gone. Try not to screw it all up."

"I'll be—"

"Good night, Seth." Summer hung up the phone and tucked it back into her pocket. "Now, where were we?" She leaned back in, wanting to give Lena her undivided attention for the rest of the night.

"The car's here." Lena nodded in the direction of the town car and the driver, standing next to the driver's side door.

"I guess we should go." Summer pulled Lena away from the wall and toward the car.

"And just where are we going now?"

"I still haven't fed you yet. The snacks on the plane don't count."

"Oh, thank God. I'm starving."

"I made reservations," Summer said as Lena took her hand and brought it to her lips. She watched as Lena kissed the tip of each finger. The jolt of electricity it sent through her entire body, forced Summer to clear her throat before continuing, "I've never been to the place, but…"

They sat in the backseat of the car. Lena intertwined their fingers and placed them in her lap. Summer looked down and realized that her hand was resting now between Lena's legs.

"But?" Lena asked innocently.

"I've heard it's great."

"And they're still open?" Lena asked and turned to face the front.

"On a Saturday? They're still open."

"I guess I don't get out that much," Lena replied.

"You are so cute sometimes," Summer said. "Will you do that thing where you put your head on my shoulder? I liked that."

Lena smiled and lifted an eyebrow. Summer's arm went around her shoulder and drew Lena into herself.

"Better?" Lena asked.

"Much."

"So, what's the name of the restaurant?"

"I never said we were going to a restaurant."

***

"We're at a hotel," Lena said as she climbed out of the car and observed the enormous building in front of them.

"We are." Summer stood next to her and placed her head on Lena's shoulder, looking up at the building. "It's a Camden property. It's one of the oldest, actually. And, apparently, it has a Nashville music theme." She kissed Lena's cheek. "It also has a well-known restaurant that provides room service."

"Room service?" Lena turned her face to the side.

"I got us a two-bedroom suite. I didn't want to assume anything would happen tonight. If we end up sharing a bed, I'd be okay with just falling asleep next to you."

"Really? You liked it that much the first time?" Lena asked as she pulled away from Summer, choosing to take her hand instead and drag the woman through the door of the hotel, while their bags were being rolled behind them by the bellboy.

"The first time?" Summer looked confused and then figured it out. "You knew I fell asleep next to you that night?"

"I woke up to go to the bathroom, and when I did, I noticed you hadn't left. You looked adorable in your sleep, by the way. I just fell back asleep beside you." Lena paused as they approached the front desk. "I was also a little disappointed to see you gone the next morning, but I understood."

"You're a hard one to read. I wasn't sure if you would freak out if you woke up, and I was next to you," Summer replied.

"I would have, but not for the reason you think. Well, I did, technically. I woke up, saw you lying there, smiled, and thought about touching you, but I got scared, went to the bathroom, then came back, and tried not to wake you up, because I didn't want you to leave." Lena paused. "I've liked having you around all the time."

"I've liked being around all the time," Summer replied and then turned her attention to the front desk agent. "Summer Taft, checking in."

"Yes, Miss Taft. We have you in our suite."

The man typed something into his computer, and Summer felt Lena's hand on the back of her neck, rubbing the muscles with her fingers and thumb. It was distracting, to say the least.

"Thank you," Summer said to him.

"And we received your called-ahead room service order. It should be in your room within the next few minutes."

"Thank you," Summer repeated and took the key card from him.

They made their way to the elevator that they shared with an old couple as the elevator made its way to their floor. Lena and Summer's floor was the top one. Once the couple had disembarked, Summer turned around and faced Lena. Her lips were on Lena's in a second, with Lena returning the kiss once the shock wore off.

They both let go of their bags and took hold of each other instead. A few moments later, the distinctive ding was heard, and the doors opened. Lena laughed as Summer pulled her out by both of her hands, forgetting they had bags to grab. Once Lena pulled those through, too, they made their way down the hall with purple and blue patterned hotel carpet. The soft lighting from the sconces illuminated the numbers on the dark wood doors. When they found their room, Summer placed the card against the reader. They heard the beep and then the click of the door unlocking. Summer went in first, letting go of Lena's hand to grab their bags first before watching the woman walk in the room.

"It smells good in here. What did you order?" Lena asked, and Summer realized the room did smell like food.

"You're going to laugh," she replied with a smile and led Lena into the living room of the suite.

It was a musician's paradise. There were instruments of all kinds on the walls and even what appeared to be a fully functional drum set in the corner of the dining room, where there was a full eight-seater table. On that table was a massive spread, and Summer hoped they got the order she had requested right. "I got us food that I thought would be fun, but I also got real food, just in case you needed that."

"Real food?" Lena laughed, and Summer took her hand as they left their bags to make their way to the table.

"You had them make grilled cheese sandwiches?" Lena asked upon seeing two of the plates.

"With pepper jack." Summer laughed alongside her while pulling Lena's hips to her own. "And I also ordered sundaes for dessert, but they made them ahead of time, so I can't throw five cherries on top this time. There's also steak, because I figured we'd be hungry, and the grilled cheeses were mostly just funny."

"Are you kidding me?" Lena asked her with a wide smile. "I'm eating all of it." She pulled back. "Wait. That's probably wrong to do on a first date… Shove food in my face?"

"You can shove food in your face all you want. I will still want another date with you, Lena Tanner." Summer kissed her cheek and then pulled away. "Have at it."

***

They laughed and ate. Summer was glad she had ordered all that food, because they nearly finished it. She had only ordered a salad at lunch with Hayden, and since that had been an awkward experience for her, she hadn't exactly eaten much of it.

"Really? That night?" Summer asked.

"Yes. I had that terrible blind date with the loud chewer, remember? I walked into The Lantern that night just expecting to hang out with my friends, and there was Summer freaking Taft sitting next to them."

There was music playing in the background, but Summer couldn't tell you what it was. She had her eyes on Lena's body, and her ears on every word the woman was saying. Lena had unbuttoned the top two buttons of the shirt that made her eyes look impossibly brighter, and her cheeks were slightly flushed. Summer wasn't sure if it was because of the wine they had been drinking, or if it was something else entirely, but the blush had crept down Lena's neck and to the part of her chest Summer could see. She had kicked off her boots, and they were lying on the sofa, facing one another.

Summer, too, had kicked off her boots, and she was possibly the most relaxed she'd been in a very long time. She had relaxed with Lena before, but she'd had these feelings that hadn't been expressed yet, so there was still tension she couldn't release. As she watched Lena slide the waves of hair behind her ear and laugh, Summer was entirely relaxed. Her hand was running up and down Lena's leg over her jeans, while Lena's hand was lying over her legs, staying still.

"Summer freaking Taft? Really?" Summer laughed.

"Yes, really. I knew Charlie and Hailey knew you, but I hadn't met you. I walked in, and there you were. You looked gorgeous, and I felt like crap because I'd had a long day at work before a shitty date. Oh, and then, there was Emma."

"What about Emma?" Summer laughed.

"Hailey thought there was something going on with you two. I thought I saw something, too. So, I just pushed my initial thoughts out of my mind."

"Initial thoughts, huh?" Summer's hand stopped moving. "What exactly were those?"

"You know," Lena replied, embarrassed.

"No, tell me."

Summer sat up a little more and slid her hand up Lena's leg, moving her own legs as she did so that she was kneeling on the sofa next to Lena. Her hand stopped at the top of Lena's thigh.

"I wanted you," Lena said with a hitched breath afterward, that made Summer's entire body clench.

"I wanted you, too," Summer confessed and lifted one leg over Lena's two. Lena's body scooted over enough for Summer's knee to rest as she straddled her. "And nothing was going on with Emma that night, or any night, okay?"

"Okay," Lena replied.

Summer leaned down and hovered over her. Lena's hands went to Summer's back but remained over her shirt, to Summer's disappointment.

"Is this okay?" Summer checked before connecting their lips.

"Yes," Lena breathed out more than verbalized.

Summer leaned down and kissed her before sliding her hand up Lena's side and holding herself up with the other one. Then, her phone rang again.

"You have got to be kidding me!" Summer exclaimed as she pulled up. "Wait. That's not mine."

"It's mine. It's just a text. I don't care. Come back." Lena pulled her back down, and Summer had to stop laughing to allow Lena to kiss her again.

"Wait." Summer snapped back up.

"Why?"

"Can we maybe take this to the bedroom?" Summer stared down at her. "Maybe change and get comfortable and then continue this?"

"Bedroom?"

"Or not. We can just stay here and–"

"I want to go to the bedroom with you, Summer," Lena interrupted. "And I want to do more than just this." She tugged on Summer's shirt.

"But?" Summer waited for the other shoe to drop.

"I think I'd kind of like our first time together to be at home," Lena replied.

Home. Lena had said *home*. She hadn't said her house or her place. She had said *home*.

"How about we change, like I suggested, do a little more of this, and just fall asleep? I wouldn't mind having your head on my shoulder tonight, if you're up for it." She kissed Lena's forehead.

"I think I'm up for it," Lena returned.

* * *

Summer climbed into the bed first while Lena changed. She couldn't believe how nervous she was, even though she knew they were just going to sleep tonight. Kissing Lena was like a gateway drug. Summer's body and mind craved more the moment they touched. She wanted Lena tonight. She wanted the other woman under her and over her. Summer wanted to see the body she had been pretending not to stare at these past few weeks.

She needed Lena, but she knew that she needed it to be right, and tonight was their first date. They just happened to be in a hotel. It didn't mean they were ready for anything more to happen. She had no problem waiting for Lena. It also wasn't just Lena that wanted to wait. While Summer wanted her, she'd rushed into things before, and it hadn't worked. She wanted it to work this time.

Lena emerged from the bathroom in a pair of warm red and black flannel pants and a white t-shirt. She was smiling shyly in Summer's direction as she shoved her dirty clothes into her roller and took a few steps toward the bed.

"Nope. No way." Summer waved her hand at Lena.

"What?" Lena stopped immediately.

"You're wearing a white shirt."

"Yeah, so?"

"I can see right through it. You have to change," Summer said.

Lena looked down at her shirt and, apparently, just realized that it was basically pointless.

"Oh, I didn't–"

"Might as well not even be wearing a shirt. If we're just going to be making out tonight, then you'll need–"

"What?" Lena interrupted this time and took another step toward the bed. Summer held the blanket up to her chin, as if to protect herself from the approaching woman. "You can't handle seeing and not touching?" Lena teased with a devilish look on her face.

"I like this side of you," Summer said, not thinking. "I mean, not the…" She pointed at Lena's chest. "I mean, I like that, too. I do, and I want–" Summer took a deep breath, while Lena laughed and slid into bed next to her. "I meant the confident side. The mocking you just did. I liked it." She turned to Lena. "It's hot."

"Yeah?" Lena asked.

"Definitely. You should try it more often," Summer said.

"Maybe, I will."

Summer rolled onto her side and lowered the blanket down a little to move more freely.

"You should wear that shirt you wore tonight more often," Lena replied as she rolled on her side, facing Summer. "I had a nice show all night."

Summer laughed and said, "You did?"

"When the lights hit it just right, I learned you wore a black bra under it."

Summer laughed again, reached her arm over Lena's side, and rested her own hand on the small of Lena's back, encouraging the woman to slide over a little closer.

"Well, at least *I* had a bra on. *You* do not. It's not fair."

"I didn't tell you to put this on." Lena tugged on Summer's gray Stanford shirt. "I can't see anything now." Lena gave a false pout that had Summer melting.

"This is definitely the best date I've ever been on," Summer said.

"Come on. No, it's not. I'm sure–"

"Stop." Summer placed her fingers over Lena's mouth. "You seem to think I've led this ridiculously exciting life, and that I do something like tonight all the time. But, Lena, that couldn't be more wrong." She leaned in, removed her fingers, and kissed Lena's lips gently. "Come here." Summer rolled onto her back.

Lena slid into her. Summer's arm went around her shoulders as Lena's head rested on her chest.

"Seth and I grew up poor. We were middle class, at best. But when our mom got sick, we had a hard time making ends meet, with her medical bills. My dad could only do so much."

"You don't talk about her," Lena said after a moment.

"It's still hard sometimes. She was sick for years, and treatments sometimes worked, but most of the time, she could barely move. She couldn't work. When Seth and I each turned fifteen, we got jobs. I worked at a fast-food place. He worked at a music store in the mall. We drove a used car our uncle gave us because we needed a way to get to and from work and school without our dad, since he worked so much." Summer rubbed Lena's back with one hand while playing with her hair with the other.

Lena's hand was lifting Summer's shirt slightly so she could drag her fingers over her stomach and hip bones. Summer was doing what she could to stay focused on the story she was telling.

"We knew Seth was smart but had no clue he was genius-smart, because we went to pretty crappy public schools, where Seth got Bs and Cs most of the time. It wasn't until he took the SAT and started taking this computer programming class, that we started to realize it. He got into Stanford."

"What about you?"

"I did well in school, so I got in pretty easily. That's when the business started. It hasn't stopped since." Summer lifted the back of Lena's shirt up so that she could feel the other woman's skin. "I've been working for the past seven years. I've traveled a little, yes, but it was for work. I've dated and had serious relationships, but I've never had a date like this."

"You've never flown someone to another state just to see a jazz show?"

"No." Summer laughed. "But that's not it." She placed her hand on top of Lena's stilled one on her stomach. "Tonight was amazing, Lena. It still is. From the moment I picked you up – and you looked so beautiful, to the car ride, where I held your hand – but really wanted to kiss you, to the flight, where we talked, and you made me try that really stinky cheese," Summer said and then paused to listen to Lena's laughter. She felt the pleasant rumbling against her body. "To sitting next to you in the club and holding your hand, feeling you pressed against me, and then kissing you." Summer exhaled. "I've wanted to kiss you for, what feels like, forever. It felt really good to finally get to do it. And then, coming here and eating a ridiculous dinner with you; and now, just lying here with you – it's the best date I've ever been on, Lena. And I can't wait for the next one. I'm kind of hoping you'll have that wavy hair and maybe even put on those glasses for that one, though."

Lena lifted her head up in laughter, rested it on her elbow, and said, "The glasses?"

"Yeah, the glasses," Summer repeated and ran her hand through Lena's hair. "It's like they amplify the power of those eyes. I'm reeled in." She smirked at Lena, who smiled back.

"Well, for me, it's those hoodies you wear."

"What? Really?" Summer laughed.

"I like my women comfortable," Lena pointed out.

"I wear one pretty much every day."

"Yes, you do. It's been difficult." Lena chuckled and lowered her eyes.

"Difficult?"

"Yes, Summer Taft, you are gorgeous." Lena looked back up at her.

"And I find you to be sexy as hell. I'm going to need your head back on my shoulder now, because I can see down the front of your already see-through shirt. Are you trying to kill me?"

Lena's laughter rang out in the room. Summer joined her with the light laughter of her own, as Lena's head returned to its resting place.

"Do you want to watch something?" Summer asked.

"Not really," Lena said.

"Listen to something?" Summer asked.

"Like what?"

Summer reached for her phone, which she'd plugged in to charge for the night. She scrolled through her music and found the playlist she had just created it. She pressed play and felt Lena tense and release against her.

"How's that?" Summer asked about the jazz she had downloaded and played at a low volume as she set the phone back in place.

"Perfect," Lena replied in an exhausted voice. "I know I promised you more making out, but–"

"Go to sleep." Summer chuckled with Lena coiled tightly around her.

Lena's leg slid between Summer's, and her hand rested under Summer's shirt on her abdomen.

"What time do we have to be up tomorrow?" Lena muttered.

"Whenever we want. It's a private plane, Lena," she reminded.

"Oh, right? Sorry, I get forgetful when I'm tired."

"You get cute when you're tired. I've noticed it before."

"It's funny: we've basically been living together, so we've noticed stuff already."

"I think it's kind of perfect." Summer ran her hand through Lena's hair again and pressed a kiss to the top of her head. "Now, get some sleep."

"Good night, Summer Taft."

"Good night, Lena Tanner."

CHAPTER 16

W<small>HEN</small> L<small>ENA</small> <small>WOKE UP,</small> S<small>UMMER</small> was
pressed against her back and lightly kissing her neck.

"I thought you said we could wake up whenever we
wanted," Lena said groggily after several more moments of
enjoying the kisses and light caresses of Summer's hand on
her stomach.

"I didn't tell you to wake up. I'm perfectly capable of
entertaining myself until you do," Summer replied.

She, apparently, had been awake for a while, because
her voice showed no signs of sleep.

"Your entertainment seems to have woken me up,"
Lena said as a kiss was more firmly placed on her neck
behind her ear.

"Not sorry," Summer whispered into her ear. "And
you should know that I debated about waking you up by
sliding my hand under your shirt a little further, but then,
decided to go this route instead."

"Well, I'm glad you seem to be able to make decisions
now," Lena joked and turned over in Summer's arms.
"Good morning."

"Morning." Summer leaned in and pressed a kiss to
her lips.

Lena's eyes closed at the action. Her hand moved to

the back of Summer's neck to pull her closer. Their lips began the now-familiar dance of slow and tentative, leading to fast and intentional. Summer's tongue slid along Lena's lower lip. Lena rolled over onto her back, bringing Summer with her as she did, encouraging the woman to get on top. Summer straddled her waist and leaned down to move her lips to Lena's neck just as the sound of a phone could be heard.

"Oh, come on!" Lena recognized her own phone as the culprit.

"People do not seem to be in favor of this relationship," Summer joked and slid off her body. "I'm going to go in there. You take care of that. Then, we can continue this."

Summer pointed at the bathroom first, then, the phone on the nightstand, and then, between herself and Lena. She headed into the bathroom after that. Lena rolled over to the other side of the bed, reached for her phone, and saw that it was Charlie.

"Hey. What's up?" Lena greeted in a somewhat frustrated tone.

"Uh, good morning to you, too," Charlie replied.

"Sorry, I just woke up."

"You don't normally sleep in this late."

"Late night."

Lena kept her answer short intentionally. She wasn't sure what Summer wanted to tell the others about last night. It hadn't escaped her notice that the woman had used the word *relationship* a moment ago, but it had been one date. Lena was pretty sure neither of them was ready to call what they had a relationship.

"Feel free to say no to this."

"You can't start it off like that." It was Hailey's voice.

"Am I on speaker?" Lena asked.

"Yes, and I never should have let her tell you about this. I have someone I think you would like to meet," Hailey replied.

"You do?"

"Yes, her name is Heather. She's thirty-five and works with Charlie at the firm."

"She's in the legal department, technically," Charlie added. "But she's great."

"Anyway, she is single. We've spent some time with her at different work events for my girlfriend, who hates when I try to play matchmaker like this, but she loves me anyway. Heather's a lawyer, obviously. She's originally from Connecticut – which reminded me of you, and she's very smart and funny, and–"

"I'm going to stop you there. I'm not interested," Lena interrupted.

"You don't even want to meet her? We can set it up so it's a double date or a group night at Windy's or BBZ's, or even The Lantern," Hailey replied.

"I told you, Hails; she's into Summer," Charlie reminded. "You *are* still into her, aren't you?"

"Yes, I am. So, I'm not interested in meeting Heather."

"Well, that might be a problem… Because I kind of told her that you were amazing and that you'd meet us at BBZ's tonight. Ember and Eva will be there, and maybe Alyssa and Hannah, since Alyssa's mom is in town and is taking care of the kids, and–"

"You told her that?" Charlie questioned her girlfriend. "Sorry, Lena. I didn't know she'd gone rogue."

Lena laughed and heard the water stop in the bathroom, which likely meant Summer would be returning momentarily.

"It's okay. I'm not interested in dating Heather, but that doesn't mean you shouldn't invite her to hang out if you guys like her. I'm not sure about tonight, but I'll let you know later, okay?"

"Sure. Just text me. I'm sure we can find someone else for her to date. Hailey might be starting a matchmaking service on the side. Heather could be her first client," Charlie said.

"I am not. And sorry, Lena. Charlie told me you liked Summer, but that you weren't planning on doing anything about it. I just figured maybe you and Heather would hit it off," Hailey said.

"I understand. And I do have to go, though," Lena said.

"Text us later," Charlie reminded.

"I will."

Lena hung up and tossed the phone on the unmade bed just in time for Summer to emerge.

"What did she want?" Summer asked, and it looked as if she had brushed her hair, washed her face, and likely, brushed her teeth.

"To go to BBZ's tonight," Lena shared and stood. She stretched her arms over her head and then watched as Summer admired her. "I was non-committal, but I'm going in there now." Lena pointed to the bathroom. "Hailey was on the call, too. They might be inviting you next." She headed toward the bathroom, applying a kiss to Summer's cheek as she walked past.

"Should I be offended that they called you first?"

"No, they probably just figured you were more likely to find a date than I am," Lena said and closed the door behind herself.

***

Summer flopped back down on the bed, while Lena took her time in the bathroom. Lena's phone vibrated, and thanks to her position, she could see the message on the screen. It was Charlie, saying she was sorry for waking her up. Summer smiled at that one, but then, she noticed one underneath it. She was only able to see it for a moment before the phone dimmed again, but it was from someone named Vanessa. It said she was sorry for texting so late and that she would love to go out with Lena. It also mentioned having fun at coffee. That must have been the text that came in last night, while they were otherwise engaged. Summer felt her heart immediately sink in her chest. Lena had had coffee with someone and hadn't told her. She had also, apparently, asked Vanessa out after that coffee.

Summer hadn't even thought of anyone else since she had met Lena. Lena, however, seemed to have others on her mind. Summer wasn't sure how she felt about that. She was ready to go all-in with Lena. Summer had no problem taking their time with the relationship steps, and she didn't want to date other people. She also knew she didn't like the idea of Lena dating someone else, but Lena was a free woman. They had made no promises to one another.

"Hey, sorry about the interruption. I'll make sure to scold our friends appropriately later. Can we pick up where we left off?" Lena asked as she re-entered the bedroom.

"Actually, we should probably get going." Summer hung her legs off the side of the bed. "Check out is at noon. I think I'm going to hop in the shower. You can go after me, if that's okay." Summer stood.

"Oh, sure," Lena replied.

Summer walked past her and into the bathroom. For a moment, she pressed her back against the door and exhaled. She needed to keep the immense feeling of disappointment buried, because they still had a three-hour flight. Oh, and then, there was the fact that she was still staying at Lena's house to deal with. That should be interesting.

***

Lena picked her phone up off the bed just as her notification went off again. There was a message from Charlie, that she dismissed, and there was also one from Vanessa. It must have been the one she had ignored earlier so she could feel Summer on top of her without distraction.

"Shit," Lena muttered to herself just as the shower turned on in the bathroom.

Vanessa was nice, but she was no Summer Taft. If

Vanessa had sent the original text asking Lena out, this would be easy for her, but Lena had been the one to text her. Now, she wanted to text her back that she wasn't interested anymore, but that would be rude. It was Sunday, though. She would focus on enjoying the rest of this weekend with Summer, get home, and maybe go out with the group, where she and Summer could tell them that they were dating.

Tomorrow morning, she would stop by Strange Joe's to tell Vanessa that things had changed. It was better to do something like this in person. She couldn't exactly call her right now, or even later, because Summer was still staying with her. That thought brought a smile to her face. Summer would be going home with her. Tonight, Summer would be staying in the master bedroom with Lena, instead of in the guest room.

***

Lena climbed into the plane first and made her way to the same sofa they'd occupied less than twenty-four hours ago. Summer joined her, but she sat at least a foot away. The woman also faced the other side of the plane and had barely made eye contact with Lena since they had left the hotel. The drive over had been mostly silent, which was not like Summer at all. And they'd also barely touched; considering how they woke up this morning and the fact that Lena knew if Summer had pushed for things to go further than their make-out session last night, Lena would have let her. She felt powerless to resist Summer when she was on top of her like that.

"Hey, is everything okay?" Lena chanced to ask.

She reached out her hand and brushed Summer's hair back so she could see her face more easily.

"Everything's fine. Why?" Summer asked simply. "I think I'm going to take a nap. Is that okay? I'm still tired from last night."

169

"Do you want to use my lap as a pillow?" Lena asked with a smile.

"I'm okay."

Summer stood and made her way to one of the plush private plane chairs they had no need for yesterday. Lena was left sitting on a sofa she now had no need for, and watching Summer – the woman she had only just admitted to herself she was falling in love with, pull away after an amazing night together.

The problem, as Lena saw it, was that Summer's indecisiveness seemed to have gotten in the way, for some inexplicable reason; and Lena's lack of confidence made it difficult for her to confront Summer. So, instead, Lena took a seat on the other side of the plane, wanting to give Summer her space.

Every so often, Lena would chance a glance in the other woman's direction. Summer's eyes were closed, as if she were sleeping. But Lena had watched her sleep before. She knew what it looked like to see Summer truly at rest. This was not Summer Taft at rest; this was Summer Taft in an internal battle. Lena only wished the woman would include her in her thoughts. She had faith that if Summer did, they'd be able to figure things out together.

***

Summer knew she was being petulant. That was a word she usually reserved for her brother, but it fit her at the moment. When they deplaned and climbed into the car, she knew Lena had grabbed onto her mood. Things had shifted between them. Summer didn't know what to do, though, because, despite how much she wanted to fix the riff, she wasn't ready to move past it. Seeing that text message from another woman really threw her off. The experience she'd had on their date was nothing short of miraculous. Summer had never felt anything like it before, and she thought she finally had that with Lena. She hated being one of those women who expected commitment immediately; and she wasn't, normally. She was usually the opposite, in fact. When previous boyfriends and girlfriends had wanted her to commit early in a relationship, Summer had suggested they play things by ear.

As she looked over at Lena, though, Summer wanted nothing more than to be with her and only her. Summer had known the woman for a few weeks, and she had spent nearly every moment of those weeks thinking about her. She had finally gotten what she wanted, and now, she was ruining it. Was this what the people she'd dated felt like in the past, when they wanted to date exclusively, and she wasn't ready for that? If so, she felt for them now, because this did not feel good.

The car pulled them into the driveway of Lena's house, the place that had come to feel like home to her. Lena got out. Summer, however, remained inside.

"Are you coming in?" Lena asked after a moment.

"I left my stuff at my apartment," Summer explained while leaning out. "I did my laundry, repacked, and then left the damn bag there."

She hadn't done it intentionally. She'd been nervous and had a hard time picking out what to wear. She'd made a decision, earlier in the day, and then changed her mind a hundred times before finally deciding on the outfit she'd worn. She had left the apartment without her bag and hadn't thought about it since, until they had pulled up to the house.

"You have your roller bag."

"But I just packed stuff for the night. The rest of my stuff is in my big bag. I'll go back to my place and grab it."

"You need to do that right now?" Lena's frustration was growing.

"I'll go grab it and come back. That way, I can just stay after."

"I'll go with you," Lena offered.

"No, you stay here," Summer replied and placed her hand on the door handle. "I'll call Seth, take care of a few things, and come back after, okay?"

"Fine," Lena replied and straightened her lips into a line.

"Are you going to meet Charlie and Hailey at BBZ's?" Summer asked her.

"Probably not. I'm, suddenly, not feeling like socializing," Lena answered and was presented with her bag by the driver, who then climbed back into the driver's seat and started the engine.

"I get it. I'm pretty tired, too," Summer said when Lena didn't ask her the same question. "I'll see you later, okay?"

"Sure." Lena pulled her bag toward the front door while Summer watched.

Lena's posture reminded Summer of Linus van Pelt from a comic strip *Peanuts*, dragging his blanket around. Summer had done that to her. She hated herself for it, but she also didn't know how to pull herself out of this funk, either. She knew that if she hung around the house, her mood wouldn't improve their situation. She needed some time away from Lena, to try to figure out how she felt about Lena seeing other women. But, just the thought of Lena kissing another woman or doing something more than just kissing, made Summer feel nauseous. She rested her head against the back of the seat and couldn't believe how deep she'd gotten herself in just a few weeks.

***

At 7:14, Lena walked into BBZ's. She saw the group immediately but hesitated to head over right away. Lena needed to put on her game face first. She shouldn't have come, but Charlie had been somewhat persistent. After the sixth text, asking Lena to come out with them, she had given in and agreed.

Lena had waited for Summer to show up at the house, but the woman never arrived. And when she started getting ready to come out, Lena had picked up the phone to text Summer and let her know that she had decided to go out for one drink with the girls. After she typed the message, though, she ended up deleting it. Summer clearly needed something, and that something was not Lena at the moment. If the woman wanted space, Lena would just give it to her.

Lena's phone rang in her purse just as she was about to walk over to where Emma, Charlie, and Hailey were sitting – in a large booth across from Ember and Eva. Hannah and Alyssa were at the bar, ordering for everyone. Lena stopped walking and pulled her phone out of her pocket. When she saw the name, though, she thought about declining the call, but she had already gotten herself into a confusing mess, so she answered it and decided to be an adult.

"Hey," she greeted and took a few steps back outside, where there was less noise.

"Hi," Van replied. "You actually just answered my question," she said just as Lena emerged from the bar and stood on the sidewalk.

"I did? What question?"

"Did I just see you walking into a bar?" Vanessa asked. Lena looked up and spotted Van about twenty feet away outside of a restaurant, with two other women. "Like I said, you just answered it."

"Hey," Lena repeated her initial greeting.

"I thought I saw you walk in." Van pointed toward the bar entrance. "We were just finishing up dinner. This is Brynn and Robbie." Van pointed at her two friends. One was lighting a cigarette for the other. "That restaurant is their place." She pointed behind them at the restaurant they'd just exited.

"Nice to meet you," Lena said.

Both women nodded in reply as they shared the cigarette.

"They're just taking a break before they go back inside.

They both smoke, which I think is gross, but it gives them an excuse to step outside once in a while. I'm convinced that if they were non-smokers, they'd never leave the place."

"I see. Well, I can't say I've ever been there, but I'll have to check it out."

"Did you get my text last night? I'm sorry it was so late. I just got done putting away deliveries and closing up. We're open late on Saturdays. I usually don't wrap up until after midnight."

"I did, yes. I was going to reply, but I figured I'd just see you tomorrow morning for coffee, and we could talk then," Lena answered honestly.

"Did I interrupt you?" Van motioned to the bar's entrance again.

"I just got here. I'm meeting some friends inside." Lena watched as Van ran her hand through her hair. "Do you want to join us?"

"I don't want to intrude on you and your friends."

"It's okay. It's a big group," Lena replied and internally fought with herself as she did.

She didn't want to be rude to Van. It wasn't the other woman's fault Lena was in a bad mood. While she'd known so completely that she didn't want to date Van because of how Summer made her feel, Lena hadn't yet expressed that to Van.

"I'm only staying for one drink. They kind of bullied me into coming out with them," Lena added.

"That's okay. I can do one drink. I'm about ready for bed myself." Van pulled the door open. "After you." She turned to her friends. "I'll catch you guys later."

The women nodded. As Lena headed into the bar, it was, apparently, either with a friend or a date. She didn't know if it was a date now. They had agreed to go on a date, and they were together at a bar... Had she ended up on an accidental date with Van when all she wanted was to go home and see Summer?

"Can I get you something to drink?" Van asked.

"Oh, I can get it," Lena replied, not wanting Van to buy her a drink only to then reject the woman later.

"It's just a drink, Lena. It doesn't have to mean anything."

"It's not–"

"Hey, there you are." Hailey approached from behind Lena. "You're late. We're on round 2 already."

"Hey, Hails." Lena turned slightly to see that everyone, save Hailey, was at the back booth. "Sorry, I got caught up."

"My fault." Van raised her hand to take the blame.

"And who is this?" Hailey asked Lena. "I'm Hailey, by the way." She reached out to shake Van's hand.

"This is Vanessa. She goes by Van," Lena introduced.

"Nice to meet you, Van." Hailey kept her inquisitive eyes on Lena. "We're over there. I was just getting a refill for Charlie and me. I lost a bet."

"What was the bet?" Van asked her.

"She bet me that Summer would come. I told her I didn't think she would."

"Summer, the season?" Van questioned with a smile.

"Summer, the person," Hailey replied. "Our friend."

"Summer's coming?" Lena gulped and felt the room suddenly get a lot smaller.

"I thought you two would be coming together. She's still at your place, right?" Hailey asked and then looked over Van's shoulder. "There she is. Hey, Summer!" Hailey walked to greet her, leaving Lena staring at the floor.

"You okay?" Van asked when she noticed Lena's change in demeanor.

"Hey." Summer's voice caused Lena to look up.

"Hi. Long time," Lena joked.

"Yeah," she replied.

"I'm getting a drink," Lena stated and took the few steps to the bar.

"Will you get Charlie and I our usual?" Hailey asked and walked back to the table without waiting for an answer.

"I'll get it," Summer said to Lena.

"No, I've got it." Lena turned around to meet Summer's eye.

"I'm Vanessa," the woman introduced herself after a moment.

Summer had a look on her face Lena didn't fully comprehend, but it looked like recognition. Did they know one another?

"Vanessa?" Summer questioned and then looked back at Lena. "I'm Summer."

"You look familiar. Have we met before?" Van asked her.

"I just have one of those faces, I guess." Summer's eyes were back on Lena. "I'm going to the table."

"Do you want a drink?" Vanessa asked.

"Hey, Zack?" Summer yelled at the man behind the bar. "Can I get two shots of tequila and whiskey neat?"

Zack, Ember's older brother and the bar's owner, nodded in Summer's direction and then began pouring her the shots and the whiskey. He placed all the glasses on the bar. Summer dropped a couple of bills before grabbing them between her hands and walking toward the table.

"Did you guys need something else?" Zack asked Lena after a moment when he realized she and Van were still standing there.

"I think those were just for her," Van replied. "Can I just get a beer? Whatever light beer you have on tap is fine. I'm not picky."

"Sure. You, Lena?" he asked.

"Martini. Dry. Actually, can you give me that and a shot of rum?"

"No problem."

"I thought you were here for one drink."

"I changed my mind." Lena waited for her drinks.

Once Van had her beer and Lena had her martini and a shot, Lena downed the shot, tossed the money for all their drinks on the bar, and then headed to the table where the rest of the girls were waiting.

CHAPTER 17

SUMMER DOWNED ONE SHOT after the other before Lena and her date, Vanessa, made their way over to the booth that now had an additional two chairs at the end of it to accommodate their group. Summer had been able to squeeze in next to Emma, but she was still on the end of the booth. Which meant, that the two chairs Charlie and Hannah had dragged over, would go to Lena and Vanessa. Lena sat next to Hannah, though, which struck Summer as telling because Lena could have sat next to her. Their knees would have been *touching* instead of Vanessa's *knocking* with Summer's.

"Sorry," Vanessa apologized and then pulled the chair back a little.

"Everyone, this is Vanessa," Lena introduced. "That's Ember and her wife, Eva. That's Alyssa and her wife, Hannah." Lena pointed at each woman in turn. "And Charlie and her girlfriend, Hailey. You already met... Summer." She paused before saying Summer's name. "And this is Emma."

"Oh, are you Summer's girlfriend?" Van asked of Emma.

"No," Emma stated.

"Emma has another woman," Hailey shared.

"I do not. I told you, I told her no," Emma replied to Hailey's comment.

"I swear I've seen you before," Van persisted with Summer.

"She's Summer Taft," Charlie said.

"Oh, that's how I know you."

Summer hated when people said that. *'That's how I*

177

know you' was one of the things she heard fairly regularly, and it was so misleading. No one that ever said that, had actually knew her. Only her brother knew her well.

Lena knew her more than most, and Summer was looking forward to the other woman knowing more about her than anyone else – including Seth, because that was what happened when you fell in love with someone and shared your life with them. They knew you. They understood you better than anyone. Summer had no idea how much she was missing that until she met and started opening up to Lena.

"So, how do you two know each other?" Eva asked Lena.

"Vanessa owns the coffee shop next to my office. I'm kind of a regular."

"And I kind of hit on her."

"Really?" Charlie asked.

"I gave her my name and number on a cup," Vanessa replied. "It was a pretty lame move, but I'd seen her in a lot, and finally decided to do something about it, I guess."

Summer wanted to vomit.

"So, you two are dating?" Hannah asked while Alyssa put her arm over the back of the booth around her.

Summer missed doing that with Lena already.

"Oh, no," Lena objected, and that got Summer's attention. "I mean, we're not…"

"We haven't gone out yet. I was at a restaurant with my friends next door, and saw her come in," Vanessa said.

"And now you get to hang out with all of us… Lena, you guys can go. I know we kind of used guilt to get you to come, but–"

"I'm just staying for a drink. I'm pretty tired," Lena interrupted Charlie.

She lifted her martini to her lips and took a long drink. Summer finished her whiskey.

"I'm going to get another." Summer stood and lightly bumped into Vanessa as she walked past her.

It wasn't intentional. It might have been the alcohol

she'd down so quickly, starting to kick in. She ordered from another bartender and glanced down when her phone buzzed. She saw Hayden's name on the screen and set the phone on the bar, not answering it. She just wanted another drink.

"Hey." Lena approached and leaned on the bar next to her.

"Hi," Summer offered in soft response.

"I had a shot. And I just drank an entire martini, after not eating anything since breakfast, so... I'm starting to feel the alcohol kick in. Will you please tell me what the hell is going on?"

Summer's phone chimed that a voicemail had been left by Hayden.

Lena looked down at the phone, "Hayden?"

Summer downed her two shots and then turned to Lena.

"You and your date seem to be getting along well," Summer replied.

"My date?" Lena checked and then glanced at Vanessa, who was chatting with Hailey. "Van?"

"Van? That's her nickname?" Summer hated the tone she was using.

"She's not my date, Summer," Lena corrected. "She told you what happened. I was coming in here; she saw me. I thought it would be rude not to invite her."

"But, you were going to go out with her."

"What are you talking about?" Lena asked.

She then stopped Summer from consuming the next two shots the woman had requested by holding up two fingers to the same bartender. He had poured the shots quickly and placed them in front of Summer, but Lena pulled them away.

"Stop it and talk to me."

Summer exhaled a dramatic breath.

"I saw your phone this morning, when Charlie texted, and you were in the bathroom. I didn't mean to, but I caught the text from *Van*, over there, that she had fun on your coffee date, and that yes, she would love to go out with you."

Lena stared at the woman in front of her, for a moment, and then downed one of her shots. She slid the other to Summer, who took it and allowed the alcohol to once again, burn her throat.

"Why didn't you say anything?" Lena asked.

"Because *you* never said anything," Summer replied. "It's fine. You don't owe me any explanation. I just didn't know you were seeing anyone else, and I–"

"I'm not," Lena interrupted.

Hayden's number flashed across the screen again. This time, it was a text message. Summer glanced at it, but he'd only left a text asking her to call him when she could. He wanted to continue their lunch.

"The guy cannot take a hint," Summer said and stuffed the phone into her pocket.

"What hint?" Lena asked.

"We were supposed to have a business lunch yesterday, and it was weird. I think he was hitting on me or something."

"Hayden hit on you? He wouldn't do that... He knows..."

"He knows what?" Summer asked.

"He knows that I like you," Lena retorted and not nicely. "He's one of my best friends, and yesterday, before you came to pick me up for our date, I called him. I told him about it and how much I like you."

"You did?" Summer asked so softly, she wondered if Lena heard her over the music.

"Yes, I did. Summer, Vanessa and I had coffee on Friday before you and I had lunch. She had asked me out before. Don't get me wrong... She's great. She's also nice, and I like her, but I was just trying to do something to get my mind to focus on anything other than you. At coffee, she was asking me questions about myself and doing the normal, getting to know someone thing. All I kept thinking about was that I didn't want to share those things with her. I wanted to share them with you. I didn't know how you felt. I was too scared to ask until that night at the house."

"But she said you asked her out."

"I did. I texted her on Friday before you and I had a night of grilled cheese sandwiches and movie watching. I'd forgotten about it. I'd planned to see her tomorrow, when I went in for coffee, to tell her that I'm not interested. I just felt like I should do it in person, since, technically, I asked her out."

"Oh, wow," Van said from behind Summer.

Summer and Lena both turned around to see Van standing there, holding an empty martini glass and a half-empty beer glass, which she set on the bar between them and then stood back.

"Van, I'm sorry," Lena said.

"No, it's okay." Van held up her hands in defense. "I actually interrupted, so me hearing that is my fault." The woman paused and lowered her hands. "And I appreciate the whole, 'tell me in person thing.' Most people wouldn't do that." She glanced at Summer. "So, you two are…"

"Trying to figure things out," Lena said when Summer couldn't.

Summer was beginning to regret the amount of alcohol she had consumed much too rapidly.

"I understand." Van looked back at Lena then. "I'm going to go. Can you tell your friends I had to leave or something?"

"You don't have—"

"I do," Van interjected. "I'm okay, Lena. I hope you know you can still come to the shop, and it won't be weird. You too, Summer."

"That's very adult of you," Lena said, and Van smiled at her.

"Well, I find it's best to just hit things head on whenever I can. I'm glad I found out now that you're into someone else. I'll see you around." Van waved at both of them and headed out of the bar.

"I kind of like her now," Summer said.

Lena turned back, laughed at her, and said, "Now that she's gone?"

"No, that was pretty mature of her. I wish I could have been that mature about ten hours ago."

"Me too," Lena replied with a smile.

"I got jealous. I'm sorry. I know you can date whoever you want. We've had exactly one date, but I just got jealous. I hated thinking about you with someone else."

"I know the feeling. I had a hard time thinking about you with Emma, and then Hayden, and–"

"Wait. Hayden? Why would you–"

"It was after you guys started working together. He and I went to dinner, where he said you were attractive, smart, and funny. He's not wrong. But he also said that the only thing keeping him from dating you was the fact that you were a client; and I guess he had someone else he was dating, but they weren't exclusive."

"I'm not his client anymore. He got promoted," Summer replied.

"He told me. That's why I'm a little worried that you were right, and he *is* hitting on you; which makes me want to punch him in the face," Lena said.

Summer found it adorable.

"No, I want to punch him in the nuts," Lena changed her mind.

Summer then put her hand on Lena's forearm and said, "I don't like Hayden. So, regardless of whether or not you punch him, I don't want to date him."

"You want to date me?" Lena asked, and Summer found her eyes completely mesmerizing.

"Yes, I do. I only want to date you, Lena. I'm all-in. That's why I acted the way I did today. I thought, for the first time, I'm all-in with someone, and they don't feel the same way."

"I do." Lena placed her hand on Summer's cheek. "I am. I'm in, Summer."

"Yeah?"

"Yes." Lena's hand ended up on the back of Summer's neck. "I'm sorry about Vanessa. I'm sorry about Hayden, and Emma, and everything else. I just want to go home... Will you please come home?"

There was that word again. Summer smiled at the sound.

"I have to get my stuff at my place," she replied.

"Then, call the car. I'll go with you to get it. I'm not taking the chance that you don't come back again."

"I'm not exactly avoiding you anymore."

"I'm not worried about that. You are obviously drunk. You might pass out on your couch."

Summer laughed and pressed her forehead to Lena's.

"I'll call the car. You, say our good nights." Summer pulled out her phone.

"What should I tell them?" Lena asked.

Summer pulled her forehead back, turned around, and saw that every single set of eyes at that table was on them. Hailey, Eva, and Hannah all looked at them dreamily, while Charlie, Alyssa, Emma, and Ember gave them knowing and 'good for you' glances.

"I think the secret's out. Maybe just say good night," Summer suggested.

She then turned back to Lena and kissed the woman gently on the lips. After that, Lena headed to the table, while Summer ordered a car for them. Lena could feel the blush forming on her cheeks and spreading down her neck and chest.

"So, you came with one girl, and now you're leaving with another?" Charlie asked with a smirk.

"I didn't come here with Van. She was outside and saw me. And yes, I'm leaving with Summer," Lena replied.

"What's going on there?" Hailey asked, pointing between Lena and Summer.

"We're dating, I think," Lena said, beginning to feel the alcohol really take effect.

"You think?" Ember asked.

"We went on a date last night, and now we're going home."

"Home?" Eva asked with her head on Ember's shoulder.

"She's been staying with me while she's on vacation," Lena said.

"Some vacation," Alyssa joined in.

"Stop, babe." Hannah lightly slapped Alyssa's knee. "Go. Have fun."

"Yeah, have fun," Charlie teased.

"You are all incredibly mature." Hailey laughed. "Seriously, she's totally into you."

"And you're totally into her." Charlie looked at Lena.

"Go be totally into each other," Ember said. "If you know what I mean."

"We all know what you mean, babe." Eva rolled her eyes at her wife. "And you're better than that snarky remark."

"I know. But I've had a few drinks; I'm not on my A game," Ember replied.

"This is great." Hailey was, apparently, excited. "I mean, look around. We've got married with kids." She pointed at Hannah and Alyssa.

"Guilty." Hannah raised her hand. "And I'm lame because I miss them already."

"I do, too." Alyssa gave her wife her famous puppy-dog face. "We are lame."

"We've got just plain married." Hailey pointed at Ember and Eva.

"Hey, we're not just plain anything," Ember retorted.

"That was much better, Em." Eva kissed her wife's cheek.

"And we've got single and looking." Hailey turned to point at Emma.

"Single and not looking for my ex; looking for someone new," Emma said.

"In a new relationship... Relationship?" Hailey glanced and pointed at Lena.

"Yes," Summer spoke for her from behind, and Lena felt arms around her waist pulling her back slightly.

"Oh," Lena exclaimed as Summer's arms tightened over her stomach and her head rested on Lena's shoulder. "Hi."

"Hi. The car is on its way." Summer kissed her cheek.

"And we've got newly engaged," Hailey announced.

Everyone's eyes moved from Lena and Summer immediately as cheers rang out in the group.

"Really?" Ember asked.

"Finally!" Eva exclaimed.

"Wait! Who asked whom?" Ember asked. "We had a bet." She pointed between herself and her wife.

"Charlie asked me, but I had a ring for her already," Hailey said and lifted her hand.

She then placed a ring on her ring finger, and Charlie did the same.

"They're perfect," Eva said.

"I can't believe you two didn't tell me." Ember seemed moderately offended.

"You're our best friend," Charlie said. "Her best friend *and* my best friend. It didn't seem right to make you keep a secret for the both of us."

"Yeah, because I've never done *that* before," Ember replied sarcastically.

"I'm happy for you, guys. We were just heading out though." Lena turned her head to the side. "We should stay, Summer."

"No, you guys go ahead." Charlie waved them off. "You're both about to be super drunk anyway."

"I saw you down two shots the second you sat down," Ember said. "Are you sure you're okay to get home, Summer?"

"I called for a car. And we'll be fine," Summer replied.

"Go home and have fun." Hailey wrapped both arms around Charlie's neck. "The four of us can double date sometime this week. You can buy us dinner to celebrate." She kissed Charlie's cheek.

Lena laughed as Summer pulled back on her body, moving her toward the door.

"Congratulations!" Summer practically yelled on her way out. "I'm so happy for you two."

Lena was practically cackling. She almost tripped over her feet as they danced with Summer's.

"What she said," Lena echoed and gave up her struggle to allow Summer to pull her through the door. "Summer," she exclaimed as soon as they were outside.

"Lena," Summer mocked right back. "You know what I just realized?"

"What?" Lena asked as she placed her arms around Summer's neck and pulled her in.

"You've never been to my apartment." Summer pecked Lena on the lips and happily pulled away as the car arrived to take them there. "Let's go."

"Oh, you're really drunk right now, aren't you?" Lena laughed as they climbed into the car.

"I am. I'll regret it later, I'm sure. But, right now, I'm having fun." Summer turned toward Lena as they sat in the backseat. "Wanna make out with me?" She wiggled her eyebrows at Lena and placed a hand on her thigh.

"Yes, I do." Lena leaned in, immediately capturing Summer's lips.

***

Summer practically stumbled into her small apartment. Her bag was still right where she had left it. She felt Lena's arms behind her, pulling her back, as she'd done to her in the bar.

"I am very drunk," Summer said with a laugh.

"So am I. We should not have attempted to drown our sorrows in alcohol and then make up immediately after." Lena moved Summer's hair aside and placed a kiss on her neck.

"We really did not plan our make up properly." Summer invited the kiss by tilting her head, allowing Lena to continue to press her lips over Summer's sensitive skin. "We should get my stuff and go. The car is waiting."

"And then, we go home?" Lena kissed her again.

"Yes," Summer whispered.

"Can I get the tour of this place first?" Lena requested as she removed her lips.

"No," Summer replied and turned around in her arms. "That just delays us getting home. So, here's your tour."

She waved one arm in the air with a flourish and then, took her big roller handle in the other hand. Lena laughed at her in a new laugh Summer hadn't heard before. It was, apparently, Lena's drunk laugh. And Summer loved it.

"You're a terrible tour guide," Lena replied as her laughter died down.

"I'm never here, anyway." Summer pulled on her bag. "And when I finally find that house I'm looking for, this place will be gone for good. So, there's no point in the tour. Come on. I want to go home."

Lena smiled at the woman and followed her back to the car, where their driver lifted Summer's bag into the trunk, and they drunkenly got back inside.

"I haven't been this drunk in years," Lena said as Summer reached for her cheek to pull her closer.

"Neither have I." Summer went to kiss her, but Lena pulled back. "Something wrong?"

"No, you're just… you're fun, Summer. You're really fun."

"I'm fun?" Summer pulled back even more.

"No, stop." Lena pulled her back, placing both of Summer's hands in her lap. "I don't mean you're a fun time, or I'm only having fun with you. I really like you. Part of what I like about you is how fun you are. Do you know how long it's been since I've had actual fun? Since I've met you, I've had an entire planetarium to myself; I've made sundaes in my kitchen while making a mess; I've watched an 80s movie that I never thought I'd watch all the way through; I've eaten about a hundred grilled cheese sandwiches; I laughed while we sampled wine together; I flew to Nashville to see one of my favorite artists, and then, had a full-on banquet in a hotel suite." Lena took a deep breath. "I've had so much fun. I've laughed more than I have laughed in... maybe ever. And I like it."

"I like it, too. I like having fun with you," Summer replied.

"But, you know what I've also noticed?" Lena asked as the car moved them toward the house.

"What?"

"That I like the other stuff, too." She played with Summer's hands in her lap. "I like the quiet moments we've had. I liked just having you next to me the other night, while I was working; or falling asleep while you watch something on TV. I like this, Summer. I like us."

"I like us, too."

"Then, please don't disappear again." Lena was taking them to a more serious place than Summer's intoxicated brain was prepared for. "If you think something's going on, just ask. Please don't go."

"Okay. I'm sorry."

"And I'm sorry for not telling you about Van."

"Van is a stupid nickname," Summer replied.

Lena laughed at her and then wrapped Summer's arm around herself so she could slide in next to the woman and burrow her head into Summer's neck.

"Are you back to hating her now?" Lena asked.

"Maybe. I can't decide," Summer replied while Lena laughed into her neck.

CHAPTER 18

"OKAY. LET'S GO." Lena lifted Summer's bag up the stairs for her, since Summer was barely able to make it up the stairs on her own. "You're a mess."

"I have my moments," Summer replied as she held onto both banisters to steady herself.

"Honey, are you okay?" Lena laughed after getting Summer's bag safely up the stairs.

"The spinning has started," the woman replied, and Lena headed back down to help her the rest of the way up.

"So, I was thinking... you'd sleep in my room tonight, instead of the guest room."

"Yes, please." Summer sank into Lena's arms.

Lena held onto her while moving backward into her room.

"Why aren't you this drunk right now?" Summer muttered into Lena's neck.

"I think you've had more than me... Plus, I had a martini. You had whiskey, and you downed it. I, at least, took two whole minutes to finish my drink." Lena sat Summer on the side of the bed. "Can you get yourself into your pajamas?"

"No." Summer flopped backward onto the bed over the blanket, while Lena laughed and leaned down to pull off the woman's shoes.

"Then, can I at least take off your jeans and get you in your shorts?"

"I can sleep in my underwear," Summer replied.

She began working the button on her jeans, though clumsily. Lena gulped at the sight. Despite the fact that

189

Summer was incredibly drunk, Lena found herself trying not to get turned on at the woman lying on her bed, attempting to take off her jeans.

"Let me help you."

Lena reached down just as Summer unzipped them and grabbed the belt loops to pull down. Summer wiggled her body until the jeans were no longer attached to her. Lena moved to place them on her dresser. She did her best to avoid the vision that was Summer Taft in her black bikinis and a t-shirt on her bed. Summer's legs spread just slightly, and her eyes closed, trying to avoid the light in the room.

"I'm going to take my bra off," Summer said, sat up, and wobbled a bit.

Lena moved to Summer and placed her hands on the woman's shoulders to stabilize her while Summer removed her bra from under the shirt. To Lena, it seemed as if she was doing it as slowly as possible, making her feel like she needed a cold shower to keep herself from making a move. When Summer tossed it onto the floor, Lena pushed her back on the bed and watched Summer close her eyes again. Lena moved to her drawers and pulled out pants and a shirt to wear.

"Keep your eyes closed." She stripped her jeans off and replaced them with a pair of sweats.

"If I open them, the room will spin."

Lena changed into a t-shirt and then moved to the bathroom. She grabbed the glass she kept there and filled it with water. When she returned, Summer was on her side, nearly in the fetal position.

"Here. Drink this." Lena set the glass on the table and then sat herself on the side of the bed, placing a hand on Summer's back and rubbing it in slow circles. "Summer, come on."

"I just want to sleep."

"I promise, I will let you sleep. I just need you to drink this first," Lena coaxed and lifted the back of Summer's shirt so she could run her hand along her skin. "Hey, if you drink this right now, I will let you pick the next movie we watch."

"Even if it's a bad one?" Summer muttered.

"Sure." Lena laughed, and Summer opened her eyes and smiled.

"Your eyes are pretty."

"So you've said. Please, drink this."

Lena lifted the glass, and Summer lifted her head. After a few minutes, Summer finished the water. Lena stood, refilled the water, and downed a glass herself. Then, she refilled it again, grabbed the ibuprofen they would both need in the morning, and placed the full glass on Summer's side of the bed, in case the woman needed it in the middle of the night. She placed a couple of pills next to it for her, too, climbed in beside her, adjusted the blankets, pressed the button to turn off the lights, and felt Summer slide in next to her and rest her head on Lena's shoulder.

"I'm sorry I got so drunk we couldn't do anything," Summer said after a moment.

"It's okay. We can plan date number two tomorrow, when I get home from work."

"Oh, God! You have to work tomorrow," Summer replied.

"Yeah, I do. So, we should get some sleep, okay?"

"Okay." Summer lifted her head and looked down at Lena. "Charlie and Hailey are engaged."

"Yes, they are," Lena replied, wondering where that comment came from.

"Earlier, I said that we were in a relationship. When Hailey made that comment, I said yes. I was a little drunk. I probably shouldn't have just said that."

"You seem to be sobering up a little."

"The spinning has stopped, but I still feel it," Summer said while still looking down. "We've only been on one date."

"I know."

"But I don't want to date anyone else, Lena."

"I don't either."

"Is it too fast?"

"Maybe." Lena shrugged and then ran her hand up Summer's arm to her neck and held it there. "But I don't care."

"We haven't even had sex yet," Summer added.

Lena smiled and rolled her eyes.

"Well, we might have had tonight… But you ran off, because you thought I was interested in someone else. And I let you, because I was afraid of what might happen if I actually confronted you about it. Then, we both got drunk, and I don't want our first time to be something we did while drunk."

"Me neither." Summer leaned down and kissed her nose.

"But don't think it's escaped me that you're in your underwear right now." Lena lifted a playful eyebrow when Summer pulled away to see her face.

"Should I put pants on?"

"No way. Lie back down. Let's get some sleep."

"Be my girlfriend?" Summer asked.

"You know, I've never technically had one of those."

"Really?"

"I dated a woman for a couple of months, but it wasn't exclusive."

"Can I be your first girlfriend, then?" Summer asked with the kind of sincerity that Lena rarely saw in others.

"Yes." She smiled and watched Summer do the same.

Summer leaned down and kissed her lips gently, at first, before parting her lips and waiting for Lena to do the same. They both knew it wouldn't go further, but Lena enjoyed the fact that Summer was half on top of her. She particularly enjoyed the small whimpers that came from Summer as the kiss continued. When Summer finally pulled back, she took in Lena again.

"Beautiful," she whispered and kissed Lena's forehead before lying on her back. "Come here."

Lena rolled on her side and moved into Summer.

"Good night," Summer said.

"Good night." Lena kissed Summer's neck and closed her eyes.

***

Summer woke up earlier than she had wanted. Lena's alarm hadn't even gone off yet. It was way too early, and her head was pounding from the impending hangover. She turned to her side and noticed the water and pills Lena had laid out for her. She thought to herself about how lucky she was, and then downed half the glass with the pills before turning over slowly to see that Lena was still asleep. It was only 5:45. Summer had no reason to be awake this early on a Monday, when she was still on vacation, but she decided to take advantage of it. She slid out of bed and made her way into the bathroom, where she washed her face with Lena's stuff, hoping she wouldn't mind. Then, Summer remembered that her toothbrush and toothpaste were in the guest bathroom. She refilled the water glass after finishing the other half and an additional full glass, and moved it to Lena's side of the bed, placing it there next to the pills Lena had left out for herself.

Summer made her way down the stairs and into the kitchen, where she searched the fridge for something that would make a decent breakfast. She located two eggs and bacon, which would work just fine. She began cooking and started on the coffee. By the time she had bacon on a paper towel to soak up the grease, she'd set the island with two plates, steaming coffee cups, and glasses filled to the brim with grapefruit juice. The toast popped up from the toaster, and Summer reached for it, not knowing how Lena liked her toast, either, and then turned back around to see a groggy Lena standing in the entryway of the kitchen, with a smirk on her face.

"I would have asked you how you like your eggs, but I didn't want to wake you up," Summer said.

"You're cooking in your underwear," Lena replied.

"I guess I forgot to put pants on." Summer looked down and realized she'd forgotten to throw something on over her bikinis.

"I'm going to like having a girlfriend," Lena said and sat down on her usual stool.

Summer smiled at her and walked around to Lena's side of the island, placing slices of toast in front of her bacon and eggs.

"Good morning." Summer leaned down and kissed her. "I think I successfully cooked food without burning anything."

"With a hangover? That's impressive," Lena said with a lifted eyebrow.

"I made over easy. Is that okay?" Summer asked.

"It's great. Thank you." Lena placed a hand on the back of Summer's neck and held her girlfriend in place. "How are you feeling?"

"A little better, thanks to the pills you left out, but my head still hurts. I think I could sleep all day."

"You could, you know? You're on vacation," Lena replied and let go of Summer so she could sit next to her. "I wish I was on vacation."

"Me too." Summer turned to her just as she was about to sip her coffee. "We'd have more time together."

Lena smiled, and then Summer noticed her eyes flit down to her legs.

"You should always eat breakfast in your underwear," Lena suggested.

"I'll keep that in mind." Summer laughed and took a drink. "Do you think you have time for lunch today? I could stop by and pick you up again."

"That sounds nice, but I have a lunch with my directors. I might be able to squeeze you in for dinner, though," Lena said.

"I can pick you up when you're done with work, and we can go to someplace nice."

"Or, I can come back here, bring some take out, and we can eat it while we watch a movie and try another one of those bottles of wine," Lena suggested.

"That's what you want?"

"To be alone with you? Yes, that's what I want."

"Maybe we should revisit the wine idea for tonight, though. I might not be up for more alcohol."

Lena took a bite of her eggs and laughed.

"Non-alcoholic beverages only, then."

"Okay. That sounds nice. You're taking the car, though, right?" Summer asked.

"You need to stop lending me cars. A girl could get used to being chauffeured around."

"What's wrong with that?" Summer asked.

"I guess nothing," Lena replied and smiled into her juice.

"I saw that." Summer placed her free hand on Lena's pajama-covered thigh. "It's okay to get used to it, you know?"

"It just feels weird, sometimes."

"To be driven around?"

"No, to use your account to be driven around," Lena said.

Summer could only laugh as she crunched on some particularly crispy bacon.

"Babe, have you not noticed that I've been living in your house?"

Lena smiled and finished off her bacon.

"It's not the same thing."

"What's different about it?"

"I'm not paying for you to live here."

"Lena, it has nothing to do with money. I like the fact that it's safer than the alternative. Besides, you could afford an account yourself, couldn't you?"

"I grew up in a place where people used money to get what they want. I kind of still work in a place where that's the case. I have a hard time understanding when someone does something with it that's not motivated by anything else."

"Well, it is motivated by something," Summer replied.

"My safety?" Lena asked with a knowing smile.

"That, and the fact that it gets you home faster, so I get more time with you."

"I thought you were going to say something else."

"Like what, exactly?" Summer asked suggestively.

"You're really going to make me say it?" Lena asked, and Summer just laughed. "Fine. So, you weren't using it to try to get in my pants?"

Summer continued her laughter as she finished her coffee.

"Well, if I were, it would have failed so far." She pushed her plate away.

Lena cleared her throat. Summer thought it was out of nervousness, which made her concerned about their banter. Had she taken it too far? Lena stood and pushed her stool back. Summer grew even more concerned for a moment, but then Lena slid Summer's stool back with a strength Summer didn't know she possessed. She took Summer's hand and turned her so that Summer's back was against the island. And just like that, Summer was no longer concerned that she had taken her joke too far, because Lena's hands were on her waist, and she, herself, was being lifted onto the counter. Her hands went to Lena's shoulders to steady herself, and her eyes met the blue orbs staring back at her, dark with thoughts she hadn't possessed only moments ago.

Lena's hands were on the inside of her thighs, pulling them apart. Summer suddenly felt very nervous about the fact that she was only wearing underwear that she now definitely needed to change. Lena moved between her legs and slid her hands up Summer's shirt, stilling them on her abdomen, before leaning in and starting a dangerously slow, amazingly satisfying kiss. Summer's hands went into Lena's hair. She felt the natural waves she liked so much as she gripped Lena a little harder and pulled the woman even closer. Lena's stomach was now flushed to her center, as Lena's hands slid around Summer's back, and Summer had a hard time resisting the possibility of friction. She moaned into Lena's mouth and decided not to be embarrassed by it, because her body felt so good.

Summer's hands moved to Lena's back and then her hips, and she tugged Lena further into her body. Her hips reacted when Lena's lips moved to her neck and began sucking on her pulse point. She felt one of Lena's hands move to her thigh and then slowly, slide to the inside of it and stop. Her entire body was pulsing with desire, wanting nothing more than for Lena to continue sliding it just a little further.

"This was a bad idea," Lena said against her neck, and then Summer felt her tongue dance its way to her earlobe, and Lena's lips sucked it into her mouth.

"Feels pretty good to me," Summer managed to get out.

"I have to go to work," Lena reminded, and then her other hand slid up Summer's shirt and stopped just below her breast.

"No, you don't. Call in sick. We can do this all day," Summer said.

Lena pulled back, and Summer felt the warm pressure against her disappear. She reached her hands out for Lena's, who had removed her hands entirely from Summer's body and had them hanging at her sides.

"Come back," Summer asked her.

"I want to," Lena replied and stared at Summer's lips. "But, I need to go take a very cold shower now, and get ready for work."

"I cannot believe you got me going like that, and you're just walking away." Summer laughed and slid off the counter, pulling Lena back into her body. "I might have to finish what you started solo after you leave for work."

Lena's eyes got big, and her lips parted. Summer thought for a moment that her ploy had worked.

"Do it in my bed, if you do." Lena wiggled her eyebrows. "I'll take care of myself in the shower," she teased.

"Not fair!" Summer pushed the laughing Lena back away from her. "Go, take your shower. I'll clean this up."

"You're talking about the dishes, right?" Lena mocked, and her eyes lowered to Summer's legs.

"Oh, my God!" Summer exclaimed.

Lena laughed all the way upstairs. Summer gripped the island for a moment while leaning over it. She smiled at the realization that this could be her life. She could wake up next to Lena and make her breakfast. They could eat together, talk, and then do other things as well. And those other things felt very good. Summer's body was coiled, tight, and craved more. But she wouldn't actually do anything to take care of herself, despite her earlier joke with Lena. Summer knew she would be able to come, but it wouldn't feel nearly as good as having Lena touch her.

She'd always been someone that had a healthy sexual appetite. She liked sex as much as the next person, but she'd rarely found herself in a situation where she'd call herself horny or hard up for it. As she clung to the countertop, though, she could only describe herself with those words, because it was more than wanting at this point. She needed Lena.

Summer released her hands from the counter and began working on the dishes as a means to distract herself. She focused on the hot, near scalding water as she cleaned the pans. When she had loaded the dishwasher and closed the door, she had no more distractions left. She headed up the stairs to the sounds of the shower turning off. The bedroom door was once again, open.

Summer knew Lena would be heading out of the bathroom soon – likely, wrapped in a towel, with her hair wet and dripping. She grunted under her breath and stared at the floor while walking into the room, because her bag had been pulled in there the night before.

"I'm in here. Not checking you out, though," she said so that Lena would be aware of her presence.

"Where are you taking that?" Lena asked of Summer's bag that Summer was pulling.

Summer stared down at the floor.

"Are you in a towel right now?"

"Yes." Lena laughed. "Is that why you're staring at the ground?"

"Yes. I'm taking this to my room."

"Summer, leave it here," Lena replied.

"Don't come close to me, all fresh out of the shower and only wearing a towel," Summer warned her as she felt Lena approach.

Lena took the handle of the bag from her as she laughed. Summer caught sight of bare feet, legs, and then, the hem of a white towel. She just had to look up.

"You're killing me," she said when she took in the sight of Lena's skin glistening with water droplets.

"Summer, *this* is your room now," Lena replied. "I mean, at least while you're staying here. You can use my bathroom. You don't have to use the guest room."

"Should we maybe revisit me staying here?" Summer asked without really wanting to ask. "Since we're dating now."

"We can, but can it wait until tonight? I have to finish getting ready."

"Sure," Summer replied.

Lena left the bag where it was and headed back toward the bathroom.

"But, for the record, you're staying here tonight no matter what, right?"

"I guess I am." Summer smiled at the thought.

"Good." Lena turned her head just slightly so that Summer could see her eyes for a moment, and then, she disappeared into the bathroom.

CHAPTER 19

LENA HATED HAVING to leave Summer at home to go to work. Her head was still feeling the remnants of the hangover. She told herself she'd never drink that much that quickly again, but especially, not on a Sunday night before work the next day. She popped a couple more ibuprofen just before heading out to her lunch with the directors. She did this monthly, as it gave them a chance to have a meeting outside of the office, and it was a way for her to recognize their hard work. Her lunch went a little long, and she was more than exhausted after her next meeting. She needed a caffeine pick-me-up and thought about the terrible office coffee. It just wasn't worth it. She considered going to Starbuck's, but decided that if Van could be an adult about this whole situation, she could, too. She headed down to Strange Joe's instead.

Lena had gotten there, apparently, at the same time everyone else needed caffeine. The line was nearly out the door. She focused on responding to a text from Summer while she waited in it. She was a woman with a schoolgirl crush. She was giddy and smiling all the time. Summer's message had asked Lena what she was doing. Lena typed out that she was getting a much-needed cappuccino. Then, Summer's message came in along with a picture of her with a lifted inquisitive eyebrow. The text underneath it was a question about where Lena was getting that coffee. Lena replied that she was at Strange Joe's, but that she was just here for the coffee. She saw the three dots in a bubble, indicating that Summer was responding, but before the message could come in, she heard Van's voice.

"Hey, stranger," she greeted and then stocked a bag of coffee on a shelf above the condiments bar.

"Hey." Lena looked up.

"When I didn't see you this morning, I thought things might be awkward now, and you'd stop coming in." Van approached Lena in the line.

"I wanted to come in, but I didn't have time. This is the first chance I've had." Lena's phone chimed with Summer's response.

Van glanced down at it in Lena's hand and then back up at Lena.

"It really is okay, you know?" the woman said. "I didn't expect us to just jump into something serious. I would have been okay with you telling me about Summer."

"It wasn't like that." Lena took another step toward the register as the line moved. "I liked her, but I didn't think she liked me. We just met a few weeks ago. She was a friend of a friend. We started spending more time together, and I realized that I liked her. You did the cup thing, and I didn't know how to respond... I'm still getting used to this whole thing. I'm a little slow." Lena laughed lightly. "And I had fun with you on Friday, but that night, I was with Summer. I finally decided to just ask her out and let the chips fall, I guess."

"And she was into you, too? I think that's great, Lena."

"You do? You're being so cool about all this. I asked you out, and you said yes, and then this happened." She took another step forward with Van in tow.

"Like I said, I didn't expect it to turn into anything serious, at least not right away. I would have been fine with going out on a date even if you were going out with other women, or in this case, one woman. Also, not all lesbians are crazy and dramatic about this stuff. It's not like I planned on us moving in together after our first date or anything." Van laughed.

"Well, thank you," Lena replied and pretended it was funny.

"It seems like you two aren't doing the date other people thing, though, I take it."

"No, we're not."

"Bummer for me," Van said with a smile. "Maybe you and I could be friends."

"I'd like that."

"I'll get your cappuccino," the woman said and took a few steps away from Lena to go around the counter.

"I'm paying for it this time," Lena replied.

"Yeah, you are. That's the least you could do," Van responded with a playful wink.

***

Summer took a very long shower in the morning after Lena left. That helped release some of the tension in her body, but she also knew she needed another activity to help with the rest of it. She was hoping that activity would be taking place in a few hours, when Lena got home.

"It's weird – being in Lena's house for the first time, and she's not here," Hailey said.

Hailey passed her the plate from their sandwiches. She had made her way over to Lena's on a late lunch break before she would head to Detroit for some meetings at that office the next day.

"It is?"

"It's not weird for you, being here without her?" Hailey asked. "I mean, I know you two are dating now… But you weren't when you first started staying here, right?"

Summer smiled and nodded that they should retire to the living room to finish their chat.

"No, we only had our first date Saturday night. And

no, I never felt weird being here without her, even in the beginning."

"I would have," Hailey said as they sat on the sofa.

"I think it's this house." Summer slid one leg under the other as she got more comfortable. "I just felt totally at home here the moment I saw the place."

"Really?" Hailey asked.

"Yeah, I can't explain it. It's like, I pulled up in the car, and I had finally made it home after a very, very long trip." Summer glanced at Hailey, who was smiling at her. "What's that look for?"

"Nothing. It's just that's how I felt about the house Charlie and I built. I saw it in the design process, and we visited the site almost daily, but when we actually got there, and it was done, and we were moving in, it was like that for me. For Charlie, too, I think. We just felt completely at home."

"Then, you get it."

"Yeah, but a part of that for me was the fact that Charlie was there, too. She's my real home. Our house is amazing, and I never want to leave it, but it's not just the brick, the wood, and the tile. It's the fact that I'm there with the love of my life."

"Your fiancée now," Summer said.

"Exactly." Hailey smiled. "I want us to grow old and raise our kids there. I want our grandkids to stop by and play in the backyard. That's why it's really home." She paused. "Is that part of why you like this place so much?"

"Because I want my grandkids to play in the backyard?"

"You know what I mean."

Summer laughed but stopped when she realized Hailey was serious.

"Oh, I don't know. I like Lena; I know that part. I really like her. I have since I met her. I just don't think I understood it completely that night." Summer laughed. "That night, when we met at The Lantern, after you guys left, and it was just us, Lena suggested we help each other find people."

"What?" Hailey asked.

"Like, we'd be wing-women for each other. I said yes. I guess, for a minute, I thought it would be fun and maybe I'd meet someone, but almost immediately, I realized that I said yes because I wanted an excuse to hang out with her again." Summer took a deep breath. "I invited her to this book signing and played along with the whole thing about finding someone for her, but I didn't really want to. Then, we went to the planetarium, and it was just us. I kept staring at her." She looked at Hailey. "Have you seen those eyes? They're, like, a color I didn't know eyes could be. Like, they're nowhere on the ROYGBIV spectrum, you know?"

Hailey laughed and said, "You've got it bad, girl."

"I do," Summer agreed. "I guess maybe she *is* part of it."

"Part of why you like this place so much?" Hailey asked.

"I've never actually had someone that I wanted to come home to, or someone I wanted to come home to me. I've been texting her non-stop today. I'm sure it's annoying the shit out of her, but I miss her. I can't wait until she gets home."

"You're so cute right now." Hailey patted Summer's thigh before removing her hand. "Are you in love, Summer Taft?"

"I don't know. Maybe."

"You *do* know," Hailey accused. "You love her!"

"I've known her for a few weeks. I can't love her yet, Hails."

"Yes, you can. Ask Charlie... If anyone can tell you that love at first sight is a real thing, it's her. I am so lucky she waited for me to get my crap together. She could have found another girl at any time and–" Hailey stopped as Summer lifted an eyebrow at her. "Oh, yeah..."

"You realize both my girlfriend and I have made out

with *your* fiancée, right?"

"Gross. No offense," Hailey replied.

"It could have been worse. We both could have slept with her," Summer said.

Hailey smacked Summer's leg and replied, "Stop it!"

"I'm just saying that there *was* no other girl for her, Hailey. Sure, she had dated, but she wasn't going to end up with anyone. I mean, if she made out with both Lena and me, and turned both of us down, she was only ever going to marry you. I can attest that Lena is an amazing kisser; like, fireworks good. And I've been told a time or two that I am also an amazing kisser."

"Would you stop talking about making out with my fiancée, please?"

"It was only once," Summer said and was promptly slapped again. "Okay, I'm sorry."

"You realize you're basically living with Lena now, right? You're in love with her, and that's great, but you're supposed to be searching for a house. Are you even still doing that?"

"Kind of."

"Kind of? Are you two just going to make this official and move in?"

"I don't know. We're going to talk about it tonight." Summer paused. "And I hope it's a short conversation."

"What? Why? Because you don't want to leave?"

"Because I want to have sex," Summer replied before thinking about it.

"Is she that good at that, too?" Hailey laughed at Summer's explanation.

"I don't know. I want to find out. I'm going crazy, Hails. I've never wanted someone like this. I can't stop thinking about her, and what I want to do to her, and with her, and for her to do to me, and with me, and it's... I've just never been like this."

"You two haven't–"

"No," Summer interrupted. "But it's not like we're

behind. We just had our first date on Saturday. I almost screwed the whole thing up yesterday. We would have last night, but we were both way too drunk. This morning, it almost happened in the kitchen, but she had to go to work."

"In the kitchen?" Hailey asked. "Where in the kitchen? We just ate lunch in there, Summer."

"Please, I've eaten in your kitchen. Are you really trying to tell me you and Charlie never get naked with each other in there?" Hailey's face reddened in response, and Summer continued, "That's what I thought. We didn't, but I really wanted to. And, Hails, I know it's crazy, but I don't want to leave this house. Is it wrong that it already feels like my home?"

"No, it's not wrong. I actually think it's pretty amazing, Summer. You've found her, and she's your home. She just happens to own a house that you love, too. But, I'm telling you, it's not the house itself. Think about it like this. You are very rich, right?"

"Yeah."

"You could literally build a replica of this house anywhere in the world. You could buy the house next door just for the land, tear the place down, and then build this place, put in the same furniture, same décor, and the same flowers in the backyard. Would it feel the same, though, if Lena wasn't there?"

Summer thought about it and glanced around the room.

"No," she said after a moment. "I think I need to go back to my damn apartment."

"What?"

"I am crazy about her, and I love this place, but I want to move in here when we're both ready for that step. I don't want to be here because I was staying here when we started dating."

"You should talk to Lena and find out where she's at, before you make any decisions."

"I will," Summer said.

"Can we talk work for a second?"

"Sure."

"Seth's back in office."

"Has he screwed something up already? It's been, like, six hours."

"No, but I was just curious as to how long your vacation might be."

"Honestly, I don't know. I haven't really thought about it. I figured I would just take some time off and get caught up on schoolwork, which I have, and then relax a little and go back when I was ready. Why?"

"And you're just going to stay here? You're not going on a real vacation?"

"How is this about work?" Summer asked. "Plus, I just started dating Lena. I don't want to go on a vacation without her."

"That's so cute," Hailey said. "I know how worn out you were before. Your heart just didn't seem in it. I want you to take the time you need and come back when you're really ready. We can take care of things while you're gone. That's all I wanted to say."

"My heart wasn't in it?" Summer asked.

"Summer, it kind of seemed like maybe you hated your job, there, for a while."

"It did?"

"I don't think other people noticed, but I'm your friend. I could tell. When I first started working for you, you seemed okay with your position. I've watched you since then, and it just doesn't feel like this is really what you want to do. Seth basically left you holding the bag, and it got worse."

"Well, he's back now. And he knows he's not allowed to just take off like that again."

"Summer, you're twenty-seven years old. You're incredibly wealthy. You don't have to be the CEO of a company you and your brother founded if you don't want to. You know that, right?"

"I can't just leave him, Hailey. Even if I wanted to find something for myself, he can't take care of himself and a whole company."

"Summer, he is your older brother. He should be taking care of *you*; not the other way around." Hailey stood. "You deserve to do what you want. Make a new company or write that book I keep fielding and declining offers for. Or, don't work at all. Maybe you could be a housewife, and when Lena comes home, you have dinner on the table for her."

"All right, calm down." Summer rolled her eyes.

"Just think about it, okay? I have to go home and say goodbye to Charlie for the night so I can go to Detroit. I hate not falling asleep next to that woman. Even when we were just friends, I loved sleeping over at her place. Just having her in the same apartment was enough to make me sleep better. Oh, my God! How did I not know I was in love with her?"

"I have no idea." Summer shook her head.

"I thought I just loved sleeping on her comfy couch. What is wrong with me? I'm making her take tomorrow off so she can just come with me. We can plan wedding stuff on the drive."

"That sounds like fun," Summer replied sarcastically.

"You know you're a bridesmaid, right? You'll have to participate in this stuff, eventually." Hailey waved a finger at her.

"Great." Summer winked at her. "I'm kidding. You know I'm there when you need me."

"Good. Ember is going to officiate, because we can't tear her in two and have her on both of our sides. You're on mine. I'm pretty sure Lena's going to be on Charlie's. You two keep it all together at least until after our wedding, okay?"

"You're hilarious." Summer stood. "Get out of my house."

Hailey's eyes widened as she said, "*Your* house, huh?"

"Goodbye, Hailey." Summer motioned for the woman to head out the front door as she laughed silently.

"Have fun with Lena later. I want details," Hailey said as she opened the door.

"Definitely not," Summer retorted and held the doorknob as Hailey walked outside.

She heard her phone ringing from where she'd left it in the kitchen and smiled at the thought of Lena calling her to tell her when she would be home. Summer jogged into the kitchen to see that it was actually her brother.

"Hey, Seth. You're not leaving already, are you?"

"Sum, something's happened," he replied completely lacking his usual spirited tone.

"What's wrong?"

"It's Dad."

CHAPTER 20

LENA TEXTED SUMMER that she was on her way home. She asked the woman if she was interested in either Chinese or Thai, or if they should just order pizza. Summer hadn't yet responded, which was strange, because she'd been texting her pretty much non-stop all day. Lena had thought it cute. She'd gotten a few pictures of Summer doing various activities. There was one where Summer held a pen between her teeth, wearing Lena's glasses as she mock-studied. The second one was the one Lena got at the café, and another one came in later, when Summer was making sandwiches for Hailey and herself. Lena hadn't heard from her since. The car needed to stop for the food soon, or the decision would be made for them, and they'd be ordering pizza. Lena picked up the phone and decided to call her.

"Hey, I'm on my way home. What do you want me to pick up?" she asked when Summer's voice greeted her hastily.

"I'm not at home," Summer replied.

"Where are you?" Lena asked, a little confused.

"My dad had a heart attack," Summer replied. "I'm just getting on a plane to head to California. I'm sorry. I would have called you earlier, but I've been on the phone with Seth and my aunt since I found out."

"Oh, my God, Summer. Is he okay?"

"They don't know yet. He's in surgery right now. I'm hoping to get there by the time he gets out."

"What do you need from me? What can I do?"

"Nothing. I'm sorry about tonight. I know we had–"

"Hey, it's okay. I'm just sorry, Summer. Are you sure there's nothing I can do?" Lena asked.

"Unless you're a cardiologist and you haven't told me, there really isn't. We're about to take off. Can I call you when we land? Actually, no. Maybe when I'm at the hospital or when I know something or–"

"Summer, call me whenever you want, okay? I'm here. I'll wait up. Whatever you need."

"Okay. Thank you. I'll call when I can," Summer replied.

"Okay."

"Bye."

"Bye, babe," Lena said and then felt like she wanted to say something else, but she didn't want the first time she said those words to a woman, to Summer, to be when she was dealing with a major family crisis.

Lena arrived home a few minutes later to an empty house. She missed Summer already. It wasn't just that they had a date night planned and that she hoped they would have their first time tonight. It was that Summer's stuff was gone. The bag Lena had only just carried back up the stairs had disappeared with Summer. The woman had taken her things out of the bathroom, too. Lena understood that she had done that in haste, because of the emergency, but she missed her girlfriend all the same. She wasn't sure how long Summer would be gone. She knew not to even ask. But she also knew that when they would have talked that night, about Summer staying or going, Lena was going to ask her to stay.

She knew it was crazy. They'd only just met and were beginning their relationship, but she wanted Summer there with her. Lena had thought about it as she responded to emails at the office. Summer could keep her apartment, and if something went wrong between them, the woman could always go back. She could even still keep looking for a house. But if it took her some time to find one, Lena would be okay with that. She had smiled, earlier that day, at the thought of Summer telling her one day that she would be canceling the search for the house, because she wanted to move in permanently; or even Lena, herself, asking her to move in permanently.

Lena let out an exasperated sigh as she changed into her pajamas. She pulled out her laptop, ordered pizza, and tried to distract herself with work, while she waited to hear back from Summer. She brought up the financial analysis about the vendor they were considering for their locations. There were three companies still in the running for spaces in four stores. They'd add to that number of locations over the next three to five years, depending on the success. The problem Lena was seeing was that the big brands already had their partnerships. Starbucks was in a lot of Target stores and several other grocery brands. They weren't all that interested in O'Shea's. Wells Fargo and other banks already had their presence and were only interested in ATMs and not full locations. The three companies Lena had to choose from were interested, but they wanted lower rental rates for the space and a high brand-licensing or franchise fee. She was being pressured from the COO to consider dropping this idea entirely and just offering more O'Shea's products in those spaces, but Lena liked the shared space idea. She just needed to find the right partner. In her mind, she defined the right partner as a company that didn't see the partnership as a favor to O'Shea's. O'Shea's would be working with a company that would benefit from using the space, and O'Shea's would benefit from having them there. Then, it hit her.

"Van, hey," she greeted Vanessa after thinking through her idea and checking out the Strange Joe's website for a few minutes.

"I didn't expect to hear from you so soon."

"I know. Are you busy right now?"

"We're about to start a staff meeting. Can I call you back when it's over?"

"Yeah, that's fine," Lena agreed. "Or, I can come back into the city, and we can talk about it in person."

"What's the *it* you're referring to? And what do you mean, back to the city?"

"I'm in the burbs," Lena replied. "And I think I have a business idea for you."

"A business idea?"

"Yeah, it's not totally fleshed out yet. You might not want to do it, but I just thought of you and Strange Joe's, and it made sense."

"Okay, well, I live in the burbs, too. Well, I live with three other girls in the burbs, because that's the only way I can afford it, but I can stop by when we're done here."

"Really?"

"Yeah, if you think it's that important that it can't wait until tomorrow."

"I do. I have to finalize it before I present it, and I present it on Friday."

"Okay. Well, text me your address and give me, like, an hour?" Van asked.

"I'll keep working on it until then."

"Okay." Van laughed. "This is weird."

"I know. Sorry, but I promise I'll explain it to you when you get here."

"All right, I guess I'll see you soon."

"Great." Lena hung up the phone just as her pizza arrived.

She turned the oven on low and put it inside. If she was making Van come all the way out here on a whim, she could at least save dinner for her. She spent the next hour working out her idea in her mind and on paper, while checking her phone religiously, knowing there was no way Summer had landed already but being impatient to hear back from her girlfriend all the same. When Van arrived, Lena pulled out the pizza and brought it to the living room for them to share.

"This is a nice place," Van said as Lena re-entered the

living room with the pizza, paper plates, and waters for both of them.

"Do you want the tour?"

"Maybe later. I'm kind of really curious about this idea you have." Van paused and took the plates off the pizza box while Lena situated it on the table. "And thanks for the pizza. I haven't eaten yet."

"You came all the way out here at the last minute."

"I live, like, ten minutes from here, actually. You're on my way home."

"Oh, then, I'll take my pizza back," Lena joked and then looked at her phone.

"Is everything okay? You've looked at your phone, like, five times since I got here."

"Summer's dad had a heart attack."

"Oh, God."

"She's on a plane right now. I'm just waiting nervously for her to land and tell me how he is."

"Are you sure you want to do this now? I can—"

"I am, yes. I need a distraction. I can't do anything to help her, and it's driving me nuts."

"Okay, I will help distract you, then. What's this idea?"

"O'Shea's has retail space for a third-party company in four of our locations."

"Okay?"

"I don't just want to partner with anyone. The companies that are interested either want major deals and discounts, or think they're doing us some kind of a favor, which isn't the case." Lena took a breath and slid a piece of pizza onto a plate to pass to Vanessa before doing the same for herself. "I want to find a company that will benefit from this, and that will work with us and not against us."

"And I'm here because…"

"Because of Strange Joe's."

"My shop? You want to put my shop in your stores?" She took a bite of her pizza with wide eyes.

"I'm thinking about it. Van, you could have a brand.

You could start with four stores in O'Shea's. You'd have less overhead, and it's a smaller footprint than your current location, so fewer employees. You could even promote some of your current employees to oversee or manage the new ones."

"Okay, wow! Hold on." Van set the plate down. "I can't afford this. I still have to pay off the initial business loan, along with my student loans, remember? I have three roommates. What makes you think I have the money to set up shop somewhere else?"

"I think I can help you there, too."

"How?"

"The partnership with a company like O'Shea's will all but guarantee you another loan. I was also thinking that maybe I could be an investor."

"You want to invest in Strange Joe's?" Van asked.

"I'd want to see the financials and the business plan first, but I've actually been looking for an investment opportunity for a while. I have money from my family. I make good money at my job. I've been searching for something I could put money in, that I'd actually like. I like Strange Joe's. I've been going there since I got to Chicago."

"Really?"

"I had my first interview for O'Shea's there. I got there extra early and downed a cappuccino before the HR person even arrived. I've gone there almost every day since. I'm not going to lie, sometimes, I go to Starbucks when you guys are really busy. But I like your coffee shop, Van. It's busy almost every time I go in there. You've got to be doing something right."

"I guess, yeah."

"I think we can help each other. If you're not interested, that's okay. We can just eat pizza and talk, and you can go home. If you are, we can start talking about some details to see if it would even work," Lena said.

"It's my company, Lena. I wouldn't just hand it over to O'Shea's or you."

"I understand. And that's not what this would be. I promise. You would be the primary shareholder and the decision-maker. O'Shea's isn't looking at ownership."

"I'd need to talk to a lawyer before–"

"Absolutely," Lena agreed.

Van seemed to be considering for a moment, before she reached for her pizza.

"Okay. I'm willing to see if there's a match."

Lena and Van shared her laptop for the next few hours, working on the first draft of a business plan. Van seemed to be more than interested in expanding and creating a Strange Joe's brand. Lena was excited. After talking business with Vanessa, she knew the woman knew her stuff. Van had an MBA, which was more than Lena had. She also had great ideas and wanted to add community involvement to her business once they could afford it.

Lena felt like it was a place she could invest in and not only see a profit one day, but it would be something she could be proud of, too. That mattered to her even more. Her phone rang just as they'd lost all of their energy. Lena knew they would need to wrap up if she was going to be able to wake up on time for work the next morning.

"Hey... How are you?" Lena greeted Summer immediately.

"Grateful for the private plane that got me here so fast," Summer replied, and she sounded as exhausted as Lena felt.

"Where are you?"

"I'm in the waiting room, with Seth. Dad's still in surgery. I don't know anything yet."

"I'm so sorry, Summer. I feel totally helpless here. I can't even hug you," Lena replied.

"Hey, I'm going to go," Van said after sliding on her shoes. "I'll talk to you tomorrow, okay?"

"Yeah, thanks," Lena said and returned her attention to Summer. "How are you?"

"Who was that?" Summer asked.

"Who was what?"

"Who's with you?"

"Oh, Van's here."

"Where? Your house?"

"It's a long story, but we're putting together a business plan," Lena replied.

Van waved at her as she opened the door, exited, and then closed it behind her. Lena rose to lock it up for the night.

"A business plan? When did this happen? You and I were supposed to have a date tonight."

"Summer, this doesn't matter right now. Your dad matters."

"Yeah, you're right. Seth and I are going to stay here until they kick us out, whenever that is. Then, I'll head home until we can come back."

"Okay. I don't know how long you're going to have to stay, but do you want me to come out there? I can catch a flight on Friday after work and stay the weekend. I don't have to… It's totally up to you. I won't be offended if you want me to stay out of the way."

"I can't even think of that right now," Summer replied. "I haven't talked to him in a while, and the last time I did, we fought. That's all I can think about right now. I'm sorry."

"Babe, *I'm* sorry. I'm here."

"I know. I should go."

"Will you call me when you find anything out?"

"It could be late for you."

"I know. I don't care."

"I will if I can."

"Okay," Lena said.

"I'll talk to you later."

"Yeah," Lena agreed, and the line went dead.

CHAPTER 21

SUMMER WAITED IN THE ROOM for another hour while her father was still in surgery. It wasn't actually a room. It was more of a hallway, with four ancient plastic chairs that were bolted both to the floor and the wall and had silver scratch marks all over them over the initial black coating. Seth was sitting to her right but had left a chair between them, that was now filled with empty hospital coffee cups and wrappers from their vending machine dinner. His dark hair was mussed, and his equally dark eyes were closed. There were many times in their lives where people thought Seth and Summer were twins. They looked so much alike and were usually together growing up, that it made sense to make that assumption. That made Summer think of Lena and Leo, and she closed her eyes at the selfish thought that entered her brain. She was supposed to be lying next to Lena right now, after making love for the first time. She was supposed to be holding her, kissing her shoulder and neck, and whispering sweet nothings in Lena's ear, or even saying something funny to make the woman laugh so she could feel the reverberations against her own skin.

Instead, Summer waited for her father to come out of an emergency heart surgery and had to just deal with the timing of it all, along with the fact that the last time she'd seen her father had been too long ago. They'd fought about the fact that he wouldn't throw her mother's stuff out, even after all this time. He had kept their bedroom as a shrine to his deceased wife, along with all of her belongings. The house was in utter disrepair, and he had no money to fix it. The stubborn bastard wouldn't accept any money from either Seth or Summer. She'd yelled at him for it. She'd yelled at her own father for having too much pride. He could lose the house they'd grown up in, when he had children who could buy him a hundred houses each. The only money their stubborn father had accepted from them was used to pay off her mother's medical bills so that he could spend his money on the mortgage and other living expenses. Summer found herself getting more and more infuriated at the man that was currently under anesthesia.

"So, Aunt Donna is at the house. She's going to take care of Mo for us," Seth said while putting his phone back in his pocket.

"That's good," Summer replied without really paying attention.

"She'll come back tomorrow, during visiting hours, but wants us to update her when he's out," he continued. "Are you listening, Sum?" He tapped her shoulder.

"Yeah, sorry." Summer turned to him. "Aunt Donna is taking care of the dog and wants us to update her. Got it."

"There's some paperwork they need us to fill out. I did most of it, but there's some stuff I don't know. Can you take a look?"

"Sure," she answered, and he passed her a clipboard that had been on the other chair.

"This isn't exactly how I pictured our reunion," he said once Summer had it in her hand. "I thought I'd get settled back in, you'd come out here, and maybe I could convince you and dad to get in the same room for dinner one night."

Summer stared down at the words that appeared to be in a foreign language to her heavy eyes and tired brain. She reviewed Seth's work and then added a few things he had left blank.

"You'd have to convince him. I don't have a problem eating dinner with him. I just wish he would listen to me and take the damn money I don't even need so that he doesn't lose the house he and mom built together and we grew up in," she replied.

"I know. I get it."

"You don't seem to care as much about it as I do," Summer retorted.

"Hey, that's not fair. Just because I'm letting the man make his own decisions doesn't mean I'm happy about it."

"I know. I just don't understand it."

"He lost the love of his life and went a little crazy there. You and I can't understand that. We've never felt anything like that before," Seth said.

Summer turned back to him again.

"That was profound," she replied.

"Thanks for the surprise," he joked. "Let's talk about something else. We can't change his mind. Even if we could, it's not like we can do it right now."

"Yeah, you're right." Summer flipped one page up so she could review the next.

"So, what's going on with you? How's Chicago?"

"Chicago's great," Summer answered and checked a few more boxes.

"Great?" Seth knocked her arm. "Hey, talk to me."

"What do you want, Seth?" she asked a little louder than necessary. "My father's having an emergency surgery, my brother spends more time traveling the world than at the company he founded, while I have to sit behind a desk I don't really want and make decisions that impact all of the employees, while the board tries to get me to hire a *real* CEO. I finally found a house I love. And it's owned by a woman I'm falling in love with. But I haven't told her, and I don't think we can just start living together, so I have to find some place I like less. I finally start dating her and think I might actually get this whole love thing for the first time ever, we're about to take our relationship to the next level, and I get a call from you, telling me about dad. I have to leave her at home, where she's visited at night by a woman she kind of dated and that probably still likes her. For all I know, they're taking that step right now with each other, while I'm filling out hospital forms," Summer said it all in one breath and then forced the necessary oxygen back into her lungs. "I'm so tired, Seth. I'm tired of running a company with little to no support from you. I'm tired of trying to finish school while I do it. I–"

"Hey, hold on there." Seth turned his entire body to her. "One thing at a time." He put his hand on his sister's shoulder. "I honestly don't know where to start... Your rant was pretty extensive."

"I know. I'm sorry."

"Let's start with work, okay?"

"Fine."

"Sum, do you want to be the CEO of our company?" he asked plainly. "I know I've been gone a lot this year, and I suck. I get it." He pointed at himself. "But, every time I talk to you about work, you seem like you kind of hate it. Now, you're on this last-minute vacation, but you're not actually going anywhere. What's going on?"

"I don't know." Summer sighed. "I guess I've been feeling a little out of place lately."

"Out of place?"

"Seth, this thing was your dream," she reminded. "I helped in the beginning. I loved it then. I loved working with you and making this thing happen. But now, it's happened, and I don't know what I'm still doing."

"You're in charge, Summer. You're good at it."

"Maybe, but it's not where my heart's at."

"Sounds like your heart is not somewhere else, but maybe with someone else."

"Lena Tanner," she replied with a sudden smile.

"Yeah?"

"I am crazy about her, Seth. I'm supposed to be with her right now. It's kind of driving me nuts that I'm not."

"Why isn't she here?" he asked.

"We just started dating. I didn't think it was fair to tell her to drop her life and fly across the country just to sit in the hospital."

"Is she crazy about you?"

"I think so."

"Then, I doubt she would mind, Sum."

"She offered to come this weekend if I'm still here."

"That's good."

"Yeah. I've been staying at her house since before it started, though. I think I need to move out so that, maybe later, there's a chance I can move back in officially," she said.

"What does she think about that?"

"I don't know. We were supposed to talk about it tonight."

"Bummer," he replied. "Well, you can talk about it later, I'm sure. Is that the step you were talking about?"

"Huh?" Summer asked and finished the paperwork she had been working on.

"You said you were about to take a step."

"We were going to have sex," she said.

"Summer! Gross! I don't want to know that!" He covered his ears like a toddler who didn't want to listen to his mom yelling at him.

"Hey, you asked." Summer smirked at him. "It would have been good, too," she teased and laughed as he recoiled.

"That's enough. New topic." He waved her off.

Summer kept laughing. It felt good to laugh, given all that had happened.

"I want to finish school, Seth."

"You *are* finishing school."

"No, I mean, that's the *only* thing that I want to do."

"You want to quit work and just finish Stanford?"

"I think so. I've only been on vacation for a few days now, and it's like I can breathe again. I talked to my advisor, and because they've basically built the program around me and my schedule, I can finish in Chicago. I want to go for my MBA later."

"You've never talked about that before."

"Not with you, no, but with the people at school I have. And I can afford to do it without working, which isn't a luxury most people have. I think I'm going to work on that book people keep telling me I should write and see what – if anything, comes from it. But I don't think I want to be the CEO anymore."

Seth seemed to consider her words and said, "Well, shit."

"I know. This is not how I planned on telling you. Honestly, I don't know if I was going to tell you at all."

"That's stupid, Sum." He turned back to her. "If you don't want to do this, I don't want it for you. Let's just take care of dad and then talk about what's going to happen, okay?"

"Yeah, that sounds good."

"I'm glad about the girlfriend thing. Just never tell me about the sex thing again." He held up one finger and then another as he rattled items off. "And what was that about another woman being in her house tonight?"

Summer thought of Vanessa with her floppy hair and her earrings that seemed a little too much for someone that wasn't in high school. She thought about her being in Lena's house, sitting on the sofa with Lena, where Summer usually sat, and laughing with her about stuff Summer should be laughing with Lena about. She felt a rush of frustration and anger.

"I don't know. I can't worry about that now," she said after a moment.

She trusted Lena. They'd said they were together, that they were exclusive, and she didn't think Lena would do anything to jeopardize that, but their relationship was still new and, therefore, vulnerable. She wasn't entirely sure about Van, though, since she didn't know her at all. But what she did know of her, was that she seemed to take the rejection well. Maybe she took it a little too well, though, and she was waiting for Lena to be alone so she could try to change her mind. Lena had been at the coffee shop earlier that day. Summer decided she definitely hated Van again.

A doctor, dressed in pale-blue scrubs with the mask

around his neck, approached them from behind two swinging doors that led to the surgical wing of the hospital. Summer stood immediately without thought, feeling like she needed to be standing for whatever news the doctor would be delivering.

"Taft family?" he asked.

"That's us." Seth stood next to her and placed his hands in his pockets.

"I'm Dr. Maddox. I'm the surgeon who's been assigned to your father's case."

"How is he?" Summer asked.

"He suffered a pretty severe heart attack. We had to perform an emergency triple bypass. This treats the blocked arteries by helping to increase the blood flow to the heart. We take veins from other parts of the body and use them to reroute blood around the clogged artery."

"Is he okay?" Summer asked, knowing she could look up the details of a triple bypass online later.

"He's in recovery now. He's stable, but we'll need to monitor him here for the next few days. We'll keep running tests, and if everything looks okay, he should be able to go home after that. He will also have to make some lifestyle changes. I'll have one of the nurses come by the room and review those with you later."

"Can we see him?" Seth asked and removed his hands from his pockets.

"He should be in his room in about an hour. You can see him then," the doctor replied.

"Thank you," Seth answered for both of them.

The doctor nodded and headed down to the nurse's station in the middle of the hallway to fill out some paperwork. Summer felt like she couldn't sit any longer. She had sat on the plane and then in the uncomfortable plastic chairs for hours.

"I need real food," Summer said.

"Me too. Want me to go grab something?"

"No, I got it. I need to move. Do you want your usual

from In-N-Out?"

"Yeah, thanks. I'll call Aunt Donna."

"I'll be back before he's out of recovery."

Summer dropped off the paperwork with the nurse at the station and made her way to the elevator and then immediately outside, where she inhaled the fresh air for the first time in several hours. She climbed into the town car she'd signaled from upstairs, and had the driver take her to the nearest In-N-Out so she could get her usual double-double. It was probably the one thing – outside of her family, that she missed about California.

She checked her phone and noted the time. It was already 9:45 p.m. Pacific, which meant it was even later in Chicago. Lena would be asleep, or she should be asleep at the very least, since the woman had work tomorrow. Summer thought about calling her, but she didn't want to wake her. And, truthfully, she also didn't have the energy for a conversation. She hadn't planned on revealing all that to Seth. She just hadn't realized she had felt all that until she blurted it out.

She ordered their food and had the car take her straight back to the hospital. She had her aunt drop her bag off at her dad's house earlier, so she would have to go there later, to pick it up before heading home, but she also wanted to check on Mo, her dad's eight-year-old German shepherd. Her aunt would likely be exhausted, since she was the one that had to call the ambulance during lunch when the attack happened.

She texted Lena before heading back up to the waiting area that he was out of surgery, and they didn't know much yet. A few minutes later, Summer was in the middle of her burger when Lena texted back that she was thinking of her. Summer smiled at the message and responded that she'd be leaving the hospital once she'd checked on her dad and that she didn't want Lena to wait up.

"I missed this." Seth bit into his burger.

"Me too. And I can't believe I'm admitting this, but I

missed you."

"I missed you, too, Sum." He bumped her shoulder with his own, and they waited until the nurse came over to tell them they could see their father.

Summer and Seth went into the room silently. Summer stood back, while Seth immediately went to his bedside and looked down at him. Summer crossed her arms over her chest. Her dad had always been such a strong man. He'd been a blue-collar worker, a manual laborer, his entire life. She'd thought he was a Superman when she was younger, as most kids do of their fathers. Now, though, he looked like the villain that Superman had destroyed, after a long hard-fought battle. He had tubes coming out of his body and was connected to the machines that beeped and IVs that dripped liquid into his veins. He was wearing a hospital gown, and Summer could see some of the bandages that lay on his chest, covering his new surgical scars. Summer felt her mouth go dry. She listened to the steady beeps and thought about how fragile life really was.

The last time she'd been in a hospital was when she watched her mother finally fade away. She, too, had been wearing a gown and had been hooked up to similar machines and tubes. The smell of antiseptic had also been in the air. The stillness and quietness only amplified the steady beeps that then began to slow down and fade altogether. She had held her mother's hand, while Seth stood behind her, with his hand on her shoulder. Her father, the man currently in the bed, had been on her mother's other side, clasping tightly to the arm of the woman he loved. Summer remembered that more than anything else that day. She could easily see both of her father's dry and calloused hands, gripping onto her mother's pale and weak arm, as if by doing that he could make her stay; as if he could, somehow, while connected to her – through sheer force of will, keep her alive. He couldn't, of course, and Summer cried while her mother died.

She stood off to the side for several minutes before

Seth finally turned around and reached out his hand to her. Summer hesitated before taking it and allowing him to pull her over to the bed. Her father had the tube on his face attached to his nose, providing him with consistent oxygen. Summer felt like maybe she could use consistent oxygen, too. She gulped and stared for several more minutes, while Seth did the same, before the nurse returned and told them it was time to go. Visiting hours were over.

***

"Hey, sweetie," her aunt greeted Summer at the front door and brought her into an immediate hug. "How is he?"

"He's asleep. We'll go back in the morning, for visiting hours," she explained and walked inside the small living room she used to spend her evenings in with her family.

"I've been trying to clean up. I swear, my brother is a terrible housekeeper," Donna exclaimed and returned to a giant black trash bag she had, apparently, been filling with old take-out cartons.

"Mo!" Summer kneeled on the floor when Mo, the beautiful black and tan shepherd, ran at her from the kitchen and delivered a strong bark. He jumped up and placed his front legs on her shoulder, as was their greeting custom. "I missed you, too, buddy." Summer allowed him to lick the side of her face before he jumped down and ran off. "Are you sure you're okay taking care of him? I can take him with me."

"I'll be fine. Your uncle comes back from Seattle tomorrow. We'll take him home with us until your dad's better. He can play with Roxy and chase Gizmo."

"If he gets to be too much–"

"We'll be fine, sweetie." Her aunt picked up more boxes and shoved them inside the trash bag. "I put your luggage in your old room, just in case you decided to stay here tonight." Donna nodded toward the hallway that led to the bedrooms of the ranch home.

"Thanks. But, if it's okay with you, I'm just going to go to my place."

"Of course."

"We're going back tomorrow morning, for visiting hours."

"I'll make sure everything is taken care of here and with Mo, and I'll be there when I can," Donna replied.

"Thanks." Summer stood. "I'm going to go grab my stuff."

"Okay, honey."

"And you don't have to clean up. I'll take care of it before he gets home."

"I'm his older sister. I've been cleaning up his messes since he was born. I can handle this," she replied.

Summer smiled at her aunt and entered the hallway, where she saw the old family photos that lined both walls. Her mother and father, at the wedding thirty years prior, gave way to pictures of infant and then toddler Seth, before the pictures of infant and then toddler Summer joined them. There was a collage of their trip to Yosemite, which had been before her mom had gotten sick. Summer barely even remembered it.

She passed her parent's bedroom and stopped in the open doorway. Her mother's clothing was still hanging in the closet, and that door was open as well. Summer moved inside and tried to close it, but her father's dirty laundry was in the way. She pulled the hamper out of the closet and piled the clothes that were on the floor into the overflowing bin. Then, she closed the closet door, not wanting to see her mother's old dresses hanging there, unworn in years.

She turned to see that her mother's makeup table, that the woman rarely used after getting sick, was still against the far wall, with expired, half-used makeup resting atop it. Summer doubted her father had even dusted it since her mother's passing. She found the room sad and depressing. She felt stifled there and needed to leave. So, she headed toward her old room in search of her bag and her sanity.

Her old room hadn't had an occupant, officially, since Summer had been in college. She had lived at home part of the time, because her scholarship hadn't covered everything, and she could save money that way. Her old twin bed, with plaid comforter and sheets, still remained made and, likely, untouched since the last time she'd stayed the night. Summer had tried to hire her dad a maid or housekeeper, but he'd refused that, too. She'd hired one covertly a few times anyway, and made sure they were there while her dad was out. Summer had dealt with his frustration about it later, but at least the house was clean.

She had an old dresser against a wall. Her old desk still remained with an old PC on top. She actually laughed when she saw that, remembering it had been Seth's first, and it was actually the computer he had developed his code on in the beginning. Her bag was resting against the closet door. Summer pulled it until she was back in the living room, where Mo greeted her with his chew toy. She left the bag, opened the back door, and threw the toy, watching him run after it and play with it for a minute.

"You ready to go?" her aunt asked.

"I have a car waiting. I can send it away and stay if you–"

"I'm going to be calling it a night soon anyway. You can go home."

"Okay." She reached out and hugged her aunt, and then, headed out to the waiting car.

**

Lena tried to sleep, but she missed Summer's body next to her. They'd only fallen asleep together a few times, but she was already addicted to the feeling of Summer's body connected to her own. She clutched at the pillow Summer had used only the night before, and took in her girlfriend's scent. It was floral, and Lena now knew it as distinctly Summer Taft.

She tossed and turned for a while, checking her phone repeatedly in case she missed a text from Summer. She'd turned her volume up all the way, but still, her mind would not rest unless she checked the phone every five minutes. By two in the morning, Lena could check no longer. Her eyes were heavy, and she finally drifted off.

***

Summer arrived at her house in completely and utterly exhausted. When the driver pulled up and helped her with her bag, Summer stared at the house she had left behind as if it was a place she had never been to before. It felt foreign to her. Her Palo Alto home had turned into a layover more than anything. It had furniture, dishes, and decorations, like any house would, but most of Summer's more personal objects and clothing were already in Chicago.

She unlocked the door and moved slowly inside, feeling the weight of emotions from the day. It had started so positively, with her cooking breakfast for Lena, and then Lena lifting her onto the counter and lighting her nerve endings on fire. She'd had a nice day around the house and then, with Hailey. In an instant, though, everything had changed. Her father was in the emergency room, and Summer was back at the house that had never felt like home.

She climbed the stairs, while dragging her bag behind her, and moved to the shower first, where she cleaned herself for the second time that day. She changed into her shorts and t-shirt, slid under her comforter, and checked her phone for messages from either Seth or the hospital. Finding none, Summer thought about texting Lena again, that she was in bed, but she was too tired and didn't want to chance waking Lena.

Instead, Summer plugged in her phone to charge and turned on the playlist she'd created the other night. If she couldn't be near Lena tonight, she could at least listen to the music Lena loved, and be reminded of her.

CHAPTER 22

"Hey," Lena greeted with sleep reading in her tone.

"Hi, babe," Summer replied. "It's so good to hear your voice."

Lena sat up in bed and checked the time with one eye opened. She had gotten about four hours of solid sleep. That would have to do.

"You too. How are you?"

"I've been better, but I'm hanging in there," Summer told her. "I'm at the hospital already. I just stepped outside to call you."

"How's your dad?"

"He's awake, but in and out. They just took him to run some more tests. Seth went to the office, because one of us should be there. I told him I'd call if anything changed. He was here first thing, and they got to talk for a few minutes before dad fell back asleep."

"How long will he be in the hospital?" Lena asked, knowing Summer would likely be remaining there at least until he was back at home.

"They're saying until Friday right now, but that might change, depending on the test results. Honestly, I kind of want them to keep him for a while. At least, if he's here, I know he's eating regularly and being taken care of."

"Is there anything I can do?" she asked.

"Not really," Summer repeated her same response from the day before. "How are you?"

"Worried about you, but otherwise, okay. I miss you," Lena said.

"I miss you, too," Summer replied. "So, how's Van, the woman with the terrible nickname?"

Lena laughed and said, "You're not jealous, are you?"

"She was at your house late at night. I'm in another state. I don't know... Should I be?" she asked.

"Summer, no," Lena confirmed. "I told you that it was a business thing."

"What business do you two have together?"

"Nothing yet... But I had this idea come to me last night, while I was trying to distract myself from worrying about you... It turns out, she lives nearby and could over. We talked about business the entire time, I promise. I am not interested in Vanessa at all, okay?"

"Yeah, okay. Sorry... I'm not normally the jealous type."

"It's okay. You've got a lot going on." Lena paused and bit her lower lip. "Summer, I have to be here this week. I have an important presentation on Friday, and it has to do with the Van thing, but I will hop on a plane the moment it's over and come out there. But, like I said last night, I don't want to get in your way. We just started dating, so I understand if–"

"Please, come," Summer interrupted, and her voice sounded so small.

"Yeah?"

"As soon as you can. I had a really hard time falling asleep last night. I've been thinking a lot and realizing some things. I would just like you here. I miss you like crazy."

"Realizing some things?"

"About my life, my future, and everything that entails." Summer sighed audibly into the phone. "Not about you. Not in a bad way, at least. You're a part of that future."

"Good. I want to be."

"My dad should be out of the woods by the time you get here. We'll probably be bringing him home. It might be chaotic. Are you sure you–"

"Yes, I'm sure," Lena interrupted back. "I'll book a flight when I get to the office."

"No, don't. I'll book you on our private plane."

"Summer, you have enough to worry about."

"I have an assistant, Lena. I'll text her and have her get in touch with you to make the arrangements, okay?"

"Okay."

"I should get back inside. He'll be back soon, and I have to grab something to eat."

"Okay. Call me later?" Lena asked.

"I will. Have a good day at work. I hope whatever business thing you're working on with Van works out."

"Thanks. Me too. I'll fill you in when things calm down a little for you, okay?"

"Yeah. I'll call you later. Bye, babe."

"Bye, babe," Lena repeated back and hung up.

She liked the way Summer called her *babe*. She liked the way it felt to get to call Summer that right back.

***

Summer spent the remainder of her Tuesday in the hospital, watching her dad fall asleep, wake up periodically, and then fall back asleep. When he was awake, he was rarely cogent. Their conversations amounted to him asking for water or the nurse. Summer sat in a straight-backed vinyl chair in the corner, listening to music on her phone or reading the book she'd brought with her from the house. She also started a moving to-do list for herself and decided she'd wait to make the official plans until she determined how long she would have to be here with her dad. She, likely, would have to store what she decided to bring with her to Chicago until she found the house she wanted. So, she looked up local storage places and bookmarked a few she was interested in. Then, she sat back as much as she could in that terrible chair and thought about how nice her collection would look in Lena's office. But that would come much later at this rate, since they'd only been on one actual date. Summer predicted they'd be living together within the next three to five years, if this frustrating pace was any indication.

Seth met her at the hospital around four, and they stayed for a bit longer before they decided to meet their aunt at her house for dinner. Summer enjoyed the company of her family and the home-cooked meal, but she also couldn't stop worrying about her father. The nurse had explained to Seth and Summer, prior to them leaving for the night, that he'd have to drastically change his diet, exercise more, but start off very slowly, and change other pieces of his life that Summer knew he wouldn't want to change. She worried that she might lose him even after all this, due to his inability to make those changes.

***

Lena hadn't heard from Summer in a while. She was starting to worry. As she worked on the proposal for Strange Joe's in the office, Lena stared down at her phone for the millionth time since last night, when she'd fallen asleep after sending a third text, asking if Summer was okay and not hearing back. This morning, she'd resisted because of the time difference, but by mid-morning her time, Lena had called. It went straight to voicemail. She'd sent another two texts and then decided she'd try another source.

"Hey, Hails."

"Hey, what's up?" Hailey replied.

"Have you heard from Summer?" Lena asked.

"Not since yesterday. She texted that her dad was sleeping but stable," Hailey said.

"I got that one, too, but I haven't heard from her. She promised me she'd check in."

"I'm sure she's just busy, Lena. Don't read too much into it, okay?

"I know. I'm just worried."

"If she reaches out, I'll tell her to call you," Hailey said.

"Thanks," Lena replied, feeling a little defeated.

"Hey, can you talk to Charlie for a sec?" Hailey asked. "We're driving back from Detroit. You're on speaker."

"Sure. Hey, Charlie."

"Hi. Sorry about Summer and her dad," Charlie said.

"Me too."

"Listen, Hails already talked to Summer about this, but I was hoping since she was going to be a bridesmaid on Hailey's side, you'd be one on mine."

"Oh, really?" Lena replied, a little surprised.

"It's kind of perfect, if you think about it. You two can walk down together."

"It is, yeah," Lena said and hoped against hope that it really would be that perfect by the time of the wedding. "Sure. I mean, of course."

"Good. Thanks. Hailey's going crazy with the whole wedding-planning thing. I'm kind of just along for the ride."

"Hey, you love me. Don't forget that," Hailey tossed in. "Plus, we got together during Eva and Ember's wedding festivities, if you remember correctly. So, you should love weddings."

"I surrender," Charlie mocked, and Lena listened as Hailey laughed at her.

"We have no idea when it's going to be yet, so keep your entire calendar open for the next two years or so," Hailey added.

"I will." Lena laughed.

"And if Summer checks in about business stuff, I'll tell her to call her girlfriend, but I'm pretty sure you'll be her first call as soon as she's able to make one."

"Thanks. I'll let you two go. Drive safe."

"We will. I'm driving," Charlie said. "Ow!" Lena heard Charlie exclaim, and she assumed Hailey had punched her lightly in the shoulder.

"Bye." Lena laughed and hung up.

She finished up the document she had been working on and slid her computer into her bag before heading down to Strange Joe's for her meeting with Van. The other woman had brought her own computer to the meeting, which they held in the back office. They walked through her financials and history, along with some of the information about O'Shea's and the locations where Strange Joe's would fit. They sipped on Strange Joe's coffee while they worked, until Lena finally saw Summer's name appear on her phone.

"Hey," she greeted instantly and stepped outside the small office.

"Hi. I'm sorry. I used my phone all day yesterday, and I fell asleep before I plugged it in, so it died. I just woke up, plugged it in, and saw your messages."

"Oh, it's okay," Lena replied, suddenly feeling terrible about thinking the worst. "How are you? How's he?"

"I haven't been to the hospital yet. I'm going to grab breakfast and head over. He should be awake by now and be a little more alert."

"And you? How are you?" Lena repeated her initial question and sat in an empty chair at one of the tables.

"I've been better. I'm sorry for not calling."

"It's okay. I understand. I was just worried."

"Am I interrupting you at work?" Summer asked.

"I'm working, but you're not interrupting."

"My dad is a stubborn asshole, by the way. You should know that before you get on that plane," Summer said after a moment of shared silence.

Lena laughed and replied, "Please, you haven't met my parents yet."

"Yeah? Stubborn, too?" Summer's tone lightened.

"Not really stubborn… They just have giant sticks up their butts."

Summer laughed a weighted laugh, but at least she laughed.

"Hey, can I ask you a favor?"

"Of course, you can," Lena replied.

"I don't know how much longer I'm going to be here, but I don't have much to do outside of sitting in the hospital room during visiting hours and doing school stuff…" Summer paused for a second. "I'm thinking about boxing up some of my stuff. My books, mostly. Anyway, I don't want to send them to my apartment, because I'm never there."

"Send them here," Lena said.

"Are you sure? I can send them to the office. I can even wait. I'm just a little bored, I guess."

"Summer, send them here. If they get here when I'm there with you, I'll have my neighbor put them in the garage. She has a key and helps watch the place when I have to go out of town for work. She won't mind."

"Not Van, though, right?" Summer teased.

"No, not Van." Lena turned to see the woman they were currently talking about heading behind the register to help a customer. "Summer, she and I might be working together, though. That's not going to be a problem, is it?"

"No, it's not. I'm just messing with you." Summer paused. "I'll pick up the books when I get back and move them into storage until I find a house."

"Oh." Lena forgot about the whole Summer moving into her own home thing.

"I know we didn't get a chance to talk about that before I left. Maybe we can when you get here."

"Sure," Lena replied. "Hey, I miss you."

"I miss you, too," Summer replied. "Can I call you tonight? We can just talk for a while about anything other than what's going on here." She sighed. "I don't want us to lose trajectory, Lena."

"Trajectory?"

"I'm here, you're there, and we were just starting to figure things out… It's been a crazy couple of days, but I don't want us to stop… progressing."

"Neither do I." Lena smiled. "Call me whenever you want."

"And you'll be alone?" Summer asked. "And I don't mean that in a jealous way. I just want to be able to talk to you. Maybe we could FaceTime."

"I'll be alone, and that sounds great. I miss your face," Lena admitted.

"Will you wear those glasses?" Summer asked with a mischievous tone.

"Will you wear a hoodie and those shorts?"

"Definitely." Summer laughed.

"Then, you've got yourself a date," Lena replied.

"I can't wait. I have to go get dressed and get to the hospital."

"Okay. I'll talk to you tonight. And let me know if anything changes with him today."

"I will. I–" Summer stopped mid-sentence, leaving Lena wondering what she was originally going to say. "I'll talk to you later," she completed.

***

"Hey, Dad," Summer greeted her father, who was sitting up, trying to eat Jell-O.

"Morning," he greeted gruffly. "This stuff is terrible. They only have lime. Who likes lime Jell-O?"

"I imagine a lot of people, or they probably wouldn't make the stuff." Summer sat down in her chair. "Seth's stopping by later. He had a meeting."

"You're the CEO. You don't have meetings?"

"I was on vacation when this happened; still am."

"I've got to get out of here soon, Summer. I can't just lie around like this. I gotta get back to work."

"Dad, you can't just go back to work. You had a triple bypass."

"I'll be fine. The doctor said I could go back to work." He dropped his spoon and Jell-O on the tray.

"He did? When?" Summer challenged.

"Yesterday," he replied. "He said I have to take it easy for a bit, but then, I can go back."

"Well, I'll make sure to get a more definitive timeframe than you did, and we'll see."

"Summer Taft, I am your father. I'm a grown man."

"You're a stubborn asshole, Dad." Summer leaned forward. "You don't listen to anyone. You make your life harder than it has to be, and you're here because of that." She stood. "Do you want anything from the gift shop? A magazine or—"

"I don't suppose they sell cigarettes."

"No, Dad. The hospital gift shop does not sell cigarettes. You couldn't smoke them in here, anyway. Oh, and you just had heart surgery! You can't smoke anymore."

"Why are you in such a bad mood?" he asked, apparently not understanding why she'd be upset that he asked for cigarettes. "You haven't been around in months. I didn't even think you'd come."

"To the hospital?"

"To California. You seemed happy in Chicago. Seth said you were staying there."

"I am, but you had a heart attack, Dad. Did you really not think I'd come?"

"You seemed pretty upset with me the last time you were here."

"Because you're living in the past," Summer retorted. "The house is a disaster, Dad. You're going to lose it. You know that, right?" Summer paused. "Aunt Donna said you're probably going to have to move in with her."

"I am not. I just need to get back on my feet and—"

"And the bank will foreclose," she interrupted. "Dad, you have two children that have more money than we know what to do with, and—"

"I'm your father. That's not how this works. I don't want your money."

"You don't *want* it, but you *need* it. Why are you doing

this? Why are you not letting us help you?"

"I need to be able to take care of myself, Summer."

"But you're not, Dad. You're not taking care of yourself. You're eating fast food every night and not cleaning the house. The place looks awful. You take better care of Mo than you do of yourself."

"I'm doing all right."

"Says the man in the hospital bed." Summer walked toward the door. "I'm going back to the house, and I'm hiring a maid to come clean it top to bottom."

"You are—"

"Doing it, and you can't stop me." She turned back to him. "And when you're out of here, you're staying at my place, while Seth and I talk to the lawyers about your finances and see what has to be done to save the house, since you refuse to leave."

"Summer!"

"No, I'm done putting up with this crap from you, Dad. This isn't what Mom would want for you. You know that. Seth will come by to see you later. Aunt Donna said she'd be by, too. If you need me, have the hospital call me." She left the room.

CHAPTER 23

"THERE THEY ARE," SUMMER said. "You should wear them more often." She pointed through the screen to Lena's glasses.

"Let me see… Did you keep up your end of the deal?" Lena watched as Summer pulled her iPad back a little so Lena could see the hoodie and shorts. "Nice." She winked at her.

"How was your day?" Summer asked.

"Can I get the tour?" Lena asked back. "I never got the tour of your apartment."

"Why? I don't actually live here, either," Summer said. "So, how was your day?"

"It was good, actually."

Lena went on to explain the idea she came up with in more detail so Summer would know that she and Van were only going to be business partners once everything was approved.

"The lawyers are reviewing everything now, but from what I can tell, it looks good. I think it's going to work. I've got the presentation ready to go for Friday if it does. If it doesn't, I've got the backup vendor I know they'll approve."

"That's amazing, Lena. You've done all that in, like, two days."

"How's your dad?"

"I thought we weren't going to talk about that." Summer squinted her eyes.

"We don't have to, but I'd like to know."

"He's the same personality-wise, unfortunately." She

241

inhaled and exhaled deeply. "He's stable and will be released on Friday afternoon."

"Still acting like a jerk?" Lena asked.

"I spent most of the day at the house, helping the maid I hired to clean up. And we're still nowhere near done," Summer explained. "I think there's mold. I have an inspector coming out tomorrow to check. But if there is, and it's bad, he can't move back in there until it's gone. The maid is the one that found it. She said she's not going back until it's gone. I can't blame her for that."

"You shouldn't be in there, either."

"I won't go back in until I know how bad it is. I packed my books up when I got back here. I'll send them overnight tomorrow morning. They should arrive before you leave."

"I'll take care of them."

"Thank you. I really appreciate it."

"You don't have to thank me."

"Yes, I do. You've been great with this whole thing." Summer let out an exasperated sigh. "I'm just so tired, Lena."

"I know, honey."

"No, I mean, I'm really tired." She leaned back and ran her hand through her hair, which was down and perfect. Lena missed touching it. "I don't want to be the CEO anymore. I don't want to have to deal with my pain in the ass father anymore. I want my brother to step up and actually run this damn company he started and stop running around the world. I want my dad to be okay. I want him to take care of himself. He won't, so I have to. That's not fair to me, because I don't want to be here any longer than I have to. I want to be there. I want to be with you. I want to be with my friends. I want to be home."

"Home?" Lena asked.

"With you." Summer shrugged her shoulders. "I know it's crazy, but that's how I feel. Hailey helped me realize it the other day. I feel at home when I'm with you. I think it's one of the reasons why I like your house so much. I do like the house, but I like it more because you're in it. I liked the few days I was there, when you came home from work, and we ate dinner and just talked. I've never had that."

"I liked that, too. I want it again," Lena replied.

"I don't know how long this vacation thing will last," Summer said. "But I'll find a place when I get home. Maybe you can stay over there sometime. We can go back and forth. I'm sure I can find something I like. I can try to make sure it's close—"

"Summer," Lena interrupted her and watched the look of confusion on the woman's face. "Did you not just hear what I said? I said I liked it. I want it again."

"I heard it."

"You don't have to rush to find a house. You don't have to rush to do anything you don't want to do," Lena explained.

"I know, but…" Summer faded, and Lena could tell she was holding back.

"Summer, just tell me what you want. Don't worry about how I might take it."

"I can't. It's too—"

"Too crazy? Too soon? Too fast?" Lena interrupted again. "I don't care." She laughed. "I never expected to find someone like you, Summer. I thought I'd be in a dead-end marriage for the rest of my life. When I finally got out of that, I barely had enough courage to try to talk to a woman. Then, I met you. You turned my world upside down." Lena laughed lightly. "And I like it. I like you. I more than like you. I don't want to pressure you or anything, but it's okay with me if it takes you a while to find a house." Lena took off her glasses because she wanted to make sure Summer could see her intent in her eyes.

"It is?" Summer smiled.

"Yes."

"I'll keep my apartment, though. The lease isn't up for a while, so if you change your mind or if something—"

"Okay. Okay."

Summer smiled at her and said, "I'm kind of crazy about you."

"I'm kind of crazy about you, too," Lena replied with an eyebrow lift. "Now, tell me more about all these life decisions you're working on."

"It's exhausting. I've never had to come up with a plan for myself before. I was twenty when this whole thing started; younger even, because Seth started coding when I was still in high school. We've always been close. He included me in everything." Summer explained. "Even though in some ways, I'm ahead of everyone else my age, I feel like I'm way behind in others. It's just really starting to bother me."

"I get that."

"You do?"

"I got married in college and was ahead of most of my friends for a while there, but then it felt like I was behind, because they'd all gotten jobs and moved up in them or had kids. Their lives were progressing; mine stayed the same. My husband turned into my roommate. So, yes, I understand what it's like to feel like you're ahead but behind at the same time."

Summer smiled at her and pulled the screen closer.

"I wish you were here. I just want to hold you."

Lena smiled back at her and said, "Me too. Friday isn't that far away."

"It feels like forever. You realize this is basically the longest we'll have been apart since we met?"

"I guess I hadn't."

"Oh, I'm putting a key in the sconce next to the front door for you, in case I'm at the hospital when you get in."

"Okay," Lena replied.

"Your flight's all taken care of, right?"

"Yes, I'm good. I'll be there around five, your time."

Summer stared at her for a moment, and in that moment, Lena swore she could see the longing in her eyes mixed with the exhaustion the woman undoubtedly felt.

"So, let's talk about something else," Summer suggested. "I'm thinking… embarrassing childhood stories. Got any?"

They stayed on FaceTime for over an hour before Summer had to go, because Seth was calling with an update on the business. Lena let her go but hated doing it. She looked around her bedroom and realized how empty it felt without Summer in it; which was crazy, because it had been her bedroom for years prior to even knowing Summer Taft. Summer was right, though. Home wasn't a building. It was a person.

***

Summer had fallen asleep around midnight, after a long talk with Seth about one of their VPs, who had made a poor decision with one of their distributors. She had hoped to sleep in a little before having to head over to the house to meet the mold inspector. She wondered how long her father had been living with it, and made a mental note to have the doctors check his lungs, too.

Unfortunately, Summer had woken up early, and as her eyes made their first appearance, she realized she smelled something. It took a moment for it to register that it was coffee.

"Seth, you don't normally wake up before nine. What are–" She stopped as she entered her spacious yet mostly empty kitchen.

"Hi," Lena greeted her and placed two mugs of steaming coffee on the counter.

"Hi," Summer replied breathlessly before taking six long strides toward her and engulfing Lena in a hug. "What are you doing here?"

"You just seemed like you needed a hug," Lena said with a small laugh as she felt Summer squeeze her tighter.

"I did." Summer's arms were around Lena's neck, and after enjoying the feeling of being cradled by her girlfriend for another moment, Summer pulled back and stared into her eyes. "I missed you."

Lena was dressed in her comfy jeans and a Stanford t-shirt that Summer recognized as her own. She must have left it behind. Lena's hair was down and wavy, and she looked perfect.

"I missed you, too."

"How are you even here?" Summer asked as her fingers played with the short hairs on the back of Lena's neck.

"I flew."

"You were supposed to fly here on Friday." Summer ran her hands over Lena's abdomen, as if trying to confirm that she was actually touching her.

"I know. But you looked so lonely last night; I couldn't stand seeing you like that. I hopped on a last-minute flight out of O'Hare to SFO and got in about an hour ago. I didn't want to wake you. I let myself in and found your room just to check on you. I thought about joining you but didn't want to scare you. You went to bed alone, after all. I thought I'd make us coffee and then head up there."

"What about work? You had a presentation." Summer put her fingers in the belt loops of Lena's jeans, while Lena's hands were on the small of her back, under Summer's shirt, rubbing soothing circles.

"I still do. I'm going to do it remotely. I can do a video conference from here. It's not a part of the original plan, but it will work," Lena replied.

"You didn't have to do that. I don't want to jeopardize anything for you."

"I *did* have to do that, because you're my girlfriend, Summer, and you needed me. I told them I had to work remotely tomorrow, and they understood. Van's attorneys approved the paperwork. O'Shea's legal team is checking stuff out today. I told them that I'd be available for emergencies or updates, but that I'd be out of the office today. I thought I could help with the house, assuming there's no mold and—"

Summer didn't want to hear more. She couldn't believe she'd even waited this long. Her lips found Lena's and she pulled the other woman's body flush against her own. Lena hadn't been expecting it, so it took a moment for her to begin kissing Summer back, but once she did, it was fevered and fast. Her hands were under Summer's shirt and all the way to her shoulder blades, trying to pull her even closer. Summer's hands had moved under Lena's shirt as well, but they were on her abdomen and sliding slowly to cup the underside of Lena's breasts. At the soft moan Lena let out, Summer moved them higher, to take both breasts into her hands over Lena's bra. She was the one who moaned this time, and she squeezed Lena's breasts gently, while Lena's lips moved to her neck.

"Upstairs," Summer whispered and began backing up, taking Lena with her.

Their hands had to find purchase elsewhere, as they walked out of the kitchen and up the stairs toward Summer's bedroom, but their lips attempted to remain connected during the trip. When they made it into Summer's room, she pulled away from Lena for a moment and stared first, at swollen lips and then, at impossibly teal eyes.

"Are you sure?" Lena asked her. "I swear, I didn't come here for this." She lifted the corner of her mouth.

Summer found it adorable.

"You're wearing my shirt," Summer said.

Lena looked down, tugged on the t-shirt, and said, "You left it at home. I've kind of been wearing it."

"Will you take it off?" Summer asked softly.

Lena met her eyes and then slowly pulled up on the old Stanford shirt until it was over her head. She held it in her hand for a moment before tossing it to the floor, leaving herself in her jeans and a white lace bra. Summer let out a long exhale and took a step toward her.

"Much better." She smirked. "God, I've missed you."

Summer reached for Lena's neck, pulling the woman's back into her body and meeting Lena's lips with her own.

Lena responded immediately. Summer wrapped her arms around Lena's back and began fussing with the clasp before she was able to undo it. She moved her lips down to Lena's jawline and slowed her kisses as she reached Lena's neck, applying soft kisses to each spot repeatedly before moving onto another. She could feel Lena's hands on her hips. Two fingers from each of Lena's hands had slid just beneath the waistband of her shorts and stopped there. Summer's tongue emerged and toyed with Lena's earlobe, causing the woman in front of her to gasp.

Summer took that as an opportunity to pull away slightly, leaving enough room between their bodies for her to pull down on Lena's bra straps and remove the garment from her girlfriend's body entirely, tossing it to the floor. Lena wasted no time and pulled Summer's shirt over her head, tossing it as well, and they took a long moment to stare at the others' form.

Summer's right hand lifted on its own and touched Lena's collarbone before sliding down. Her eyes followed it as the pads of her own fingers glided against the supple skin and then, the pebbled nipple that hardened at the touch. Her other hand joined in the exploration of Lena's breasts, while Lena stood patiently, with her chest rising and falling as Summer's fingers danced over her skin in an attempt to familiarize herself with the flesh she wanted to always be touching now.

As they stood there, bare from the waist up, Summer wanted to melt into Lena's body. She had never in her life felt that kind of a pull to another human being. Her hands drifted to Lena's jeans, and she began working on the button when her phone rang on her bedside table. She looked toward it only for a moment before returning her eyes to Lena's and sliding the zipper on the jeans down. The phone continued to ring, while Lena's hands moved to Summer's neck to pull her back in. The phone stopped ringing as their lips connected, but only for a second, before the ringing started back up again.

"You should get that." Lena pulled her lips back, but Summer was insistent and reconnected them before walking Lena backward toward the bed.

When Lena's legs hit the back of it, Summer reached down to her jeans and tugged on them until Lena fell back on the bed. Summer smiled at the sight of the bare-chested woman, with white bikinis now on show as the jeans had bunched around Lena's lower thighs. The phone died once more as Summer kneeled down to remove the jeans entirely. She tossed them aside with the rest of Lena's clothing and stood, removing her own shorts, before climbing on the bed on top of Lena, forcing the woman to slide back against the headboard. The phone started up again.

"Oh, my God!" Summer exclaimed just as she was about to place her thigh between Lena's.

"Summer, get it. It's okay," Lena told her and gripped Summer's waist, applying a small tug to the right to get her to move toward the phone.

"The phone Gods do not want us to have sex." Summer grunted and reached for her phone. "Seth, this better be an–"

"Summer, he's in surgery," Seth interrupted. "Dad's been rushed back into surgery. You need to get to the hospital."

"What?" Summer questioned as she straddled Lena and held the phone to her ear.

"Something happened. I don't know. A rupture, or maybe the doctor said it was a clot; I don't know. I just got here, and it happened. And I don't know what to do now. I…" Seth continued, but Summer didn't hear what he was saying.

***

Summer appeared almost catatonic above her. Lena's

hands were still on her waist, but she slid one to her stomach to apply comfort. Summer's hand lowered with the phone. Lena wasn't sure what to do for a moment. She took the phone from Summer's hand and noticed the line was still active.

"Seth, it's Lena," she said. "Summer's girlfriend," she added. "What's going on?"

They dressed quickly. So quickly, in fact, Lena had ended up wearing the shirt Summer had been wearing initially, and Summer ended up in the Stanford t-shirt, after hastily throwing on a sports bra, because she couldn't find a regular one fast enough in her bag she'd still yet to fully unpack. Lena could only stand by and watch as Summer tried to gather her things and then again, sit and watch as they sat in the town car on their way to the hospital.

It was about a twenty-minute drive, but Lena guessed it felt a lot longer for Summer, who was biting her nails and staring out the window for the entire ride. Lena tried to reach for her hand, but Summer was too anxious to keep still. Lena settled for sitting close to her, pressing her side into Summer's so that the other woman could at least feel her presence.

When they arrived, Summer practically ran out of the car. She made it through the sliding glass doors of the hospital entrance before remembering Lena was with her. Lena didn't take offense. She actually felt bad about slowing Summer down, so she sped up her feet to meet her at the bank of elevators, where Summer pressed the up button at least ten times before the elevator arrived to carry them to her dad's floor.

Summer tapped her foot nervously on the floor of the elevator as it moved. Lena reached for her hand, not knowing if it was the right thing to do in that moment, but also not caring. Summer immediately responded by intertwining their fingers without looking over at Lena. Lena squeezed their now linked hands in a show of solidarity as the door opened. Summer didn't break the contact as they exited the elevator. She pulled Lena along with her down the white, plain-looking hallway. There were nurses, doctors, and orderlies moving briskly around them, as Summer directed them both toward a man who Lena knew to be Seth Taft – by the many pictures, articles, and other paraphernalia out there about him and the family. Even if Lena hadn't seen any pictures of him before, she would've known him to be Summer's brother. She hadn't necessarily put it together prior to this moment, but they could be twins.

"Seth, what happened?" Summer asked immediately when they were within earshot.

"I don't know. They said he had been fine when I got here. Then, he started clutching his chest, and the nurse ran in. They took him back to the operating room after that. I've been waiting for an update since."

"I thought he was okay. He's supposed to be getting out tomorrow," Summer replied.

"I don't know, Summer. Maybe I should have gone to med school." He glanced over at Lena and then down at their still joined hands. "Hi, I'm Seth."

"Lena," she introduced herself and gave him her right hand to shake, which he did.

"Sorry, I should have… Seth, this is Lena Tanner, my girlfriend."

"I gathered." Seth nodded at Lena. "I thought you were in Chicago."

"I flew in last night," Lena replied.

"Just in time to sit and wait again," Seth returned.

Lena turned to see that Summer looked pale. She wondered when the woman had eaten last, and guessed it was likely a while ago. She squeezed Summer's hand again and got her attention.

"Can I get you guys anything?" she asked but looked only at Summer as she delivered it. "Coffee? Breakfast?"

"I already ate, but I could use a coffee," Seth replied first.

"You're not sending my girlfriend on a coffee run, Seth," Summer replied in a frustrated tone, likely reserved for her one and only brother.

"Yes, he is." Lena turned to her entirely. "And I'm getting you breakfast, too. You haven't eaten." She leaned in and kissed Summer's forehead. "Let me help."

"You are helping," Summer insisted. "Please, stay with me," she whispered against Lena's lips. "I'll have someone from the office bring us food." She pecked Lena's lips lightly and then turned to Seth, who was watching and smiling at them both.

"She's right. We do both have highly-paid assistants. I'll have mine get us something." He pulled out his phone. "What are you guys in the mood for?"

Summer sat in the same plastic chair as the first day and night she'd spent in the hospital. This time, Lena was next to her, holding her hand and allowing Summer to rest her head on her shoulder. Despite the fact that her father had just come out of emergency surgery, his second in a week, Summer felt better knowing Lena was there. She could feel the steady beat of Lena's heart as she clutched to her side. It helped steady her own. She'd also felt Lena's phone buzzing repeatedly with emails, texts, and calls. Lena had yet to remove it from her purse. Summer wondered, for a moment, if she was going to get into any trouble for leaving Chicago in the middle of a big deal. Lena seemed calm and unconcerned, though, so Summer decided to put her focus on her father, who was now in recovery. The doctor had explained that they had needed to install a stent to help prop the artery open and decrease the chance of another blockage. Summer felt calmer when the doctor told her that her father would still likely be able to go home soon and that it was a relatively common complication.

Summer's phone buzzed. And she would have been like Lena, and let it go to voicemail, but it could have been her aunt or uncle wanting an update on her father. She pulled it out of her pocket and saw that it wasn't a relative.

It was the mold inspector calling about her appointment. They had explained they would call when they were thirty minutes out when Summer booked the appointment, since they couldn't commit to a specific window.

"It's the mold inspector. I'm just going to cancel," Summer told Lena.

"Let me handle it." Lena took the phone out of her hand gently and put it to her ear. "Hello?"

Summer watched as Lena went into professional, get stuff done mode, and told the inspector someone would be there by the time they arrived, and if they weren't, they should wait. Summer would have gotten turned on, were it not for their location and situation.

"You don't have to take care of this," Summer told her when Lena handed the phone back over.

"I'll go, let them in, and come right back when it's done." Lena held out her hand. "Do you have the keys?"

Summer handed them over without thought and asked, "Are you sure?"

"Can you just send for the car and give the driver the address?" Lena asked her. "I'll pick up food on the way back, okay? Are you going to be okay without me?"

"I'll be okay," Summer confirmed and added, "but only temporarily." She gave Lena a wink.

"I'll be back as soon as I can." Lena kissed Summer's forehead.

"Take your time. I know you have work you're missing to just sit here with me," Summer replied.

"You're more important than my job, Summer." Lena pressed her lips to Summer's cheek this time. "I'll be back soon." She looked up at Seth, who was working on his laptop. "You, take care of her while I'm gone."

"She's better at taking care of me than I am of her." He looked up at Lena and then glanced at Summer, who rolled her eyes.

"Then, I think it's time for some improvement on your end there, don't you?" Lena lifted an eyebrow.

Summer smiled and laughed silently before turning to see how her brother reacted. Seth seemed surprised, at first, but then nodded and shrugged. Lena kissed Summer's lips once more and stood, gathering her purse. She then gave Summer a quick smile before turning to walk down the hall. Summer ordered the car on her phone and turned to see that Seth was watching Lena walk toward the elevator.

"Hands off. She's mine," Summer told him.

"I like her for you," he said and returned to his laptop.

"You do?"

"You usually date weaklings. She's definitely not a weakling." He didn't look up from his computer.

Summer turned to see Lena get into the elevator and wave back at her, offering a smile again.

"I love her, Seth."

"I know."

The door closed. Summer turned her attention to the wall in front of her, where there was a stock photo of a family of four staring back at her. The mother and father were behind the little boy and the little girl. It was an advertisement for some kind of prescription medication, but Summer had been drawn to the image because of the family. It reminded her of her own. She realized how much she missed her mother, how much she loved her savant yet immature brother, and how much she loved the father that she almost lost.

CHAPTER 24

LENA WALKED the mold inspector out of the house. She had been permitted to go back in after he did his initial review and found that it was only a small amount. It could be cleaned and removed immediately. Lena had given him her credit card information so as not to have to bother Summer, and then walked him out. She'd stayed inside the house to take the garbage bags outside. Summer and the maid from the day before must have stopped as soon as they had spotted the mold, because there were four large, black trash bags in the kitchen. She had also seen one of the neighbors pulling out their own bins, so she surmised that garbage day was Friday and pulled the bins, brimming with garbage, to the curb, where it would be picked up. She would have stayed longer to clean more, but she promised Summer and Seth food. She did make one stop, though, and went back to Summer's house where she picked up the several boxes of books she had noticed that morning. She had the driver take her to a place where she could ship them to Chicago. She called her neighbor on the way back to the hospital to ask her to put them inside when they arrived, and then, picked up lunch for the three of them before heading back to the hospital.

Lena was exhausted by the time she arrived, carrying carry-out bags of burgers and fries. She wasn't sure what Seth ate, but she got a burger and a cheeseburger for him, just in case, and a burger and a salad for Summer, in case the woman wanted a healthy option. Lena had gotten a burger for herself and fries for all of them, and leaned back against the elevator wall. She closed her eyes as it lifted her up, wondering if she would pass out right there, considering she had hopped a plane in the middle of the night, had a hard time sleeping on board, and then hadn't slept since.

It was already late afternoon. Lena had been up for nearly thirty-six hours. She shook her head sideways rapidly as the doors opened, to try and wake herself up, then plastered a smile on her face, and headed toward the chairs that were now empty.

"Excuse me, I'm looking for the room number for Mr. Taft," Lena said to a nurse when she noticed Summer and Seth weren't where she'd left them.

She thanked the nurse that told her where to find them and headed that way. When she arrived in the doorway, she saw Summer sitting in the chair, and Seth at his father's side. Summer appeared to be in shock, or maybe she was just as tired as Lena; Lena couldn't tell. She also wasn't sure what to do, because Summer's dad was awake, and he and Seth were talking. She didn't want to interrupt. Lena looked back to Summer, who must have heard her or somehow felt her arrival. The woman smiled and took a deep breath when she saw Lena.

"Come in," she encouraged and stood.

Seth turned around at Summer's words and noticed Lena there.

"Hey, welcome back," he greeted and moved to take the bags out of her hands.

Because he was closer, he got to her before Summer

and pulled the bags away just in time for Summer to reach for Lena's waist and pull her in for a hug.

"Hi," Summer greeted again, now that she was up close.

Lena's arms went around Summer's neck, and she pulled the woman in after kissing her cheek.

"Hey, sorry I was a little longer than I'd planned," Lena said and felt Summer squeeze her before pulling back.

"Do you want to meet my dad?" Summer asked her after stroking her cheek. "He's kind of a dick, but I'll tell him to be on his best behavior."

"I heard that," her father said.

"I know." Summer turned and tugged on Lena's hand for her to follow. "I wanted you to hear that because I don't want you to be a dick right now." She took Lena around to the other side of the bed. "Dad, this is my girlfriend, Lena. Be nice."

"I am nice," he replied and lifted his right hand off the bed slightly. "Archie Taft."

Lena took his hand and gave it a gentle shake before releasing it.

"It's nice to meet you," Lena said.

"Summer's never introduced me to any of her girlfriends," he said after a moment.

"Dad," Summer said.

Lena smiled through her momentary thought that Summer had probably introduced him to some of her boyfriends, but she pushed that out of her tired mind.

"She hasn't introduced me to anyone, now that I think about it," he added.

"I think it's time for you to get some sleep." Summer squinted at him, and Lena felt her hand on the small of her back as Summer's head landed on her shoulder. "When you sleep, you can't talk," she added, and Lena laughed.

"I just woke up. And it looks like you brought lunch." He nodded in the direction of the bags Seth was going through on the small table in the room.

"Yeah, not for you." Seth lifted his head and said.

"Come on," Archie tried.

"Dad, no way." Summer's hand slid covertly up the back of Lena's shirt and rested there for a moment, until Summer's fingertips grazed her skin, and Lena was transported back to what they had been doing that morning before the emergency phone call.

"Fine," he deflated. "So, Lena, what is it that you do?"

"I'm the VP of Operations for O'Shea's Grocery Mart."

"VP, huh? Not bad, Summer." He winked at his daughter.

"That's enough." Summer dropped her hand from Lena's back and lifted her head. "Lena and I are going to go and eat our lunch in the cafeteria." She then looked at Seth. "Do not give him any of your food."

"Please, like I'd want to deal with your wrath," Seth replied sarcastically. "He's eating hospital food."

"Good." Summer returned her glance to her dad. "We'll be back. You, behave."

"Lena just got here. Can't I get to know her a little?"

"Later."

Summer took Lena's hand and entwined their fingers. She grabbed the bag that Seth held out for them, and they left the room.

"Your dad seems interested in me," Lena remarked with a smirk as they arrived at the elevator.

"You *are* very interesting." Summer smirked back as they walked. "He's just excited, I guess."

"Because he's never met any of your girlfriends?" Lena asked as she leaned her back against the wall again.

"He's never met any of my boyfriends, either, if that's what you're thinking." Summer read her mind. "He's always been accepting of me. I've just never had anyone I wanted to introduce him to."

"You didn't have to introduce me to him. I would have waited outside the room."

"Lena, stop." Summer placed her free hand on Lena's chest and stood a few inches away. "I wanted him to meet you. I wanted Seth to meet you." Summer leaned in and kissed her. "You must be exhausted."

"I'm tired, yeah," Lena downplayed.

"Thank you for flying all the way out here, for getting us food, and taking care of the mold thing." Summer's eyes got big. "I forgot to ask… How did it go?"

The elevator opened, and they left to go in search of the cafeteria.

"They were able to clean it. I just had them do it. I hope that's okay."

"It's gone?"

"They didn't have another appointment right away. I convinced them to take care of it while they were there. It's all clear now."

Summer took Lena's hand and linked their fingers again.

"You are amazing. How much was it?"

"Doesn't matter."

"Lena…"

"Summer…" Lena turned and stuck her tongue out at her girlfriend. "I took care of it."

"He's my dad. I should–"

"You should focus on taking care of him and yourself. It's not a big deal. Let's eat." Lena pulled her toward the sign that told her the cafeteria was to the left.

"You really are amazing."

Lena sat at a long table that was empty. Summer sat across from her, pulling items out of the bag.

"I'm starving. I didn't know what you'd want. I got you a burger and a salad, just in case," Lena said.

"I'll probably eat both. I'm starving, too. I'm going to go by the house after we eat and finish the cleanup," Summer stated and snagged a fry. "The doctors said he could still go home Saturday."

"Saturday? Really?"

"Seth exaggerated the emergency. I mean, it *was* an emergency, but it wasn't that big of an emergency. My dad was already here, so they were able to take care of it before it got bad. The doctor is still convinced he'll be okay. If he wasn't near a hospital, it could have been worse, but they say by Saturday afternoon – tests pending – we can take him home." Summer ate another fry. "Unfortunately for me, Seth is supposed to fly to Detroit on Sunday, so I'm going to have to stay here and keep an eye on him."

"Seth can't stay?" Lena asked and opened the foil her burger came in.

"He can, but he's working. And I'm still technically on vacation. Not much of a vacation anymore, though."

Summer bit into the burger she'd unwrapped. Lena watched her girlfriend as she ate, realizing how unbelievably responsible the woman in front of her was. Summer was twenty-seven, the CEO of a massive tech company, the youngest child, the little sister, and was still, somehow, holding both her family and a tech empire together.

"Ask him to stay, Summer," Lena muttered.

"Huh?" Summer took another bite and set down the burger. "I need a drink. Iced tea?"

"Summer, ask Seth to stay and help you," Lena repeated.

"It's okay. I'm used to it."

"Summer, you don't have to hold the whole world up for everyone else," Lena persisted. "Ask Seth to postpone his trip and stay to help you. No one at the company will think anything less of either of you for helping your dad recover from a heart attack."

Summer stood and headed to the glass case where there were bottles of water, soda, and teas. She pulled out two bottles and paid the woman at the register, while Lena watched. When Summer returned, she sat next to Lena instead, and opened both Lena's tea and her own.

"Do you want me to drop you off back at my place before I head to my dad's?"

"No, I'll go to your dad's place with you. Why did you change the subject?"

"Are you sure? I can take you back first, and you can take a nap or do some work if you need to."

"Summer Taft, stop." Lena took her hand. "What's wrong?"

She used her free hand to slide Summer's hair behind her ear. Summer looked down at their joined hands and then back up.

"I was so scared, Lena."

"I know, honey." Lena leaned in, and her forehead met the side of Summer's head.

"When Seth called this morning, I thought that he was gone, and I'd never get a chance to say goodbye, like I did with my mom. That the last time we had talked, we still weren't getting along." Summer paused and sighed. "I don't think I want Seth to stay and help."

"Why not?"

"Because he and my dad have always had a special bond. He doesn't always listen to Seth, but he listens to him more than me. At least when my mom was around, I had her, but he's all I've got left, and…" Summer faded while Lena wiped a tear from her cheek.

"You want some time alone with him," Lena replied softly.

"I do." Summer turned toward Lena. "I think I want to stay here for a week, maybe. That will give me enough time to set up long-term care for him and check out his finances. I'm not giving him a choice this time, Lena. He has to take care of himself."

"He does," Lena agreed.

"I know this isn't great for us: me – here, and you – there, but I promise, it won't be for any longer than it has to be."

"Hey, you do what you need to do." Lena kissed her lips. "I'm not going anywhere."

"Are you sure? You're beautiful, and hot, and smart,

and funny, and hot, and cute, and adorable, and you could find someone with a little less family drama."

"You said hot twice in there." Lena laughed quietly, because she didn't want to interrupt the silence in the otherwise noiseless room.

"You are hot twice." Summer winked at her. "And all the other things, too."

Lena smiled at her, lifted a fry from the box they came in, and held it to Summer's lips.

"Eat," she encouraged, and Summer did. "I'll head home on Sunday, as planned, unless you want me to leave earlier. I can leave on Saturday if you want to have more time with him."

"Stay until Sunday, please." Summer chewed. "I know this is not exactly how you planned to spend your weekend. It's going to be a lot of waiting around. But if you can stay, I'd like you here."

"Then, I'll stay," Lena replied. "And don't drop me off. I'll help at your dad's. It'll be faster if it's the two of us. It's too late to take a nap, anyway. If I do, I won't be able to sleep tonight, and I need to be rested for tomorrow."

"Your presentation?" Summer turned to face her food and then pulled it across the table so she'd be eating next to Lena instead of across from her.

"Yeah, I'll have to do a little work tonight, based on what came through today."

"You were very popular earlier," Summer said. "Your phone was going crazy."

"The attorneys have approved everything. I had my financial advisor review Van's financials and the business plan. He's convinced it's a good idea. We're going ahead with the plan," Lena replied.

"What exactly is the plan? You haven't filled me in on all the details yet," Summer asked.

"I'm going to invest in Strange Joe's." Lena took a few fries and dipped them into Summer's newly poured ketchup before eating them.

"You're investing in her company?"

"You know how you are very rich?" Lena asked.

Summer laughed and ate another fry before saying, "Yes."

"Have you ever heard of TanAgro?" Lena asked.

"The agricultural company?" Summer seemed to be trying to remember something she already knew. "It's in biotech, right? Based in New York?"

"That's where the corporate office is, yes," Lena said. "My family owns it."

"You own it?!" Summer had just bitten into her hamburger and nearly spat out her bite as she exclaimed.

"I don't. Well, not technically. My family does. My dad is the CEO, but it's been family business for over twenty-five years. It started as organic farming before organic farming was the new thing," Lena began. "There are farms in upstate New York and now more places around the country, too, but that's how it all started anyway. The past five years, though, the focus has been on cleanroom produce farms. It's actually safer to eat, and there are no chemicals and pesticides. The food lasts longer, too." She paused for a bite of her own burger. "Anyway, my dad's family has had money since they first came here, probably on the damn Mayflower. Now, they have these produce rooms all over the world. It's been very profitable. I am, technically, on the board, though I rarely attend meetings. Cale does most of the work and voting when it comes to that. He's set to take it over, because I don't want to, but I have a large trust fund outside of the company. I also have the company money, and I have a job as a VP," Lena said while watching Summer listen intently. "I'm very well-off."

"Well-off? How well-off?" Summer asked.

"I rarely touch the money I have. And since I'm continuing to accrue it, I need to find a way to invest it." Lena avoided the topic of her actual bank account total for a moment. "Strange Joe's is a great opportunity. I'll be a 49% owner, but Van will keep 51% and maintain primary shareholder status."

Summer glared at her for a moment and then took a long drink of her iced tea. She capped it and turned back to Lena with her hands clasped in her lap.

"You're just telling me this now? Afraid I'd be after your money?" She smiled.

"No, I haven't told anyone here." Lena laughed. "Anyone in Chicago, I mean. No one outside of my family really knows about it. Well, our friends in Connecticut do, and Damon does, but I don't talk about it because it's not really a part of my life. The truth is that on paper, I am a millionaire." Lena bit her lower lip.

"That's cute." Summer leaned forward and kissed her. "You can't even say that you're rich without getting all nervous."

"I don't consider myself rich, I guess. Honestly, my grandparents left me a large trust fund that my dad just added to. I got it when I was twenty-five. I never touched it, because Damon and I didn't need it. He had his own money and had a well-paying job. It's just been sitting there for years. Some of it's on the market, obviously. I bought my house and paid for all the renovations, but outside of that, I don't use it. I started considering investment opportunities about a year ago, but I hadn't found anything I was interested in, until now."

"Van's place?" Summer lifted an eyebrow.

"Still hate her?" Lena rolled her eyes.

"Yes, but not because of this. If this is what you want to do, then I'm happy for you. What happens next?"

"I have to get O'Shea's to approve letting her use their space. If they do, then we're moving forward that way. It makes the most sense. If not, I'm still going to invest. We'll just look into other options."

"Sounds great, babe." Summer said and took another bite of her burger. "Just not too many late-night work sessions in the house with Van when I'm not there, okay?" Summer smiled a wicked smile. "Unless she's in a very serious relationship." Summer ate a fry. "Like, marriage serious; but not so far into the marriage that they're no longer having sex, and she's looking for it elsewhere. She seems like she could be one of those girls."

Lena laughed and did not hold it in this time.

"Oh, my God!"

"I'm just kidding." Summer stated and then shrugged. "Mostly."

***

Summer pulled in another chair so that Lena could join her in the room with her father. Seth had returned to the office after eating and calling their aunt to check in. Summer held Lena's hand to her lips and kissed it before placing it on the armrest between them, while Lena scrolled through emails and messages on her phone.

"Summer?" Archie whispered as he stirred.

"I'm here." Summer stood and approached his bed.

"When am I getting out of here?"

"Saturday."

"I can't stay in here for two more nights."

"Yes, you can," Summer told him. "You don't have a choice, Dad."

"You know what I mean. I'm going stir-crazy in here."

"I'll bring you stuff from the house. What do you want?"

"Mo," he stated.

"Dad, I can't bring the dog to the hospital," Summer replied with a glare.

She heard Lena chuckle lightly behind her and resisted turning around.

"I don't know, then," Archie shared.

"How about that iPad I bought you?" Summer suggested.

"I haven't taken it out of the box."

"I know. I found it in your room. I'll set it up for you

265

tonight and bring it tomorrow. Want me to put some old episodes of M*A*S*H on there for you?" she asked.

"That would be good. Start at the beginning, though," he replied.

"I will. I'll get you the first season at least, okay?"

"Okay."

"And I'll download some Springsteen, too."

"The Boss?" His eyes got big with excitement.

"I'll put him on there for you. Anything else you want?"

"Beach Boys?"

"Done."

"And that app your brother plays sometimes, with the candies."

"Candy Crush? You want Candy Crush?" Summer asked.

"He let me use his phone earlier. It passed the time."

"Okay. I'll put that on there for you. Lena and I are going to go to the house, okay?"

"My house?"

"Yes, Dad. We're going to your house. I'm trying to clean it up before you get home."

"Summer, don't go throwing things out when you don't know what I–" He tried to sit up, but gave up immediately.

"Dad, I'm throwing out garbage only. I'm just straightening up things. You had mold in there. Did you know that?" she asked.

"Mold? No, I didn't," he objected.

"Yes, you did. It was in the kitchen and in the bathroom. Lena spent her morning at your house with an inspector and cleaning crew getting it out of there. You should thank her." Summer moved over slightly so Archie could see Lena sitting in the chair.

"You did that?" he asked Lena.

"I just met the inspector. Summer set it up," Lena replied.

"Thank you," he replied and then looked at Summer. "Leave your mother's stuff–"

"Alone; I know. We'll talk about that later, okay? And we're talking more about the money situation, too, dad," she said.

"I don't–"

"Nope. Shut up." Summer turned to Lena. "You ready?"

"Sure." Lena stood.

"This isn't over, Dad. We're talking about this more. You're making big changes whether you want to or not." Summer pointed at him. "I got you magazines to get you through tonight. I'll be back tomorrow with your iPad." She leaned down and kissed his cheek. "I love you."

"I love you, too; even though you're a pain in the ass."

"I get it from you," Summer said and took Lena's hand, leading her out of the room.

CHAPTER 25

"LENA, YOU LOOK so tired. Are you ready to put the computer away now?" Summer asked as they lay in bed.

"You put the iPad away, and I'll put the computer away," Lena replied.

"I can't, with you in those glasses."

"What?" Lena laughed and pulled the glasses off her face, turning to Summer.

"I'm so fucking tired," Summer admitted. "But I love you in those things. I get... going," she admitted and then wiggled her eyebrows.

"We said not tonight," Lena said.

"I know, and I can't. But I just want you to know that I want to." Summer set the iPad on the table next to the bed and rolled on her side. "How's it going? Are you ready for tomorrow?"

"I think so." Lena closed the laptop. She leaned over the side of the bed and placed it on the floor. "Is it okay if I do it from here tomorrow?"

"Of course," Summer replied.

Lena rolled on her side to face Summer, sliding her arm under her head on the pillow.

"Are you going to be okay at the hospital by yourself? You're not going to try to fist fight your bed-ridden father, are you?" Lena placed her free hand on Summer's waist and tugged her a little closer.

"Not unless he starts it." Summer gave her a mischievous smile. "I'll be fine. I'll be thinking about you and your presentation, though." Summer's hand went to Lena's waist. "So, now that I know you're crazy rich, I expect some changes to occur in our relationship," she said with her eyes closed and a wicked smile.

"Oh, yeah?" Lena laughed and closed her tired eyes, too. "Like what?"

"I want to do that *Indecent Proposal* thing, where they throw money on the bed and have sex on it."

Lena's eyes shot open, and she laughed, pulling Summer closer to her.

"We could have done that before. You're crazy rich, too."

"True, but it's more fun when the money belongs to someone else," Summer shared and pressed her forehead to Lena's.

"Money is gross. We're not having sex on top of it," Lena replied.

Summer laughed. Lena felt it and loved it.

"We should probably have sex first before we start adding things to it. There's clearly a conspiracy against us getting it on."

Lena laughed again and said, "How romantic."

"I was all about romance this morning; until the phone call."

"I know you were. It was sweet," Lena shared. "I liked how you looked at me, how you touched me."

Summer grunted, and Lena opened her eyes, but Summer's were still closed.

"We need to stop talking about it. I have no energy, but that's not stopping my hormones, and I have a vivid memory. I'm seeing you on the bed topless, and in that cute underwear."

"Let's just go to sleep," Lena chuckled.

She felt Summer roll over to face away from her, and then Summer's hand was pulling Lena's arm over her waist and onto her stomach. The woman held it there, and Lena pressed her face into Summer's neck.

"Good night, Lena Tanner."

"Good night, Summer Taft," Lena whispered.

***

Lena had to wake up extra early, because of the time difference and the need to coordinate with Van and the attorneys prior to her presentation. Summer slept later, but then, she left for the hospital. She had wished Lena luck with work, and Lena wished her luck with her father. Lena dressed for work, as if she would be going to the office. She straightened her hair, put on her makeup, and then set herself up in Summer's office. By noon, she was ready for the presentation she would deliver virtually with the other VPs and their CEO. Two hours later, it was finally over. She closed the computer and breathed a sigh of relief. They'd approved her proposal.

Lena dialed Summer to tell her the good news.

"Hey! How did it go?" the woman asked immediately.

"It's approved," Lena said with a smile.

"Babe! I'm so proud of you. That's amazing," Summer replied.

"It is, yeah."

Lena felt better. Just hearing Summer's voice and hearing how happy she was for her, made Lena feel like she could do anything.

"How do you feel?" Summer asked.

"Really good. It feels really good, Summer."

"Listen, I'm at the hospital. They've just finished some tests, and my dad looks pretty good. He's being released tomorrow morning. I need to go over to the house and get it ready," Summer said.

The previous night, they had finished cleaning, but they still had to go grocery shopping to stock the place with healthy food. Summer also wanted to try to at least make sense of his financial paperwork before he was out of the hospital and could put up more of a fight.

"I still have some work to do here. I have to send documents around to everyone and make a few more calls to get things going before Monday."

"Can you come to the house when you're done?" Summer asked. "I'm going to hit the store first. I have to wait for Seth, who's coming by after work. I told my aunt I'd go over to her house and set up her new router."

"Router?" Lena laughed.

"She and my uncle are not good with technology. Honestly, no one in my family is. It's a wonder Seth and I turned out how we did. Their old one stopped working. I told her I'd come over and take care of setting up the new one. It won't take long."

"Sounds like a very busy day for you," Lena replied and leaned back in the desk chair.

"Shaping up to be that way." Summer sighed. "We can have a late dinner over there if you're up for it? Order a pizza, maybe."

"Can we make out in your childhood bedroom?" Lena smirked to herself.

Summer laughed and replied, "If you want to, but I doubt it's going to add any excitement."

"It would still be nice to kiss you where you spent your early years," Lena proposed.

"Only if one day, I'll get to see the mansion you grew up in," Summer replied.

"You can see the house, but my room is gone, so we won't be making out in it."

"Did your parents turn it into a home gym or something?"

"No, they tore half the house down about ten years ago and remodeled the whole thing. I think it was something my mom needed to do after Leo. His room was next to mine. After the accident, she kept it as he had left it for a few years, but then, she decided it was time to move on. Instead of just giving away his stuff or throwing on a fresh coat of paint, she tore down half the house."

271

"Wow. I guess I'll have to settle for pictures, then," Summer replied.

"I guess so."

"Come by when you're wrapped up there."

"I'll pick up the pizza on the way. Do you have a favorite place you haven't had in a while?"

"Marco's is pretty good. It's about ten minutes away from the house. I usually order the meat lover's, but sometimes, I just get mushrooms and–"

"Summer?"

"Yeah?"

"First thing that comes into your mind… Favorite pizza, go!"

"Mushroom," Summer stated as if it should have been obvious to everyone.

"Then, I'll get mushroom."

"I see what you did there." Summer chuckled at her. "Getting me to make a decision."

"Well, it worked," Lena said.

"Don't get too excited… I'm still pretty indecisive. Pizza isn't a big deal."

"I don't know… You've made some pretty big decisions lately." Lena thought out loud. "Dating me, for example."

"That's been a good one. Took me a couple of weeks to get there."

"You're about a decade ahead of Hailey."

Summer laughed loudly at that.

"That's true. She did take forever," Summer remarked about Hailey's feelings for her fiancée.

"You've decided to help your dad get things together, and you decided to quit and focus on school for a while."

"Last night, I told you I was *thinking* about it."

"You know you've already made up your mind. You just have to admit it to yourself. For what it's worth, I think all of those decisions are good decisions." Lena's phone alerted her to another caller. "Hey, I have to go. Our VP of sales is calling."

"Okay. I'll see you later."

"Tell your dad I said hi," Lena said.

"I will." Summer hung up.

***

Lena knocked on the door with one hand while holding onto the pizza in the other. After several knocks and no response, she pulled out her phone and dialed Summer's number. Her workday had gone on a lot longer than expected, but that seemed okay for Summer, because her tasks had taken nearly as long. Apparently, the shower in her dad's bathroom required a new showerhead, because her father hadn't ever cleaned the old one. The resulting water pressure was just above a trickle. Summer made the trip to the hardware store to purchase a new one and installed it herself. Lena was exhausted yet again and wondered if there would ever be a time when she wouldn't be tired.

They had agreed to eating dinner and fixing up Archie's room to make it ready for his arrival. It had been cleaned and somewhat organized by them already, but it had extra furniture and boxes in it that needed to be moved or gone through still, to find out what was in them, so that he could get in and out of the room easily, which was necessary in his condition. Lena remembered the key she had used before and found that it was right where she'd left it. She opened the door just as Summer's voicemail picked up. She hung up the call to enter the house.

"Summer?" she called out but received no response.

Lena placed the pizza box and the oversized bag she had brought with her down. She got it so that she could bring along a bottle of wine she had grabbed at Summer's house on the table, in the sparsely and outdatedly furnished living room. When Lena glanced into the kitchen and saw no one, so she proceeded down the thin hallway, stopping periodically to take in the adorable pictures of baby Summer and then awkward pictures of teenage Summer, while she looked into the bathroom, Seth's old room, and then Summer's old room, to see that her girlfriend wasn't in any of them. At the end of the hall, Lena finally found the other woman sleeping on her father's bed. Summer had a pile of clean laundry in a basket on the floor and some folded items on the end of the bed. She had a t-shirt in her hands, and her hands were in her lap, as if she'd fallen asleep while trying to fold the shirt.

Lena just stood in the doorway of the room and took her in. Summer's face was tense, even though she was asleep. Lena wondered if she was having a nightmare or maybe just a dream that was a little too realistic, because Summer's other muscles appeared tense as well. She moved toward the bed and silently removed the already folded clothes, placing them on top of the dresser that was missing one of its small legs and was being held up instead, by a part of a red brick.

Lena sat on the floor of the room next to the bed and began pulling shirts, shorts, jeans, and, unfortunately, boxer shorts, along with socks that looked like they'd seen better days, out of the basket. She folded them one by one and placed each item on the floor until she had nearly finished the basket. Then, she felt a hand on her shoulder.

"What are you doing?" Summer whispered.

"Hey." Lena turned her head to the side to see Summer leaning down with tired eyes. "I was just finishing up."

"I fell asleep."

"Yes, you did. I didn't want to wake you." Lena placed the last pair of now matched clean socks on the floor and lifted herself to sit on the side of the bed next to Summer. "I brought pizza. You hungry?"

"I don't think so." Summer rolled onto her back and stared up at the ceiling. "I feel like I need another twelve hours of sleep."

"We can just go back to your place, then. We can eat the pizza there."

"I need to finish up. I have to put all this away and–"

"Tomorrow morning, you can go to the hospital to pick him up, and I'll come here and put the stuff away. It's already folded. Come on. Let's go put you to bed."

"Why are you the best?" Summer asked and forced herself into a sitting position.

Lena smiled and pulled on Summer's hands to get her to stand.

"I don't know."

Summer wrapped Lena in a hug and pulled her closer.

"What would I do without you?" Summer asked and pressed her lips to Lena's neck before pulling back to rest her forehead against Lena's.

"You did fine before you met me," Lena replied with a gentle kiss to Summer's lips.

"I don't want to be without you again, though," Summer pecked her lips again and uttered so softly, Lena barely heard the words.

"You won't be," she replied.

***

"Take your shirt off," Lena ordered when they made it to Summer's bedroom after a fast dinner of pizza and beer.

"Excuse me?" Summer lifted an eyebrow and turned around to find Lena standing right behind her.

"I'm going to give you a back massage. You need it." Lena's hands went to the hem of Summer's shirt, and she lifted it until Summer's arms went up in the air so she could pull it off.

"Let's just change and go to sleep. You don't have to-"

"I want to. Let's get you into your shorts first," Lena interrupted.

Summer smiled and moved to her bag on the floor.

She pulled out her shorts and slid off her jeans, replacing them with the navy-colored sweats she'd cut off long ago.

Lena took her turn in the bathroom, brushing her teeth and getting ready for bed after changing her own clothes. Summer had only snuck a short peek when Lena pulled her shirt and bra off to change into a t-shirt. Anything more than a short peek would have gotten her even more turned on than she already was just by that short look. Yet again, though, the emotional and physical toll of trying to get her father's affairs in order had gotten the best of her. As much as she wanted to take Lena to her bed and explore every inch of the woman's skin, Summer wanted their first time to be special. She also had hope that it would be Lena's last first experience with anyone. She wanted it to matter.

When Summer emerged from the bathroom, she found Lena on her knees, facing the headboard of the bed. She had grabbed a bottle of lotion from somewhere and appeared to be waiting for her.

"Hey." Summer made her way toward the bed. "Where do you want me?"

"Lie down. Take off your shirt first," Lena repeated her original command.

Summer did as she was told and removed her shirt. She stood next to the bed and watched as Lena's eyes moved greedily up and down her body.

"Second thoughts?" Summer smirked.

Lena cleared her throat and said, "No. Just…" She looked down and then pointed at the bed. "On the bed, please."

Summer ended up on her stomach, with her hands under her head. She felt self-conscious for a moment, because Lena wasn't doing anything yet, but then, Lena's hands, covered in lotion, made their way to her skin. Lena slid them up and down Summer's back, at first, to coat the skin with the lavender-scented lotion Summer had been given as a gift years ago in one of those lotion and shower gel sets.

It was supposedly aromatherapy, but Summer hadn't gotten any therapy from any aroma that she could recall. Lena's hands were gliding to the small of her back and circling in patterns that had Summer closing her eyes. Lena was straddling her legs. Summer felt her against her. She wished she had the energy to roll Lena over and take her, but she knew that even if she did, Lena didn't. They had both been overly extended, thanks to the week's events.

Lena's hands moved to her middle back, where she applied a little more pressure, working tense spots out of the muscles there. Summer's back had been in pain since the first few hours in those rough plastic chairs. When Lena's hands pressed into the muscles under her shoulder blades, Summer exhaled both because of the tension released, and because Lena had to move herself up in the process and was now straddling Summer's ass, applying firm and focused pressure to her shoulder blades. When Summer made sounds of both pleasure and pain from the tension released, Lena alternated to her neck muscles and then back to her shoulder blades. Summer felt the hands drift low again. Then, Lena was pulling down on her shorts.

"Can I?" Lena asked with hesitation in her voice.

It was Summer's turn to clear her throat.

"Yes," she turned her head to the side to whisper.

"I'm just going to massage you, okay?"

"Okay," Summer replied unconfidently.

She felt Lena slide back. Lena's hands were on the waistband of her shorts. They pulled down. Summer lifted herself slightly so that Lena could slide them off entirely, along with her underwear. Summer heard Lena gasp, once the clothes were hanging off Summer's ankles. Then, she repositioned herself, straddling Summer's thighs. Summer heard the lotion bottle open again. Moments later, Lena's thumbs were applying focused, firm pressure to her ass. Summer moaned when Lena found a particular spot that had never been massaged before. She let out a deep exhale as the tension left her body. Lena continued her work until she had worked out the tension not only in Summer's back but in the rest of her body, too.

Then, Lena slid off Summer and pulled her shorts and underwear back up, lifting Summer's hips to make sure they were properly in place before encouraging Summer with her hands to roll over.

"Better?" she asked and picked Summer's shirt off the floor.

"So much," Summer replied as she rolled.

Lena handed her the shirt. Summer lifted her body only enough to put it on before flopping back down onto the bed.

"And I'm doing that to you one day," Summer stated.

"Sounds good." Lena laughed as she walked into the bathroom.

Summer pulled the blanket and sheets down. When Lena returned, Summer noticed the lotion bottle was gone, and Lena had washed her hands to remove the excess.

"I can't believe how good that felt," Summer said.

"Yeah?" Lena climbed into the bed next to her.

"Were you a masseuse in a past life or something?" Summer rolled onto her side to face her.

"I don't know. Maybe. I don't remember my past lives." Lena winked at Summer and held her arm out.

Summer took the hint and rested her head against Lena's chest.

"Tomorrow's going to be crazy," she said.

"I know." Lena ran a hand under Summer's shirt.

"There's something I want to tell you, but I'm kind of worried about how you'd take it…" Summer gulped after saying that.

"What?" Lena asked and kissed her forehead. "You can tell me anything."

"It might be too fast."

Lena didn't say anything for a moment. Summer felt Lena's body tense, and she grew worried that she'd scared the woman, and she hadn't even said it yet. Then, Lena relaxed, and her hand on Summer's back moved again. Lena's free hand topped Summer's on her stomach, and she dragged it up and down Summer's arm.

"I love you," Lena said in a whisper.

Summer immediately lifted her head to stare down at her girlfriend.

"You do?" she asked, with her heart racing.

"Yeah." Lena looked terrified while she waited to hear how Summer would react.

Summer could only smile as she met Lena's eyes.

"That's what I was going to say to you," Summer replied.

"I thought it might be." Lena finally smiled back up at her, and then, ran her hand over Summer's cheek.

"It's crazy, isn't it?" Summer shook her head from side to side. "We just met and started dating. I've never felt this way before, Lena. I'm crazy about you. I think about you every minute of every day."

"It is crazy, but it kind of fits us," Lena suggested.

"What do you mean?"

"We're crazy." Lena laughed for a second. "It's as if, separately, we're not crazy. But since we've met, we've gotten crazy, but in the right way." She paused. "I've never met someone I felt this way about. I've had very few relationships in my life; only a couple in high school and college before I started dating Damon. Since him, though, I've only been on a few dates." Lena's hand landed in Summer's hair. "I did the traditional thing before. I met someone, we went on dates, at some point we had sex, and then, we either took other steps in the relationship or not. That's how it usually goes, right?"

"That's how I've done it," Summer replied.

She continued to take in Lena's eyes. There were these little darker blue flecks in them Summer hadn't noticed before. She wondered how she had missed them until now.

"We're not like that," Lena said. "We met because our friends knew each other. Then, we hung out as friends who were trying to hook each other up with someone else. We also kind of moved in together accidentally. Then, we kissed and went on a date, where we kissed again. We almost stopped there, but then we made up. You came here because of your dad, and I followed you. And now, we're here."

"And we still haven't had sex." Summer gave her a playful glare.

"No, we haven't. But we will. I'm okay with it taking time to get there. I'm okay if it happens when you get back home. I know how I feel, Summer. And it is crazy, but the reason I think it's so crazy, is that I thought I knew love. I thought I loved Damon. I thought that's what it was. But if it *was* love, it pales in comparison to what I feel for you. Yes, it's fast, but for once in my life, I'm going to be a person that's brave and just admit how I feel. I love you."

"I know what I want for the first time in my life," Summer replied softly. "You've made me think about myself and the things that I want to do and don't want to do. I know what I want now. I know that you're a part of that. I love you," Summer finally said it out loud.

CHAPTER 26

W HEN LENA LEFT to go back to Chicago on Sunday, they exchanged '*I love you*' as their new goodbye. Summer realized that was how it would be from now on. Whenever they parted, she would likely say the words and hear them in return.

Lena had been right. They were not a typical couple at all, but both of them had tried typical before. It hadn't worked. It never made either of them happy. They had talked a lot about their previous relationships Saturday evening. While Archie slept in his bed, they continued to organize his stuff and reviewed his financial documents. Archie had been his typical stubborn self but had at least been on better behavior since Lena was there. Summer could tell he was trying not to embarrass his only daughter, and she worried that he was reserving stuff for after Lena went home.

Luckily for Summer, sleep was his primary activity for the better part of the afternoon and evening. He woke only to eat and go to the bathroom. Dinner was prepared – thankfully – by her aunt, in the now cleaned and fully stocked kitchen. Her uncle and Seth joined them and brought Mo back over. Her father seemed to immediately perk up when the dog arrived. His smile made Summer feel better.

***

"You miss her like crazy, don't you?" Charlie asked Lena as they ate lunch at Windy's on Tuesday.

"It's been two days. What's wrong with me?" Lena sipped on her water.

"Nothing's wrong with you. You're happy, Lena. This is what it means to be happy." Charlie took a bite of her sandwich. "Look at Hails and me. It's crazy. I can't sleep when she's gone. Last week, I went to Detroit with her because I didn't want to be in the house without her."

"Yeah, but you and Hailey were pre-destined or something. You two were always going to happen," Lena replied.

Charlie stopped eating and stared across the table at her.

"Who's to say you and Summer weren't?" She turned toward the front door. "There she is."

Lena thought about Charlie's comment, while the woman stared at the door Hailey had just walked through. Lena hadn't thought about that. She had been so caught up in the fact that she had fallen for Summer so quickly, and that she missed her girlfriend when she wasn't around, she had never thought that maybe they were just as pre-destined as Charlie and Hailey. Was that why it felt so different with Summer?

"Sorry I'm late," Hailey said and sat next to Charlie. She then leaned in immediately and kissed her. "I see you started without me." Hailey grabbed a potato chip off Charlie's plate.

"You told us to start without you," Charlie replied.

"I know. I'm just giving you a hard time. It's kind of my job now."

"*Now?*" Charlie shot back at her while Lena looked on. "When have you ever *not* given me a hard time?"

"True." Hailey turned her attention to Lena. "I hear congratulations are in order."

"They are?" Lena asked.

"Professionally and personally. You signed a deal or something."

"I'm an investor in a coffee place now. We're putting them inside O'Shea's stores. It should be a good move for me and for the company."

"That's amazing, Lena," Hailey said. "Although, I'm more excited about the personal thing."

"What personal thing?"

"Summer called me yesterday to share the news that you two exchanged some words." The woman took a drink of Charlie's soda.

"She did?" Lena smiled.

"Words?" Charlie looked at Hailey and then at Lena.

"I told her I loved her," Lena said. "We were lying in bed, talking, and she seemed nervous, like she wanted to tell me something but was worried. I decided to tell her first."

"Confident, weren't you? Knew what she was going to say?" Hailey asked.

"I thought she might. It's hard to explain... It felt like every time we said goodbye, either in person or on the phone, something was missing. Like there was something we weren't saying that we were supposed to be saying."

"You said it first?" Charlie asked. "That surprises me."

"It surprised me, too," Lena said. "I've only said it to one other person, and he said it first back then. Everything's different with Summer. I can't explain it. She makes me feel more like the whole version of myself. It's as if she makes me more confident in who I am or who I was meant to be. I don't know. Maybe that's stupid."

"It's not stupid," Charlie replied immediately. "I know exactly what you mean."

"You do?" Hailey asked her.

"You know I do," Charlie replied. Hailey's arm went around her back, allowing Charlie to rest her head on Hailey's shoulder. "It's like, you are who you think you're supposed to be, and then, you meet someone that makes you doubt that because they make you better. They make you who you were supposed to be all along."

Charlie couldn't see Hailey's face from her position, but Lena could. Hailey's head was down, and her hand around Charlie was playing with the woman's short hair. Her other hand was toying with the straw wrapper on the table, but her face was bright, with a wide smile and light eyes.

"That's love, Lena," Hailey said after a moment. "I'm glad you two aren't dancing around it, like we did for all those years."

Lena watched Charlie's face this time. Her eyes closed briefly. Lena wondered if she was taking that moment to breathe in Hailey's scent. Charlie then smiled and opened her eyes. They held on Hailey for a minute before returning to Lena.

"Me too," Lena said. "We made it, like, three weeks before we just gave into it."

"You asked her out, too. And now, you're professing love first. Summer Taft has definitely worked her mojo on you." Charlie laughed.

"Hey, guys." Emma approached their table with a woman Charlie didn't recognize. "I didn't know you'd be here."

"Hey, Em," Hailey greeted. "What are you doing here?"

"Grabbing lunch. This is Jennifer. She just started at work; moved here from St. Louis." Emma motioned to the woman standing next to her.

Jennifer was portly and probably in her mid-forties. She had long black hair and brown eyes. And she also seemed a little out of place.

"It's her first day. I told her I'd take her to lunch," Emma added.

"Nice to meet you, Jennifer," Hailey replied.

"These are my friends: Hailey, Charlie, and Lena."

"Do you want to join us?" Charlie asked and leaned

up, so she was no longer resting on Hailey's shoulder.

"No, thank you," Jennifer answered. "I'll just grab something to go, if you don't mind." The woman glanced at Emma, who then looked at Hailey and Charlie for a moment before rolling her eyes while making sure Jennifer couldn't see.

"Go for it. They take to-go orders at the bar." Emma nodded in that direction. "I'll stay with my friends, if that's okay."

"Sure." Jennifer didn't stop at the bar but instead, left the restaurant.

"What the hell was that?" Charlie asked.

"My guess?" Emma sat next to Lena. "She isn't a fan of *the gays*." She pointed between Hailey and Charlie. "Did you see how she looked at you two, all cuddled up over there?"

"Well, that's stupid," Hailey stated.

"Yeah, I don't think I'll be spending any more time with this new Jennifer. And I think she'll be okay with that once she finds out I date women, too. She probably already has, since I associate with you two, same-siders."

"Same-siders?" Lena asked her.

Hailey and Charlie laughed.

"It's what servers in restaurants call annoying couples that sit on the same side of the table; usually, all over each other," Hailey explained and glanced at Emma. "And for your information, I just got here. Lena was over there. Charlie was on this side. I needed to steal food, and I didn't think it was fair to steal Lena's when I could take Charlie's. So, I sat here."

"What's mine is yours." Charlie slid her plate over. "I'm only a little offended that you sat here for the food, though."

Lena smiled at the banter between the couple. It reminded her a little of the new banter she shared with her girlfriend, and she looked forward to having more time together to develop it even further.

"Where's Summer?" Emma asked Lena.

"She's still in California, taking care of her dad," Lena replied and dug into her salad.

"Is he doing okay?"

"Yeah, he's doing really well, actually. I hope she can come back at the end of the week, but I don't want to pressure her to do so, if he still needs her there."

"Well, tell her I said hi next time you talk to her. Now, I need to order something. I'm starving."

"Me too. I can't eat all of Charlie's food," Hailey agreed. "Let's order at the bar. Probably faster."

***

"Dad, I'm not arguing with you about this. We are lending you money. That's the end of this conversation." Summer stood up from the small and very old sofa in her dad's living room. "I'm tired of arguing with you. Seth and I have money. You need money. Call it a damn loan, if you really want, and pay us back. I don't care. You're taking the money, or you're going to lose the house."

"I'd rather lose the house than take money from my children, Summer." He slammed down the glass of water he'd been drinking.

"What? How does that even make sense in your head, dad?"

"What did I just walk into?" Seth asked when he entered the house.

"Your sister is being unreasonable," Archie replied.

"Unreasonable? You're the one being unreasonable!" she shouted. "I stayed to help you get things in order, Dad. I have a life to get back to in Chicago. I have a girlfriend to get back to. But I'm here, trying to help you get back on your feet. Why can't you just accept the help?"

"It's probably not best to fight with the guy when he just had a heart attack, Sum." Seth closed the front door of the house.

"I'm going to bed." Archie stood slowly. "We're done talking about this."

"Oh, no, we're not," Summer objected. "But we can talk about it tomorrow."

Archie labored past her and down the hall. Summer settled back down on the sofa, and Seth joined her.

"I know he's a pain in the ass. Thanks for taking care of this stuff," Seth said.

"Thanks for staying here an extra couple of days before heading to Detroit," she replied and turned to her brother. "I appreciate it."

"I haven't done much. I've mainly just brought food."

"Well, sometimes, that's very helpful."

"Sum, we should talk."

"About?" Summer didn't like his tone.

"I'm not going to Detroit this week."

"Why not?"

"We moved up the negotiations with the vendors in the Philippines. I need to go there, to check the factory for the new hardware and sign the paperwork. It can't wait."

"Well, I guess that's good. Offering our own hardware is the right decision. That's why I approved it."

"And then, I'm going to go back to India, to check on the engineers and the office there because I'll be somewhat closer."

"And just how long is that going to take?" She lifted an eyebrow.

"I'll be in the Philippines for at least a week. I'm thinking I need at least three weeks with the engineers. We're reworking the entire structure of the team, using the pod approach, and changing how we do QA. I need to be there."

"Seth, that's another month away."

"I'm not going on vacation, Sum. This is work," he replied.

Summer sat up and put her face in her hands.

"That's how the last trip started, too. You went for

work, and instead of coming back, you toured half of Europe."

"I won't do that this time. I promise, I'll be back. I put off going until Thursday of this week so I could stay and make sure Dad was okay, but I really do need to be there. I'm not trying to flake, Summer."

She leaned back, leaving her hands in her lap, and said, "Maybe I wouldn't be worried about you doing that if you didn't do it all the time, Seth."

"I know this isn't what you want, but it is what's right for the company. I'm the CTO. It's the job. Summer, can you just stay on as the CEO for a little bit longer? When I get back, we can start the search for your replacement. It would just be delaying the change by a little."

"A little? I can't exactly say no, Seth. I *am* the CEO." She considered her options. "I'll make sure Dad is okay this week. If he's good, then I'll come back from vacation and get to work." Summer remembered something. "Wait. What about the convention and the meeting?"

She was referring to the week-long technology convention they were not only attending this year but also sponsoring and hosting in the convention center that was literally across the street from the HQ. This was their first attempt at something like this. And, originally, Seth was slated to attend many of the events. Summer had planned to make a brief appearance – if at all – the moment she found out Seth would be returning. They also had a major investor's meeting in three weeks. Seth had been scheduled to deliver the presentation regarding their move to include hardware along with their software and app offerings. Again, Summer had planned on attending, but her role would have been fairly minimal compared to Seth's, since he would be going through all of the technical information.

Summer realized in that moment, how little she actually wanted to be the CEO. She should have been clamoring to be the presenter at that meeting; to attend one of the largest tech conventions in the world and unveil their new products. But Summer hadn't been interested enough to try to steal that from Seth. In fact, she had been the one to beg him to do all these things. It was one of the main reasons Summer kept encouraging him to return from his European track. She couldn't believe in that moment, how long her heart hadn't really been in this business and how long she had thought about leaving but stayed anyway.

"You can handle all that, Sum. The speech for the convention has already been written. Hailey and her team put it together. They've even written the introduction for the investor's meeting already. They just need to change a few things, and you'll be fine. I'll have Palmer deliver the tech specs for you. He's the best Director of Engineering we've ever had. He can actually command an audience, and not just a keyboard."

"Seth, that would mean I'd have to be here for at least two more weeks. I'm supposed to be back in Chicago."

"I'm sorry, Sum. If you want, I can see if one of the other officers can handle at least some of it, but I don't think that's the best idea. You planned to be here, anyway."

"I planned to come for the Friday of the convention, just to make an appearance, stay the weekend, and then do the Monday meeting. I wasn't going to be here for that long, Seth."

"You can still go back to Chicago. I get it; Lena's there. Just stay here with Dad for the week and go back, like you planned. Then, come back for the convention and stay for the meeting. I should be back after–"

"Should be?" Summer stood. "Should be? That's not exactly inspiring, Seth, especially given your track record."

"Summer, I love you, but I'm done apologizing for this." The guy stood. "I appreciate the job you've done, especially when I went on vacation, but I'm entitled to take vacations, just like everyone else. And I'm also lucky because I can afford to take them all over the world." He ran his hand through his short dark hair. "You're the CEO. I'm not. That means you have more responsibility than I do.

I'm sorry if you don't want it anymore, but I am going away for work, and then, I'm coming back. If you want to resign tomorrow, do it, but stop blaming me for not liking the job or going on a vacation. It's not my fault you've never done that yourself."

"I couldn't do that, Seth, because you were always on one, or Mom was sick, and Dad needed help, or I had to run the company because you told me I'd be the right person for the job."

"I'm sorry I gave you bad advice, then, Sum," he replied a little agitated. "I'm not excited about missing the convention *I* helped plan and enjoy attending every year. I'm not excited about missing the investor's meeting. I'm going because I have to go. It's the job of the CTO. If you don't want to do your job, then quit. We can handle the backlash until we can find someone that actually wants it."

He turned to walk to the door.

"Seth…" Summer tried but failed to say other words after saying his name.

"What? You act like I'm trapping you in this. When we first started this, I thought you'd be good at it. I thought you liked it. But it's clear that you don't anymore. That's okay. But make a decision, then, Sum. Get out if that's what you want, but stop blaming me."

"I'm sorry," she replied.

"I know. Me too. I know I've been flaky sometimes, but I'm not the kind of guy you've had to clean up after. I've owned up to my responsibilities. I know you don't always see that, but even when I was on vacation, it's not like I didn't check in with my team. I didn't drop the ball on anything." He looked down and then back up at her. "I know you sometimes feel like the older sibling. And I get that I act like the younger one, sometimes. But I'm not Dad, Sum. He's an asshole, for sure, and he's also a mess, but I'm not him."

"I know you're not."

"I was going to come over here and see if you wanted

to play Mario Kart, like old times. Dad still has the console and stuff in the garage. I saw it the other day. I thought it would just be something fun we could do together before I leave."

Summer smiled at her brother and replied, "Sure. But I get to pick your character."

"That's not fair." He opened the door to go outside and get the console. "I get to pick the course, then."

"Fine, but you're Peach."

"Enjoy all those banana peels I'll throw at you from first place." He winked at her and headed to the garage.

CHAPTER 27

LENA HADN'T HEARD from Summer since Wednesday night, when they spoke only briefly before the woman had to help her dad change a bandage, and Lena needed to get some sleep. It was now Friday. Summer was due home Sunday night.

They had texted, but with the time difference and Lena's heavy workload since the deal was approved, it had been difficult to have more than five minutes alone to talk to one another. Summer had been staying at Archie's in her old bedroom, to be there in case he needed something in the middle of the night and to take care of Mo for him. She had told Lena that Archie was doing well, and that she should be able to leave on Sunday, as scheduled, but Lena hadn't been able to get any more than that out of her. Summer seemed distant and burdened with something.

"Hey, we have a problem." Gideon Lee, the Chief Legal Counsel for O'Shea's and one of her favorite people at work, entered Lena's office.

"What's wrong? I was just heading out. I'm having dinner with a friend tonight."

"You're an investor in Strange Joe's?" he asked upon sitting down.

"I am. It's in the paperwork."

"I know. I saw it. Honestly, I thought about turning the deal for the O'Shea's locations down, due to the conflict of interest. You work here. You would be making a profit on the locations inside the stores. I didn't, though, because it's you. I know you, and also I reviewed all the other options for other partners, and this is the smartest one for the company."

"Okay... Then, what's the problem?"

"Henry saw the paperwork, too, and reported it to O'Shea."

"Henry?" Lena groaned.

Henry was the VP of Development. He did not like that part of Lena's responsibilities intersected with his own, and that most people deferred to her judgment over his. He was on his way out and knew that everyone else knew it.

"He's making a play?" Lena asked.

"Trying to save his job, probably. I told our illustrious CEO that I don't see a problem here, but he's insisting we review the other options again and then make a final decision."

"Great," Lena retorted sarcastically. "What does that mean?"

"He's having Henry's team take the lead this time. Then, they'll send it up to me, but O'Shea wants more involvement to make sure this is the right choice."

"I'm out of the decision-making process even though this is the best option?"

"I'm sorry, Lena. I tried." He leaned forward. "They could still go with Strange Joe's. It really is the best partnership option for us. The profits, the PR for the community outreach you included, and the jobs it would create – it all works well with our mission."

"What if I take myself out of the picture? Vanessa, the owner, could get a business loan to afford the initial buy-in. It would still work," Lena said.

"Sure, but do you really want to do that?"

"Not really. But I also don't want her to suffer because I'm involved." Lena leaned back in her chair and caught the time on her wall clock. "I have to run. I'm going to be late as it is. How much time do I have to make a decision?"

"They're going to meet on Tuesday and hope to have a final recommendation to O'Shea by Friday. We'd go from there. Do you need a ride to your dinner? I brought the car today."

"No, thanks. I have one," she said.

"You bought a car? When?" He followed Lena out of her office.

"No, it's my girlfriend's. Well, it's a service, but she insists I use it."

Lena smiled widely, despite the bad news she'd just been given. That was the first time she had used the word *girlfriend* at work, and it felt good.

"Girlfriend? When did this happen?"

"Recently. She's in California right now, but she gets back on Sunday. I can't wait."

"Really? Well, maybe we can have the two of you over for dinner sometime. It's been way too long." He told her.

"Sounds good," Lena replied by the elevator. "I'll see you on Monday. And thanks for the heads up, Gideon."

***

"Dad, can I talk to you?" Summer asked softly as she stood in the door of her father's bedroom.

"Yeah, come in."

The man had been in a bad mood since their fight earlier in the week, but Summer hadn't had the energy to fight him anymore. They had gotten along – at best, throughout the rest of the week, but that had given Summer some time to figure out a different way to approach him and also come up with her next steps.

"I have some things I want to go over." She sat on the edge of the bed and held the papers she had brought in with her.

"Not this again, Summer." He noticed the paperwork.

"Dad, I talked to the bank yesterday. They're going to foreclose on the house unless you can make the balloon payment. You have thirty days, and that's it. The way I see it, there are two options. Option one, is that you let me take care of the mortgage outright, so you don't have to worry about it again," Summer said.

"Summer—"

"Hear me out. I know how much you hate that idea. So, I'm guessing that leaves us with option number two."

"Which is?" he asked.

"Let the bank foreclose. I'll buy the house from them. I already talked to the agent. They said it would be going up for auction. If I can buy it at their price before that, it's mine. Either way, you can still stay."

"Summer, I don't want you to–"

"You don't have a choice. I'm sorry. I've seen all your accounts. I know how much you make at work. It's nowhere near enough, on top of your new medical bills." Summer turned to face him, while still sitting on the edge of the bed. "It's one of those options, or you won't have a home, dad."

Archie leaned back against the propped-up pillows.

"I haven't had a home since your mom died, Summer," he replied after a long minute. "I let this place go. I know that's my fault. If she were still here, she'd hate what I'd turned it into. I don't know how to do this without her. I know you just want to help. I let my pride get in the way sometimes, but you're not a parent. You can't understand what it's like. You want to take care of your children. They shouldn't have to take care of you; or at least not until you're old and gray. I'm neither old nor gray."

"Not yet." Summer winked.

"I don't know how to let people help me, Summer. I never have. Your mom was the only one who knew how to get through my thick skull."

"I'm part of her, and I'm part of you. I think that gives me a head start over other people. I know this is a lot, but if you don't want to lose–"

"The house?" he interjected and looked around the room. "I think the reason I'm having a hard time with this place is that there are too many memories of her here. I can't seem to get rid of her stuff, but it's more than that. I can still feel her here."

"Me too," Summer agreed.

"And, as good as that is – and is it good, it's also bad."

"I understand."

Summer did understand. She could still feel her mother's presence in the kitchen, where she used to make brownies for Summer and Seth. She'd let them sneak one right out of the pan before she would allow their father to have one. That had been before she had gotten sick. Summer could still see her mom pale and thin on the sofa, watching TV, with bottles of pills and water on the coffee table.

"I don't think I can let you buy this house, Summer," he told her.

"Dad–"

"I can't let you because *I* don't want to live here anymore. I think that's why I've let it go, and why I haven't tried."

"You don't want the house?"

"This heart attack has had me thinking. I've just been going through the motions here. I've been stuck. I don't want to be stuck anymore."

Summer smiled at her father and replied, "Dad, that's great."

"I don't know what to do. Should I get an apartment?"

"We'll find you something. And you have to let Seth and I help you, at least until you're back to work full-time, and we get a better idea of what you can afford on your own. Oh, and we're taking care of your medical bills. That's already done. You can't argue," she said.

"I guess I can't." He squinted his eyes at her. "Maybe you do have more of your mother in you than I've given you credit for."

"What do you want to do with her stuff?" Summer nodded toward the closed closet.

"Just give me some time to adjust to it all being gone, okay?" He turned back to Summer. "And then, we can go through it. You should take anything you want. Seth should, too. We'll give the rest to charity."

"And one more thing," she added, hoping to catch him

in a good mood.

"What?"

"I want to go back to Chicago."

"Go. I'm fine here." He immediately waved her off as if she'd be leaving that exact minute.

"Not right now," she replied and laughed. "Seth's gone for a few weeks, and I'll be back, but Aunt Donna can't be here every day. I've hired a nurse to come check on you, and a dog walker to help with Mo."

"I don't need—"

"It's not for forever. She isn't a live-in one or anything. She'll just stop by once a day to check on you. She'll help with whatever you need. I've set up your iPad with a grocery delivery service. Just order what you want, and they'll bring it to the front door. Aunt Donna said she could come by Sunday nights, Tuesday nights, and Thursday nights for dinner and to help clean, if necessary. I'll be back for the convention. We can work on your living situation in the meantime and figure something out. I think the best situation is that I buy the place from you before they foreclose. It would just be so that we could sell it ourselves, and we wouldn't have the foreclosure on any records."

She waited for a moment while he seemed to be thinking hard about how to respond.

"That all sounds fine," he reluctantly agreed. "You've taken care of everything, I guess."

Summer let out a massive breath as she felt a tremendous weight lifting off her shoulders.

"I love you, you know?" she told him.

"I know," he said. "I love you, too."

***

Lena met Hayden at the restaurant only five minutes after their agreed-upon time. She hadn't seen him in a while, and he called to check up on her, so they decided to have dinner at one of their usual haunts. They had caught up on life since the last time they had talked, while they ate their appetizers, but now that they were in the middle of their entrées, Lena had a question she had been wanting to ask but had been putting off.

"So, I have a question for you."

"Shoot," he replied and stuck asparagus in his mouth.

"Did you hit on Summer?"

Hayden nearly choked.

"What?" He took a sip of his water. "Why would–"

"She said that the last time you guys saw one another, you were acting differently. I know about your 'no dating clients' rule, but you'd just gotten promoted and wouldn't be handling her account."

"Lena, I didn't hit on Summer." Hayden swallowed. "I promise. I'll apologize to her if I was acting strangely, but I wasn't hitting on her. I knew how you felt about her. And I knew how she felt about you. I wouldn't do that to you."

"Okay." Lena slid her fork around her Brussel sprouts. "I didn't think you would, but–"

"I wasn't trying to date Summer. I was trying to get her on board with my new company."

"What?"

"I got the partnership. That came with a nice bonus that I planned to use to form my own agency. I already have a partner. I was planning to ask Summer if she would be interested in a business partnership or an investment, just to get us started."

"Oh. Why didn't you ask me?" Lena asked him.

"You and I are friends. I didn't want to bring money into it. I know you make good money at your job, but I also know you just paid for a house upfront and all the renovations it entailed. I assumed you didn't have much left over for something like this. Usually, when people make those moves, that's their primary investment. They're not looking for a start-up real estate agency to help."

Lena laughed and said, "Summer thought you were flirting. I can't wait to tell her how wrong she was, by the way. If this is your dream, Hayden, and you need help, I'm sure we can figure something out."

"We were able to get a business loan. That's one of the reasons I called you. I wanted to celebrate." Hayden lifted his wine glass. "I'm branching out on my own. I'm resigning next week, and we've already found our new offices."

"Hayden, that's amazing. Congratulations!" Lena lifted her own glass along with him, suddenly celebrating not only his success but the fact that he hadn't betrayed her trust by trying to sleep with Summer.

"Oh, and Lauren and I are together officially now. I have a girlfriend."

"So do I," Lena replied and clanged their glasses together.

"Congratulations all around, then." Hayden laughed. "We're definitely getting dessert."

***

Lena felt a lot of competing emotions by the time she had said goodbye to Hayden. They'd gone out for drinks after their dinner. Lauren had joined them, giving Lena the chance to meet her for the first time. She liked the woman, and Hayden seemed perfectly smitten. That made Lena miss Summer, but she had to put that out of her mind because she wanted to celebrate Hayden's success. When they had parted so the two of them could get to Lauren's place, she had gotten a text from Charlie, saying that she, Hailey, and Emma were at The Lantern. Lena was only a five-minute walk away, so she joined them. It turned out to be pretty fun, because watching Hailey try to help Emma meet women was entertaining.

When Lena ordered a car, she dropped Hailey and Charlie off at their place and finally made her way home. She missed Summer even more after watching Charlie and Hailey together and seeing Emma hit it off with someone. Lena was also worried about the deal and needed to come up with a new plan, or figure out how to break the bad news to Van.

She had had a good time that night, though, and decided that would be the prevailing emotion that would carry her off to sleep. She needed more fun like that in her life. She unlocked the front door and dropped her bag by it, as always. Her phone buzzed before she could even stand up all the way again. Lena pulled it out of her purse and saw it was a text from Summer. She hadn't heard from her girlfriend for the past several hours, but that had been their norm lately.

Summer's message was only a, "Hello."

Lena stared at the phone for a second and then took a few steps into the living room as she was about to reply. Then, Lena felt the other woman before she even saw her, and when she finally looked up, she gasped.

"Hi," Summer said out loud and offered an adorable wave.

"What are you doing here?" Lena asked.

She was still. She couldn't move. She hadn't expected to see Summer until Sunday night at the earliest. Summer was the one that made the move toward her. She looked beautiful. She was wearing jeans, with a gray collared button-down. Her hair was down over her shoulders. Lena felt like she'd been in her own clothes for three days, and that her hair must look terrible.

"I took care of my dad. I set stuff up for him, and he kicked me out." Summer smiled and stood a foot away from Lena. "In a nice way. He kicked me out in a nice way."

"How–"

"He told me I should come see you." She reached for Lena's hips. "We can talk about it later, but... Can we just go upstairs?"

"Yeah, just let me hug you." Lena pulled Summer into herself and hugged the woman close. "God, I missed you," she said into Summer's neck.

"I missed you, too. I hopped on a plane as soon as he

was settled. I couldn't wait until Sunday." Summer held onto Lena's waist, and after a moment, she pulled back enough to stare into Lena's eyes. "Upstairs?"

"When did you get here? Why didn't you call? I was out with Hailey, Charlie, and Emma. I would have come home if I knew you were here."

Summer didn't respond. She just pulled Lena by the hand up the stairs and into the bedroom.

"I got in about fifteen minutes ago, and I wanted to do this first."

Summer motioned with her free hand to the room, which was filled with candles, illuminating the dark space. Their welcome light flickered all around them. There must have been at least thirty white candles. Some of them were tea candles, and other ones were larger, but all of them created a warm, inviting atmosphere; and Lena began to understand.

"I had to buy them in California, because I knew by the time I got here, everything would be closed. Luckily, I fly private, so no one asked any questions when I brought a big bag of candles on board." Summer turned to Lena, who was still in awe of the room.

"You did all this?"

"Lena, I love you." Summer held onto her waist again. "I love you. I've missed you this week. There's still a lot we need to talk about, but I don't want to do that right now." She ran a hand over Lena's cheek and then held it against her neck. "You said you wanted our first time to be in your bed."

"Really?"

"Unless you're too tired. Seems like you had a long day." Summer ran her hand down Lena's chest and held it softly between Lena's breasts.

"You're the one that flew across the country; and no, I am not too tired. I feel like I've been waiting for this forever," Lena replied. "Can we do one thing first, though?"

"Anything."

"Turn off our phones."

Summer laughed at that and shrugged. She had her phone in her back pocket, so she took it out, held the off-button down, and then slid her finger across the screen, while Lena did the same with her phone. When Summer was done, Lena grabbed their phones and placed both on the dresser before returning to stand in front of Summer.

"That may have been the best idea you've ever had." Summer began working on the buttons on Lena's shirt.

"I don't want any distractions tonight." Lena lowered her head, following Summer's movements as each button was released. She could not only see the buttons, as they were pulled from their catches, but also two trembling hands. "Summer, what's wrong?" Lena asked and placed her hands over Summer's, stilling them. "You're shaking."

"I'm nervous," Summer confessed without looking up to meet Lena's eyes.

"Why? You've–" Lena cut herself off, unable to determine the best way to say that Summer had done this before.

"Confession time?" Summer looked up at Lena now, and then dropped her hands to Lena's gray slacks, pulling the other woman toward herself a little more with fingers through Lena's belt loops. "I've never done this before."

"What?" Lena replied and was certain shock rang through her expression. "Been with a woman? You've had–"

"Yes, I've been with women," Summer interrupted with the clarification. "Not many of them. Three, to be exact. I've had sex with three women."

"Then, what were you talking about?" she asked.

"Lena, I've never had sex with someone I–" Summer lowered her head again.

"With someone you love?" Lena chanced.

Summer's eyes met her own again. There was clarity there that hadn't been before.

"Yes," Summer whispered, and Lena's arms went around her neck.

"Do you want to wait?" Lena asked.

"I've waited long enough. I just wanted you to know that's why I'm nervous. The stakes are high this time."

"Summer, I've never had sex with someone I love, either. Damon doesn't count," Lena explained after seeing Summer's look of confusion. "Even though I loved him, I couldn't love him with all of me. I'm gay. I held an important part of myself away from everyone, including him. As the years went on in my marriage, I knew I had never been *in* love with him. I loved him, yes, but not the kind of love I feel for you." Lena paused and dug her hand into Summer's hair. "I'm in love with you. I don't think I've ever really been in love before now."

That revelation seemed to make Summer more confident in her stare, and her hands returned to their place on the last two buttons of Lena's shirt before she slid it off the woman's shoulders and let it fall to the floor.

Lena had experienced confidence problems of her own in the past. She'd had Summer to help her get through some of them, but she was certain that she had never used her own experience to give someone else confidence like this. That made her fall even deeper in love with the woman in front of her.

Summer lifted the white undershirt up and off Lena's body, leaving her only in her white bra. Lena cursed herself for grabbing an old bra out of the drawer that morning, instead of putting on something a little more alluring. She hadn't expected Summer until Sunday.

Lena's hands were on the move. When Summer's lips hit her neck with soft, satisfying kisses, Lena's hands couldn't hold back. They worked Summer's buttons more quickly than Summer had worked her own. Within moments, Summer's shirt was spread open, and Lena had her hands on Summer's stomach. She gave a little push, and Summer lifted her head back in understanding. Her shirt, too, was left to fall on the floor, leaving the woman only in her bra, which Lena pulled off hastily.

It was as if Lena couldn't wait another moment before she had Summer Taft beneath her body. She had waited, and wanted, and almost had her for too long. The familiar pulse started to beat between her legs. Summer must have felt a pulse of her own, because her hands quickened at Lena's back, pulling off her bra. Then, her lips were on Lena's.

They were moving fast with Lena's lips, and then harder, too, as Summer backed herself up to the end of the bed while her hands worked Lena's pants now. Lena allowed Summer to undo her button and zipper before she shimmied her body out of the dress slacks and then kicked them the rest of the way off. She pressed Summer's legs against the bed and held onto her waist while giving her another little push. Summer sat and pulled Lena's body to her lips. They were on the other woman's stomach while Summer's hands covered Lena's breasts, but Lena felt Summer everywhere. Her nerves were on fire in a way she had never experienced. She felt the warmth and wetness in Summer's kisses dance across her skin, leaving cold in their wake.

Summer's hands were lightly tugging at taut nipples and then squeezing Lena's breasts. Lena's eyes closed of their own accord when Summer's lips met a nipple and took it into her mouth. Lena gasped, and her hands went to the back of Summer's head to coax her on. Summer sucked and nipped before moving her lips to the other nipple to repeat the motion.

Lena needed to be lying down. Her legs were shaking. She hadn't done this in a while, and her body was more than ready to be touched, but it was more than that. She craved Summer in a way she had never craved anyone before in her life. So, when Summer was about to move her lips again, Lena's hands went to her shoulders, and she gave Summer a push onto the bed.

***

Summer was lying topless on Lena's bed, gawking up at the beautiful, nearly naked woman in front of her. Her lips were swollen already from the attention they'd just paid Lena's taut nipples, but she wanted more. She wanted to lose herself in this woman. She watched as Lena leaned over her and reached for her jeans. The button was undone and then the zipper. Lena's eyes met Summer's as she pulled the jeans down her body and then off entirely. Summer was left in her black bikinis while Lena was in pink ones.

Summer could see how wet Lena was from her position, thanks to the light color of the panties the other woman wore. She wanted to do more than just see it. She wanted to touch it, to taste it, to revel in every bit of Lena Tanner. Lena's eyes came back to Summer's. Summer saw a little nervousness there, and for a second, she wondered why, but then, Lena's hand rested right beneath her belly button. Lena's thumb was touching the waistband of her underwear and sliding up and down. She was wordlessly asking if she could remove them. Summer nodded.

Lena used both hands to drag Summer's underwear down her body before returning to lean over and kiss Summer heatedly. Summer wanted more. She pulled down on Lena's panties, giving her the hint. Lena pulled them off her legs herself and then finished climbing on top of Summer. They kissed as they both shimmied to the top of the bed, where Lena's body crashed into Summer's.

"Oh, God," Summer let out the moment she felt breasts against her own and hips pressing into her.

It was the first time they had both been completely naked in front of the other; the first time they'd felt their hips against each other like this, with nothing between them. Summer held onto Lena's neck as Lena continued to kiss her. The kisses slowed when Lena's hand slid to the outside of Summer's thigh and stilled. Summer moaned when the hand slid further inward, and Lena's tongue darted out of her mouth to slide across Summer's bottom lip. Lena sucked it into her mouth and then pushed gently on

Summer's thigh to get her to spread her legs. Summer did as wordlessly commanded, and Lena's hips pressed into her, while her mouth moved to Summer's neck.

"I've wanted you since that first night," Lena whispered into Summer's ear before capturing the woman's earlobe between her teeth.

Summer felt Lena's center press into her own as Lena's hips rocked, still slow, down into her.

"You feel really good."

Summer knew she sounded breathless already, and they had only just begun, but she decided that if she was going to share this experience with Lena, she would share all of herself, even the nervousness. She wouldn't be embarrassed by how Lena made her feel.

"Can you look at me?" she asked of Lena.

When Lena lifted her head up and connected their eyes, Summer couldn't hold it in even if she'd wanted to.

"Beautiful," Summer said as she noticed the tiny flecks and then felt Lena's hips roll into her, forcing her own eyes to close.

"Yes, you are," Lena whispered and reconnected their lips.

Summer wondered when Lena would touch her where she really needed her to, but Lena seemed content to go at this pace. Summer wouldn't want to rush this, despite the thudding pulse between her legs that only seemed to amplify every time Lena's hips rolled into her.

Summer's hands were on Lena's back, sliding up and down slowly over the smooth skin. But when Lena's rolls moved only slightly faster, Summer's hands cupped Lena's ass and helped her apply more pressure. Lena's breathing was faster as her lips once again, connected with Summer's throat, and her tongue slid down to Summer's collarbone. Lena shifted her leg, placing one thigh now between Summer's.

"Yes," Summer let out as she felt Lena's wetness on her own thigh.

It was such a foreign yet welcome feeling to her, that she almost forgot about her own arousal now coating Lena's thigh as she continued to rock into the other woman. Lena increased her pressure in both the thigh rubbing against Summer and in her movements, pressing down to increase the friction for her own benefit.

Lena's lips moved lower, causing her to slow her writhing, but while Summer missed that consistent contact, she was happy when Lena's lips attached themselves to her nipple. She had never felt particularly sensitive there, like some women seemed to be, but maybe that was because her past lovers didn't do whatever it was Lena was doing to her. The sucking Lena was applying to her right nipple, combined with the light twisting she was doing to the left, had Summer squirming beneath her. The nerves in her breasts seemed to be connected to the ones much lower, that were currently sliding against a thigh.

Her orgasm began to build, and Lena hadn't actually touched her with the pressure and speed she normally required to get off. Summer had never had an orgasm from a thigh between her legs, but as Lena moved to her other nipple to begin her work again, Summer felt herself about to come. She wasn't sure how to say it. She had never had this happen before. It normally took time for her to reach orgasm. That was true even when she was touching herself. Her body required certain touches, and not everyone could get her there. Hell, Summer couldn't get herself there, sometimes.

"Are you okay?" Lena pecked Summer's nipple gently and then lifted her head to meet the woman's eyes.

"I'm just..." Summer gripped Lena's ass again and pushed her into herself. "I'm almost—"

"Yeah?" Lena lifted herself up and kissed Summer hard while she rocked down into her at a faster pace. "Really?" she asked when she pulled up for only a second to give Summer some time to answer.

"I'm sorry. I—"

"Don't apologize," Lena insisted and met Summer's forehead with her own. "Come for me."

"I don't want to. I want you to touch me," Summer gasped out as she felt herself on the precipice of an intense orgasm.

"I will, I promise. But come for me now."

Lena pulled back so that she could look at Summer's body. Summer felt her hips acting on their own, rising to meet Lena's thigh. She then looked at Lena's center that was grinding into her own, and that was all it took. Her head jerked back. Her hips jerked up and froze, while her eyes closed, and her mouth opened.

"Yes! Don't stop!" Summer screamed out.

Lena didn't stop. She continued sliding her own thigh along Summer's wet, hard clit at the same fast pace, while Summer remained frozen in place. When Summer yelled out in release once more, Lena slowed her ministrations to allow her girlfriend to come down fully. When Summer opened her eyes, after what felt like several minutes, Lena was looking down on her with all the love in the world.

"You're amazing," Lena said and kissed her lips sweetly.

Summer was having a hard time breathing. She knew it was because of the orgasm's intensity, but somewhere along the way, she also registered that it was because she had never been looked at before, how Lena was looking at her now.

"I love you," Summer said after a moment.

"I love you," Lena replied and kissed her again.

***

Lena couldn't believe what she had just witnessed. Summer, coming while under her body, was both the sexiest and most amazing thing she had ever seen. The woman was beautiful, and Lena wanted to do that all over again, except she wanted more of her girlfriend this time.

Summer seemed to finally be back down to earth. She lifted her head and noticed that Lena had stopped moving against her. Lena wanted her own orgasm, and she had definitely been close when Summer came beneath her, but she'd stopped moving because she wanted to watch more than she wanted to feel her own release in that moment. Lena felt her body begin to rock again on its own, but she still wasn't ready. She hadn't touched Summer how she had been dreaming about touching the woman. Lena wanted that more than anything. So, she slid her hand down between Summer's legs and finally felt her.

"What are you—"

Lena cut Summer's question off with a kiss and dragged her fingers through Summer's wetness. Summer gasped and let out a guttural moan when Lena stilled two fingers at her entrance while toying with her clit with a flicking of her thumb. Lena took that as a good sign, and she slid her fingers inside while kissing Summer's neck. She had found a spot that seemed to be particularly sensitive and sucked while thrusting her fingers, using her hips to apply more pressure.

Summer's hips lifted up in time with her slow thrusts and curling fingers. Lena alternated curling with sliding in and out, and changed the pace of her thrusts every time Summer's hips started moving faster, and her hands gripped onto Lena's body harder. Lena wanted to make this one last. She slid her fingers out when Summer's moan vibrated in her throat, and then used her fingers, coated in Summer's arousal, to slide on either side of her girlfriend's clit, not applying any significant pressure.

Summer was getting impatient. Her hips were lifting, searching for pressure and friction to help get her there. Lena smirked into Summer's neck and sucked on her pulse point just as she pushed back inside, deeper this time. She pushed her thigh into her fingers as well. Lena's thrusts increased in speed and strength because of that. Summer was grunting more than moaning at this point, and Lena realized that the woman was nearly there. As much as Lena wanted to make it last, the sounds Summer was emitting were too much. She wanted to hear her release and feel it on her fingers.

Summer did not disappoint. She yelled Lena's name and a few expletives Lena hadn't ever heard her girlfriend utter as she came. Again, Lena allowed her to ride out her pleasure as she kissed Summer's throat, jawline, and mouth. Summer's entire body relaxed beneath her.

"Hi," Lena greeted somehow nervous, even after what they'd just shared.

"Hi," Summer replied, apparently feeling the same way. "I want you." She ran her hand through Lena's hair.

"You have me," Lena replied and kissed her.

***

Summer wasted no time in flipping them over. She had wanted to be on top of Lena like this for what felt like forever. She knew that Lena had to be close already, given what she'd felt like against Summer's thigh moments ago. She also knew Lena would likely come quickly the first time. She decided to embrace that and moved her lips to Lena's nipples and then back to the stomach she'd kissed earlier, before sliding lower and spreading Lena's legs.

Lena was watching Summer as she slid lower and placed her hands on the inside of Lena's thighs. She pushed them further apart, met Lena's eyes, and slid her tongue through the slick heat between Lena's legs.

"Oh!" Lena closed her eyes, dropping her head on the pillow.

Summer repeated the motion several times before applying subtle pressure with her tongue as it moved. Lena was definitely close. Summer paused to look at Lena's sex. She saw her glistening with arousal, swollen, and hard. Lena was ready. Then, Summer watched Lena's hands as they gripped the sheets, preparing for what was to come.

Summer smirked as she lowered her head back down, pulling Lena's clit between her lips and sucking hard and fast.

Lena's hips bounced up once and then twice. Summer flicked her tongue from side to side and then up and down, and the hips jerked again while Lena moaned. Summer lowered her tongue and pressed it flat, sliding it back up. She knew Lena was there as she sucked her girlfriend in again, harder this time, and Lena's hips bucked into her mouth, encouraging her on. Summer released one of Lena's legs and slid her hand under her mouth.

Her fingers went to Lena's entrance, and just as Lena screamed about God, Summer entered her and filled her completely. Lena gasped at the very unexpected contact. Summer couldn't believe how good it felt to be inside her. How had she waited this long to do this? She thrust her fingers deep inside and curled them as she continued sucking. Lena's body began thrashing harder against her mouth. The woman's hands both went to the back of Summer's head to keep her in place. Summer curled her fingers against Lena in time with the sucking motion and felt her come completely undone. She then slowed her movements when the grip on the back of her head went from painful-but-worth-it, to gentle. Lena was rubbing the back of Summer's head lightly, while Summer's tongue was still lightly grazing her.

"I want to do that again," Summer said and looked up at Lena, who still had her eyes closed. "You ready yet?"

Lena laughed a deep, satisfied laugh and said, "You might have to give me a few minutes."

"I can do that." Summer kissed the inside of Lena's thighs before lifting herself up and kissing her stomach, moving up to apply gentle kisses to Lena's nipples and her neck before meeting her lips.

"I can't believe we finally…" Lena stopped herself and rubbed Summer's back as Summer pressed down on top of her.

"Neither can I," Summer said into Lena's ear.

They remained like that for several minutes before Summer finally rolled off of Lena and remained on her side, holding her own head up with her elbow. She ran curious hands over Lena's now clammy skin, while Lena's eyes remained closed. Summer wondered if anyone had ever appreciated Lena's body like this. She could stare at it all night. She could touch her all night just like this, applying gentle caresses and allowing Lena to feel her gratitude for being able to see her like this, exposed and satisfied.

Summer slid her hand between Lena's legs, after several minutes of adoration, and brought the woman to another orgasm, enjoying being able to watch her this time. The rise and fall of Lena's hips and chest were enough for Summer to need another release of her own. Lena must have realized this, too, because her eyes were open and connected with Summer's as she came.

Summer was certain she showed her intense arousal and desire in her stare. Lena pulled Summer on top of herself, and Summer straddled her hips. Lena watched Summer rub against her stomach and come after only a few hard and fast movements. Summer liked that Lena watched her get off. It was a new brand of excitement she'd never experienced. She wanted to do that again and, likely, again after that.

***

Lena's body was shifting. Her eyes remained closed, and she was very much groggy from sleep, but she knew that her body was shifting somehow. Her legs were also moving, but she was in bed. It took her another full minute to determine that the shifting had something to do with Summer's hand sliding up and down her thigh, moving inside, and then down and back up again, ever closer to Lena's center. Lena kept her eyes closed, not wanting to betray the fact that she was awake. She didn't want the touches to stop.

Summer's finger ran along Lena's hip bones and back down to her thigh in an attempt to coax Lena out of her slumber. When Lena's hips lifted ever so slightly on their own, Lena could swear she sensed a smirk on Summer's face, despite her eyes still being closed. Summer said nothing, but she dragged her finger to the apex of Lena's thighs and slid it up and then down through dark blonde curls, not touching anything that would offer Lena release.

"Admit that you're awake, and I'll continue," Summer said.

"I don't want you to continue. I want you to do something else," Lena replied in a husky voice.

"Oh, you do, do you?" Summer asked in a sing-song tone. "What exactly do you want me to do?"

Summer's lips were on Lena's shoulder, migrating toward her neck.

"I want you to roll over onto your back," Lena began and opened her eyes to see Summer now staring down at her with an inquisitive expression. "And I want you to spread your legs."

Summer dipped her finger into the wetness that had already begun to build.

"Are you sure? Your body seems to want something else." She wiggled two extremely sexy eyebrows at Lena and repeated her movement.

"My body can wait. My mind wants you." Lena lifted Summer's hand and removed it from her body, to Summer's surprise.

She rolled Summer onto her back with a push and climbed on top of her. Summer let out a wicked laugh as Lena spread her legs by pushing her thighs apart. Lena hadn't done this last night. She wanted nothing more than to wake herself up by going down on her hot girlfriend, who was already more than ready for her. Lena glanced up at Summer's eyes. They were staring down at her with need. Lena wondered how long the woman had been awake, waiting for Lena to join her just so that they could do this again.

They had fallen asleep earlier but had woken later, somehow at the same time, reaching for one another again. They came together with Summer grinding down into Lena, while her fingers were buried inside Lena's body. Lena was so exhausted from the week, the late night, and their activities, that it felt more like a very vivid and very welcome dream than her reality. That was probably because she'd dreamed about this exact scenario many times since meeting Summer Taft.

Lena's tongue met Summer first. Summer's hips jerked immediately. Lena smirked this time and answered her earlier internal question. Summer had been up for a while, apparently. The woman was wetter than she had been last night, and her clit was swollen and in need of attention. Lena devoured it; aware of Summer's responsive body and sounds by the alternating guttural moans and gasps, and the fact that Lena had to place an arm over Summer's stomach to hold her down and in place.

Lena's own arousal burned in her belly and settled between her legs. She was nearly hanging off the bed, and her hips began to move down as she matched Summer's hips moving up in time. As Summer let out a particularly loud scream, and Lena squeezed her own thighs, she knew she was close to getting off herself as she then started to squeeze repeatedly, allowing her clit to have some relief.

Quickly, she lifted herself from between Summer's legs. Summer's head shot up in shock at the loss of contact. Lena didn't say anything. She just shifted lower until her knees were on the floor. Then, she yanked Summer's legs toward herself, hard enough so that Summer's center was at the end of the bed and in front of Lena's greedy mouth again. Summer's chest was rising and falling rapidly. Lena took full advantage of the view for a moment as she spread her girlfriend's legs wider and leaned in to slide her tongue as deep as it would go inside Summer's body.

"Fuck!" Summer shouted.

Lena almost laughed at the swear word coming from the woman, but she kept herself in check to focus on sliding her tongue in and out. She used one hand on Summer's breast, kneading it and twisting the painfully erect nipple, and her other hand, to give Summer's clit attention with soft rubbing, followed by circling it with two of her fingers.

Summer's hips were firing like bullets off the bed. Lena recognized that her orgasm was near. She slid her tongue back up and refocused her mouth on Summer's clit while sliding her fingers inside, where her tongue had just been. Now, both of her hands were on Summer's breasts, full and firm, and smooth as silk. Lena's body craved contact, but she had knelt down on the floor to focus on Summer. She squeezed her thighs harder, not to try to come but to stop her pooling wetness from dripping down her thighs while Summer came in her mouth.

Lena twisted Summer's nipples lightly. Summer's hands unclenched from the fists they'd been in and settled on top of Lena's, pushing Lena to twist and squeeze more as she continued to come. Lena's thrusts and ministrations against Summer's clit slowed as Summer came down, and then they stopped, when Summer's hands went to the back of Lena's head and encouraged it up.

"What?" Lena asked with a wicked grin.

"I can't take anymore," Summer laughed.

Lena kissed the inside of each thigh and then the woman's hips and stomach just below Summer's belly button. Her tongue swirled around it before sliding up Summer's abdomen and between her breasts. Summer sat up on her elbows while Lena moved to stand in front of her. Summer's eager eyes took in the nude woman in front of her. Lena's eyes took in the rise and fall of Summer's chest, still faster than normal, and watched Summer close her legs and beckon her forward with a long finger that Lena wanted inside herself.

***

Summer had had sex with three women prior to Lena Tanner. She'd had girlfriends; more than three, of course, but she was young when she figured out her bisexuality. Her first girlfriend had turned out to be less into women the further along they'd gotten. While Summer had been ready to take that step, she had kept them rounding first base for a while, until she dumped Summer for a boy and never looked back.

Her two long-term relationships with women, that actually escalated to sex, had both been good initially, as most relationships were. The first one, Adelyn, was a lesbian who, it turned out, wasn't a big fan of going down on women. Summer hadn't wanted to pressure her into doing something she didn't enjoy or wasn't comfortable with. Their sex life had been adequate, at best, and later, non-existent. Summer's next and last long-term girlfriend had been Megan. She had no problem with any sex act, really, but Summer had always had difficulty coming easily. So, she normally faked it to spare her feelings.

The third woman Summer had been with hadn't been a girlfriend at all but had been Emma Colton. Their experience was rushed, heated, and driven slightly out of Emma's need to try to get over Eli and the alcohol they'd both consumed. Emma hadn't gone down on Summer, and Summer hadn't done that to her.

Only one of Summer's boyfriends had been able to use his mouth to make her come, but it had been lackluster and only left her wanting more. Later, she'd even questioned if it had been an orgasm at all.

Lena was different. Summer planned to not only tell the woman how much, but to, hopefully, make her body feel just as good. Lena's tongue and lips had found spots Summer hadn't found during her own explorations. Summer's body was still thrumming from her orgasm, but as she sat up straight, all she wanted, was to make Lena's body thrum the same way.

She pulled Lena's hips toward herself and encouraged Lena to straddle her lap. Summer held her in place as she felt Lena's wet center press against her. Lena didn't move her hips to search for friction. She seemed to want Summer to lead now. Summer had no problem giving her girlfriend exactly what she wanted. Her lips pulled a nipple between them, and she sucked while Lena's arms wrapped around her shoulders and pulled Summer closer. When Summer switched to the other nipple, she let one hand slip between their bodies to cup Lena's sex, which caused the woman to jerk into her hand. Summer nipped at the pebbled bud in her mouth and slipped her fingers inside Lena on the second jerk of Lena's hips.

"Yes," Lena let out.

Summer felt Lena's hands gripping the back of her neck and pulling slightly on her hair. Lena rocked against her hand, causing Summer's fingers to slide deeper inside and then almost out, while, at the same time, Summer's palm pressed hard against Lena's clit. Summer held onto Lena's back and cupped her ass while Lena rocked and jerked against her. Summer's lips found the woman's pulse point and sucked before finally meeting Lena's lips, as Lena looked down at her and gripped her face with both hands, lifting Summer's lips to her own. Summer's tongue met Lena's, and they danced, as Summer felt the walls begin to tense and pulse around her fingers.

"Come for me," Summer ordered softly between kisses.

And Lena did. Her hips moved so quickly, Summer could no longer support her in their position. She lay back and allowed Lena to ride her fingers to continue her orgasm. Summer held onto her hip while Lena rocked, and Summer was certain she had never seen anything so sexy in her life. Then, Lena dropped her hands on each side of Summer's head and continued grinding her hips down into Summer's body. Summer was certain, again, that she had never seen anything so sexy in her life. Lena was letting go. She was taking what she wanted, what she needed, and there was something so very primal about it. Summer could watch it every day for the rest of her life and not get enough.

As Lena's nipples were brushing against hers, Summer felt her body react when she had not expected it to. Lena's rocking wasn't even hitting her in a spot that would do anything for her, normally. Summer's fingers and wrist were starting to hurt, but neither of those things mattered, because just as Lena seemed to come for a second time, Summer's own orgasm built, and she was shooting over the edge, lifting her hips in time with Lena's.

When Lena crashed down into her body, spent and sweaty, pressed against her, Summer's breathing was just starting to slow down from the intensity of her own orgasm. Summer clutched Lena to her body, enjoying her warmth, her softness, and the sound of Lena's still rapidly beating heart against her chest.

"I love you," Lena whispered into her ear.

"I love you, too," Summer whispered back.

CHAPTER 28

LENA HAD FALLEN back to sleep after their most recent round of lovemaking, and then, woke to the sounds of Summer leaving the bed. She opened her eyes and rolled to see Summer's naked backside heading into the bathroom. She turned to check the time and noticed it was already noon. They'd failed to have breakfast, and it was now lunchtime. At that thought, Lena realized how hungry she was. But the idea of the two of them leaving the bedroom wasn't appealing. She felt as if she'd discovered herself last night, and again, this morning. She had never had orgasms like this before.

The fact that it was with Summer, the first person she ever really loved with her whole heart, her whole self, made it feel that much more amazing. Lena silently wondered if that was why it had been so good, to begin with. Maybe she was always supposed to be with Summer, and their sex was supposed to be this good because of their feelings for one another. Lena thought about the fact that she was almost thirty-seven. She finally, for the first time in her life, knew what it was like to love and be loved in return for all that she was, and to feel that manifest physically in the intimate acts shared between two people. Summer emerged from the bathroom, rubbing her eyes adorably. Lena watched with a smile as the woman lowered her hands and realized Lena was awake, lying on her stomach and staring at her.

"Did I wake you?" Summer asked as she sat on the side of the bed and ran a hand along Lena's spine.

Lena's eyes closed for a moment as she enjoyed the light caress of the fingers sliding along her skin.

"Yes. How do you plan to make it up to me?" she teased.

Summer smiled, leaned down, and kissed the spot between Lena's shoulder blades.

"I can order us food, since I'm sure you're hungry. I don't think either of us is up for cooking."

"Can we eat it in here?" Lena questioned and rolled over onto her back.

"That's up to you. This is your bed." Summer stood and walked over to the dresser where she had placed their phones the night before.

Neither of them had exactly jumped at the opportunity to turn them back on, so Summer passed Lena her phone first, and then, turned her own on. Lena regretfully turned her phone on but placed it on the table without glancing at any of the notifications.

"It's your bed, too, you know?" Lena sat up when she noticed Summer sitting up and staring at her phone.

"Is it?" Summer turned her attention from the phone to Lena. "I know we talked before, but are we really just going to…"

"Live together?" Lena asked and ran her hand through Summer's hair. "It's funny, because I didn't live with Damon until after we were married. I thought we should wait until we were engaged. Then, I doubted that would even happen. When he proposed, I accepted more out of fear than anything else. He wanted to move in right away, but after the accident, I told him I needed some time. Then, it just made sense to wait until after the wedding." Lena paused and toyed with strands of Summer's hair. "I was so scared back then, of living with someone else. I was afraid that if I lived with him, he'd find out who I really was, and that I was hiding something from him. I didn't even know what I was hiding. I hadn't figured it out yet, but I thought I'd be found out."

"And now?" Summer asked softly.

"Now, I'm not scared," Lena stated confidently. "I'm scared in the way that I think everyone gets scared when they start a new relationship and take the big steps, but I'm not scared beyond that. That's a big deal for me. I feel like you were supposed to be here all along. When you were gone, the room was missing something." Lena then looked around the bedroom. "And it made no sense at first, because this has been my room since long before I ever met you. But now, I get it."

"You do?"

"I think it's always been your room, too." Lena smiled at her.

"So, I live here now?" Summer asked with a smile.

"Yes, you live here now," Lena stated.

"Okay." Summer's smile grew bigger. "Now, I just have to move all my crap in."

"Not right now." Lena leaned in and offered Summer a kiss. "Put your phone away." She tried to cover the screen with her hand so Summer couldn't see it.

"I'm trying to order us food, babe." Summer laughed. "You do want to eat, don't you?"

Lena wiggled her eyebrows and slid down Summer's body.

"Yes, I do, actually."

Summer nearly cackled as Lena pulled her down into a lying position and spread her legs for the second time that day.

**

Summer and Lena spent the rest of their Saturday in bed, enjoying one another in new ways between meals and breaks. They spent their evening going through Summer's books and organizing them in the office. They'd have to find bookshelves for them, but in the meantime, the books would rest on the floor. Summer made them sundaes again, around midnight, which Lena told her was excessive, but Summer didn't listen. Instead, she scooped ice cream into bowls while Lena looked on and laughed as some of the chocolate syrup somehow ended up on her shoulder, and

Summer just had to lick it off.

"Have you ever had sex on this counter?" Summer asked as she lifted Lena up the same way Lena had lifted her before.

Lena laughed as one of Summer's hands tugged at her shirt to remove it while the other one reached for the syrup again.

"I don't think I've ever had sex outside of a bedroom," Lena admitted.

Summer pulled back and met her eyes just as Lena lifted the shirt over her head and tossed it aside.

"Really?"

"Damon was pretty traditional, and I think I've had more sex today than in all the years since my divorce."

"Yeah?" Summer smirked at her and held the bottle upside down, allowing the rich brown syrup to drip down between Lena's breasts.

"Yeah." Lena gasped as Summer's tongue met the bottom of the slow-moving stream and licked up, spreading the chocolate as she did. "I've never done *this* before, either."

Summer spread Lena's legs, loving the feel of the woman's soft skin on the inside of her thighs as she kept her hands there and moved between the two smooth legs.

"I think we should change that right now." Summer's tongue met Lena's pulse point before she sucked the same spot. "And then, we can do it in every room in the house."

Lena let out a laugh and then stifled it as Summer's hand found her center over the bikinis she had put on when they left the bedroom to come downstairs. They hadn't gotten properly dressed all day. The most clothes they'd had on involved a bathrobe of Lena's, that Summer had thrown on to meet the delivery guy that brought the food, and she had been naked under it.

Summer didn't give Lena time to say no because she could feel the woman beneath her hand was more than ready. While she licked chocolate off her girlfriend's shoulders, neck, and breasts, Summer slid her fingers into the blue panties and toyed with the wetness, while Lena leaned back and allowed her.

***

"Hey. Did we know you were coming?" Summer asked when she opened the front door on Sunday mid-morning to see Hailey and Charlie standing there.

"That's so cute. You're using *we* now." Hailey walked in, and Charlie followed her.

"She said she called you," Charlie said of her fiancée.

"She lied," Summer replied as she closed the door behind them. "Lena's out back, talking to Van. What's up?"

"Van?" Hailey asked as they made their way into the living room.

"They're working together," Summer explained and followed behind them, still a little curious as to why her friends would just show up like this without calling.

"I did try to call you, you know?" Hailey, apparently, read her mind. "Your phone was off… again."

Summer smirked at the fact that they'd turned their phones off again that morning, when they didn't want to be interrupted having sex on the sofa Charlie and Hailey were currently sitting on.

"Sorry. Is something wrong?"

"No, nothing's wrong. We were just going to take you guys to lunch. Em and Eva are going to join us. We thought we'd try to at least narrow down a date for the wedding." Charlie turned to see that Hailey was smiling.

"I can check with Lena. I'm not sure how much longer she'll be. Van only got here a few minutes ago." Summer glanced out the back window, where she could see Lena and Vanessa leaning over a laptop at the patio table. "Before I do, though, can I just gush like a schoolgirl with a crush for a minute?" Summer plopped down unceremoniously into a chair across from them.

"That good, huh?" Hailey asked with a lifted eyebrow.

"Hails, I never knew it could be this good," Summer replied.

"The sex?" Charlie asked.

"That too." Summer smiled back. "We haven't even known each other that long, but it feels like we have. I owe you big time, Charlie." Summer turned her attention to the pixie-haired woman to Hailey's right.

"You do?"

"I wouldn't have met her without you. You and I met, and you and Lena met. All this time later, she and I meet. I think that's how it was supposed to happen. I feel it." She placed her hand on her heart. "It's like everything I've done in my entire life, has led me to her." She kept her eyes on the back of Lena's head and her wavy blonde hair. "Am I crazy?"

"No, you're in love. And I think it's great," Hailey stated and took Charlie's hand. "To change the subject for a second, though, what's going on at work, Summer? Seth's gone again. You're back here, but he told me you're doing the investor's meeting and the conference."

"I don't want to, but I am. He's coming back this time. And even though he's said that before, I actually believe him this time. I haven't told Lena yet, but I'm going back later this week."

"You just got here," Charlie said.

"I know, but I have to do this right." Summer's eyes turned to Hailey. "I'm going to resign."

"What?" Charlie sat up.

"I win." Hailey turned to Charlie. "Back rub for me tonight."

"Explain," Summer said.

"I told Charlie that I thought you'd resign within the next three months. She bet you'd go back and forth about it, but would stay for at least another year. I win." Hailey winked at Charlie. "Forty-five minutes of your hands on my back with that expensive coconut lotion."

"She acts like that's a big loss for me." Charlie winked back at her.

"You guys were taking bets on me?"

"You have a tendency of saying you're going to do something and then not do it. Then, you talk about how you've made the right decision only to change your mind again. Can you blame us?" Charlie asked.

"It took you weeks to decide on the curtains you wanted for your very temporary apartment. You bought them, hung them, changed your mind, and returned them," Hailey said.

"You have curtains in your apartment?" Charlie asked.

"No, I decided not to get the curtains after all. And I concede your point, but this is different."

"Why?" Hailey asked and leaned forward, matching Charlie's posture.

"I'm ready now. I talked to Seth about it. I think he's ready to be on his own there. I want my own place in the world, and I can't have it there. I've always just been Seth's little sister, who wouldn't have gotten the job otherwise. I've put up with it for this long, but I want something different for myself. I want more."

"What will you do?" Charlie asked.

"Finish school and then, figure it out after that." Summer looked back outside. "Be with her. Live here."

"Here?" Hailey asked.

"It is crazy, right?" Summer wondered out loud.

"It's only crazy if you think it's crazy. Do you think it's crazy?" Hailey replied.

"No. I think it's right. I want to move in officially and stop looking for a house here. And I'm not going to look for a place in Detroit because I won't be working for the company anymore. I'll sell my place in Palo Alto, or at least rent it out. I just want to be here with her. I don't want to waste any more time without her," Summer said.

"I think that's great. Now, can we grab your girlfriend and Van, if we have to, and go get lunch? I'm starving, and

I want to get this wedding-planning started," Charlie said.

"People always think I'm the girly one of the two of us. But, babe, you definitely give me a run for my money sometimes." Hailey leaned over and kissed Charlie's cheek.

"I'll see if Lena wants to go. No promises." Summer stood and headed toward the back door, leaving the two lovebirds on Lena's couch.

No, it wasn't Lena's couch. It was her couch, too. It was their couch. Summer smiled at that thought and opened the door to see Lena immediately look up and smile at her.

"Hey, Hails and Charlie just showed up. They wanted to know if we could go to lunch. Ember and Eva are going to be there. They want us to start wedding-planning."

"Oh." Lena turned to Van, who had only just looked up from the laptop.

"It's cool. I think we're about done here. I need to run everything by my attorney, anyway," Van said.

"You can come, too, if you want. You've been invited," Summer told her.

"No, I should get going. I'm closing tonight, since one of my managers needed the night off. I'll just head in a little earlier. I'll call you when I hear back from the lawyer, but I think this is a good idea."

"Me too." Lena stood. "So, where are we going to lunch?" she asked Summer.

"I didn't get that far," Summer replied.

She held out her hand for Lena to take, while the woman clutched her own laptop between her body and her arm. They headed inside the house, with Van in tow, and then, into the living room.

"Hey, did we know about this lunch thing?" Lena asked.

"*We* again, huh?" Hailey glanced at Summer, who just rolled her eyes at her friend.

"Did I miss something?" Lena questioned with a glance in Summer's direction and a squeeze to the hand she was still holding.

"No," Summer replied quickly but playfully.

"I'll see you later," Van said to Lena. "And it's nice to see the two of you again," she said to Hailey and Charlie.

"Van, you're single, right?" Hailey asked her.

"Oh, God. Here she goes again..." Charlie stood, pulling Hailey up with her.

"Yeah, I'm single. Why?" Van asked.

Lena set her computer on the coffee table.

"I'm going to get my purse. You good to handle this?" Lena asked Summer.

"I'll keep her in line," she replied.

"Van, call me later?" Lena asked.

"I will," Van replied and then returned her eyes to Hailey.

"My friend, Emma, the one you met her at the bar–"

"I remember."

"She's single, too."

"Oh," Van replied knowingly.

"We're going to The Lantern with her on Friday night. You should come with us."

"Because you're trying to set us up?" Van questioned as Lena laughed and walked off.

"It's better if you just lean into it." Charlie took Hailey's hand. "We'll be in the car. You guys can ride with us if you want."

"I was just suggesting that–"

"Hails, not everyone wants to be set up with someone," Charlie interrupted and pulled Hailey toward the front door.

"I should get going. Thanks for letting me borrow her today," Van said to Summer.

"She's really excited about this investment thing. So, I hope it works out."

"Me too. It's a huge opportunity for the business, but she'd be giving up the investment."

"What?" Summer asked.

"Because of the conflict of interest thing her company

brought up."

"Conflict of interest?" Summer asked.

"I'm sure she'll fill you in, now that we have a plan." Van gave her a small wave and followed Hailey and Charlie out.

Lena swayed back into the room, seeming awfully chipper for someone without an investment. Summer waited for the door to close behind Van before turning to Lena.

"Hey, what's this about – you giving up the investment in Strange Joe's?"

Lena stopped a foot in front of her, seemingly surprised.

"I was going to tell you about it tonight, after Van and I got a plan together. Plus, you and I have had other things on our minds this weekend." Lena wiggled her eyebrows.

"True. But, what happened?"

"Some asshole at the company cried conflict because I'd be an investor and an employee at O'Shea's. He's just out for my blood. He has been ever since he found out about my family."

"Your family?" Summer asked and headed toward the front door to open it for them.

"We own TanAgro. And TanAgro does a lot of business with grocery stores; that includes O'Shea's. My grandfather, actually, is golfing buddies with the CEO of the company." Lena walked out the door past Summer, who followed. "He thinks I got the VP job because of nepotism, but he doesn't know that when I applied for the job, I actually had a different last name. I was Lena Durant. I only changed my name back to my maiden one after. I was in the process of doing it when I got the job. The people who interviewed me had no way of knowing who I was. But that hasn't stopped him from creating the gossip that they did, and that I'm not qualified."

"I think your success speaks for itself." Summer took Lena's hand as they watched and waved at Van, who pulled out of the driveway and walked in the direction of Hailey and Charlie, who waited for them.

"He's technically right. I can't argue with him on the ethics of it all. I made some changes to the original plan so that everyone comes out a winner."

"But you're not an investor?"

"No, I'm going to loan Van the money privately and at a cheaper rate than any bank would. O'Shea's doesn't need to know where she gets the money from, anyway. She'll be able to afford the initial overhead, and I'm not losing out on being an investor completely. We're just doing it differently. I will own 25% of the company, and any of the money due to me will actually go into a charitable organization I'm going to set up and name after Leo." Lena smiled as she arrived at the car door and opened it for Summer. "I'll fill you in on the rest later, but it's a good idea, and it's going to help people, too."

"That's amazing, Lena." Summer leaned over and kissed her sweetly.

"Gross. Get in the car, you two," Hailey scolded.

CHAPTER 29

"I MISS YOU," Lena told the screen.

She was lying in bed, setting up her new iPad case that she had purchased specifically for her FaceTime dates with Summer during their time apart.

"I miss you, too. Tell me how it went. I'm dying over here." Summer was sitting on her sofa, waiting for a pizza to arrive, since it was hours earlier in California.

"They're considering it. I don't have a definitive answer yet," Lena replied.

"I thought you said you'd have an answer today," Summer returned.

"I thought I would." Lena adjusted herself in bed so she could lie on her side and still see Summer's face. "They seemed to be okay with the idea. The boss is pretty big on Chicago. He grew up on the South Side and is a self-made man. Any time he's able to see a profit and somehow also help people, he doesn't require much convincing."

"Then, why no answer?" Summer asked.

"I think he was just putting on the show to appease the rest of the VPs. He'll tell me tomorrow. I'm pretty sure it's a go."

"Have you told Van yet?"

"No, not yet. I don't want to get her hopes up. I told her it went well, but that they're still considering."

"That's nice of you. Hey, what are you sleeping in tonight?" Summer nodded with a smile.

Lena smiled back at her and pulled on her t-shirt.

"Yes, it belongs to you," she replied to Summer's real question.

"I like when you wear my clothes," Summer said and continued smiling. "So, can you come here this weekend?"

"I don't think I can, Sum." The smile left Lena's face. "I have a mountain of paperwork to do for one of our new locations. If the deal is approved, I'll need to keep up the momentum and get everything ready to go by Monday so that we can move forward. O'Shea is a fast mover once he makes a decision."

"Sounds like my polar opposite," Summer retorted.

"No, you have hard times with decisions themselves. There's a difference," Lena suggested. "And I haven't seen you having a hard time with any big ones lately."

"I'm here vacillating between leaving this job tomorrow, or staying on for the next few months."

"Why?" Lena asked.

"Because I don't want to leave anything undone," Summer replied.

"I hate to tell you this, babe, but anytime you leave a job, you'll be leaving more than one thing undone. The higher up you are, the more things will be left behind for others to work on in your absence; but that doesn't mean you shouldn't leave."

"Do *you* want me to leave right now?" Summer asked her with lifted eyebrows.

"What? No," Lena told her definitively. "I want you to do what you want. I love you, and I'd like you here with me, but I understand what a job like that entails. I'm a VP myself, but I grew up with CEOs and politicians. I get how much work goes into it. I get that you want to stay around for a while longer – or at least until Seth gets back, to make sure everything is as finished as it can be when you do leave."

"I sat in my office today, and I felt completely out of place," Summer began. "It was like the chair belonged to someone else. That's always a little how it's felt, but it was even worse today."

"Why do you think that is?"

"I guess because I know it's correct now."

"What do you mean?" Lena squinted at her through the screen.

"It feels like I've been in the wrong place for years now. I've decided to leave, and the chair knows I'm an imposter. The office knows I don't belong."

Lena chuckled at her and said, "Those are inanimate objects. They don't emote."

"You know what I mean, though. I'm going through the motions again, like Hailey has told me before. I hate that because that's not me." Summer let out a long sigh. "I'm the person that tries and excels, and doesn't just do something because it's required or because it's expected of me."

"You need to find something you want to do, Summer. You're allowed to enjoy your job."

"I know. I just don't know what that is." She turned away from the screen. "Pizza's here. Do you want to watch me eat it?" She turned back to Lena.

"I should get ready for bed. I have an early day tomorrow."

"Okay. I love you."

"I love you, too. Call me tomorrow," Lena replied.

"I will. Good night." Summer tapped the screen, froze for a moment, and then disappeared entirely.

Lena missed her immediately, but she folded up her new case and set it off to the side. It was still too early to go to sleep, but she was more than tired. The week so far, had been long and hectic. She had continued to work and present on the Strange Joe's deal, while also trying to balance all her other responsibilities. She had stayed late at the office every night and had gone in early each morning. It was strange to Lena because that, in and of itself, wasn't a new thing to her. She had always been early to the office and last to leave since she started at O'Shea's.

Since meeting Summer, though, she'd found a reason to sleep in a little longer and get home earlier. She realized, as she climbed into a hot bath to try to relax her tight muscles, that they'd never gone on that spa date Summer had proposed and booked. Lena decided she would book one for them when Summer got home. She also thought about how much they appeared to balance one another out. Summer made Lena more confident in her personal life, and made her realize there was more to life than her job. Lena believed she'd helped Summer with some tough decisions recently. She wondered, as she sank into the water, how Summer felt about that. Did she, too, find that they'd made one another better?

***

"Hey, Dad," Summer greeted her father as she entered the house, carrying groceries for him.

"Just in time. Jeopardy's on," he replied and motioned with the remote toward the TV.

Summer smiled at her father and continued on into the kitchen, to drop off the three bags.

"I haven't watched Jeopardy since I was a kid, Dad," she replied as she began to unload.

"It'll be like old times, then," Archie replied from the living room.

When Summer's mom had gotten sick, the woman wasn't able to leave the house much. They couldn't afford anything other than the standard channels back then. That meant a lot of *Wheel of Fortune* and *Jeopardy* after dinner. Unfortunately for Summer, she associated those shows and other alike programs with her mother's sickness and chose not to watch them anymore.

"I'm going to make you a salad with grilled chicken for dinner," she informed.

"And a burger?" he yelled from the living room.

"You wish." She laughed.

Summer had been in California for four days now and had spent more time with her father in that time than she had in the years prior. During their time together, they'd shared meals and told stories of happier times when Summer and Seth grew up. They had sorted through her mother's clothes and personal items, and had stacked them into piles.

After they had eaten dinner, they returned to the bedroom. She and Archie made additional progress with the boxes, and Summer carried some out to the garage to be picked up by the charity they had contacted, while the others would be there, awaiting Seth's return. She would take the ones that belonged to her now back to the house to ship to Chicago.

"I was thinking about something, and I wanted to run it by you," Summer shared after they'd retired to the living room for the night.

"Let me guess. It's about the house," he replied.

"Yes." She turned to her father, sliding a leg under her as she did. "I had an idea."

"Another one? You're just full of ideas lately," he teased.

"I'm moving to Chicago." She ignored his last remark.

"I know that, Summer."

"And I'm going to be resigning from the company when Seth returns."

"I know that, too."

"Do you want to stay in this house, Dad?" she asked quietly.

"What?"

"If you had a choice to stay here or to go, which would you choose?" Summer asked. "I can pay off the house. We can fix it up, put money into it, or you could move somewhere else."

"Where? An apartment or something? I don't want to take any more of your money."

"You could move into my house. I'm going to sell it, anyway. I don't need it. It's paid off and brand new. It's bigger than this place, but it's not a Hollywood mansion," she said.

"I can't take your house, Summer." He turned slightly toward her, placing his arm over the back of the couch.

"Why not? You wouldn't be taking any money. It's already paid off. You could do whatever you want to it. I have no emotional attachment to that place. The backyard is big enough for Mo, and it even has a pool, which you could use for exercise when the doctor clears you."

"It's your home, Summer," he replied.

"No, it's not." She smiled. "My home is in Chicago. She's blonde and about my height. She lives in this amazing house that I fell in love with the moment I walked in. That's my home. This place was just a house I bought because it seemed like I should buy a house. Dad, you could make it your home, though." Summer looked around. "I know this place is home to all of us, but it has some bad memories in it that make it hard to find the good ones."

"That's true." He lifted both eyebrows and dropped them back down a moment later. "And you really wouldn't care?"

"I want you to be in a decent house. That place is more than decent. I want you to start moving on with your life. This house isn't really a place for that." Summer placed her hand on top of his rough one.

"I'll think about it."

"That's all I can ask." She squeezed his hand and gave him a smile.

"Are you staying here again tonight?" he asked after a moment.

"No, I'm going to get back. I actually have some reports I need to review and sign off on some stuff before tomorrow. I'm going to take care of that and call Lena to say goodnight."

"She's good for you. I'd like to spend more time with her now that I'm healthy. Is she coming here anytime soon?" he asked.

Summer couldn't help but smile at her father's approval of her girlfriend.

"No, she's busy at work. Once I get there and settle in, though, I can arrange for us both to come back for a visit."

"Good." He stared at her thoughtfully. "Is she the one, Summer?"

"The one?"

"How I felt about your mother? She was the one. There will never be another one like her."

"Oh, I don't–"

"Yes, you do. You know it in your bones. That's what your mom said to me. She said when you love someone like you'll never love anyone else, you know it deep down inside. It hits you in the gut, like a punch. That's the signal you're supposed to pay attention to. Most people don't," he explained.

"You did," she replied with a smile.

"I didn't, at first." He laughed. "I felt it right away, but I was young and naïve. I thought I wanted to be single and date as many women as I could." He let out another deep laugh. "She was persistent, though. When we were just starting out, she told me she wanted to be exclusive. She didn't date a man if he was dating other women. I told her that I needed some time, and she said that was fine, but that she wouldn't wait around for me." He paused. "I took the night and called her the next day."

"Really?"

"I didn't really need the night. I was just too stubborn to agree with her right away."

"What was it that did it for you?" she asked with a smile.

"The thought of her finding someone else while I was being an idiot," Archie replied immediately. "Just imagining your mom with another man, while I sat on the side and watched them fall in love, was enough. I proposed less than a year later. I only took that long because I needed to save up money to buy her a decent ring."

Summer hadn't seen her father smile like that in a very long time.

"That's a great story."

"So, is Lena? Did you get the gut punch?"

Summer contemplated his question and slid her hand off of his to join it with her other hand in her lap while she did.

"I did. I got punched repeatedly."

"Yeah?" He seemed surprised.

"When I first saw her, it was her eyes that did me in. You've seen them."

"I have."

"They're gorgeous. I could swim in them." Summer paused. "The second time was when I walked into her house. I felt it immediately. It was like home to me, and I'd never even been there. Every room is how I'd want it to be, and she's there in it with me."

"And the third time?"

She squinted her eyebrows, wondering how to tell her father this part.

"When we kissed for the first time. I felt fireworks. I was consumed." There was also the fourth punch, but she'd keep that one to herself, because that one hit her the first time they'd made love. "It feels epic, Dad."

"It is epic, Summer." He paused. "I know I don't seem the type to believe in this kind of stuff, but your mom made a believer out of me. If it can happen to me, it can happen to anyone. I'm happy for you. Your mom would be, too."

"Thanks, Dad."

"Now, I'll think about the house thing, but if I agree to this, that tile in the kitchen has to go. I can't deal with all that pink."

Summer laughed, knowing her father would be taking her house, and she'd be going home.

CHAPTER 30

SUMMER STARED at the computer. She read the words in the email but failed to take in the actual content. She was tired. She was tired again. She'd been up late the night before, chatting with Lena after putting in a twelve-hour day to help make preparations for the convention and the investor's meeting. She had woken up early to talk to Seth about his progress overseas, and she felt like she hadn't had more than three hours of sleep a night in over a week.

Her weekend with Lena hadn't helped of course. They'd spent every free moment touching one another and had gotten very little sleep. Summer knew she needed to take better care of herself, but she wasn't sure when she'd find the time. She checked the time on the computer and gave up all hope of getting any more work done. She would grab a quick dinner in the employee cafeteria downstairs, that she frequented whenever she was too lazy to cook or pick something up, and she would go to the house to see what else she needed to pack up before calling Lena for their FaceTime session.

It hadn't been that long since she'd seen her. It was Friday afternoon, and they had only parted on Sunday, but it felt so much longer. She wanted Seth to wrap up his business so she could wrap up her own, get out of here, and get back to her girlfriend. They were at the beginning of their relationship. This was supposed to be the part where they spent all their time together. They should be getting home from work and having dinner in, or going out for a date night before coming home and taking a shower together *before* and probably again *after* having hot sex on all the surfaces. Summer grunted in both disappointment and frustration that she couldn't have that tonight.

When she got to her house, she took a quick shower instead of a relaxing bath she really wanted, because she had a call scheduled with the convention organizer that she had postponed for the past two days. After Hailey sent her the third text, begging Summer to not put it off any longer, Summer had relented. The call was a lengthy one, but it had accomplished the task, which had her feeling appreciation.

The organizer was polite and professional; Summer appreciated that, too. They'd meet in person on Monday, and they would be spending a lot of time together up until the convention and during as well. Her name was Keira. They had met in person once already this week. Keira had long blonde hair. When Summer met her, she had it pulled back into a single braid that ran down her back. She had blue eyes, and they were radiant, as was her smile. But those eyes and that smile could in no way compare to Lena's; the eyes and the smile Summer dreamed about each night. Summer sensed that Keira was more than happy to be dealing with her instead of Seth for the convention and found herself guessing at Keira's sexual orientation when she felt a hand on her forearm and the laugh Keira laughed that was a little too loud whenever Summer said something that wasn't really that funny.

After the call ended, Summer sat outside on her deck and enjoyed the warm night air that often came with living in California. She had a nice enough view and a glass of red wine in front of her. She then placed her phone on do not disturb so she could have just ten minutes of silence from her technologically focused world, and took in the sounds of the outside instead. Northern California, at least where she lived, anyway, wasn't really known for crickets, but the strong breeze picked up the leaves and branches of the trees and tossed them about, supplying her with soft sounds to close her eyes to. She closed her mind to thoughts about work and her father's health. She closed herself to the worries about the upcoming meeting and the convention, and thought only of Lena and the house they now shared. Summer wondered what the other woman was doing, but she resisted the urge to text. They'd FaceTime later. Then, Summer fell asleep and missed the attempted FaceTime call and the three other calls and ten texts from Lena. It was after 11 p.m. Summer's time – which meant it was even later for Lena, but when Summer stared down at the phone and noticed the worried tone of the texts, she didn't bother listening to the three voicemails or worry about Lena being asleep.

"I am so sorry," Summer greeted without a hello. "I fell asleep, and I had my phone on do not disturb."

"Are you okay?" Lena's worried voice asked.

"I'm fine. I'm sorry. I was just sitting outside, enjoying the quiet, and I fell asleep," Summer replied, stood, and headed back inside the house. "Did I wake you up?"

"I couldn't sleep. I was worried. I thought about texting Seth or your dad... But I didn't want to wake or worry your dad, and Seth's on the other side of the world right now."

"I'm sorry, babe. I just wanted ten minutes, and I ended up scaring you." Summer closed the door behind herself and turned off the lights as she walked around the downstairs and made her way upstairs toward her bed. "I'm sorry I missed our call."

"I'm just glad you're all right," Lena returned, and Summer could hear the exhaustion now in Lena's tone.

"I'm tired, and I wish I was with you right now, but other than that, I'm okay." Summer climbed slowly.

"I wish you were here, too. How are things going there? You had that meeting today."

"With Keira, the convention organizer, yeah. It was just a phone call, though. I put it off so it wouldn't have to be a meeting." Summer finally made it to her room.

"Why?"

"Because I just didn't want to deal with it." Summer explained but left out the part about Keira's possible flirtations. She could have been reading the situation wrong, and there was no sense in mentioning it to Lena, when it meant nothing to Summer anyway. "That's how I've been feeling a lot lately."

"It'll be over soon, though, right? You'll be back?"

"Of course." Summer flopped down onto her bed. "Of course, Lena. Did you think I wouldn't be?"

"No, I just worry that they might find a way to suck you back in; and I promise, I'm not worried for me. I mean, I want you here with me, but I also know how unhappy you are there. I want you to be happy. I just don't want them to try to make you stay by laying a guilt-trip on you or something."

"I'm coming home to you as soon as I can. I won't let them suck me into anything here. I talked to Seth early this morning. Things are going well there. He should be back at least a few days early. He might even be back earlier. I may have laid a guilt-trip on him, actually."

"You did?" Lena laughed a little.

"We're doing the investor's meeting next week instead. I moved it up. Seth didn't object."

"You can just do that?" Lena asked.

"I can, for now. I'm the boss."

"For how much longer?" Lena's tone reflected both concern and hope.

"I'm resigning at the meeting."

"I thought–"

"I was going to wait until after Seth got back, but I think the best thing to do is tell them and the board that there will be a change in leadership. I told Seth this morning, and he's good with it. It gives everyone a chance to find a replacement." Summer let out a deep sigh. "I'll keep up appearances with the public at the convention, and until we find a replacement, but then, it's done. I'll be in Chicago permanently. I'll finish my undergrad, apply to schools there for my MBA, and figure out what I want to do with my money and for the rest of my life. I'm twenty-seven and about to be jobless."

"You could become a world traveler, like your brother," Lena suggested.

"Only if you come with me." Summer smiled at the thought.

Lena chuckled and said, "Someday, we'll plan a trip."

"Someday, huh?" Summer questioned with a playful tone.

"Yes, someday. We can take time to plan it. You'll be done with school. I won't be so busy at work."

"Oh, my God! I completely forgot." Summer shot up in bed. "Did you find out yet or are you still waiting?"

"On the deal?" Lena asked.

"Yes, on the deal." Summer laughed.

"We found out today. I was going to tell you during our call."

"Tell me now. Yes or no?"

"It got approved. We start the real work on Monday," Lena replied.

"That's awesome, Lena. I'm so happy for you. How's Van? Is she excited, too? Will she stop using that lame nickname now that she's franchised?"

"I doubt it. She's excited, too, though. It's a great thing. I get to invest in something and help people, too."

"It *is* a great thing, babe. I wish it didn't mean you had to stay there and work so hard, because I miss you, but I'm really happy for you."

"I miss you, too."

"I don't think I'll be able to get there this weekend." Summer explained. "With the meeting being moved and the convention coming up, it's going to be all hands on deck here. My aunt and uncle want to do a family dinner, and I just don't think I can get back."

"Oh," Lena said, and then there was a moment of

silence. "Sure. I get it."

"Can you come here?" Summer asked.

"Um… not really," Lena replied.

"Not really?" There was another long pause, and Summer wondered what was causing the pauses and silences, but she didn't know how to ask. "Work again?"

"Yeah, work," Lena answered, but there was something off about it.

Summer squinted for a moment, thinking about how to find out what had happened.

"Are you okay?"

"I'm just tired. It's late."

"I should let you go. I'm sorry we couldn't talk earlier."

"I know. Me too. I love you. Sleep well," Lena said.

"I love you, too." Summer thought about just how much that statement was true. "So much, Lena."

"I know. I'll talk to you tomorrow."

"Okay, good night."

Summer heard the phone click. She pulled it away from her ear, and it took her a while to get to sleep.

***

Lena rolled onto her side and placed her phone on her bedside table. She regretted not telling Summer what she probably should have told her. She was upset with Summer now, and she probably shouldn't be. It wasn't Summer's fault. She had been incredibly busy with work and her dad, and still trying to talk to Lena every night while they began their relationship. It wasn't like Lena could really be mad at her for forgetting her birthday.

***

By Wednesday, Lena's excitement over Strange Joe's and the deal with O'Shea's had unfortunately lessened, as the amount of work that went along with it increased. It didn't help that she was still avoiding the conversation about the weekend with her girlfriend, because she hoped Summer would somehow magically remember that Lena was turning thirty-seven on Friday. They were a new couple. Things had been harder with Summer's departure and workload, but they'd had the whole birthday conversation the night of their first date. That wasn't all that long ago. She'd been surprised that Summer hadn't at least remembered and mentioned it. It wasn't like she was expecting a big production. It would have been nice to spend it together, but Lena understood that wasn't likely. They could celebrate it later. But Summer hadn't even remembered it.

Lena tried not to think about it as they made arrangements for Strange Joe's and visited O'Shea's locations. She pushed it out of her mind as she called her parents and told them about her plans to set up a foundation in Leo's name.

It was interesting to Lena that the age difference between herself and Summer hadn't seemed to be a problem or even worth a mention. They were basically ten years apart, with Lena turning thirty-seven in a few days and Summer still having months to go before turning twenty-eight. It hadn't ever come up between them or even with their shared friends. It felt right between them. The difference didn't seem to matter.

She had spoken to Summer a few times since their middle of the night talk, but their chats had been brief or interrupted. Summer's investor's meeting had been Tuesday afternoon. She'd given them the heads up to her resignation. Lena had been equally busy and hadn't been up for long talks. Things were a little awkward now. Lena knew it was her fault. She wasn't normally this passive-aggressive. She hated that she was being that way now, but she couldn't bring up the fact that the reason she couldn't go to California for the weekend was that, this week, Charlie and Hailey had decided to plan a party at their house for her.

Lena had mentioned to Charlie on the phone Monday

night that she hadn't had a birthday celebration of any kind in a long time. Charlie said that wouldn't work for her, or Hailey, and insisted. Ember and Eva would be there, along with Alyssa and Hannah. Hayden was invited, and he would be bringing his girlfriend. Zack, Ember's big brother, and his wife Grace would both be in attendance as well. Van had been invited as well, and when Lena had spoken to Charlie about it, she'd ensured her that she'd talk to her girlfriend and invite her. Lena didn't want them to know that Summer had forgotten. She'd honestly planned on telling Summer, but she didn't want the woman to feel pressure to come back when she had stuff to finish up there. By Wednesday night, Lena was too tired to talk to anyone. She texted Summer goodnight and turned her phone off. She needed a solid eight hours, if she was going to get through the next two days at work and the long weekend without the woman she loved.

CHAPTER 31

"HI, SUMMER. How are you?" Keira greeted Summer with another smile that was just a little too wide.

"I'm good," Summer answered her directly, not wanting to encourage her anymore.

It had been four straight days of Keira touching her arm just so and laughing that too hard of a laugh over and over again. Summer was done with it. She just wanted the whole convention to be finished so that she could move on with her life. They had already ensured everything was on track with the venue, that the plans were underway for the main stage, and finalized the keynote speech she would be delivering in Seth's absence. Summer felt like she didn't really need to be involved in all of this, but that Keira was, perhaps, exaggerating how important it was that she takes part in and approve everything.

"I was thinking about going into the city this weekend. There's this band playing at one of the bars in the Castro. I have a friend that can get us in with no cover and get us pretty decent seats," Keira said as they arrived at Summer's office Friday afternoon.

"I'm not much of a band person," Summer lied.

"We could grab a bite, then. There's a place next to the Ferry building I really like. I did an event for them once. I can probably get us a good table with a nice view." Keira sat in a chair in front of Summer's desk, while Summer placed her laptop in her bag. "You're probably able to do that all the time, though, right? So, it's not like a big deal to you."

"I guess so, yeah," Summer replied and pulled her bag over her shoulder. "I'm sorry, I need to cut this short. I have to head out."

"Oh, sure. Sorry." Keira stood. "So, is that a no to dinner, then?"

"It's a no, yeah. Sorry, Keira. And I don't want to presume anything, but if you're looking for a date, I'm unavailable. I have a girlfriend."

"You do? I'm sorry, then. I asked one of your directors. He said you were single. I am really embarrassed right now." The woman's cheeks took on a shade of deep red.

"Don't be." Summer walked around her desk to stand in front of Keira. "Really, it's no big deal."

"That probably happens to you a lot, too, huh?"

"What?"

"Getting hit on. I mean, you're gorgeous, and successful, and rich, and–" Her blush deepened. "That's not why I was interested. I'm not after your money or anything. God, I'm suddenly very bad at this."

"I understand. It's okay. I don't tell everyone in the company my personal business, but yes, I'm in a relationship, and it's serious. I'm sorry if you were misled, though."

"No, it's fine. I understand." Keira headed toward the door of the office. "I'll see you next week for the final preparations."

"Keira?"

"Yeah?" The woman stopped and turned back to Summer.

"Can you involve Hailey in this stuff and, maybe, leave me out of anything I don't have to be there for or approve?" Summer asked.

"Oh, sure."

"It's just that this really isn't my thing." Summer tried

to soften the blows she was delivering to Keira today. "Hailey's much better suited for it. She has a team of people that, I'm sure, can be of more help than I can. I was kind of hoping to just show up, wave, make a speech, and go home."

"I'll talk to Hailey and see what she wants to take on or delegate." Keira nodded in understanding and gave a small defeated wave before leaving.

Summer waited for a bit as she watched Keira head to the elevator. The doors closed, and Summer headed in the same direction. She needed to get out of the office, but she didn't want to have to face the awkward ride down with Keira after that exchange.

***

Lena wrapped work early on Friday for the first time in forever so that she could head home and change before leaving for Charlie and Hailey's house. It was really convenient that they had built their place so near to her house. She wasn't sure if she was required to bring anything for a party held in her honor, but she had been brought up to be polite and always bring a hostess gift no matter what. She had settled on two bottles of wine. Lena had been told it would be a casual affair and had chosen a pair of comfortable jeans with a black and white striped sweater and black boots. She had left her hair down and wavy, and as she climbed out of the car to a gust of wind that blew it back, she thought about how much Summer loved her hair like this.

She had only received a text from Summer earlier in the day, saying she would be meeting with the convention planner most of the day and would be unavailable, but that she would call Lena when she could get free. Lena was disappointed. She hated the fact that she could have just reminded Summer why this day was important, and that it would have been nice to just hear her girlfriend's voice, but she would tell Summer tonight, when they would talk after the party. Or, maybe she would tell the woman tomorrow, depending on how late the party went.

Lena also hated the fact that she wasn't excited about talking to her girlfriend. She had always been excited to talk to Summer. She headed toward the door, after saying thank you to the driver, and was greeted immediately by Charlie, as the woman opened her front door and took a few steps outside into the cool night air.

"It's the birthday girl! Happy birthday," Charlie said a little louder than normal, due to their distance.

"Thanks. I brought wine."

"Why? It's your party." Charlie looked confused for a moment. "Where's Summer?" she asked as Lena made it to the front porch.

"She couldn't make it. She's still in California," Lena stated but left out the fact that she had never told her girlfriend about the party.

"What? I thought you said she was coming," Charlie replied and crossed her arms over her chest.

"We thought she could, but the convention is coming up. Things are hectic there. It's no big deal. I'm not really much for birthdays anyway. This whole party was your idea." She pointed at Charlie and winked.

"Yeah, yeah." Charlie pulled her in for a brief hug. "Get inside. Almost everyone is here. We're still waiting on Van, Hayden, and Lauren. Alyssa and Hannah are in the living room with the kids. They couldn't find a sitter. Hailey's in the kitchen, making something with mushrooms. There's wine and beer in there. Ember and Eva are in the living room, too, playing with the kids and pretending they don't want their own." Charlie laughed. "At least Hails and I are honest about how much we want them; and soon. Those two keep pretending like they're actually going to wait until Ember's done with school. Please." The woman rolled her eyes.

"I think they will," Lena replied and passed her bottles

to Charlie. "It's obvious they want them, but I can see Ember waiting. School takes a lot out of a person."

"Not Em. She's a genius. It's like a cakewalk for her. Oh, Emma's coming, too. Zack and Grace are on their way. They're bringing more liquor from the bar, and food from the bar, too, I think. I don't know. Ember worked it all out with them."

"This really is all too much. I don't need all this. It's not even really a big birthday," Lena said.

"Hey, can you do me a favor?" Charlie changed the subject.

"Sure."

"Can you head to the backyard for me? I have a cooler with ice out there that needs to be brought in," Charlie asked.

Lena thought it sounded a little strange to ask *her* to bring in a cooler, but she nodded and watched Charlie head off in the direction of the kitchen, while Lena did as requested and headed to the backyard. What she found there instead, were white twinkle lights hanging along the top of the fence that surrounded the yard. They were connected in the center of the yard by a thin near-invisible pole, thanks to the darkness. The lights had been connected to the house in five places and were pulled toward that pole along with strands that had been connected to the top of the fence. There must have been hundreds of gleaming white bulbs illuminating the backyard with the tables and empty chairs, and light jazz music played over the speakers Lena couldn't see.

What she could see, though, was her girlfriend, Summer Taft, standing in front of that near-invisible pole, wearing a black cocktail dress and matching flats. Her smile was wide and beautiful. Her dark hair was down and over her shoulders. Her hands were clasped together in front of her body in a somewhat nervous pose.

"You thought I forgot, didn't you?" Summer asked as her smile grew wider.

"You're here?"

"Who do you think gave Charlie the idea to host a party?" Summer moved her hands and walked toward Lena. "I will admit that I forgot, temporarily," Summer added. "When we talked last weekend, I was so tired. I wondered what made you seem distant. You seemed sad about something. It took me until the next morning to figure it out. I'm so sorry." She now stood a foot away from Lena and placed one hand on Lena's cheek. "I've been working like crazy so that I could finish everything up, but that's no excuse. I thought about telling you that I'd be here, but I wanted to at least try to make up for my temporary memory loss and surprise you."

"You did. I'm so happy you're here," Lena admitted and pressed her forehead against Summer's. "So, Charlie was in on it?"

"Charlie and Hailey got it started, but everyone inside knows. That's why they're in there and not out here. I wanted to have a minute with you first." Summer leaned her lips into Lena's and pressed them together gently.

Lena reveled in the feeling of having Summer pressed against her like this and responded to the kiss. Summer's hands wandered to Lena's back and pulled her closer, while Lena's went around Summer's neck and did the same. Lena wasn't sure for how long they'd been like that, but she guessed it was a while, because she heard the sound of applause and shouts of encouragement from her friends coming from behind her.

"I guess that minute is over." Lena laughed.

"Can we come out now?" Hailey asked in a pleading tone.

"I think you did that a while ago there, Hails," Ember replied to her.

"You can come out here," Summer said loudly. "We'll have more time later," she said to Lena and pecked her lips gently.

"What did you think of your girlfriend's surprise?"

Hailey asked Lena when she approached.

"I had no idea." Lena stared at Summer. "I thought you forgot. I felt bad, because I should have just reminded you."

"It was hard this whole week, because I made plans to come out here, but I could tell you were upset with me. I didn't want to ruin the surprise, though."

"I'm just glad you're here." Lena pulled Summer in for a hug. "I've missed you like crazy."

"Did I miss the party?" Emma asked as she made her way through the sliding glass door into the backyard.

"Just getting started, actually," Charlie replied.

***

Summer sat next to Lena at one of the tables, holding her hand against her thigh, and it just hit her. She looked around at all her friends. Emma was talking to Lauren, Hayden's girlfriend, while Ember and Eva were whispering back and forth to one another at the table next to them. Hayden was on Lena's other side, and the two were discussing Lena's deal and Hayden's new company. Van was on Hayden's other side and seemed a little out of place, but she hadn't spent a lot of time with the whole group, so that was understandable. Alyssa was sitting on the ground with the twins. They played with some of the toys they'd brought with them. Hailey was sitting in front of Charlie, between her legs, just watching the toddlers, while Charlie held her from behind. When Zack and Grace had arrived, they brought more alcohol and food, and they were now sitting next to Eva and Ember. Summer turned to see that Lena was now staring at her with a wide grin on her face.

"I love you," Summer told her, but kept her voice quiet.

"I love you, too." Lena squeezed her hand. "You are the best birthday present I've ever gotten."

"Oh, I'm your present, am I?" Summer asked.

"Yes, you're my present." Lena laughed. "How long are you staying? Do I get you for the whole weekend at least?"

Summer smiled at her and said, "You get me forever if you want."

Summer leaned in close and pressed her lips just under Lena's ear, eliciting a tiny gasp that only she could hear.

"You know what I meant," Lena breathed out.

"I'm going back on Monday morning. And I'm only staying through the end of the week to wrap up stuff with my dad and the house."

"What about the convention?" Lena asked and turned her head.

"She's ditching me," Hailey announced from her seated position after, apparently, overhearing Lena's question.

"What?" Lena asked Summer.

"Seth is coming back in time. He called me while I was flying here. He's finally interested in taking on more than just the small stuff in the engineering world. I think he might be finally growing up. He said he even missed home and was looking forward to getting back to the office. That's the first time I've ever heard him say that before."

"So, he's coming back, and you..." Lena didn't finish the sentence.

"I'm staying here." Summer smiled at her. "Hailey's going out there to make sure everything goes well and that my brother really does follow-through. They're going to start interviewing my replacement next week. I can finally come up for air, and I want to do that here, with you."

"Are you sure about this?" Lena asked and squeezed her hand.

"For the first time in a long time, I am 100% sure that this is what I want. I'm not equivocating over it or coming up with excuses to do something or not do something. I love you, Lena. I love my life here." Summer sighed as she looked around. "I finally have a great group of friends."

"Amen," Charlie agreed.

"I still need to learn to keep my voice down, apparently, though." Summer laughed and placed a hand on Lena's soft cheek. "I don't know what exactly I'm going to do after I finish school, but I know that no matter what it is, or where it takes me, I want you there."

Lena blushed. Summer loved that shade of red on her.

"I want that, too," Lena muttered quietly.

"All my stuff is being shipped to your house. After this week, we'll basically be living together. I still have the apartment, technically."

"Get rid of it. I don't want a backup plan anymore, Summer. I don't want one of us to have a place to flee, because I don't want either of us to flee. I want to live with you. I want to make a home with you," Lena said.

"I'll help my dad finalize everything and come back here to you and to *our* house." Summer put the emphasis on the word and liked how it sounded. "Lena, you and me…" She motioned with her finger between the two of them. "We're epic."

Summer felt the tension in Lena's body release. She smiled at her girlfriend as she recalled the conversation she'd had earlier with her father about finding the one person you were meant to be with. He'd had his and unfortunately lost her. Summer would do everything in her power to make sure that her person – the one she was supposed to be with forever – never left her.

"Epic?" Lena questioned softly.

"What all these people have, Lena…" She looked around the space. "We have it, too. That kind of love that just seems right and powerful and meant to be; that's us." Summer kissed Lena's lips gently. "I may be indecisive at times, but there's no decision to be made here, because it was made for me maybe before I was even born." Summer kissed her gently again. "I was meant for you, Lena Tanner."

"And I've waited a very long time for you, Summer Taft." Lena paused. "Like I said before, best birthday present ever." Lena leaned in and pressed a sweet kiss to Summer's lips.

"This isn't your present," Summer whispered and then turned Lena's head slightly so she could continue to whisper in her ear. "Your present is in my suitcase. I have to take it out and put it on for you later."

Lena's blush increased. Summer felt the hand – that was still on her thigh – tense while she looked down to see Lena's thighs squeeze together.

"Really?" Lena cleared her throat, trying to cover her reaction.

"Really," Summer continued to whisper. "It's in two pieces, and is soft and a little on the see-through side. I was thinking I could put it on, and then, you could take your time taking it off."

"Yes," Lena whispered.

"How long do you think this party is going to last?" Summer whispered again.

"Too long," Lena huffed out in frustration.

Summer laughed.

EPILOGUE

"YOU SURE ABOUT this?" Summer asked.

"It's a good opportunity. I'm sure," Emma replied.

They were at Emma's going away party that Hailey was hosting for her.

"Well, at least you're moving somewhere I go a lot." Summer shrugged.

"That's true. You can always come to visit."

"Oh, we will. Lena wants to buy something in the city, anyway." Summer nodded in the direction of her girlfriend, who was talking to Hailey and Charlie in the kitchen.

"You two have been on a buying spree lately. What is that now? You're up to three houses?"

"We have this one, but I guess that's technically just Lena's. Then, we have one at Cape Cod. It's a nice summer place for us. It just needs to be restored before we can really take advantage of it. She wants a place in San Francisco so we can have a place to stay when we're there that's not at my dad's house or Seth's place."

"I'm just happy I'll be seeing you guys sometimes. It's always hard, starting over. I hate to leave Chicago and all my friends here, but San Francisco is calling my name."

"We'll miss you, but we're out there every few months, visiting the family, so we'll see you all the time." Summer reached out and hugged her friend.

"You'll have to show me around, then. Despite the fact that I'll be the one living there full-time, I'm guessing my workload will be pretty heavy, to start. And you grew up there, so you're more well-versed in everything."

"Fine, but you're buying dinner." Summer winked.

"Deal."

"I'm going to go grab my girlfriend. We should really be heading out. We have an early day tomorrow."

"Well, I guess I'll see you in Frisco."

Summer winced and said, "Oh, don't call it that. They hate that there."

Emma laughed.

"Babe, you ready?" she asked Lena as she wrapped an arm around the woman's waist.

"I'm ready. Did you say goodbye to Emma?" Lena turned.

"Yeah. You?"

"I said my goodbye earlier. See you guys later?" She turned to Hailey and Charlie.

"Sure. Have a good night." Hailey winked at Summer.

"What's with the wink, Hailey?" Summer asked of her former employee and closest friend.

"Nothing," Hailey answered, but her tone revealed a bit of mischief.

"Come on." Lena laughed and pulled Summer along.

"What was that about?" Summer asked Lena when they were out of earshot.

"I don't know," Lena answered, and they both climbed into the car Summer had called for them.

***

When they arrived home, Summer immediately went to the kitchen, and Lena knew what she was doing. It had become a ritual of sorts during the first year of their relationship. Whenever Summer went straight for the

357

kitchen after they'd been out, she was heading for the freezer.

"You okay about Emma leaving?" Lena asked as she sat on the stool and watched Summer pull out a carton of vanilla ice cream from the freezer and then move onto the chocolate syrup and cherries.

"I'm going to miss seeing her all the time, but she's right. It's a great opportunity for her. She'll be working for the Health Department and teaching part-time, which is something she's been interested in for a while. I think she caught the bug from Eva, actually." Summer grabbed the ice cream scooper out of the drying rack.

They had done this so often, it rarely made it back to the cutlery drawer.

"She'll make more money, and it's a great city," Summer continued.

"It is," Lena agreed.

She watched her girlfriend prepare their sundaes with precision. They had lived together for the entirety of their relationship and had never looked back. It was now one year later. Summer was finished with her undergrad degree and was about to embark on her MBA at Northwestern. Lena was doing well at O'Shea's, and her non-profit in Leo's name had already done so much good work for the city, that she had considered it a huge success. Strange Joe's was doing incredibly well and was now in nine locations in the Midwest.

"We'll see her a lot, anyway. My dad demands quarterly visits now." Summer pointed the scooper at Lena accusatorily. "That's because of you, by the way."

"I can't help it; your dad likes me." Lena laughed a little. "Hey, I wanted to talk to you about something."

"Okay..." Summer dragged the word out in obvious concern. "That's not ambiguous."

"Wait here." Lena laughed at her girlfriend's tone.

"Okay," Summer said again.

Lena went up the stairs and into her office, which was

really more Summer's office now than her own, and she liked it that way. Summer's books were on the shelves now and in just the right order. The woman had a thing with the order of her books. It didn't really make sense to Lena, but she left it alone. She went to her desk and pulled out what she was looking for. She knew Summer rarely actually went into any of the desk drawers, so she hadn't bothered hiding it. Lena went back downstairs and headed toward the kitchen, where she watched Summer place two bowls in front of the stools.

"I added five cherries for you," she told Lena before she even saw her.

"And I'll eat none of them for you." Lena sat down, placing the paperwork in front of Summer.

"What is this?" Summer looked at her and then down again.

"Just read the first page."

Summer picked up the small pile of pages in front of herself and lifted them to read.

"Lena…"

"What do you think?"

"This is a business," Summer stated.

"It could be, yes." Lena began. "We don't have to do it, or we can just do it part-time. I don't plan on quitting O'Shea's anytime soon. I know you're about to start your MBA program, but I thought this could be something we could share."

"You want to start a venture capital firm with me?" Summer turned to her.

"Well, Strange Joe's turned out well. Hayden's business is also booming, and we both played a part in that. You and I have enough money to start a company like this on our own. We could help people like Seth, Van, and Hayden, who have big dreams and good business plans but don't have the money to get things started."

"Is that what Hailey was winking about earlier?" Summer asked.

"No, that's something else."

"So, you do know what was up with her?" Summer pointed the papers at Lena.

"I do. And I'll tell you in a second. But, what do you think about this? Feel free to say no, or even to just say no right now. I drew up the paperwork so you could see what it could look like if we went through with it."

"*Taft Investments*," Summer read from the top page where Lena had to identify the name of the company to draw up the paperwork. "Why just Taft, though? Shouldn't it be *Taft & Tanner* or *Tanner & Taft*?"

Summer looked over at Lena, whose face was now a bright shade of red. Lena had tried to hide it, but there was no way she could.

"Because I want your name one day," Lena revealed. "This isn't a proposal or anything, but I know that if we do that, I would want your name, Sum. Why bother putting Tanner on there if I won't be a Tanner someday?"

***

Summer gulped as she stared at her girlfriend. Summer wasn't afraid of commitment, or even of getting engaged and married to the woman she loved more than anything. But, just the thought that Lena Tanner wanted to become Lena Taft, was enough to make Summer go silent for a moment. They had talked about this, sure. They had been together for a year. They had watched Hailey and Charlie say, 'I do' as they stood on opposite sides of the aisle, smiling mostly at one another instead of at their friends, who were exchanging rings and vows. But they hadn't yet made it official or even talked about it seriously with any kind of timeframe in mind. That was until recently, when Summer talked to her father again, and he gave her the ring he had once given her mother. He told her it was for Lena, and that Summer's mother would be happy to have the woman wear it when Summer was ready.

"Sum?" Lena interrupted her thoughts after a long silent moment.

"Sorry, that just caught me off guard," Summer revealed.

"Oh, we don't have to call it—"

"No, I want to. I want to." Summer set the pages down in front of her now melting ice cream. "I want that."

"The business?"

"All of it," Summer shared.

She thought about going to school and working with Lena side by side, helping other people start their own businesses and maybe doing some charitable work on the side, like they'd been doing with Leo's foundation. That sounded like the best way she could think of to spend her time. She wanted that. She wanted all of it.

"So, you think it's a good idea?"

"I do," Summer said and then realized that those two words had kind of a different meaning at the moment.

"There's something else in there." Lena motioned with her head toward the papers.

Summer picked them back up and rifled through a few pages, until she landed on one that looked different from the others.

"The house?"

"Your name is on it now. I thought it should be official. It's our home; not mine."

Summer looked up and around the space. Then, she looked back at Lena.

"You put my name on the house?" she asked.

"We have the place in Cape Cod, and we're about to buy one in San Francisco… But, this is our real home. It just seemed wrong, not to have your name on it. So, I had it added. It's paid for, so it wasn't as hard as I thought it would be to do it without you knowing."

"Lena, thank you."

"You don't have to thank me. I should have done it a long time ago."

361

Summer stood. She set the papers down on the counter.

"Can you give me a minute?" she asked.

"Sure, but–"

"Just one." Summer ran off without waiting for a response.

***

Lena sat in her chair, wondering what had just happened. She stared down at the melting ice cream and scooped all the cherries Summer had added to her bowl into Summer's instead.

"In here," Summer's voice called from the foyer. "No, wait! Out here."

The front door opened. Lena turned and stood to see Summer walking out into the front yard.

"Summer, where are you going?"

Lena hurried down the hall and out the door to see that Summer was standing about halfway down the driveway.

"Here," Summer said and pointed at the concrete under her feet.

"What are you doing? Get inside. It's late," Lena replied.

Summer was only lit by the streetlights and the light over the garage.

"This is where I knew," Summer stated.

"Knew what?" Lena chuckled and headed toward her.

"That I loved this house. I got out of the car, that first time you brought me here, I looked up at it, and I knew that this was my home."

Lena smiled at her and said, "It is."

"And I would've taken you to the first place I knew I loved you, but it would probably be closed by the time we got there."

"Where's that?"

"The Lantern," Summer stated as if Lena should have known that. "The first time I saw you, I knew. I questioned it, because that's what I think we all do when we fall in love at first sight, but I saw those eyes, that wavy blonde hair, the way you walked into the room, and I knew. Then, I heard your voice, and I knew again. I got to know you, and I knew again, and again; and that was it."

"What was it?" Lena's tone reflected the serious turn of the conversation as Summer took several large steps toward her.

"No indecisiveness," Summer announced without context. "I could plan it, and make a big show, but that's not who we are. We're just us, and I love us."

"I love us, too but, Sum–"

"Lena Tanner, will you please become Lena Taft?" Summer held out her hand.

The woman had been holding a ring box in it that Lena hadn't noticed before, thanks to the darkness of the sky and Summer, keeping that hand mostly out of view.

"Summer, I didn't–"

"This isn't about the name of a company or anything else. This is what I want." Summer opened the box. "This was my mom's ring. My dad gave it to me the last time we were there. I want you to wear it, Lena. I want you to become Lena Taft." She paused and let out a deep breath. "I love you. Will you please marry me?"

"Yes," Lena let out. "Yes," she repeated a little louder.

"Yes?"

"Yes."

Lena reached for Summer and pulled her in for a kiss that started off slow and steady but turned passionate and fast. One of the sprinklers in the neighbor's lawn kicked on and pulled them out of their revelry. They started laughing.

"Can I?" Summer asked.

"Yes." Lena lifted her hand so that Summer could place the ring on her finger.

It wasn't a perfect fit. Summer's mom's finger was a

little larger than Lena's, but they would get it fitted. Despite the size, the ring looked like it belonged there.

"I can't believe this," Lena said after Summer lifted her hand to her lips and kissed the ring on Lena's finger. "I had this whole thing planned out."

***

"What?" Summer looked up at her.

"I had this whole proposal thing planned. It was in three steps. Tonight was the first step, with the whole business name thing, just to see what you thought about it. I was going to take you to get a dog, since we've been putting that off. We'd have the dog for a while, and then, I was going to do a whole cute proposal involving the dog and—"

"Oh, my God!" Summer laughed. "That would have been adorable."

"Yes, it would have." Lena scowled playfully at her. "But, I'm pretty happy right now, so I'll forgive you for ruining the whole thing."

"Did you have a speech prepared or something?" Summer smiled at her.

"I did, actually. I wrote it down."

"I need to read it," Summer said.

"You can." Lena pulled Summer's hands and walked backward so they could go back inside the house. "On our wedding day."

"What? That's not fair."

"You ruin my proposal plan, and *that's* not fair?"

"I was in the moment." Summer giggled.

"I'll give you the speech in private before the ceremony," Lena said. "I'll give you one line to hold you over, though, if you want."

"I do want," Summer replied as Lena stopped their progress.

"You make me brave, Summer Taft. You make me

brave enough to propose to the most amazing woman I've ever met in my life, and I love you." Lena shrugged. "That's two lines, I guess."

Summer stared at Lena for a moment.

"I love you, too. So, are we still getting this dog, even though I ruined the whole thing?"

Lena laughed that deep laugh that Summer loved.

"We can go tomorrow, if you want."

"I do."

"Save that for the wedding," Lena said as they headed back inside.

Made in the USA
Monee, IL
16 March 2021